Dead
RED

ALSO BY TIM O'MARA

Crooked Numbers

Sacrifice Fly

Dead
RED

TIM O'MARA

Minotaur Books ⚓ New York

DEAD RED. Copyright © 2014 by Tim O'Mara. All rights reserved. Printed in the United States of America. For information address St. Martin's Press, 175 Fifth Avenue, New York, N.Y. 10010.

www.minotaurbooks.com

Design by Omar Chapa

Library of Congress Cataloging-in-Publication Data

O'Mara, Tim.
    Dead red / Tim O'Mara. — First edition.
        pages ; cm. — (Raymond Donne mysteries ; 3)
    ISBN 978-1-250-05863-8 (hardcover)
    ISBN 978-1-4668-6299-9 (e-book)
    I. Title.
    PS3615.M37D43 2015
    813'.6—dc23
                        2014032394

Minotaur books may be purchased for educational, business, or promotional use. For information on bulk purchases, please contact the Macmillan Corporate and Premium Sales Department at 1-800-221-7945, extension 5442, or write to specialmarkets@macmillan.com.

First Edition: January 2015

10 9 8 7 6 5 4 3 2 1

For my daughter, Eloise Bushmann O'Mara.
Right up to the moon—and back.

Acknowledgments

I WISH TO THANK THE COMPUTER School family once again, for making it a joy to go to my day job, and the folks at The Center School, for making my daughter feel the same way. (Okay. It's a tie.)

I'm forever grateful to Mike Kunin and all the amazing people at Ramapo For Children. Please check out their Web site, www.ramapofor children.org, to see how you can help to continue the magic they perform year in and year out at summer camp for so many kids.

This book owes much to the few hours I spent with Detective Don Carney of the Special Investigative Squad of Nassau County Police Department, also a Gunnery Sergeant in the United States Marine Corps Reserves. That's right—a real-life American hero.

Thanks to the real Dr. Amy Burke for her generous donation to the Computer School and for being such an interesting character. I am grateful to Events Manager Anne Harson at New York City's Upper West Side Barnes & Noble for treating me like one of the big shots. I proudly selected as my 2013 Teacher Hero Contest winner Linda Marsh-Eells, whose entries thanking her heroic teachers Mrs. Burke and Mr. Corbin were from the heart. Thank you, Harry Tilton, PI.

The public libraries and their dedicated librarians across the country constantly amaze and humble me. Not to play favorites, but I wish to single out Mary Barrett of the Newport (Rhode Island) Public Library; Missouri public librarians Madeline Matson of the Missouri River Regional

Library in my second home of Jefferson City, Patricia Miller of the Columbia Public Library in Columbia, Sherry McBride-Brown of the Calloway County Public Library in Fulton, and Karen Neely of Southern Boone County Public Library in Ashland; the staffs of the Merrick, Bellmore, Uniondale, Long Beach, and Roslyn Public Libraries on Long Island, New York; Maria Redburn of the Bedford Public Library in Texas; my neighborhood librarian, Sandra Chambers, of the New York Public Library Columbus Branch; and Mary Ellen Fosso and Jude Schanzer of my hometown East Meadow Public Library. Hooray for socialized reading!

Get a group of writers together and pretty soon the conversation will turn to how much we all are in debt to the great independent booksellers. Among those I wish to heap praise upon are Robin and James Agnew of Aunt Agatha's in Ann Arbor, Michigan; Scott Montgomery of Mystery-People in Austin, Texas; Adrean Darce Brent of Mysterious Galaxy in Southern California; Mystery Mike (and Little Mike—*Bang!* You're dead.) of Carmel, Indian; Loren Aliperti of Book Revue in Huntington, New York; McKenna Jordan and John Kwiatkowski of Murder By The Book in Houston, Texas; Jonah and Ellen Zimilies of [words] in Maplewood, New Jersey; The Mysterious Bookshop in New York City; Lexi Beach and Connie Rourke at Astoria Bookshop in Queens, New York; and Vivien Jennings of Rainy Day Books in Fairway, Kansas; Cheri LeBlond and Acia Morley of Mysteryscape in Overland Park, Kansas; Alice Hutchinson of Byrd's Books in Bethel, Connecticut; Randy Schiller at Left Bank Books in St. Louis, Missouri; and Jenn Worthington of Word in glorious Greenpoint, Brooklyn. Support your local indie!

Joan Hansen of www.menofmystery.org has been responsible for putting so many of us writer guys in front of so many women readers. We all owe you so much.

My mid-Missouri peeps continue to make me feel like a Show-Me State native and have helped sell a lot of this New Yorker's books. Special thanks to CC McClure of Downtown Book and Toy in Jefferson City; Brian and Danielle Warren of Well Read Books in Fulton; Brooklyn Pizza, also in Fulton; Warren Krech and John Marsh of KWOS Radio; Paul Pepper of KBIA Radio; Jack and Tom Renner; the late, great Wyn Riley; Cameron's Café in Holts Summit; and the entire Bushmann clan.

Thanks again to my agents, Maura Teitelbaum and Erin Niumata, for having my back and "representing." St. Martin's/Minotaur Books continues to make me feel like a pro. Thanks to Hector DeJean for still putting up with my questions. A big shout-out to Matt Martz, my patient and wise editor, who makes me a better writer with each book. You will be missed, my friend.

You know that lonely, secluded writer image? It doesn't work for me. I continue to depend on my first reader and fine friend Mike Herron. I've enjoyed many good times with Sharon and David Bowers, Maria Diaz and the staff at El Azteca Mexican Restaurant, Wayne Kral, Harold James, Drew Orangeo, Charles Salzberg, Tommy Pryor, Lynn Marie Hulsman, Jim and Josephine Levine, the Stokes Family, Linda Hanrahan, Ramon De La Cruz, Cari O'Leary and Family, "Aunt" Lisa Herbold, and "Uncle" Rob Roznowski. A special tip of the hat to Kevin Sieger—thanks for the tour of Long Island's South Shore and years of friendship.

I'd like to salute all the owners and bartenders at my favorite gin joints, especially Teddy's, Cornelia Street Café, Alfie's, d.b.a., and 2A. A big thanks to Margery Flax of the Mystery Writers of America for all you do for us writers. Lending their support yet again were Ann Marie Offer of *Something to Offer,* John Kearns and The Irish Writers & Artists Salon, and Andrew Meyer of WBGO in Newark, New Jersey.

Thanks to Maggie and Elise Williams for all their encouragement. Cheers to my father-in-law, Les Bushmann, who's always there with a wise and insightful comment when (and even when not) needed. Like me, Les married way out of his league. My books and I owe much to my mother-in-law, Cynthia Bushmann, who brings her considerable editing talents and keen proofreading eye to each of Raymond's stories.

Thanks to my brother Jack and his family. I appreciate my sister Ann inviting me to Skype for the first time with her book club in Torrance, California. (Sorry about the pizza joke, but I still live in New York.) My little sister Erin keeps making her big brother look good with her wonderful marketing and design skills.

Every one of my novels benefits from the experience of my brother, Sgt. Michael O'Mara of the Nassau County Police Department. Not only did he share his cop expertise with me once again, but this time around he also introduced me to Lowtide. I'm glad he did.

Kudos to my mom, Patricia O'Mara, for talking up my book to everyone she meets and learning to raise her hand when she wants to ask a question during my readings.

Eloise, read the front of the book, kiddo. This one's for you. (Yes, Daddy's tearing up.)

My wife, Kate, makes my life—and my books—so much better. Don't edit this next line, sweetie. I love you. Thanks.

Dead
RED

Chapter 1

I NEVER HEARD THE SHOT THAT killed Ricky Torres.

We were talking in the front seat of his cab, when the driver's-side window exploded and Ricky fell face-first into the steering wheel. I leaned over and the rest of the windows blew apart, sounding like someone had thrown a pack of firecrackers into the taxi.

That's when everything went white.

"Jesus Christ, Doc. How mucha that blood is his?"

I tried to open my eyes, but they wouldn't obey. My head was throbbing. I felt cold and wet all over. I was lying down, not in my bed. Something harder. Somebody was touching my head. Someone else was blowing a dog whistle. *How could I be hearing a dog whistle?*

"None," somebody said. "He's very lucky."

Lucky?

"His eyes are moving," the first voice said under the high-pitched whine. "That's a good sign, right?"

"We'll know more when he gets back from X-ray," the second voice said. "Right now, if I had to guess, I'd say he's suffered a concussion, at the least. There's also the possibility of a cranial fracture."

Silence for a few seconds. "You mean he broke his head?"

"Not exactly, Chief." There was a pause. "Aide?" he called.

Chief? The only chief I knew was my Uncle Ray. Why wasn't he telling the guy with the whistle to shut up? I could barely make out what these two were saying—

I felt myself being moved. I got my eyes open enough to see the ceiling spinning. Whatever I was lying on had wheels. What the—?

Shit. Where the hell was Ricky?

"Ah, there he is!" someone said. "Welcome back to the world, Nephew."

My eyes were open again. They weren't doing such a good job focusing, but they were open. My ears were working just fine; the damn whistle was still blowing so I could just about hear my uncle's voice.

"Can somebody shut that guy the fuck up?" My own voice coming out like a two-pack-a-day smoker.

Uncle Ray grabbed my hand. "You talking about me, Ray?"

"No," I wheezed. "The asshole blowing the damn whistle."

"Mr. Donne," another person said from the other side of the bed. I turned and immediately wished I hadn't. Pain shot down my back into my left foot.

"Ahh!"

"Mr. Donne. I'm Dr. Watson. It's best if you keep your movements to a minimum for the time being." He took my other hand and held the wrist, checking my pulse. "I take it you're hearing a high-pitched whistle?"

"You mean you're not?"

"What you're experiencing," the doctor said as he put my wrist down, "is tinnitus. From the shooting. It's perfectly normal and should pass in the next twenty-four hours."

The shooting.

"Where's Ricky?"

"Ricky?" the doctor repeated.

"Officer Torres," my uncle explained. "We'll talk about Ricky later, Ray. Right now you need to rest."

"He's dead," I said. My vision was returning and I could make out the general features of my uncle's face. *What time was it?* "I remember that. He's dead. I tried to—I don't know, I tried to—"

"It appears you tried to help him, Mr. Donne. And that is what saved you."

I sat up a little—another not-so-good idea—and felt the blood sprint to my head. "I know this is probably stating the obvious, Doctor," I whispered, "but I have very little idea what you're talking about."

"From what we can piece together," the doctor said, "it seems as if you attempted to help Mr. Torres after he'd been shot."

"I leaned over," I remembered. "Everything went white and then I . . ."

"Lost consciousness," he finished for me. "Some of the bullets hit the front of the cab, causing the air bags to inflate. Mr. Torres's head was projected into yours at an impressive rate of speed, causing the concussion and loss of consciousness. On the positive side, the air bag from the steering wheel forced you under and that's why—"

"The bullets went over my head," I said. "Jesus Christ. Ricky."

"He was pronounced dead at the scene, Ray," my uncle said, his hand still on mine. "There was nothing you could have done. Medical Examiner said he was more or less dead on impact."

"You get the shooter?"

Uncle Ray shook his head no. "We got lots of manpower out there, but so far no wits. Two o'clock in the AM, not a whole lotta people out. Which," my uncle said in his stern voice, "brings me to a question I'll ask you later. When you're up to it and get some more rest."

"The shooter . . . he was moving. Fast."

My uncle leaned into me. "How the hell do you know that?"

"Ricky's window. It was the first to break. Then . . ."

"The bullets hit the front of the cab," Uncle Ray repeated for me, "causing the air bags to go off. So, we got a shooter in motion. Probably with an automatic. You sure about the driver's window?"

"I'm not sure of anything, but I think so, yeah." I reached up to touch my head and pulled out a piece of glass the ER must have missed. I handed it to the doctor. "I don't know. Ricky called me. Woke me up." The past few hours—*how many?*—were coming back to me. "Said he needed to talk. Right away. I'm sorry. Can I get some water, Doc? My throat's killing me." I cringed at my choice of words. "I'm really thirsty."

"I'll find an attendant," the doctor said and stepped out of the room.

"What the hell was so damned important that Ricky hadda talk to you at two in the morning, Ray?"

"I don't know."

"Don't know or don't remember?"

I shook my head. The blinding pain and bright lights reminded me not to do that again. I reached up to feel for any more glass and felt a lump on my head.

"Both, right now. He picked me up outside my place and we drove over to the Southside."

"What the hell was he doing in a cab?"

"That's what he's been doing since he got back from Iraq." More parts of my conversation with Ricky were coming back. "He said he wasn't ready to go back to the cops, so he's been driving his cousin's cab to help out his mom with the rent and stuff."

"How much have you talked to him since he's been home?"

"Just a quick call when he got back. And then last night."

The doctor came back with a water pitcher and some cups. I guessed he couldn't find an attendant. He filled a cup for me and offered one to my uncle.

"No, thanks," he said. "Got anything stronger?"

Dr. Watson laughed, thinking my uncle was joking. He wasn't.

"Too tempting to keep it around this place." He gave me the cup. "So, Mr. Donne, as I had expected, you have a minor concussion."

"Minor?" I downed the small cup of water in one swallow. "Hurts like hell, Doc."

"Be glad it's not major, then. Anyway, I'd like to keep you overnight . . ." He looked at his watch. "Through the afternoon at any rate, for observation."

I reached up and touched my lump. *Impressive.* My vision cleared up enough for me to read the clock on the wall; almost four thirty. "You're saying all I got's the concussion, right?"

"That's what the X-rays showed, yes."

"Then," I sat up—much slower this time—"I'd rather just go home. No offense, but hospitals give me the creeps." I flashed back seven years to the week I'd spent in the hospital after my accident. That time it was my knees, not my head.

"I strongly advise against it, Mr. Donne. A concussion, however minor, can still be a serious matter. I'd like to monitor you for at least twelve hours."

"But I can sign myself out, right?"

Watson let out a deep sigh. "Yes." He was disappointed in me.

"Then give me my clothes and show me the dotted line." He gave me a look. "What?" I asked.

"Your clothes." he said. "We had to throw them away."

I closed my eyes. "Because of the blood." I wasn't asking. I'd been in the ER enough times as a cop and knew about throwing away stained clothing.

"Yes."

I looked down at the blue robe I was wearing and tugged at it.

"Just get me a matching pair of pants, and my uncle will drive me home."

"I just want to go on record," Dr. Watson said, "that I'm advising against it at this point."

"I hear you," I said. "And I appreciate it, but I want to go home."

"Okay." Dr. Watson left the room obviously frustrated and, I hoped, in search of a pair of hospital pants and the necessary paperwork.

"I can drive you home, Raymond," my uncle said. "But I don't got the time to babysit." He looked at his watch. "Gotta be at One PP this morning by seven thirty."

I leaned forward and eased my legs off the hospital bed so I could sit up. The room starting spinning, so I closed my eyes. When I opened them again, I said, "I'll call Edgar." I gave that some thought. I could call Allison, but why worry her at this time of the day? "What day is today?"

"It's Saturday, Ray, and just the fact that you have to ask kinda proves the doc's point, don'tcha think?"

"I can lie around at home just as well as I can around here."

"You need to be monitored."

"It's Saturday," I said as if I'd known it all along. "Edgar's off. He can watch me and then we'll have dinner together. Shit. I'm really hungry. That's another reason to get out of this place."

"You got his number?"

"Yeah." It took me a little while to retrieve it from my memory, but when it came, I gave it to him, proud of myself.

"I'll give him a call," Uncle Ray said. "See if he can meet us at your place and stay the day."

"He'll do it."

"I'll do it," a voice from the doorway said, and my sister, Rachel, stepped into the room. She had thrown a jacket over some gym clothes and looked as if she were expecting the worst. "I had a feeling you wouldn't be staying." She gave our uncle a hug and then stepped over to where I was sitting. She gently wrapped her arm around my lower back. "Hey, big brother."

I patted her knee. "Hey, little sister. How did you know—?"

"One of the guys phoned Dennis," she said, referring to her detective boyfriend. "Dennis . . ." She looked over at our uncle. ". . . *called* me." She took a breath. "I heard about Ricky. I am so sorry, Ray."

"Yeah," I said, letting her hug me a little harder. "Me, too . . . Fuck!"

She quickly pulled her arm away. "Sorry."

"No." My eyes started to fill, and I found myself fighting back the tears. I was not going to cry in front of my uncle in a goddamned hospital room. "It's not you."

Rachel put her arm around me again. "I know, Ray. I know. Let's talk about it at your place." She paused then added, "I'll make you a nice cup of tea."

And, just like that, her imitation of our mother made me laugh, causing my head to hurt once more and a few tears to spill down my cheeks. Rachel pulled a tissue out of her bag and gave it to me. That's when Dr. Watson stepped back into the room, the look on his face more concerned than when he had left.

"Mixed emotions," my uncle explained. "He's fine."

The doctor tossed a pair of blue surgical pants on the edge of the bed. "No, he's not," he said. He walked over and handed me a clipboard. "Sign on the bottom line and initial by the *X*'s."

"Doctor," I said, taking the pen from the clip and scribbling my name, "this is my sister, Rachel. Rachel, Dr. Watson."

They shook hands and Rachel smiled. "Like Sherlock Holmes?"

"Exactly," he said. *Like he hadn't heard that a thousand times.* "I take it you were unable to talk any sense into your brother?"

"Not for the last thirty years. But I'll take him home, make sure he doesn't nap for more than two hours, and I'll get some soup and crackers into him. If his headache gets any worse or he starts to vomit, I'll bring him straight to the ER."

"You've done this before?" he asked, sounding somewhat impressed.

"My boyfriend plays rugby," she said.

"You got your car?" my uncle asked.

"Right outside."

"Then let's get a move on." Uncle Ray offered his hand to the doctor. "Thank you, Dr. Watson. You ever get pulled over for speeding in the tristate area, just mention my name."

"I'll keep that in mind, Chief." To me and Rachel he said, "Anything out of the ordinary, I want him in the ER immediately. If not sooner."

"Yes, sir," Rachel and I said in unison.

I stood up—the floor felt wonderfully cool to my bare feet—swayed a bit, and sat back down. I counted to ten and tried it again. Better, but I needed to hold on to Rachel to get into my new pants.

"There's a big boy," Rachel whispered.

"Shut up."

"Yeah," my little sister said. "He's gonna be fine."

"The nurse will be by with a wheelchair in a few minutes," Dr. Watson said. "That," he said, holding up his hand like a traffic cop, "is non-negotiable. Hospital policy, Mr. Donne."

"Thanks, Doc. Hey," I said. "Where's my stuff?"

He pointed to a plastic baggie on a table by the window. My uncle walked over to get it. As the doctor left the room, the nurse came in with the wheelchair. I had to admit it felt good to sit down again. Uncle Ray put the baggie on my lap. As we made our way to the elevators, he said, "You both have my cell number."

"Yes."

"Any changes"—he pressed the elevator button—"you get his ass to the ER like the doc said and then call me. You hear?"

"I hear you, Uncle Ray," Rachel said.

"Raymond, I'll be by around six tonight. We can order in some dinner. Then you and I are going to have a talk."

"Don't I need to talk to the detectives or something?"

"That's one of the things we're gonna talk about. I worked it out so I'll be the one taking your statement."

"I don't know how much I'll be able to tell you, Uncle Ray. I don't—"

"We'll have a long talk," he repeated as we entered the elevator. "See what comes up." Nobody said another word until we got to Rachel's car.

Ten minutes later, Rachel pulled up in front of my building. The thought of walking up the four flights to my apartment made my stomach hurt. The thought of going back to the hospital made that pain subside. Rachel got out of the car and came around to my side. She opened the door, held out her hand, and helped me out. She gave me the baggie with my stuff.

"I saw a parking spot back there," she said. "Can I leave you for a minute to go around the block and get that space?"

"Yeah," I said and made my way to the streetlight and leaned against it. "Just make it quick, okay? I need to lie down again."

She kissed me on the cheek. "I'll be right back."

She drove to the corner, made an illegal right at the red light, and sped off. I grinned, put one arm around the lamppost, and closed my eyes. I needed to get horizontal soon. I considered vomiting right there on the street—hell, there was no one around to see me—but figured I could hold out another few minutes. *Wow,* I thought. *All the side effects of getting drunk without any of the fun.* I focused on my breathing.

In—count to five—Out—count to five. I was on my fourth round when someone grabbed me from behind, spun me, and shoved me into the post.

"Hey, Asshole," Someone said. "The fuck do you think you're doing?"

Chapter 2

"HEY, SHITHEAD!" I HEARD MY SISTER scream.

My assailant turned, and I heard the sound of something being sprayed. Some of it got onto my lips, and it tasted like last week's chili. Pepper spray. My eyes opened just as the guy's hands left my shirt and covered his face.

"Jesus Christ!" he yelled, spinning completely around toward Rachel.

"Fuck you," Rachel said. "Yah!"

My vision was still blurry, but I heard a sound like a bag being punched. Then the guy groaned, and I watched as his shape dropped to the ground. Rachel pulled her leg back and shot it into the guy's side.

"Goddamn it, Ray!" the guy moaned. "Call your bitch off."

"I am not his *bitch*," Rachel said. "I'm his fucking *sister*." She punctuated that with another kick.

"And I've got a fucking gun," the guy said. "Kick me again and I swear to Christ I will shoot you."

My vision was coming back now, and I saw a large guy with a blond crew cut reach into his jacket with one hand while the other kept him from going down to the sidewalk. Without thinking, I pushed away from the lamppost and threw my body into his midsection. I ended up sitting on the guy as he flattened out. My whole body was thumping with pain.

"Goddamn it, Ray," he coughed up some phlegm onto the cement. "Enough already. I get it. I got my ass kicked by the Donne family. Now get the fuck off me."

He managed to turn over and, for the first time, I got a good look at his face.

Holy shit.

I held my hand out to Rachel, and without saying a word she pulled me to my feet. She looked down. "You telling me you know this shit, Ray?"

"Nice mouth, sister," Jack said.

Rachel's leg went back as if to kick the guy again. I put my hand on her shoulder. "It's okay, Rache. Yeah." I looked down at my former partner, who my sister and I had pretty much just beaten up. "I know him. His name's Jack Knight. What the hell, Jack?"

"Oh, yeah, thanks Ray. I'm fine." He got to his knees. "Jim Dandy." He turned to Rachel and said, "I think you broke my fucking rib."

"Oh, I remember now," Rachel said, her breathing heavy. "This is Jack, whose favorite word is 'fuck.' "

Jack stood up slowly, grinned, and spit out a mouthful of blood. "Same kinda wiseass as your brother, girlie. Could get you in some trouble one day."

"Who's holding his ribs and spitting out bodily fluids?"

"Okay," I said. "Okay. Both of you shut up." I looked at Jack. "What the hell, Jack? I don't see you for . . . what? Two years and then—"

"What the fuck were you doing with Ricky T, Ray?"

"That's what this is about?" My head started spinning again. "Can we talk about this upstairs?"

Can we make it upstairs?

Jack shook his head and rubbed his eyes. "Yeah," he said. "I need to use the john anyway."

I reached into the hospital baggie, took out my keys, and handed them to Jack. "Lead the way. Fifth floor, no elevator."

"This could take a while," Rachel said.

"Fine," I answered as I grabbed my sister's arm. "School doesn't start for another . . . two weeks."

Jack opened the first of the two doors and held it open for us. When it clicked shut, he walked around us, lost his balance, fell into the mailboxes, and cursed again.

Rachel stiffened. "You trust this guy in your apartment, Ray?"

Jack caught his breath and opened the second door. "It's okay, little sister. Big brother here owes me one."

Whatever else Jack had said or done in the last few minutes, he was right about that.

After washing the pepper spray out of his eyes in my bathroom, Jack announced, "Nice digs, Ray," then eased himself down onto my living room futon. I was already leaning back in my recliner. He put the wet cloth my sister had given him up to his eyes, looking like he had the world's worst case of the flu. "All this on a teacher's salary, huh?"

He moved a pillow to his side, where one or more ribs may or may not have been broken, and leaned back gingerly. I caught a small smile on Rachel's face as she came back from the kitchen holding two glasses of water.

"Boys," she said, handing us each a glass.

"My landlord likes cops," I said. "Even ex ones. Gave me a break on the rent. I shovel when it snows, replace the occasional lightbulb in the staircase."

Jack took a long sip of water and closed his eyes. "That's something you and I got in common now, isn't it?"

"Decent landlords?"

"We're ex-cops," he said and registered my surprise. "Don't tell me you didn't hear I put in my papers, Mr. Donne. I thought you knew everything that happened at the nine-oh, and what you didn't know your uncle'd tell ya."

"I guess I missed the newsletter, Jack." I put my glass against my forehead and then moved it up to the lump. "What made you qui—put in your papers?"

"Take a fucking guess."

"Oh, I bet I know," Rachel said, sitting on the ottoman but leaning forward and raising her hand like a sixth grader. "You figured out with your people skills you had a better chance of winning the lottery than making detective." She paused to give Jack a smile. "How'm I *fucking* doing, Jack?"

"Nice mouth," he said, opening his eyes. "You blow Dennis with that—"

"Hey!" I yelled, sending another wave of pain to my head. I put my water on the coffee table carefully. "She's my sister, Jack. Cut it out or leave."

Jack looked like he wanted to argue the point, but I think his ribs reminded him that he'd be better off where he was for the moment.

"Let's just say," Jack said, barely moving his lips, "I decided my future lay on a different career path. So I put in my fifteen and left."

"To do what?" I asked.

Jack smiled. "I'm private now. I hung up my badge and hung out my shingle." He reached into his shirt pocket and pulled out a card. Like a magician, he flung it at me, hitting me in the chest. *Fucking Jack.*

I picked the card off my lap. It had a picture of a horse on it. "Jack Knight," I read aloud. "Private Investigations and Security."

"Have Dick, Will Travel?" Rachel asked.

Jack ignored her. "See the horse? It's a knight. Like in chess."

"Very clever. How's business?"

"That's what I wanted to talk to you about."

"But you decided to assault me instead?"

"I lost my temper," he said. "The whole thing with Ricky T, y'know?"

"How did you find out about that so quickly?"

"You think you're the only one with friends? I gotta call from a buddy at the precinct. By the time I got on scene, you both'd been taken to the hospital. I drove over," he swallowed hard, "got the word about Ricky, and waited for you."

"What the hell for?"

He looked over at Rachel and then at me. "Can we talk? Alone?"

"If you think I'm leaving you alone with my brother, you're dumber than you look."

Jack squirmed and looked like he wanted to get up again. "Ray?" he said.

"Easy, Rachel," I said. "I do want to talk with Jack."

"What the hell am I supposed to do?" asked Rachel.

My stomach growled. "Go on down to Christina's. Please. Pick up six egg sandwiches with kielbasa and—"

"I don't want kielbasa for breakfast."

"—*and* something for yourself. You can take some cash out of my wallet. It's in the baggie from the hospital—"

"I can buy breakfast, Raymond." She took two steps toward the door and turned. "The coffee should be ready. You boys can get that yourselves."

"Thank you, Rachel."

When the door shut, Jack got right to the point.

"Ricky was working for me," he said. "Has been for a few months now."

"I thought he was driving the cab."

"At night, yeah. During the day, I had him doing some of my light work."

"Light work?" I repeated. "Light work that doesn't get you killed?"

"I know. You don't think that's the only thing on my mind the last coupla hours?" Jack got up slowly and walked to the window. He looked out at the Manhattan skyline, the early morning sun casting an orange glow on the buildings. When he turned around, I couldn't tell if his eyes were showing emotion or still suffering from my sister's pepper spray. "But, I swear, Ray. It was light work."

"Jack. Sit down before you fall down."

He stepped back over to the futon and sat. I let him get comfortable before speaking again.

"Explain," I said, as if talking to one of my students.

"I needed someone to do a few building inspections for me," he said. "Most of my work—over ninety percent—is for insurance companies. Someone gets injured or's the victim of a crime in one of the buildings they cover, the company's gotta send an investigator, do a report. Check the stairs, door locks, the carpeting, lighting. All that shit. Talk to the super. See if the accident and/or crime was preventable, how much the surroundings contributed."

"You mean see how liable the owner and the insurance company are."

He nodded. "Yeah. It brings in the big bucks, but I do a fair and honest inspection, Ray. Victims' got people on their side trying to make a buck, my guys got me."

Jack sounded like he was auditioning for his own commercial.

"And you got—had—Ricky?"

"He was good at it, man. All those years as a cop, writing incident reports and shit. He did good. Never forgot the report might end up in court someday. Concise, objective." He took a breath. "And I gotta tell ya, having a Spanish guy going into the buildings the companies cover, that ain't such a bad thing."

I looked at Jack's midsection. "That why you still carry the piece?"

"You better believe it," Jack said. "Had to pull it a few times on some of these . . . citizens." When I worked the streets with Jack, the word "citizen" meant any nonwhite member of the community. "Made sure Ricky carried his, too." Jack put his arm on the back of the futon and turned more toward me. "What the fuck were you doing with him, Ray?"

"He called me. Told me he needed to talk and it had to be right away. He picked me up and drove me over to North Seventh and Kent."

He closed his eyes again. "Why the hell would he drive all the way over there?" he asked. "He's at his mom's on the other side of the expressway."

"It was two in the morning, Jack. I was more concerned with what was so important, not the location." *But now that I thought of it, it was a good question.*

"So you didn't ask?"

"No." Then something came back to me. "I do remember him saying he was working more hours and that he wanted to show me something."

Jack leaned forward. "Something on that block?"

I reached up and felt the lump on my head. I picked up my glass and pressed its cool condensation against the lump. "I don't remember. Something he was doing for you?"

"There was nothing he was doing for me that's worth talking about at . . ."

I've never known Jack Knight to start a sentence without finishing it. Now it was my turn to lean forward.

"What is it, Jack?"

He shook his head. "Nothing," he said, but not very convincingly.

"Jack? If you know something, my uncle's coming over in a few—"

"No. It's just that Ricky was doing such a good job for me, and he said he needed more hours. The cab thing wasn't pulling in enough bucks, so . . ."

That was twice now with the unfinished thought. "Jack?"

"I let him do some grunt work for me on a case," he said. "A real case."

"What's a *real* case?" I asked, and then remembered what he'd said about most of his business. "The other ten percent?"

"Yeah. A buddy of Ricky's works out in Nassau County now, lucky bastard. Their patrolmen pull in as much as our sergeants do."

"Get to the point, Jack."

"This buddy, he puts me in touch with this family. Rich white folks. Live on the water out there in Nassau. Guy's a big shit in PR in the city. About a month ago, their daughter goes missing. You probably saw it in the papers."

"Rich white girl from the Island disappears? Yeah, Jack. I think I saw it in the papers. And on TV. Folks got a website up with a reward, right?" It took a couple of beats for me to come up with the name. "The Goldens?"

"Right. Angela Golden. Look her up on GoldenGirldotcom. That's where I come in."

I brought my glass down from my head and took a sip. "Maybe it's my head, Jack, and all the shit I've been through the past few hours, but you're gonna have to go through that part for me real slow."

"Every time a debutante goes missing and the family puts out a reward, the crazies start coming out like diarrhea. That's why the cops hate fucking rewards."

"Virtue being its own, right?"

He gave me a look like I was speaking Latin. "Huh?"

"Never mind. Keep going."

"Me? I love rewards. I get to bill by the hour for chasing down every halfway-credible lead that comes in to the website. The closest thing to a clue the family could provide was that the daughter recently hooked up with a new friend. Puerto Rican, Dominican, they're not sure. The one thing they are sure of?"

I waited. "Yeah?"

"Parents said their kid tells them her new running buddy's from the Willy B. I hear that, I get Ricky T to do a little double duty. While he's out doing my accident reports, I got him asking around about 'anybody see this *chiquita.*'"

"And let me guess . . ."

"That's right," Jack interrupted. "I get to bill two clients at the same time and split the fees with Ricky. Called that a nine-point-one on the Ric-Tor scale."

The RicTor scale was Ricky Torres's rating system on everything from Spanish food to music to the girls we'd see out on the streets during our patrols. A breakfast burrito from Mickey D's was a one. My uncle being Chief of Detectives, a nine-point-five.

"How was he able to look for this '*chiquita*'?"

"I got a picture from the Goldens." Jack reached into his pants pocket and pulled out his cell. After pressing a few buttons, he handed the phone to me. I was looking at a blurry face of an obviously dark-skinned girl with a smile that could sell toothpaste, but the quality of the picture made her barely distinguishable from hundreds of other good-looking Hispanic girls around Williamsburg. "That's a blow-up," Jack explained, "of a not very good photo they found in Angela's room."

"Ricky get any hits off this?" I handed Jack's phone back.

"Nah, but he was out there trying." He put the phone back in his pocket. "All billable hours, man."

"How nice for you."

"*And* for Ricky. I told you, he wanted more hours. I guess he needed the cash."

"He ever say for what?"

"Cost of living? I don't know. Guy didn't have to shell out much green over in the Middle East. Makes ya forget how expensive the big city can be when ya get back home and gotta start paying for shit again."

"So you don't think doing your light work—or grunt work—had anything to do with Ricky being killed?"

"Ray, if I thought that, you and me would not be having this conversation. For all I know, maybe you were the target."

I hadn't even considered that and didn't want to do so now. But Jack did have a point. Why would Ricky need to involve me if he already had a photo of Angela Golden's Latina friend and his own connections inside Williamsburg?

"So," he said, "you never told your little sis about our adventure with your boy Frankie, huh?"

"Oh, yeah, Jack. I tell her every time I break the law. Maybe I'll mention it to my uncle when he swings by for dinner tonight."

"That's some funny fucking shit there, Raymond."

I closed my eyes and leaned back into the recliner. "You ever think about it, Jack?" *I know I did.* "I mean, it was a good shoot, but not exactly by the book."

"I didn't read the book as much as you did, Ray. That's why I was there that night. But, yeah, I fucking killed a guy. A guy who was about to kill you and who kidnapped your student, by the way. No one's ever gonna accuse me of being Mr. Sensitive, but you think a day goes by I don't think about it?"

I waited for him to say more. When he didn't, I said, "And . . ."

"And better him than you or the kid, okay?" he said. "Don't read too much into that. You and me were never meant to be friends. Ain't nobody who knows us don't know that. But on the street, if it's between some asshole with a gun and a brother cop? That's one of them no-brainers we learned about in the academy."

I was about to remind him I wasn't a cop two years ago, when the door to my apartment opened. Rachel came in holding two bags of the best-smelling Polish food this side of Warsaw.

"Breakfast, boys." She placed the food on the coffee table. "Don't get up." The sarcasm again. I needed some of that. "I'll get the plates and silver." She looked down at the table. "And the coffee, I guess."

"We were talking," I explained.

"I got it."

She went into the kitchen, and someone's cell phone went off. It wasn't mine, and the way Jack just sat there I figured it wasn't his. Rachel stuck her head into the living room holding my baggie from the hospital and said, "Ray. Your phone. You wanna let it go to voice mail?"

The ring didn't sound right. "I don't think that's mine, Rache."

She opened up the baggie and pulled out the ringing phone. It was not mine. Mine was—where? She stepped over and handed it to me as the ringing stopped—just reaching for it hurt my shoulder—and something else came back from last night. Before everything went all to hell, Ricky had handed me something.

Jack and I looked at each other. I pressed the phone's home button, and the screen lit up. "Fuck me."

Jack slid over to the edge of the futon. "What?"

I handed Jack the phone, and he looked at what I had. "Fuck me hard."

"Boys," my sister said. "We haven't even said grace yet."

Jack reached into his pocket, pulled out his cell, and punched some buttons. He put his phone next to Ricky's, studied them both for about ten seconds, and then turned them to me.

There, once again, on Jack's phone was the blurry picture of the girl with the great smile. On Ricky's was an in-focus image of the same girl.

Chapter 3

"I FUCKED UP, RAY."

"What kinda fuckup?"

"On the RicTor scale, about a nine-point-eight, man."

"That's a pretty big fuckup, Ricky."

"I know it. But, lemme show you something. Then tell me you wouldn'ta done the same thing."

"You two comparing cell phone sizes, now?"

"Rachel," I said. "Come here." When she got to the side of my chair, I held the phones out for her. "Whatta you think? This the same person?"

She looked at the pictures. "Could be. It's hard to tell 'cause this one's blurry, but that is the same smile. Again, hard to be sure, but in this one," she held up Ricky's phone, "she looks a bit older. Maybe it's the hair?" She took a closer look. "This girl is pretty."

I studied the picture on Ricky's phone. "Terminally." I pressed the button to call back whoever had just called, and I was sent directly to an automated response telling me the caller was unavailable.

"What the fuck are you doing with Ricky's phone, Ray?" Jack asked.

"He gave it to me." I was remembering more now. "Said he needed to show me something."

Jack shot up off the couch as Rachel was handing me back the phones. His face told me he suddenly wished he hadn't. On wobbly legs and through gritted teeth, he said, "What did he tell you, Ray? That he'd found the girl we were looking for? Were you and Ricky gonna go for the reward without me? That it?"

There's the old Jack, I thought. *Paranoid as all shit.*

"I never got a chance to see the picture, Jack. Remember? All the bullets? The concussion? Ricky getting killed?"

"Maybe all that happened after you got a look at the picture. Maybe that's why you kept the phone."

"Right, Jack. It was all a plot against you." I let out a breath I didn't realize I'd been holding. "Somebody at the scene probably found the phone, assumed it was mine, and put it in the bag." I flashed back to last night before I left the apartment. I didn't remember taking my phone.

"Tell me more about the missing girl," I said to Jack.

He got quiet for a few seconds and took a deep breath as Rachel stepped into my kitchen. "The family," he said, calming down a bit now. "The Goldens. They're offering fifty G's for info that leads to her safe return home. Like I said, they all do that, the rich ones. I was weeding out the nut jobs, but the thought occurred to me that if Ricky or me found the chick . . ."

"You and Ricky were going to split this?"

"We were practically partners. I'm not gonna cut Ricky out of something like that. Especially if he came up with something big."

I gave him a look like I didn't quite believe him, but I kept my mouth shut. Jack took the opportunity to sit back down on the futon.

"Coffee, boys?" Rachel placed two steaming mugs on the coffee table and removed yesterday's newspaper to make room for our breakfast. "I'll be right back with some plates and napkins. Try and play nice."

Jack put the wet towel back up to his eyes and grinned. "She ain't too bad when she's not spraying people with pepper or using them as a kicking bag."

"Birthday gifts from Uncle Ray. Got her the spray and a year at the gym with kickboxing lessons."

"Tell him I said thanks a lot."

"I'll do that. We're having dinner tonight."

"I'll be gone by then. Shucks."

"He'll be disappointed he missed you, too."

Rachel returned with our sandwiches. She had placed two on each plate and after putting them down on the coffee table, she went back into the kitchen and came back with her own breakfast: a big plastic container of cut-up fruit.

"You still on that diet, Rache?" I asked.

"It's not a *diet,* Ray. It's a lifestyle change."

"Oh." I took a bite of my egg and kielbasa sandwich. If I was wrong and there was a Heaven, this was what they served for breakfast. "I thought it was a diet."

"Diets don't last, Ray. I'm the expert on that. I'm just eating a lot more fruits and veggies and cutting way back on the dairy and meat. You might wanna give it a go sometime." She speared something that looked like a chunk of pineapple and put it in her mouth. As she chewed, she said, "So what's with the picture of the girl?"

"It looks like it might be the—"

"It involves a case I'm working on," Jack interrupted. "Can't say more than that at the moment."

"Because I might spill the beans?" Rachel said, pointing a pair of blueberries that were stuck on the end of her fork at Jack. "Ruin the whole case?"

"Because," Jack said, "every client deserves confidentiality. That's why we're called *private* investigators."

Rachel ate the blueberries and smiled. "That's a good answer, Jack."

"Glad you approve, little sister."

We ate in silence for another minute or so. The food was doing wonders for my body and my head. After I finished my first sandwich, I looked at Jack, who was already halfway through his second.

"I remember Ricky saying something about making a mistake," I said. "You know anything about that, Jack?"

"Do you?"

"No, Jack, I don't. That's why I'm asking you." I felt some anger rising up, making my head hurt more, so I took a bite of pickle. Whatever else had gone down between Jack and me, we had both lost a friend a few hours ago. I didn't have the strength for another argument. "Stop with the paranoid shit. Up until last night, I hadn't seen Ricky since he got back. *He* called *me*. Said he had to talk. Why we had to talk over on the Southside and whatever it has to do with the picture on his phone, I don't have a clue. All I remember is his saying last night that he'd made a mistake. I guess he figured I could help him with whatever it was."

"That's you." Jack wiped his lips with a napkin. "Officer Friendly."

"I was looking out for a friend."

"You wanna go there, Ray?" He leaned forward to put the other half of his sandwich down. "You wanna have a conversation about looking out for friends in front of your little sister here? I think she'll be real interested in hearing how far some people are willing to go to help out a friend. Or a friend of a friend?"

Jack was starting to sound like some of the kids I worked with. They'd get themselves into an argument of their own creation, start feeling the wall creeping up behind them, and then change the subject. I had to remind Jack—and myself—that we were on the same side here.

"Let's stay focused here, okay, Jack? Do you think Ricky's murder could have anything to do with the work he was doing for you?"

He took a breath, trying to get back on track. "The insurance inspections or the missing rich girl?"

"Either one."

"He never said anything to me that made me think he was in any kinda trouble. Of course, people don't open up to me like they do to you, Ray."

"We have different . . . skill sets, Jack." *Man, I could be diplomatic when I wanted.* "When were you two supposed to hook up again?"

"Not until Monday. He wasn't gonna call me unless something broke on Angela, the Golden girl. I told Ricky he could work some weekend hours if he wanted—do an inspection, take some photos, ask around about the girl—and I'd pay him for it. But I don't do Saturday and Sunday unless I absolutely have to."

"And he told you he needed money, right?"

"Fuck, Ray. Who doesn't need money?"

"But more now. You said he didn't bring it up until recently."

"Yeah, I guess that's right."

I took another sip of coffee and started in on my second kielbasa and egg. I think more clearly when I'm well fed. Rachel got up and came back with the coffeepot. She refilled all three of our cups and returned to the kitchen.

"Why so pensive, Ray?" Jack said, surprising me with the word choice.

"That's a good place for the cops to start."

"What is?"

"What was going on in Ricky's life that made him need more money?"

Jack shrugged. "He probably just wanted to get the hell out of his mom's crib, man. Guy's in his thirties, spent the better part of the last three years overseas. Living with your mom's only cool for so long, y'know?"

"You're probably right."

Jack studied my face as he took a sip of coffee. "But . . ."

"But," I said, "I don't like the timing. Ricky tells you he needs more cash, and within a couple of days, he's killed. Guy does two tours in the sandbox and this is how he ends up? It doesn't feel right."

Jack shook his head and laughed.

"I say something funny?"

"That's the rookie that used to crack us up in the locker room."

I hated when Jack called me that, but did my best not to let it show.

"Your whole *feelings* thing. Sometimes shit just happens, Ray. It's not a matter of fair or unfair. Lotta times it's being in the wrong place at the wrong time. Maybe Ricky's dead 'cause someone hates cab drivers, or ex-cops, or Marines just back from fucking Mullah Mullah land. Maybe some wannabe gangbanger was busting his cherry. Who the fuck knows? All that matters is Ricky's dead."

"You telling me you don't care why?"

"Not as much as I care about the *who*. I'll tell ya something else, Ray," he leaned forward to put his cup down, "I find out who did this before the cops . . ."

I held up my hand. "You sure you wanna say this out loud, Jack?"

"The fuck's it matter I say it out loud? It's just you and me, right?"

Rachel took that cue to return to the living room.

"There's me, too," she said.

"Don't you have dishes to do or something?" Jack asked.

"Give it a rest, Jack," said Rachel. "We know what you're thinking.

We've all seen *The Maltese Falcon*. Man's partner gets killed, he oughta do something about it, right?"

"Jack," I said, "my uncle's going to be here later. He's arranged it so he's going to take my statement. I'm going to tell him everything I know, which is not all that much, but I'm gonna have to tell him Ricky was working with you. There's gonna be a whole lot of police on this, Jack. And that's not us, anymore."

Jack considered that, picked what remained of his sandwich off the plate, and finished it in two bites. When he was done, he wiped his mouth, rolled up the napkin, and tossed it on the table. He slowly stood up and didn't speak until he got his breathing under control. Just when he was about to say something, his phone rang. He looked at the screen, gave it a puzzled look, and said, "I gotta take this." He motioned to my back deck. "You mind?"

"It's all yours." Jack went out to the deck, careful to close the sliding door behind him. Rachel gave me a look. "He's a busy guy," I said, watching Jack through the window.

"I can see why. He is one smooth operator."

"He's not all bad, Rache. Apparently, there're a lot of people willing to pay money for his skills and type of approach."

"A lot of them are overtaking foreign countries, I bet."

I laughed. "I doubt it, but I wouldn't be too surprised if he subscribed to *Soldier of Fortune*."

We both turned at the sound of the deck door sliding open and closed. As Jack put his phone away and took out his car keys, he looked like someone had just told him he was adopted.

"Everything okay?"

"Yeah," he said. "I guess. I am fucking tired." He stood, frozen in place for about fifteen seconds before speaking again. "That was my friend over at the nine-oh. The one who called me last night?"

"Yeah?"

"He told me there was another taxi cab–related shooting last night. Over in Long Island City. Right over the bridge."

I gave that some thought. "Cops think they're connected?"

"They do now."

"Why's that?"

"Both cabs are licensed by the same company, part of a mini-fleet corporation. Six cabs. They drive some themselves, lease some of them out, and hire drivers—like Ricky T—to pick up shifts. Ricky's cousin is a partner in the cab company."

I let that sink in. "What happened to the driver?"

"He's in ICU. Took one in the shoulder, but he's expected to pull through."

"How was it done?'

"Same as Ricky. Automatic weapon, shooter in motion, cab shot to shit."

"Fuck," I said.

Before I could add to that deep thought, Rachel asked, "So, what does that mean? Somebody's shooting up cabs owned by Ricky's cousin?"

"That's what it looks like," Jack said.

"So, Ricky," I added, "may not have been the target after all. The cops' job just got a whole lot harder."

"Yeah," Jack said just above a whisper. "That it did." He spun his keys around like a cowboy playing with his gun. "I gotta go. Make some calls."

"You okay to drive?" Rachel asked, unable to resist taking one more shot.

"Yeah. I think I can make it." He looked down at me. "You think you can maybe keep the Golden family out of your statement, Ray? Ricky was kinda working that one under the table, and I don't need that kind of attention right now."

"What kind of attention is that?" I asked.

"The kind that makes it tough for a small businessman such as myself to keep conducting business." Jack ran his hand over his crew cut. "I don't wanna say you owe me one, but . . ."

"I'll tell him only that Ricky was in touch with you." I got out of the chair slowly and tried hard not to make any old-man noises. "Someone's gonna get around to questioning you, Jack. Tell 'em what you think they need to know."

Jack nodded. "I appreciate that, Ray." He offered his hand and I took it. I think that might have been the first time we'd ever done that. "What'd you say before? You got two more weeks until school starts?"

"Yeah. I go back the day after Labor Day. Why?"

"Just thinking, is all. I got kinda used to having an extra body around. You know, doing those inspections for me, the interviews."

It took me about fifteen seconds to catch on. I squinted at Jack. "And you're thinking I might be a candidate for the job?"

"I know. I can't believe I'm thinking about this, but you're a hard-ass for detail and know your way around paperwork. You still got your piece?"

I nodded. "Yeah."

"Licensed?"

"I renew it every year."

"Good. You never know. You got my card. Ya start getting bored, think you could use three hundred—*cash*—for half a day's work, gimme a call."

"Jack, I appreciate what you did for me and all, but you and I? We've kind of proved that we don't work well with each other."

"That's the beauty of it, Ray. We don't barely gotta see each other. You got a computer and a printer, right?"

"Yeah."

"I'll send you a PDF of the inspection report. You fill them out and fax them to my office. I'll send them off to the insurance companies. Whatta ya say, Ray? Put some extra bills in your pocket before summer's out. Off the books, if that don't offend you."

"I'll give it some thought, Jack."

"You do that. Don't think too long, though. I'm probably gonna need someone on Tuesday," he added, closing his eyes. "If you can fill in until I get another regular . . ."

"I said, I'll think about it."

He raised his hands in mock defeat. "That's all I'm asking." He turned toward the door and stopped. "Can I have Ricky's phone?"

"Nice try. You know I gotta give this to my uncle. It's evidence, Jack."

"Had to give it a shot. Can ya at least text the picture to my phone?"

I gave that some thought and looked at Rachel.

"Take a photo of the screen," she said. Before Jack could respond, she added, "We're turning the phone over to Uncle Ray. You don't want a record of you receiving the photo by text from Ricky's phone a few hours after the shooting."

Jack gave that some thought and then did as my sister said. After taking the photo of the photo, he put the phone back in his pocket. I went into my bedroom and found my cell still sitting on the bureau. When I got back to the living room, I took my own picture of the girl on Ricky's phone.

"Let me know soon about this week, Ray. I got three inspections coming up, and I haven't even checked my e-mail today."

"I'll call you, Jack."

"Looking forward to it, Ray." He looked at Rachel. "I'll see ya around."

"I'll try and wear my good boots next time."

Jack laughed and shook his head. "Same wiseass as your brother." With that, he turned and left my apartment.

"You're not seriously considering working with him, are you?" Rachel asked as the door closed.

"You heard him. It wouldn't exactly be working *with* him. More like a freelance gig where we won't have to have too much contact."

"*Any* contact with him is too much." She accented her point with a fake shiver. She was quiet for a moment and then added, "He was involved in that Frankie Rivas thing, right? The part of the story you never told me?"

Bright girl, my little sister. "Yeah."

"You ever going to tell me the whole story, big brother?"

"Maybe on my death bed."

"Let's hope that's a long way off." She put her arm around me and gave me a gentle squeeze I accepted in spite of my pain. "A long way off."

Chapter 4

"RAY," SOMEONE SAID. "YOU IN there, sweetie?"

The question was followed by a long gentle kiss on the lips. *Nice.*

"Mom?" I said opening my eyes.

Allison raised her hand to smack me, but thought better of it. "You're lucky you got a concussion, tough guy." She put her hand on my leg, leaned over, and gave me another kiss. "How're you feeling?"

I looked at her hand on my leg. "Better now." It was going to take a while to shake off the nap. "How long was I sleeping?"

"I got here an hour ago. Rachel told me you'd been out for an hour and to make sure I woke you up." She picked up her hand and made a peace sign. "How many fingers am I holding up?"

I took her hand and brought it to my mouth. "Two." I kissed the hand. "Two really cute fingers." I inched myself up and waited for the lightheadedness to fade away. I looked around my living room. "Where's Rachel?"

"She's out on the back deck talking with your mom."

I sat up straighter. "Fuck, she's here?"

"Relax." Allison put her hand back on my leg. "She's on the phone. Has been for forty-five minutes. Judging from what I've heard so far? Your sister's doing most of the listening."

"Good. That means Mom's not thinking of driving into Brooklyn."

"She's worried about you, Raymond. She's your mother and you've been in a horrible . . . I don't know . . . incident?"

"Sure wasn't an accident." I reached up and touched the lump on my head again. I wouldn't swear to it, but I thought it had gone down in size. I flashed back to the loud pops, and the white, and the black. I closed my eyes to make them go away. "Jesus, Ally. How'd you find out?" I realized too late I should have called her myself. "Your editor call? Someone else from the paper?"

"Rachel. She called me while she was waiting to pick up your breakfast. She said you had a friend here with you."

"I wouldn't exactly call Jack a friend. Guy I used to work with at the nine-oh. We . . . haven't seen each other for a couple of years. He's a PI now and was having Ricky Torres help him out with some local jobs."

"Ricky was working for a private investigator and ends up being shot? I hope you asked the obvious questions, Ray."

"Of course. And the cops will ask him again, but he couldn't make any immediate connection. Ricky was doing routine incident reports and . . ."

"And what?"

"And now with the other cab shooting . . ."

"Yeah," she said. "That's what I was doing before I got here. I was down on the waterfront in Long Island City talking with the cops and some locals. No one saw a thing. Just like in your case. Jack doesn't think there's more to Ricky's case than the other?"

I paused before answering. "Not really."

"I don't know what that means, Ray."

I reminded myself my girlfriend's a reporter. "Jack said Ricky was asking around about another case, but he didn't go into details. Something about client/PI confidentiality, but he didn't see a connection there, either."

"You trust this . . . not-exactly-a-friend guy?"

Good question. "I don't think he had any reason to lie to me. Maybe he'll think of something when he talks to the detectives."

Allison thought about that and nodded. "You know," she said, "the media is gonna make a big deal out of this. We're still looking into the background of the other victim, but Ricky was an ex-cop and Middle East vet, shot and killed on the mean streets of Brooklyn that aren't supposed to be this mean anymore."

I sat up a little more. "By the media, I guess you mean your paper?"

"And the others," she replied, trying not to get defensive. "And local TV." She looked over at my landline. "They're going to want to hear from you. Anybody call yet?"

"Not that I know of. Maybe when I was napping, but I haven't given an official statement yet. Maybe they don't even know I was there."

"Someone does, and the others won't be far behind. How'd they let you out of the hospital without—" She caught on quickly. "Your uncle."

"Yep. He's even arranged it so that he's the one who'll take my statement."

"He can do that?"

"He's Chief Donne." I looked over at the clock on my cable box. "And he's coming over in a few hours. Can you stay for dinner?"

"Until I can't." She stood, walked over to the window, and looked out. After a while, she turned back. "I'm kind of on call at the paper."

"What does that mean?"

"It means," she began, "when a big story breaks and they have to put a lot of reporters on it, we all have to pitch in and work overtime to cover the regular stuff that happens in the five boroughs."

"Don't they have freelancers for that?"

"Yeah, Ray. And little boys and girls still deliver the newspaper by bike early in the morning before Dad leaves for work." She rubbed her eyes. "They're not even paying us for doing this, but we can't complain. I get one more speech about how lucky I am to have a job in the print media, I'll wring my editor's neck."

"Which," I leaned forward into a sitting position, "*would* be a big story and *would* result in more work for your coworkers."

Allison laughed, which did more good for me than any pill.

"Yeah. They'd forgive me for killing the boss. Probably even take up a collection for my defense. But fuck with their off time? *That* would incur their wrath."

She came back to the futon and sat next to me. Instinctively our hands found each other's, and we sat in silence for half a minute.

Allison squeezed my hand. "Whatta you need, Ray? Right now, what can I do?"

"You're doing it," I said. "I'm gonna need a shower before Uncle Ray gets here, but I think I can handle that myself."

She ran her thumb across the back of my hand and leaned into my ear. "You sure about that?"

I must have been getting better, judging from the feeling spreading across my groin. Too bad the increase in blood flow started my head throbbing again. I leaned back.

"Easy there, Ally. Too much of a good thing might not be the right approach at the moment."

"Oh, sure. Whenever I'm in the mood, you've got a headache."

Now it was my turn to laugh and that hurt, too, but I didn't give a shit. I found myself thinking how nice it would be to spend my last two weeks of summer vacation sitting on my futon with Allison. I was never much for the beach anyway. We could order in takeout, watch bad TV, save money by showering together. I was about to suggest that, when Rachel came back into the apartment. She was looking at the phone, smirking, and shaking her head.

"Mom says hi," she said. "She's having some friends over for a late lunch, so we had to keep the call to . . ." She looked at her cell. ". . . An hour and six minutes."

"What's she serving?" I asked, knowing my mother's habit of turning every conversation to food.

Rachel slipped her phone into her pocket and very seriously said, "Roast beef, salami, American *and* Swiss cheese, and some *really* nice macaroni salad that was on sale at the deli counter."

"So, she's doing okay?"

"Yes. And you're welcome."

"For what?"

"For talking her out of coming over here tonight."

"She hates driving at night. Even to go a few blocks."

"Yeah, well, this is the first time her son's been shot. Or shot *at*, I guess." My little sister's eyes filled with tears. She walked over to the window and turned to look at the skyline. *What was up with the women in my life and*

*that window? Were they embracing the view of the skyline or turning away
from me?* She took a few moments before speaking. "You need to call her
tonight, okay?"

"Yeah, I will." I got up from the futon and took a few steps toward
her. "I'm okay, Rachel." I reached out with both hands and she came over
and took them. I brought her into a hug. "I'm fine, kiddo. I got the shit
shaken out of me, but I'm gonna be okay."

"I know," she whispered. "Just don't get shot at anymore, okay?"

"I'll do my best."

She squeezed me one more time. "You'd better." She let me go, took
a step back, and wiped away some tears. "I need your bathroom," she said
as she crossed the room.

Allison came over and slipped her hand into mine.

"You realize," she said as my sister closed the bathroom door, "how
lucky you are to have Rachel, don't you?"

"Yeah. I don't think about it every day, but, yeah, I know I'm lucky."

"Good."

I squelched an impulse to tell her I was grateful for her, too. Then the
moment passed, and my buzzer buzzed. I looked at the clock on my DVR.
It was just after four-thirty, too early for my uncle. Allison went over and
pressed the Talk button. "Who is it?"

"Rachel?"

"No," Allison said. "Who is it?"

"Raymond's uncle. Who the—?"

Allison shut him off by releasing the Listen button and buzzing the
door open. She then stepped over, unlocked my apartment door, and opened
it a crack. My guess was Uncle Ray rushed through whatever meetings he
had at One PP—One Police Plaza—and then had his driver take him straight
here. Part of me was pleased that my uncle cared enough to come early.
The other part—the part that gets nervous when you're called to the principal's office—knew he was also here to take my statement. I didn't think
I'd have much to say, but my uncle had a well-deserved reputation for getting more information out of an interviewee than the interviewee knew he
had.

A minute later, there was a knock. I steadied myself as I opened the door and saw Uncle Ray had changed into a dark blue suit with a white shirt and loosened green tie. He took the suit jacket off and placed it on the back of my futon.

"Allison," he said. "Good to see you. Are you here as a . . . journalist, or as Raymond's paramour?"

"Always the charmer, Chief Donne." She surprised him by stepping over and giving him a kiss on the cheek. "I'm a girlfriend today."

"Then," my uncle said, recovering from the kiss, "it *is* good to see you. You may call me Ray. Or Uncle Ray if that keeps you from confusing me with your boyfriend."

"Thanks. Uncle Ray."

He turned to me. "Nephew. How's the noggin?"

"Good. I ate, slept, and woke up with an angel watching over me."

"Save the greeting card shit for your sister. I'm assuming you've got some adult beverages in the fridge?"

"I just picked up a nice assortment of Brooklyn beers, but I really don't think I should be drinking with a concussion, do you?"

"Nice to see you still think you're funny. That's a good sign. Don't worry yourself. I'll get it myself. Allison?"

"No, thank you."

My uncle went into the kitchen and quickly reappeared with a bottle of Brooklyn Pennant just as Rachel came out of the bathroom. He looked from Rachel to Allison, then raised his bottle to the two of them. "Thank you both for being here. I don't know what my nephew ever did to deserve either one of you, but here you are anyway."

"As are you, Uncle Ray," Rachel said.

"Yes. Now, both of you. Get out."

"Excuse me?" asked Rachel.

"I need to talk to my nephew, and it needs to be in private." He reached into his pocket and pulled out some money. He peeled off the first two bills—twenties—and handed them to my sister. "It's a bit early, but go downstairs and order us some dinner. Anything but that crap with cashew nuts." He took out another twenty. "Take your time. Have a cocktail. I'm going to need a half hour. Maybe less."

"This couldn't wait?" Rachel asked.

"It *has* waited," Chief Donne said. "And the sooner you two scram, the sooner my official business will be over, and we can all have a nice dinner."

"I already had plans with Dennis, Uncle Ray. I was hoping to spend another half hour with Ray and then head out."

"We all have hopes, kiddo. Call Dennis and tell him you might be late. If he gives you any shit, mention my name."

Rachel thought about arguing, but then seemed to remember the last few decades of losing arguments to Uncle Ray and thought better of it.

"Come on, Allison," Rachel said. "Let's go have a drink while the menfolk talk."

Allison gave me a kiss on the cheek. "See you in thirty, Ray."

"I'll be here," I said. "Get me that spicy broccoli, okay?"

She gave my uncle a look. "With or without the crappy cashews?"

"Whatever you want. Thank you."

After the door shut, my uncle sat down on the futon—leaving no room for anyone else—and took a sip of ale. "I mean it, boyo. That reporter lady is too good for you."

"Thanks, Uncle Ray." I sat back in my chair. "What do the cops know about the other shooting?"

"How'd you find out about that?"

"I have a reporter lady on payroll," I lied, not wanting to bring up Jack yet.

"Right. So far the only connection is they both involved automatic—or semiautomatic—weapons and cabs owned by the same corporation. We're doing a background check on the other driver and the partners of the corporation." He took a sip of beer and added, "Sometimes police work is like performing colonoscopies, Ray."

I knew the rest, so I finished it for him. "Look up enough assholes and you're bound to find something."

"I love it when a student remembers the little things." He gave me a proud smile. "Now, as to your role in all this excitement."

"How're we going to do this?"

He reached behind him and pulled a mini-recorder from his jacket pocket. He held it up to me. "I'll tape your statement and have it transcribed in the morning. You remember how shitty my handwriting is."

I nodded. Poor penmanship was one more dysfunction I'd inherited from my dad's side of the family. Uncle Ray placed the recorder on the coffee table and pressed a button.

"Okay," he said. "Here we go."

Chapter 5

"THIS IS NYPD CHIEF OF DETECTIVES Raymond Donne." My uncle spoke loud enough to be picked up by the voice recorder. "The time now is"—he looked at his watch—"four forty-seven." He went on to give the date and the location of the interview, and instructed me to identify myself for the record.

"My name is Raymond Thomas Donne."

"You understand that you are here of your own volition and are not at present being charged with any crime?"

"Yes," I said. "I also live here."

My uncle gave me his stop-being-a-wiseass look. "And as such you have waived your right to have a lawyer present?"

"Yes."

"Okay, Mr. Donne. Can you tell me where you were at approximately two-fifteen this morning?"

"I was sitting in a parked taxicab just off the corner of North Seventh on Kent in the Williamsburg section of Brooklyn."

"And were you alone?"

"No. I was with Ricky T—Richard Torres."

"How did you come to be at that location with Mr. Torres?"

"He called me and picked me up at my apartment."

"Which is the same location as this interview?"

"Yes."

"Was Mr. Torres in the habit of calling you early in the morning and picking you up to drive to various locations?"

"No. This was the first time."

"When had you last seen Mr. Torres?"

I gave that some thought. "About three years ago. Right before he was deployed to the Middle East."

"And you've had no further contact with him until this morning?"

"We talked on the phone shortly after he returned. That was about six months ago. But we never got together."

"What did you think when he called you and asked you to meet him so early in the morning?"

"He said he was in trouble and needed to speak to me. I asked what the problem was, and he said he had to tell me in person. When I asked him if it could wait until morning, he sounded agitated and said it had to be right away."

"And you agreed to meet with him?" That question was asked more by Uncle Ray than NYPD Chief Donne.

"A friend said he needed to talk to me. I wasn't going to wait until a more convenient time to help him."

Uncle Ray nodded, pleased with my response.

"Did there come a time after he picked you up that Mr. Torres explained what this trouble was?"

"No. We never got to talk about it."

"And the reason for that?"

I gave my uncle an icy stare. "Because," I said, "Mr. Torres was shot and killed before he got the chance to tell me."

My uncle leaned forward and turned the recorder off. "Don't give me the look, Raymond. If I don't ask, someone else will."

I shook my head. "I know. Sorry."

"Don't be sorry. Be clear, be concise, and just answer the questions asked." He turned the recorder back on. "Interview was interrupted for two minutes while the witness went to the bathroom. Can you describe the shooting, Mr. Donne?"

"I'm not sure. It all happened so quick."

"Just state for the record what you do recall."

I closed my eyes and tried to remember what had happened. If I started at the beginning, maybe some of the blank spaces would get filled in along the way.

"As I said, we were parked just off the corner of Kent Avenue and Seventh."

"Did you or Mr. Torres choose that parking spot?"

"Mr. Torres."

"Did Mr. Torres give any reason for parking at that location?"

"No. I asked, and he said he'd explain everything. It took him a while to get started. We were sitting in his cab for about ten minutes, and I remember him telling me that he had made a mistake." I closed my eyes again. "He handed me his cell phone and said I'd understand." I paused. "Oh, shit. That reminds me, Uncle Ray . . ." I pulled Ricky's cell out of my pocket and handed it to him. "The EMTs must have thought that was mine and put it with my personal belongings."

Uncle Ray turned off the machine again.

"Okay," he said. "I'm going to ask you if Ricky gave you anything, and you're going to say yes and then identify his cell phone, and I will acknowledge receiving the phone from you. Got it?"

"Yes."

He cued the interview back to pick up earlier and started again. "Interview was interrupted as the witness excused himself to get a glass of water. Mr. Donne, at any time during your meeting with Mr. Torres did Mr. Torres give you anything?"

"Yes," I said, trying not to sound rehearsed. "He gave me his cell phone."

"Do you have that phone with you at present?"

"I do."

"Let the record state that the witness has just turned over the victim's cell phone to this interviewer. Interviewer has placed the phone into a plastic baggie provided by Mr. Donne." He looked at me and shook his head, meaning "not now."

"What happened after Mr. Torres gave you his phone?"

"The next thing I remember is the sound of the driver's side window breaking. When I looked over, Ricky—Mr. Torres—was lying facedown on his steering wheel. I didn't hear anything . . . I didn't know what . . ." I closed my eyes against a sudden urge to get up and run into my hallway. I willed myself to breathe slowly.

"Are you okay, Mr. Donne? Do we need to take a break?"

"No." I took a deep breath. "I leaned over to see what had happened and then more shots were fired—a lot more shots. Like from an automatic. Pretty much the next thing I remember was waking up in the emergency room."

"Can you state how much time elapsed between the shooting of Mr. Torres and the next series of shots?"

"Not exactly. But my best estimate would be less than ten seconds."

"Did you sustain any injuries during this shooting?"

"Just a concussion. The driver's air bag went off, causing his head to crash into mine. That's when I became unconscious."

Uncle Ray thought about that for a few seconds. "Have you anything to add at this time, Mr. Donne?"

"No. That is all I remember at this point."

"Thank you." He picked up the recorder. "This concludes the initial interview with witness Raymond Donne." He turned the machine off. "Not bad, Nephew. Pretty much what you told me at the hospital. Except for the phone."

"I didn't know about the phone until I got back here, Uncle Ray."

Uncle Ray picked up the phone and pushed the button that lit up the screen. He pressed another button. "Shit."

"I know. Unknown caller. I tried that myself."

He pressed another button. "Shit. All the recent calls, same thing." He turned the phone to me. "Who's the girl?"

I cleared my throat and told the truth. "I have no idea." *Most of the truth.*

My uncle imitated me by clearing his throat. "But . . ."

"You remember Jack Knight?"

It took him a five count. "Jack the Whack?"

"That's the one."

"What about him? I heard he put in his papers a while ago. Big loss," he snorted.

"He was here this morning. When I got home from the hospital."

"You running a home for wayward ex-cops or something, Raymond?"

I decided to skip the beginning. "Jack's a PI now and Ricky's been picking up some hours for him. Doing some building incident reports, stuff like that."

"What's that got to do with the girl on the phone?"

Time for a little more truth. "Jack said it was something to do with a case Ricky was working on. A missing kid thing."

My uncle looked at the picture. "This girl's gone AWOL?"

"You gotta talk to him about that. He didn't go into much detail."

"So what the hell was Jack Knight doing here this morning?"

"Same thing you are, I guess. Just in a less official capacity. He got a call about Ricky and me, went to the hospital, and followed Rachel and me back here. He wanted to know why I was hanging with Ricky at two in the morning over on the Southside. I told him what I told you. He didn't like it and went home."

"And that's all?"

"That's all I can tell you, Uncle Ray."

"That's not exactly what I asked, Raymond."

I nodded. "Have someone talk to Jack." I reached into my pocket and handed Jack's card to my uncle. "You know Jack. He's not gonna tell me shit. But if you send a detective over . . ."

"That's what I need right now. Someone telling me how to do the job."

"Not what I meant."

"I know," he said and rubbed his eyes. He leaned his large frame back into my futon. "It's just been a long twenty-four hours, kiddo."

"For both of us."

"Right. Anyway, one thing I was able to find out was that your boy, Ricky Torres, put in his papers for reinstatement a few days ago."

That seemed to go with Ricky asking Jack for more hours.

"Any idea why he waited as long as he did, Uncle Ray?"

"Nope. But I've got someone down in Human Resources making sure that paperwork goes through last week."

"Why? What good will—?" Then I got it. "The benefits. You don't think they'd deny his family the benefits, do you?"

"We both work for the city, Ray. You have to ask that question? I'm not taking any chances with that kid's bennies going back into the city's coffers. I checked. His mom's still around, and I'll be damned if some four-eyed city bureaucrat is gonna tell her that her son—who did two fucking tours over there—died without benefits."

"And you can make this happen?"

"I can and I did. My girl over in HR knows what buttons to push to make sure the paperwork is dated last week and that it was approved yesterday."

"Which just happens to be the day Ricky was killed?"

"Actually, he was killed today, remember? Life's full of ironies, isn't it? At least this one's gonna help out the kid's mom and his brother."

I'd forgotten Ricky had a brother. Must be in college by now.

"That's good, Uncle Ray. I hope this doesn't blow back into your face."

He laughed. "That would mean some civilian Poindexter in front of a computer actually gave a damn, Raymond. Anybody wants to give me shit, I'll sic your girlfriend on them, and they can explain to the people of this city who still read newspapers how the family of Ricky Torres—a true goddamned American hero—should be denied his well-deserved taxpayer-funded benefits."

"Allison's not a cop. She's not going to bark just because you say so."

He smiled as if to say, "Yes, she will," but had the decency not to. "She hit you up for a story yet?"

"No. And I don't expect she will. She can't write about me objectively, we're dating."

"Then you can expect a call from one of her cohorts. Soon."

"And now that I've given my official statement, I won't have a problem with that." I found myself almost believing my own spin. "It's a big story. I was there and can help put a human face on it."

"Damn, boy," Uncle Ray said. "You're starting to talk like a member of the press. Best be careful before she puts a leash around your neck."

I shook my head very slowly got up from my chair. "You kill me, Uncle Ray. You got everybody figured out. Everybody fits into your little boxes." I gave him a mock-serious look. "How'd you ever get so cynical?"

"Years and miles, Nephew. When you got enough of both behind you, you'll see how wise a man your old uncle was."

"I see it now. I grew up seeing it. You're a good man, Uncle Ray. Probably the best I've ever known."

"That's the concussion talking."

"No, it's not. You are a good man. But that doesn't make you right about everything."

He stood up. "That's definitely the concussion talking." He looked at his watch. "The girls'll be back up with the food any minute. Why don't you hit the head, wash your face, and powder your nose? I'll get the plates and stuff." He looked around my apartment. "I'm guessing, what with the absence of a dining table, we'll be eating in the living room?"

"You're a damned fine detective, Chief Donne."

I went into the bathroom. The face in the mirror was definitely mine, but it seemed to have aged ten years since yesterday. I leaned in to get a better look at my eyes. The pupils were dilated—a result of the blow to the head—but not as bloodshot as I would've guessed. I ran the cold water for fifteen seconds and then splashed it on my face. With dinner about to show up, it would have to do for now. I remembered Allison's earlier offer of a shower, and hoped for a quick dinner and exit by my uncle. His words to my sister came whizzing at me through space:

"We all have hopes, kiddo."

Chapter 6

RACHEL HAD TO LEAVE FOR HER dinner with Dennis, and thirty minutes later the only remnants of dinner were half an egg roll, an unopened box of rice, and an assortment of plasticware, plates, and bowls. Allison and I cleaned up and decided not to mention dessert or the possibility of one more drink to my uncle. When we got back into the living room, Uncle Ray was leaning back, eyes closed.

"Damn," he said, rubbing his belly. "That hit the spot. You guys wanna watch a movie or something?"

Allison grabbed my hand and squeezed. I gave her a silent look that said I'd take care of it. My uncle opened his eyes.

"I'm just messin' with ya. Told my driver to meet me outside at six." He looked at his watch. "It's almost that now. I'll see myself out."

He got himself up off the futon with more than a little effort. He grabbed his jacket and stepped over to Allison. "Thank you again. I'm glad my nephew's got someone in his life who cares."

"So am I," Allison said and kissed my uncle on the cheek. "Thank you."

Uncle Ray turned to me. "Keep your head down, Nephew."

"I will, Uncle Ray."

"Any symptoms," he said, "right to the ER and call me."

"Absolutely."

He pulled me into one of his manly hugs and then eased up out of fear of hurting me. His hugs could do that even when I didn't have a concussion.

"Call your mother."

"As soon as you leave."

He looked at Allison and winked. "You better. I don't want you getting yourself all distracted and leaving it 'til the morning."

"I won't." I walked him to the door. "You and I will talk soon, I guess."

"Soon," he said and exited my apartment.

When I got back into the living room, Allison was coming out of the kitchen with a new beer. She raised it to me. "You can have *one* sip. Then call your mom."

"And then . . . ?"

She handed me the beer with one hand and reached around and squeezed my ass with the other. "Call your mother, tough guy."

I woke up in a cold sweat hearing gunfire and the sound of metal creaking. Allison and I were on top of my comforter—we'd never made it under the covers—and she was wearing my Brooklyn Pilsner T-shirt and little else. My mind kept flashing back to twenty-four hours ago: Ricky's face in the steering wheel, the sound and smell of his cab being shot up, the lights of the emergency room. There was no way I was getting back to anything resembling sleep tonight.

I rolled out of bed and went into the bathroom. I popped three more ibuprofens and chased them down with some cold tap water. My throat hurt, so I went to the freezer and treated myself to a couple of spoonfuls of chocolate ice cream. I let them slide down as I looked at the darkened skyline outside my kitchen windows. The city may never sleep, but it does rest its eyes every once in a while.

On my way back to the bedroom, my cell phone started ringing. In the dim light, it took me a few rings to find it hiding on the coffee table. I didn't recognize the number, but given the events of the last day, I picked it up.

"Hello?"

"Ray. It's Jack."

"What the—Jack. It's . . ." I looked at the digits on my DVR. ". . . Not even three in the morning. I told you, I'd call—"

"Shut up, Ray, and get dressed. We both know you weren't sleeping."

"How do you know that?"

"This your first time being shot at, right?"

"Yeah."

"My *first* time? I slept like a baby for days."

"Is that right?"

"Yep. Woke up every two hours, cried for a bit, and then hit the bottle."

In spite of my fatigue and nightmare, I laughed. "That's good."

"I'll be outside your apartment in five."

Maybe I was still dreaming? "Jack, I've got my girlfriend over. What the hell are you talking about?"

"I just got a call from that buddy of mine at the nine-oh."

"Okay . . ."

Pause. I could hear that he was in a car. "You dressed yet?"

"Jack, you're not making much sense. What's going on?"

"What's going on is you and I are heading over to the Southside."

"Why would we want to do that?"

"My buddy just told me they found a DB in the East River Park."

Please, I hoped I was dreaming. "How does that concern me?"

"Because this particular dead body," Jack said, "used to be a teenager, and next to this teenager the cops found a bike and a Beretta Px4 semiautomatic pistol. It's also less than two blocks from where Ricky T was shot." He paused for effect. "You dressed *yet?*"

"I'll meet you out front."

It took me a few minutes to convince Allison that I had not, all evidence to the contrary, lost my mind, and that I'd call her from the crime scene. Of course, she wanted to come, and of course, I said no. She seemed to go along with it, but I knew she didn't approve. I promised I'd be back for breakfast. This whole conversation took place as I was getting dressed, so I was able to keep my word to Jack and was out front in five minutes.

"Any shit from the missus?" he asked as I slid into the passenger seat of the vintage Ford Mustang he must have bought to complete the image of a PI. To his credit, this question was asked as he handed me a large cup of coffee.

"A little," I said, taking a sip. "She's on the phone with her paper now."

"I forgot she's a reporter."

"Your buddy say who caught the case?"

Jack smiled. I didn't like it when Jack smiled. "You're gonna fucking love this, Ray." He made an illegal left at the light, and I remembered I needed to buckle up. "Remember Detective Royce?"

"You're shitting me, right?" I said. Royce was the detective in charge of the Frankie Rivas case a few years ago. He knew he never got the full story of my involvement in getting Frankie home, but chose not to pursue it. It was one of those times where my last name—and another's willful ignorance—helped me out.

"I am shitting you not." Jack made a quick right and headed toward the river. "He's gonna flip when he sees your white ass, huh?"

"He's not *going* to see me, Jack. I don't know who your buddy is, but there's no way either one of us is stepping foot on that crime scene."

"Don't need to." He turned around and pointed with his thumb at the Dunkin' Donuts bag and two boxes of coffee on the backseat. *Promoting the stereotype.* "I'm bringing refreshments in exchange for the possibility of some inside info that just might be pertinent to one of the cases I'm working on."

I took another sip as I deciphered that latest bit of information. When I was done, I didn't like the conclusion I'd come to and was about a centimeter away from getting real pissed off.

"You told me that Ricky's death had nothing to do with any case he was working with you."

"I said I didn't *think so,* Ray. I'm a big enough man to admit that there's an outside chance I could be wrong."

I chose my next words carefully. "You're a dick."

"Oh, get off the fucking high horse, Cowboy. I'm still not sure if there *is* any connection, but when I hear that a body's found dead with a semi-automatic pistol by his side, and then I remember that my old buddy Raymond Donne stated that the last thing Ricky T may have heard was automatic gunfire, I've got to check it out." He took a sip and another left turn. "I know your sister was busting my balls before, but she was right: Ricky may not've been my *partner* partner, but we were working together, and I'm gonna check this shit out." He screeched to a stop in the middle of the street. Some hot coffee flew out of my cup and landed on my jeans. "You want," he said, shifting the car into Park, "I can let you out here and you can walk back home to the little lady."

We stared at each other for maybe ten seconds as I waited for the burning sensation on my leg to subside. "Okay," I said, taking some napkins out of the bag and wiping my leg. "Drive."

Jack shifted the car back into Drive. "Thought so."

A few minutes later, Jack pulled over to the curb and took out his cell phone. He spent the next few seconds typing, and then pressed a button.

"I just sent my buddy a text that we're here." He leaned into the back and reached into the Dunkin' Donuts bag. "You wanna donut before the cops get their hands on them?"

"I'm good." I pulled out my own phone to call Allison to see if there really were any hard feelings from my not inviting her to tag along.

"This guy Jack," she said. "He sounds a bit . . . unstable."

I opened my door and stepped out into the street. From where I stood, it looked like half a dozen patrol cars had responded to the call. I could also make out a few town cars; Brooklyn brass had arrived. I did not see any TV vans. Yet.

"He's not even sure this has anything to do with Ricky, but any chance for some juice and Jack'll jump."

"Just don't be holding his hand when he does, Ray."

"I'm a big boy, Allison. You get in touch with the paper?" I asked, deftly changing the subject.

"How did you . . . Yeah," she said. "They got a guy heading over. I scored a point with the graveyard editor. This is what they used to call a scoop."

"Good. See, Jack's come in handy already."

"How're you feeling, by the way?"

"I'm okay. A little dizzy, but it's early in the morning."

"Just get home in time for breakfast."

"It's on the top of my to-do list."

As I ended the call with Allison, I noticed a patrolman half walking/ half jogging over to Jack and me. When he got within five feet of us, he stopped and took off his cap just as Jack stepped out of his car.

"I thought you were coming alone, Jack," he said, scratching his head. The cop seemed to be about my age, but the bags under his eyes made him look older and told me that he'd been pulling a lot of overtime lately.

"He's a . . . friend, Roy," Jack said. "Roy White, Raymond Donne."

I offered my hand, and Roy looked at it like it was last week's tuna. "Raymond Donne?" He turned to Jack. "This is the chief's kid, Jack?"

"Easy there, Roy. Ray's the chief's nephew."

"Big diff," Roy said. "The chief know you're here?" he asked me. "Or that I called Jack?"

"Neither," I said. "Like Jack said, I'm here as a friend. There's no reason for my uncle to know anything about this. How long've you been at the nine-oh?"

"About five years, why?"

"Because I don't know you. I left a while ago."

He turned to Jack. "You bring the treats?"

Jack spun around, opened the back passenger door, and pulled out the to-go boxes of coffee and a large bag of donuts and coffee fixings. He handed them to Roy. "There's my end of the bargain."

Roy accepted them and then looked over his shoulder. "Gotta make this quick. Some of the big boys are starting to show up."

"Why's that?" I asked.

"You want the full answer, or do I *Reader's Digest* it for you?"

"You're the one working."

"Right." He put the coffee and donuts on the hood of Jack's car and walked over to the sidewalk. Jack and I followed.

"You read the papers," Roy said. "Watch TV. We been getting a lot of shit about which cases get the most attention and which ones don't. So when a . . . black youth shows up dead along the river, we treat it with the ut-most priority."

I had a comment for that, but decided to keep my mouth shut.

"Also, with the mayor's war on illegal and out-of-state guns, the guys with all the stripes wanna make sure they are all over this before briefing Hizzoner, who, I hear through the grapevine, is already on his way to the hospital as we speak to meet personally with the victim's family—as soon as they get an ID—to share their pain and express his outrage at another senseless killing involving an illegal weapon. How the family's gonna spin what their kid was doing down by the river at this hour—possibly in pos-session of some serious firepower—should be interesting to watch."

I looked at Jack and then back to Roy. "So why'd you call Jack?"

Roy gave Jack a look, not knowing how much to say. Jack spoke first.

"Roy and I have a deal. If he comes across anything he thinks might be of interest to me, he calls. It's called the private investigation *business* for a reason."

I knew that. Back in the days when I was a cop, I had a few PIs give me their business cards. They made decent bookmarks.

"But how'd he know to call you about this?"

"I put the word out on my way home from your place this morning. Any squeals involving automatic or semiautomatic weapons, gimme a shout. Roy did." He turned back to his friend. "You sure on the make and model?"

"Beretta Px4," Roy said. "Nice piece for a gangbanger. Too nice to leave behind. Worth at least three or four bills on the street."

"So, the shooter . . ." I started to say.

"Wanted the piece to be found," Jack finished for me. "And I betcha another dozen donuts that when Ballistics gets their hands on the vic's gun, it's gonna match one used in a very recent and very local shooting."

"Shit," I said, not wanting to believe where Jack was headed with this. There were too many illegal assault weapons floating around the five bor-oughs. It was a bit of a leap to say this was the one that had killed Ricky. But Jack had a point about recent and local. "Anything interesting on the DB?" I asked Roy.

"He's got some outstanding ink work running from just below his right ear down to his little finger. They're processing his prints now. If he's in the system—and that's not a very big if, if you ask me—they'll have him ID'd not too long after the mayor gets to the hospital."

"Who discovered the body?"

"Livery driver. He heard a shot while enjoying a late-night beverage along the waterfront. He was halfway over the bridge before he called nine-one-one."

"So no wits?" Jack asked.

"Nada."

Jack and I looked at each other. Neither one of us came up with anything else to say. Officer Roy White took the bag and boxes off the hood of the car and said, "Better get these over to the scene before they get cold."

"Good looking out, Roy," Jack said. "You'll let me know when anything else comes up?"

"Yeah." Roy looked over his shoulder then back at Jack. "Same deal, right?"

Jack took Roy by the elbow and walked him away from me, back toward the scene. They stopped before reaching the sidewalk, Jack said something I couldn't hear—which was the point of putting some distance between us—laughed, and patted his buddy on the back. Roy turned to leave, then stopped as if he suddenly remembered something. He said one more thing to Jack, then headed in the other direction. Jack stood there for at least twenty seconds. When he came back to where I was, he said, "Didn't wanna bore you with the details of my business, Ray. You understand, right?"

"Yeah, Jack. Private means private."

"I appreciate that." He looked at his watch. "Well, too late for a drink and too early for breakfast. I guess you want me to drop you at home, huh?"

"What was that last thing Roy said to you?"

"Just something he noticed about the vic."

"Something interesting enough to ponder in the middle of the street?"

Jack considered whether to share this last bit of information with me. He walked around to the driver's side of the car and leaned over the roof. "You remember what Roy said about the tattoos on our dead kid?"

"Yeah?"

"He noticed some more ink on the palm of the kid's left hand."

"Another tat? Gang shit?"

"No. This was real ink, like from a pen."

"What'd it say?"

"Could be nothing," Jack said, sounding like it was anything but.

"That's not an answer, Jack." I leaned on the roof of the car. Our eyes met over the top of his fancy Mustang. "What did it say?"

Jack looked down at the roof of his car. He licked his forefinger and made a circular motion along a spot in front of him. He then took his sleeve and buffed out whatever he thought was there.

". . . Jack?"

"He had the letters KT written on his hand," he finally said.

"That's it?"

"They were followed by a slash and the number seven."

KT/7? "Some gang code?"

"You still think like a cop, man."

"So you don't think it's gang-related?"

"Remember where Ricky T was shot?"

"Do I remember where—?" *Shit.* "God damn it," I said, a bit too loudly. "Kent and North Seventh."

"Underneath KT/7 was written DJ2S," he said. "And I'll betcha another bag of donuts that was—"

"The medallion number of the taxi Ricky was driving."

"Bingo, Officer Donne!" Jack slapped the roof of his car. "That dead scumbag killed Ricky T, Ray. We don't need ballistics to tell us that."

"*We* don't need ballistics to tell *us* shit, Jack. Did Roy share this with Detective Royce?"

"Yeah," he said unconvincingly. "I'm sure he did."

"We need to be more than sure, Jack. We have to know that Royce makes the connection. Sooner rather than later."

"You wanna go walk over to the crime scene and tell him, Ray? Maybe go out for a beer later and take a trip down Memory Lane?"

He had a point. "Text your buddy. Tell him what we just figured out, have him tell Royce. Officer Roy White's gonna look like a genius."

Jack smiled again and pointed at me. "That's good, Ray." He took out his phone. "That's real good."

"I know."

"Now, Roy's gonna owe me big-time."

Good for you, Jack, I thought. *Good for you.*

Chapter 7

BY THE TIME I GOT THE BAGELS, cream cheese, and coffee up to my apartment, Allison was already showered, dressed—still in my T-shirt, but her own jeans—and sitting on the futon with my laptop on her lap. It was barely five thirty, and she was hard at work and looking pretty damn cute.

"Nice field trip, dear?" she asked, not looking up from the screen.

"Let me put some breakfast together and I'll tell you all about it."

"Keep talking like that, tough guy, and I'm moving in."

I laughed, but not too loud. Allison and I had been seeing each other for the better part of a year, and to say the thought of living together hadn't crossed my mind would be a lie. As it was, we spent two or three nights a week at each other's places, but I was glad we hadn't had The Talk yet. Maybe if we hit the year mark . . . .

I put the bagels and coffee on a tray and brought it over to the coffee table. Allison held up one finger, telling me to give her a minute. I took the time to hit the bathroom and splash my face with water for what seemed like the hundredth time in the past day. My face had been feeling hot since the ER. Probably a concussion symptom I was unaware of. When I got back, I sat beside her.

"So," she said, rubbing her hand on my back, "what did you and your new friend find out this morning?"

I told her about Jack's relationship with Roy White and how the cops had found a semiautomatic pistol next to the dead kid. I left out the part about the letters and numbers scrawled on the victim's hand. As much as Girlfriend Allison would have loved that tidbit, Reporter Allison didn't need to know that yet. When I was done, she let out a slow whistle.

"Wow," she said. "You've got a career in journalism if this teaching thing doesn't work out."

"That's off the record. Whatever your guy finds out on his own is fine, but I don't know how much the cops are gonna put out there, so . . ."

"We had this talk already, Ray," she said, pulling away her hand on my back.

"That was last December, Allison. I just wanted to make sure the ground rules were still in place and acceptable."

She reached over and patted my leg. "Don't be a dick. It doesn't suit you."

"I'm not being a dick," I said—something I usually say when I'm not quite sure if I'm being a dick or not. "What were you working on when I came in?"

She leaned away from me as if I'd burped. "That's what this is about?" She looked down at the laptop and turned it toward me so I could see the screen. "I was researching shootings over the past five years like Ricky T and the other cabbie's. I didn't find much. Then I looked into how many cops are in the reserves and how many go back to the force after they get back. It's all background, Ray, that whoever *does* cover what happened to you and Ricky is gonna need. I know I can't cover your story, but it doesn't mean I can't do a little research and help out. Besides, what the hell was I supposed to do when you were out playing detective in the early-morning hours? Vacuum?"

I leaned over and put my arm around her.

"I guess you could have made the bed," I said. "Done a load of laundry?"

She laughed. "You *are* a dick."

"Let's write it off as an early-morning gaffe from a guy suffering from a concussion and a near-death experience."

"You didn't seem to be suffering much last night when I was helping with your recovery."

"I know. It was like finding out I had *really good* health insurance."

We both laughed this time, and she placed her head on my chest.

"You didn't sleep much last night."

I pulled her in tighter. "I kept hearing the gunfire," I said. "I got up a few times thinking I smelled something burning. I was wide awake when Jack called."

"Post-traumatic stress," she said. "Probably why you made the extremely wise decision to go out with Jack."

"I was so wired, I had to do something. Heading out with him was as good as anything else, I guess."

"How you holding up now?"

"Still wired and tired. I'm glad you're here."

"Me, too." She reached over and grabbed each of us half a bagel. "Eat a bit." She looked at the cup in my hand. "Coffee's probably not the best idea, but what the hell? I'll run down in a bit and get *The Times* and *my* paper."

I looked at my laptop. "I was thinking about getting a digital subscription to the *Times*."

"Yeah, well, don't do it for my sake."

"Problem?"

"I'm old-school that way, Ray. I need to hold the paper, turn the pages, get my fingers all inky."

I smiled. "I didn't realize you felt so strongly about that."

"How do you feel," she asked, "when you wanna watch a Yankees game and all that's on is the Mets?"

"Good point."

"Let's eat, go through the papers, and maybe you'll doze off for a while."

"That'd be good."

"If not, I've got some stuff in my bag that might help."

"Is it legal?"

"Prescription," she said, ignoring my weak attempt at humor. "With the hours I work, sometimes a little pill helps."

"Whatever gets you through the night, right?"

•   •   •

"I don't know," Allison was saying. "I'll check with him when he gets up."

I opened my eyes and saw Allison on the other side of the window. She was on her cell phone, pacing. I sat up, having no idea how much time had passed since I'd dozed off. As I willed my reluctant eyes to stay fully open against the sunlight behind Allison so I could make out the time on my cable box, Allison tapped on the sliding glass door to the deck to get my attention. I gave her a blank look and shrugged. She said something I couldn't hear as she came back into the apartment. She put the phone against her thigh. "Can you talk?"

Not understanding the question, I said, "Depends."

She moved the phone from her leg to her mouth. "Hold on a minute, Pete." This time she put her hand over the phone. "Can you talk to my guy Pete?"

"You've got a guy named Pete?"

She shook her head as if talking to a drunk. "A guy from the paper. You met him at the benefit last spring. We've done a few stories together."

Oh. That Pete. "Yeah," I said. "I guess. Sometime tomorrow?"

She gave me a half smile/half grimace. "He's kind of downstairs."

"That was quick."

She took a step toward me. "He was the one who covered the shooting at the river last night. He was in the neighborhood and—"

"How did he know where I live?"

"I didn't tell him where you live, Ray. Give me a little credit. He's waiting inside the McDonald's on the avenue."

We stared at each other for a few seconds, then she spoke into the phone.

"I'll call you right back." She ended the call and gave me her full attention. "He called earlier. I told him you were asleep, but would probably be up soon."

"So you sent him to McDonald's?"

"I figured it'd save time. You did say you'd talk to a reporter, Ray. You know this business. If we don't get it now, we'll get it later, and now is better."

Part of me knew she was right. The other part was pissed. I went with the part that knew she was right.

"Call him back," I said, getting off the futon. "Tell him to give me ten minutes. I need to use the bathroom and wake up a bit."

She put her hand on my neck and pulled me into a kiss.

"Thanks, Ray. Sorry."

"We all have our jobs to do. Tell him to bring me a large coffee. Half and half, no sugar. If he wants to talk to me, he's gonna work for it."

Ten minutes later I was sitting on my deck next to Allison and across the way from Pete, enjoying a coffee courtesy of their newspaper. As I only had two outdoor chairs, Pete had to stand. I know I could have told him to bring one from inside, but I didn't want to give him the idea he'd be staying long. He looked out at the skyline, complimented me on my view, and said it was nice to see me again. I said the same even though I had no recollection of meeting him the first time.

"So," Pete said. "How well did you know the victim?"

"Ricky," I said. "Ricky Torres."

"Right. How well did you know Ricky Torres?"

I gave him the quick version: we'd worked together for a stretch out of the nine-oh; after I resigned because of an on-the-job accident, we'd still see each other for an occasional beer; we'd pretty much lost touch after the Marines sent Ricky overseas; and the other night was the first time I'd seen him since he'd been back. I added that I had no idea why he had called me and that we'd barely spoken about anything before the shooting started.

He wrote that in his notepad. "Tell me what it was like being in the car when the shooting began."

I knew that question was coming, but was unprepared for the tightness in my chest that came with it. *Caught looking at a waist-high fastball.*

"You ever light up a pack of firecrackers, throw them into a garbage can, and then stick your head in the can?"

"Nope," Pete said. "Never did that."

"That's what it was like. Or close to it."

He wrote that down, apparently finding me quite quotable.

"How well did you know his family?"

"Not very. Met his mom a few times at precinct picnics. His kid brother, too. We weren't close like where we'd hang with each other's families."

He made another note. "You must have asked yourself why he called you?"

"And I still don't know. I'm sure he's got—had—lots of other friends he could've called." I thought about Jack. "Lots."

"These other friends, they're on the job? Cops?"

"Don't say 'on the job.'" I hate it when non-cops say "on the job." "Most of them, I guess."

"Maybe some from the reserves?"

"I guess you'd have to ask them."

"I plan to." He made a big deal of flipping through his notepad and looked up after half a minute. "You wouldn't have any names for me, would you?"

I took a sip of the coffee he'd bought for me. "Nope."

"I guess I'll have to talk to his mother then."

"Of course you will." The sarcasm was wide awake now. Must have been the free coffee.

He lost the smile. "What's that mean?"

Allison reached over and put her hand on my arm. "It means nothing, Pete," she said, and gave my arm a not-so-gentle squeeze. "Ray's just saying that he understands you have a job to do."

"No," I said. "What I'm not saying is why do you have to bother his mother at all? What are you going to ask her, Pete? 'How's it feel to have your son, who just returned from serving his country on the other side of the world, shot and killed less than a mile from where he grew up?'" Allison's squeeze turned into a pinch. I pulled my arm away, realizing too late I shouldn't have done that, but kept talking anyway. "Because I can answer that for you right now. Save you a trip." I stood up too quickly, raised my voice too high. "It fucking sucks, that's how it feels!" I was breathing heavy now, my vision getting blurry and my mouth drying up. It was all I could do to stay on my feet. "Next question?"

The atmosphere on the deck felt absolutely frozen. I was staring at Pete, he was staring at Allison, and I was pretty sure whom Allison was staring at. With the exception of my neighbor's pigeons returning to their coop and a truck horn blaring from the avenue, we stayed quiet for at least thirty seconds. Allison broke the silence.

"Ray?" she said, taking the risk of touching my hand. "You okay?"

Reporters, I thought. *Always asking the tough, insightful questions.*

I took a deep breath and sat back down. Pete, who was still staring at me, looked as if he'd rather be covering any other story besides this one.

"Sorry," I said to both of them. "It's been a . . . I don't know."

"It's okay," Pete said. "I hate that part of the job myself. But I'm telling a story here, Ray, and the family of the victim is part of that story." He tapped his notepad against his leg two times. "And, no, I don't ask them how it feels. I've been doing this more than a few years now. What I do is I let them speak." He leaned back against the ledge. "Speak for themselves and the victim. No offense, but I've heard some real good cops say the same thing."

I had, too. I was brought up to believe that's what police did. It's exactly what my Uncle Ray had taught me. Pete was making it hard for me to continue disliking him.

"Yeah," I said. "Okay." *Like he needed my permission.* "You have any more questions for me?"

"Not about the vic—Ricky Torres, no."

"Then . . ."

"What were you doing at East River Park early this morning, Ray?"

I looked at Allison, who gave me a look that said, "Don't look at me."

"Patrolman." Pete flipped open his notepad. "Said Chief Donne's nephew arrived at the scene. How and why did you show up there, Ray? Is there a connection between that shooting and the shooting of Ricky Torres?"

Patrolman Roy White should have kept his mouth full of donuts and coffee instead of running it off to a reporter. Didn't he know enough that he'd be putting himself, his coffee supplier, and me in the shit with that kind of loose talk?

"He told me off the record, of course," Pete added.

"Of course." I considered my answer carefully before answering. "I can't tell you why I was there." Anticipating the next words out of his mouth,

I said, "Not yet. It's probably nothing, but if it becomes something, I promise you you'll be the first to know."

"My source only told me because he originally thought your presence at the scene had something to do with the commanding officers showing up and your uncle being who he is."

"*Did* my uncle show up at the scene?"

"Not to my knowledge. Any reason he should have?"

I repeated what Officer White had told Jack and me about the brass making a big deal out of the mayor's gun control battle and correcting how black victims of violent crimes were often underrepresented in the media. It occurred to me Pete had mentioned nothing about Officer White telling him that Jack was there as well.

"Did the mayor get to the hospital, Pete?"

"Oh, yeah. Got some very quotable quotes. You'd have thought he was running for reelection already. I'm sure he'll be all over the networks tonight. Guy knows how to work the press, I'll give him that."

"He gives good TV," I agreed.

Pete looked at his notes for a few seconds and then flipped the pad closed. "I appreciate your letting me come over, Ray. I can't imagine what you've been through, and I know it's not easy to talk about."

"Thanks." I offered my hand. "Sorry about the yelling before." I gave Allison a quick glance. "I'm going to blame it on the PTSD."

"Agreed," he said, shaking my hand. He turned to Allison. "You'll e-mail me that research?"

"Soon as you leave," she said.

"Thanks. You guys hang in here," he said. "I'll see myself out."

Neither Allison nor I argued as he did just that. When we heard the front door shut, Allison turned to me. "Remember earlier? When I said *don't* be a dick?"

"Yeah?"

"Thanks for listening. You scared the shit out of Pete."

"He's a big boy. He can handle himself."

"You scared me, too, Ray. That was some outburst. I've never seen that side of you before."

"I've never been in this kind of situation before, Allison." I rubbed my eyes. "Jesus. It's finally hitting me. I could've been killed last night. I'm not sure how I'm supposed to react, but I bet anger's right up there on the top of the list."

She put her arm around me. "I'm sure it is, but you're only going to get away with this dickish behavior for so long, Ray."

"I'm not even sure that's a word, Ally."

"I'm a writer. If there's not a word to fit what I'm trying to say, I have the license to make one up."

"I'm done arguing for the day."

"Me, too."

I put my arm around her and pulled her into a hug. It was just what I needed at the moment. Then my cell went off.

"You want to get that?" Allison asked.

"Not really." I reached over anyway and picked up my phone, which was next to my coffee. I looked at the caller ID. *Shit*. He'd probably just heard the news. "I better get it. It's Edgar."

Chapter 8

IT TURNED OUT EDGAR WAS RIGHT downstairs. Maybe he'd run into Reporter Pete on his way out. As soon as he hung up, I stepped into my bathroom to pop a few more ibuprofens. Edgar buzzed and was at my apartment door in less than thirty seconds.

"Jiminy Cricket, Ray," he said after giving me a breathless, one-armed hug. I don't think Edgar did full hugs or ran up four flights of stairs much. "Why didn't you call me? I'da been right over."

"You were the first person I *thought* to call, and then my sister showed up at the hospital, Allison came over, then my uncle . . ."

Edgar looked over at Allison. "Hey," he said, nodding with his chin.

Allison smiled. "Hello, Edgar."

"Before I knew it," I said, "a whole lot of time had passed. I was gonna call you tonight." I noticed his eyes starting to moisten. I reached out and touched his elbow. "I'm okay, Edgar. Really."

He shook his head, looked at the floor, and closed his eyes. "Okay." He looked at Allison again. "I didn't mean to interrupt anything or whatever. I was on my way back from a convention upstate, heard the news, and came right over."

"It's fine, Edgar," Allison said. "What was the convention?"

Edgar's face broke out into a huge smile, as it always did when someone showed any interest in what he was doing. And a pretty woman? Forget about it.

"It was up in Albany. The annual Spy Show. Companies from all over the country and a dozen foreign countries were there. All with the newest, top-of-the-line surveillance equipment. Most of it not even on the market yet. At least not in the U.S." A lightbulb went off over his head. "Want me to run down to the car? I got the catalog and a couple of DVDs. It is the absolute coolest stuff, really."

"That's okay," I said, noticing how quickly he'd gotten over my situation. "Some other time, Edgar."

The smile faded. "I knew it. I *am* interrupting something. Sorry."

"No. It's just that I'm real tired. I'd love to look at that stuff. Maybe this week at The LineUp, huh?"

He thought about that. "Yeah, maybe. I just don't want the other guys to start ribbing me about it, Ray. They already think I'm some sort of nerd."

"The *best* kind of nerd." He didn't seem to find that humorous or flattering. "Don't worry about what they think, Edgar. *I'm* interested. I love that shit."

The smile returned. "Cool beans. Hey, what about that other cabbie shooting? The cops connect it to what happened to you and Ricky?" Edgar acted like he already knew about it, probably from his police scanner.

I told him about both cabs being owned by the same corporation. "What it all means? I have no idea."

"*Yet*," he said, trying to sound coy. Edgar did not do coy very well.

"Don't start, Edgar. This is a high-priority case. Ricky was an ex-cop vet who was planning on returning to the PD. If they connect last night's shooting vic to Ricky, it's gonna get real hot. The last thing anyone's gonna want is another ex-cop sticking his nose in where it doesn't belong." I could see where he was about to go with that. "No matter *who* his uncle is."

I could almost hear the gears turning inside Edgar's head. Once again, I was close to a case, and to Edgar, that meant *he* was close to a case.

"Ray," Allison said. "What's this about last night's shooting? You're making it sound like there's more of a connection than you led me to believe."

My first thought was to bluff my way out of it. Claim that I had misspoken and that it was obviously a symptom of stress and lack of sleep. I looked at both their faces. Neither was going to buy it, so I decided to go with the truth and told them about "KT/7" being written on the victim's hand and about the shell casings in my shooting possibly matching the gun found—or left—next to this morning's victim.

Edgar and Allison both shook their heads, contemplating what I'd just said and looking at me as if I'd lied to them. It wasn't a lie. Not really. I just left—No, it was a lie. Exactly what I'd tell one of my students. *A lie of omission.*

"Why didn't you mention that to Pete when he was here?" Allison asked. She turned to Edgar. "A reporter I work with." Back to me. "Who Ray was *supposed* to give a full and accurate account of everything he knew."

"That's not completely true," I said. "He was here to interview me about the shooting *I* was involved with. He was at the scene, Allison. If he didn't come up with the same info I did, too bad for him. And before you give me another lecture on freedom of the press, the cops haven't made an official connection yet. That'll come after they match the victim's gun with the bullets in Ricky's cab. I'm not gonna give some reporter info that may turn out to be nothing."

Allison took a deep breath before speaking. "By 'some reporter,' I'm assuming you mean Pete?"

"Who else would I mean?"

She forced a smile. "And you don't think your girlfriend would want to know?"

Edgar took a few steps back. I wished I could have stepped back with him.

"Allison. You gotta cut me a little slack here. I'm still learning how to walk this line with you. Most of the time you're my girlfriend, and I love . . . that. But when I came home after the river . . ."—*Tread lightly,* I told myself—"You have to admit: you had your reporter jones on. So much so that, when Pete called, you couldn't wait to get him half a block away from my apartment before I woke up."

As Allison considered that, I took the opportunity to glance over at Edgar, who at the moment seemed to have located something completely fascinating under one of his fingernails. I wondered how glad he was now to have stopped by on his way home from the Spy Show.

"You're right," Allison said.

I am?

"It is hard for me to turn it off and keep work separate from us. But let's be honest, Ray. You don't make it easy. In less than three years, this is the third newsworthy story you've gotten yourself involved in. You ever think about that?"

I did now. I searched my brain for the right words and finally settled on a quote I heard years ago. I think it was Hitchcock.

"Interesting people," I paraphrased, "lead interesting lives."

I could tell by the look on Edgar's face that he liked that. Allison's face told another story.

"Interesting people also come to interesting ends." She grimaced as soon as those words left her mouth and immediately grabbed my hands and squeezed. "I'm sorry, Ray. That sounded real clever in my head and then real shitty when it came out. I'm trying to wrap my head around what you've been through. It's hard. And it scared me. The reporter thing is a way I can put some distance between the shooting and me." She ran her hands up my arm. "Not between *you* and me."

I pulled her into a hug and kissed her on the cheek. "I get it, Allison. We're good. It's been a helluva weekend."

"The Master of Understatement," she said, breaking the hug and addressing Edgar. "You want a beer? Ray's got the good stuff in the fridge."

"Ray's always got the good stuff," he said, and then smiled, realizing that could be taken more ways than one. He was silent for a few seconds and made a big deal out of checking his watch. "Thanks, but I gotta go." He looked a bit embarrassed. "I kinda want to hit the Web sites and reach out to some of the folks I met this weekend."

"It's okay to stay, Edgar," I said.

"Nah, I'm good." He reached out and took my hand. "I'll give ya a ring tomorrow and maybe we can hang for a few at The LineUp."

"I'd like that."

"Okay then," he said. "It's a date." He looked over at Allison. "If you're around, maybe you can hang with us."

"I'll probably work late," she said. "This story's getting bigger, and now with the shooting in the park *possibly* connected, I might be traveling between boroughs tomorrow. But, yeah, maybe."

"Cool," Edgar said. "Mañana."

After he left, Allison and I sat down on the futon.

"He's getting better," I said. "A year ago, he'd have been too nervous to ask you to hang out with us."

"That mean he's getting more comfortable with me?"

"No. He's getting more comfortable with himself."

She leaned back and gave me a look. "You sound . . . proud, Mr. Donne."

I smiled. "I guess I am. My little guy's come a long way."

Allison put her hand on my thigh. "I'll make your little guy—"

The ringing of my landline put that thought on hold. We sat there, Allison's hand not moving, for four rings, and then the machine picked up. After my outgoing message, a voice came on.

"Ray," the voice said then paused. "Ray, this is Robby Torres. Ricky's brother? I'm sorry to be calling you on a Sunday, but—"

Allison jumped up from the futon, grabbed the phone, pressed Talk, and handed it to me.

"Robby," I said. "Sorry, I was just coming in from the deck. How's it—I mean, shit. I'm so sorry about your brother, man. You at your mom's?"

"Yeah," he said.

"How's she holding up?"

"Not good, Ray. Me neither, really. I—" He paused again and I could hear him swallow. "It's just starting to sink in, y'know? I was upstate when my mom called me, and it was fucking unreal. I mean, the whole drive down I was thinking it was a mistake and as soon as I got to Brooklyn everything would be fine."

"I know." Clearly I didn't know shit. "I guess you have a lot of family around the house, huh?"

He laughed. It may have been the most joyless laugh I'd ever heard. "Yeah. The house is packed. Got my cousins up from Jersey, already made two runs to LaGuardia to pick up some aunts and uncles. My mom hasn't come outta the kitchen for hours. She's just cooking and serving. Italian moms, right? That's how they cope."

I'd forgotten their mom was Italian. "I've heard. Listen, I'm not too far away. You need me to come over or anything, just ask."

"That's good of you, Ray, but I think we're cool right now." Another pause. "How you feeling, by the way? Heard you were there."

"I'm good, Robby." No use going on about how I was feeling. This guy's brother was just murdered. "Just a lingering headache."

"Yeah," he said. "Hey, there is something you can do."

"Name it."

"I know you're still teaching, but are you still moonlighting at that cop bar? The Roll Call?"

"The LineUp. Yeah. Why?"

"My mom," he said. "She wants to do the church thing tomorrow with just the family and then a private burial right after. She's seen that cop funeral thing too many times on TV, and she can't deal with that."

"I hear ya."

"But I convinced her we gotta do something for Ricky's friends after that. The neighborhood guys, and the guys from the job. She doesn't want anything at the house here 'cause she knows she's gonna get all overwhelmed and it'd be rude to kinda pull a Houdini on that crowd."

"So, you thinking to do something at The LineUp tomorrow?"

"I know it's short notice, but it's away from the house, Ricky always liked the place, and—"

"I'll take care of it, Robby."

There was a five-second delay. "Just like that? Don'tcha gotta call them up and check with the owner or something?"

"Mrs. Mac's a cop's widow. She'd probably be offended if we didn't have the par—something there for Ricky. I'll make a few phone calls and get it all set up. What time you thinking about?"

He thought about that. "Maybe three o'clock? Cemetery's over in Queens, and we should be done by two thirty, something like that."

"I'll make it happen, Robby."

"Jesus," he said. "That's a real load off, Ray. I mean, you sure? I don't even know how much something like this'll cost. I—"

"That's not your concern now, Robby. Take care of your mom, and I'll see you tomorrow."

"Unbelievable, man. I can't tell you how much I appreciate this."

"Tell me tomorrow. Go back to your family. Tell 'em where we'll all be at three o'clock."

"Yeah," he said. "Thanks, man."

"You're welcome." I ended the call, leaned back into the futon, and closed my eyes. "I guess you heard that."

"I did." Allison put her hand back on my thigh. "That's a nice thing you're going to do, Ray. I can see why Ricky called you when he needed help."

"Yeah. Let's hope this turns out better than that."

"Come on, tough guy." She stood up and pulled me toward the bedroom. "Let's get some rest. We both have big days tomorrow."

"I have to make some phone calls first. Why don't you get ready, and I'll see if I can get a phone-tree thing going. I still have a few numbers in my book. And the first one I need to call is Mrs. Mac."

"She'll be thrilled," Allison said and then gave me another one of those long kisses before whispering in my ear. "Don't keep me waiting too long now. I might doze off."

"That," I said, "would be a damn shame."

She gave me a gentle push away. "Start dialing, Raymond."

About an hour and a half—and six or seven phone calls—later, I brushed my teeth and headed into the bedroom, hoping I wasn't too tired to take Allison up on her offer. Unfortunately, as I opened the door I could hear that deep breathing I'd come to adore over the past months: Allison was out.

I threw on a pair of boxer shorts and a t-shirt, and slipped under the covers. Allison turned, mumbled something that sounded like, "Pablo likes cheese," and turned back the other way. I grinned, closed my eyes, and was asleep in very little time.

Chapter 9

"YOU'RE UP EARLY," ALLISON SAID after she slid open the deck door and gave me a kiss. I'd been sitting outside watching the planes and pigeons fly over for an hour, drinking a cup of coffee, and thinking about Ricky T. The rising sun behind me cast a yellow glow across the Manhattan skyline. "You sleep okay?"

"Yeah," I lied. "Just wanted to get a head start this morning. I promised Mrs. Mac I'd get to The LineUp early to start setting up. Remember Billy Morris?"

She thought about that for a second. "The guy who throws The Q?"

"That's the one. He's got his meat guy dropping off a bunch of burgers, dogs, and chicken at ten. I gotta be there to accept delivery."

"Billy Morris has a meat guy?"

"Among other things. We also have to sweep out the back area and set up a buffet table. The beer guy's coming early as a favor to Mrs. Mac."

"Doesn't she have people for this?"

"The Freddies." I explained about the twin brothers who have worked for Mrs. Mac for the past five years. What their parents lacked in baby-naming skills they more than made up for in teaching their boys a work ethic. "But they were away for the weekend and won't get to The LineUp until noon at the earliest. It starts at three."

She pulled over the other deck chair and sat down next to me. "Not exactly how you planned on spending the last two weeks of summer vacay, huh?"

"No. But it's gotta be done, and I've got nothing but time, ya know?"

"Yeah." She stood. "Listen, I got time for a shower, some coffee, and maybe a bagel." She reached up with her foot and slid it up my thigh. "Which one you wanna help me out with?"

"Well," I said, getting to my feet. "How do you take your coffee?"

She smacked my ass and smiled. "Time to hit the showers, tough guy."

"Whatever you say, Coach."

The car service dropped me off at The LineUp just as the meat truck was pulling up. The side of the truck advertised all the kinds of meat the company purveyed: duck, goat, lamb, turkey, buffalo, and ostrich. Those last two sounded interesting, but the only meats concerning me were burgers, hot dogs, and chicken. The driver and I got everything into the walk-in fridge in less than fifteen minutes. I walked him to his truck, thanked him, and gave him a twenty for his trouble. I signed the receipt and stuck it in my pocket. As he pulled away and I wondered for the first time how all this was going to be paid for, Mrs. Mac came over to me.

"Hey," I said, giving her a hug. "Where'd you park?"

"Just up the block. The meat arrived?"

"And has been put away."

"Thank you, Raymond." She took my hand and looked me in the eyes. "How are you holding up?"

"I'm okay." I said, knowing she was not going to completely buy that—she had been a cop's wife for almost forty years. "I still have a headache and I'm not sleeping too well, but I'm good."

"And you're sure you're up to this?"

"Yeah. It beats sitting around the house watching bad TV with the air conditioner blasting."

We stepped inside the bar, where the air conditioner was just starting to cool the place off. Mrs. Mac locked the door behind us and said, "You could go somewhere. Out of the city."

"I could," I agreed. "I'm a bit low on funds at the moment."

"You could take Allison up to the Catskills for a few days. I know some folks who have a house in Roxbury and won't be back until Labor Day. You'll be an hour away from Cooperstown."

I smiled at this woman who had lost her husband a decade ago to a stress-related heart attack and who could probably sell Eskimo Pies to real Eskimos.

"I'll give that some thought, Mrs. Mac. Thanks."

"Or you could go visit your mom for a few days."

"I thought the idea of getting away was to *reduce* the stress in my life."

She smacked my upper arm. "Very funny, Raymond. Now would be a great time for you to go out to the Island and see your mother. I'm sure she's very worried about you."

I looked the cop's widow in the eyes. "She called you, didn't she?"

Mrs. Mac got quiet and cast her eyes somewhere over my shoulder. When her gaze returned, she gave me a slightly embarrassed look. "We spoke last night. She said she'd like you to come out and spend a few days with her. Maybe take a day trip out to Montauk."

Three hours in the car stuck in traffic with my mother. Not exactly a day at the beach, I thought, and allowed myself a grin at the pun.

"I will call her, Mrs. Mac."

She looked at the clock above the bar. "Now's as good a time as—"

A loud beep from outside interrupted her. I looked through the glass door and saw the beer truck pulling up. *Excellent timing.*

"I gotta get that," I said. "Let's talk more about this later."

"Later we'll be busy."

"Absolutely." I unlocked the door and stepped outside to help.

A few hours later, the bar started to fill up. The event for Ricky wasn't supposed to start until three, but here it was, not even two thirty, and I'd already served about twenty people. Most of them were cops I didn't know, some working out of the nine-oh, some who used to work out of the nine-oh, and a few who knew Ricky T from the academy. Considering it was what it was, nobody had brought along a date. The guy I was talking with, Matty Something, had known Ricky and me from our rookie days.

"A teacher," he said, taking a sip from his longneck Bud. "Are you putting me on, Ray?"

"Nope. After the accident, I just couldn't see going back to the force." I gave him the one-minute version of the past six or seven years of my life, which always ended with the lines, "I'm back in Williamsburg, making your job easier."

Matty shook his head. "Good for you," he said, not meaning it. "But with your uncle's pull, you mean to tell me you—"

"Let's talk more later," I said, not meaning it any more than I had to Mrs. Mac. "I gotta hustle up some more beers for the guys and see if the grills are ready."

I spent the next ten minutes opening beers, working the taps, and putting together a few mixed drinks. I really did need to check on those grills, but I couldn't leave the bar unmanned. As if reading my mind, Mikey—the only full-time bartender at The LineUp—walked through the front door.

"What the hell, Ray?" he said, stepping behind the bar. "Mrs. Mac told me three o'clock. I thought I'd get here early and set up . . ." He looked around at the growing crowd. ". . . But Christ on a motorcycle."

"Most of these guys had the day off. They didn't feel like waiting around. Some went to the church to pay their respects, but most just came right here."

"Beat the traffic on the LIE and the tunnels," he said, referring to the fact that a good number of the NYPD live out on Long Island or in Jersey.

"Let me check the back and get a start on the food."

He slapped me on the back. "G'head, man. I got it back here."

On my way to the outside area, I got stopped and spun around by someone grabbing my belt. I felt a bit dizzy and was all ready to get pissed off when I saw it was Billy Morris. One can never get pissed off at Billy Morris. Just ask him.

He pulled me into a hug. "Thanks for doing this, Ray. I feel like I'm usually the social director for these fucks."

Billy was referring to his annual barbecue, which he threw at his house out in the Sheepshead Bay neighborhood on the other side of Brooklyn. A few years back, he had The Q here at The LineUp because his house was being worked on. That was the first time we'd seen each other since my accident, and then he ended up playing a major part in getting my student Frankie Rivas home.

"You can thank Mrs. Mac for that, Billy." We broke the hug. "As soon as she heard what it was for, she was all in."

"That's her, Ray. How you doing, by the way? I heard you was—"

"Good," I said for what must have been the hundredth time since the shooting. "Let me check the back and we'll have a beer, okay?"

He grabbed my shoulders and shook me. "You better believe we'll have a beer, son. Quite possibly many."

I stepped over to the rear door, which was open, and walked into the small backyard. The two Freddies were stoking the coals of the two grills Mrs. Mac had put out for barbecuing. Basically they were an oil drum cut in half, sitting atop metal frames. Fill 'em with charcoal, light 'em up, and about thirty minutes later you were good to go. Normally, the food at The LineUp came out of the kitchen, but for certain events—Fourth of July, Memorial Day, farewells to cops and vets—Mrs. Mac opened the back area and threw a barbecue. I tapped my watch.

The Freddy on the left said, "Five minute, we ready." The one on the right nodded in agreement.

I gave them the thumbs-up. "Just go ahead and start cooking when you think you're good. Thanks, guys."

Good. The food was taken care of, and Mikey was doing what he did best behind the bar. Debbie, the new waitress who was an NYU undergrad and the cousin of one of The LineUp's cop regulars, was putting on her apron as I stepped back inside.

"Big crowd today," she said in her usual cheerful voice.

"Yeah," I said. "Let's not forget what they're here for, though, okay?"

That took the cheer away. "Sorry."

Shit. "No. Do what you normally do. Just be mindful that these guys are here to commiserate and say good-bye to a fellow cop." I put my hand on her shoulder. "They're all gonna get various degrees of drunk. If it gets a little stupid, let me know. You can always step outside and take a break."

The smile slowly came back. "Thanks, Ray. My cousin's told me a few stories about things like this. I'll be good."

"No doubt."

I watched as she bounced over to a booth of six guys, cleared the empties, took their order, and laughed at one of their jokes. She was going to be fine.

"Yo, *maestro*!"

I turned around to see Victor Rodriguez walking toward me. He had a grin on his face that was clearly a mix of happy to see me, not happy about why. Victor was still at the nine-oh the last I heard, born and raised in the neighborhood. When I first hit the precinct he was the one who taught me how to work a corner, the difference between *mofongo* and *mondongo*, and how *las chiquitas* in tight jeans sometimes looked "like they were trying to stuff five pounds of sausage into a three-pound bag."

"Vic*tor*," I said, accenting the second syllable. "How's it going?"

"I was gonna ask you the same thing, man." He grabbed me by the shoulders. "I mean, you were *there*, amigo."

"I'm good, Vic. Today's about Ricky T, though. Not me. Okay?"

"Yeah, yeah. I hear ya." He looked around. "His family show up yet?"

"Not that I know of." I looked at my watch. "This got started a bit earlier than we thought, and the burial ended probably half an hour ago. They should be here soon. I spoke with his brother last night."

"Shit, Ray. How's he holding up?"

"Like you'd expect. I could hear it in his voice; he was being strong for his mom, but he was close to the edge."

"Yeah. They were tight, the brothers. I remember right before Ricky got sent over, we got together for a few and Robby couldn't handle it, y'know? We were saying good-bye, but he was taking it like it was *good-bye*. He left early, and the next day drove back up to school."

I shook my head. "I can't imagine. Hey, I haven't had a beer yet. You ready for one?"

"Pssht, man. I was *born* ready."

"I've heard that about you."

I stepped behind the bar, popped open a Bud Light for Vic, and poured a pint of Brooklyn Pilsner for myself. Mikey gave me a look that said he needed to talk to me. I handed Vic his beer and told him I'd be right back.

"What's up, Mikey?"

"Ray, man," he said. "What's the deal with who's paying for this? The guys are sliding me fives and tens and walking away. Sometimes it's too much, sometimes too little. I just keep saying 'Thanks' and move on to the next one."

Mikey had a point there. I needed to find Mrs. Mac. The last I'd seen her, she was heading toward her office in the back. The door was open, and I could see Mrs. Mac on the phone. I tapped the door gently and she turned. She gave me one finger and finished up her call. When she was done, she gave me her full attention.

"Yes, Raymond. How's it going out there?"

"It's fine, Mrs. Mac. We've got the whole team on board, and the food should start coming out any minute."

"Good," she said. "Has Ricky's family arrived?"

"Not yet. But there is something I need to ask you."

She got a concerned look on her face. "Yes?"

"How are we . . . I mean who's . . . ." *Smooth, Ray.* "Are we collecting money from the guys or what? How are we paying for this?"

"Well," she said, clearly relieved that money was my concern. "Billy said he's got the meat. The guy he knows gave him a deal."

"Still, that's a lot of money."

"I know. I offered to split it with him, but he said he wouldn't hear of it, and I know that's an argument I'm not going to win with Mr. Morris."

She was right about that. "What about the bar?"

She stood and smoothed out her pants. "That's another interesting thing," she said. "That's who I was just on the phone with."

I waited for a few seconds. "And . . . ."

"Jack Knight said he'd pick up the bar tab." She obviously read the look on my face. "I know. The last time he was here, he didn't strike me as the type to even buy a round."

The last time he was here, I thought, we got into a fistfight right outside on the sidewalk, when Jack got too drunk and I couldn't help playing tough guy in front of my date. About a week after that, he saved my life. Jack Knight was full of surprises.

"Anyway," Mrs. Mac went on, "I again offered to split it, and he said absolutely no. But we did agree that everything would be at Happy Hour prices."

"That's really nice of you, Mrs. Mac."

"Long as those boys take care of Debbie, Mikey, and the Freddies, I'm happy to do what I can do." She looked at the ceiling. "That's the way Henry would want it, y'know."

I realized she was actually looking past the ceiling. And she was right, her dead husband would have wanted it that way. If I was wrong and there is a Heaven, I was sure Henry McVernon was looking down with a shit-eating grin on his face.

"All right," I said. "You coming out?"

"Give me a few minutes," she said. "If I'm not out there when the family shows up, come and get me, if you don't mind."

I stepped over and kissed her on the cheek. "I don't mind at all."

"Then maybe you can come back to the office and call your mother."

"I don't know, Mrs. Mac. I'm gonna be busy for a while, I think."

"Never too busy to call your mother, Raymond."

"I'll see you in a little while," I said, closing the door on the way out.

By three thirty there wasn't an empty seat in the joint. Mikey and Debbie seemed to be moving in fast motion, every once in a while slipping a bill into their pockets or apron. I floated around and informed everyone the drinks and food had been taken care of, but not to be shy about tipping. I moved behind the bar to give Mikey a hand, and to tell him that he, the Freddies, and Debbie would be splitting the tips. That brought a huge grin and new sense of urgency to the bartender.

I was passing four longneck Buds over the bar, when the front door opened and in walked Robby Torres, Ricky T's brother. He was flanked by four guys who had to be his cousins; they all had the same noses as Robby and what seemed like one big, bushy eyebrow. The five of them were in white shirts with the sleeves rolled up, loosened ties, and dress pants. Exactly the look you'd have if you just got out of church on a ninety-degree day. Behind them was another guy who entered when they did, but he made a beeline for the jukebox.

Robby T was a miniature version of his older brother. He was at least three inches shorter and obviously hadn't spent nearly the amount of hours in the gym.

I stepped around the bar and over to the group. "Robby," I said, sticking out my hand but pulling him into a consolatory hug. "How are you doing?"

He patted me on the back. "I'm okay, Ray. It's been a while."

We separated and he turned around.

"These are my cousins," he said. *Bingo.* "I'd tell you their names, but you'd forget them in five minutes. Guys," he turned back to me, "this is Ray. He was with Ricky . . . the night . . ." He stopped talking, but his cousins figured out where he was heading. We all shook hands, said how nice it was to meet each other, and waited for Robby to get himself together.

"Sorry about that." Nobody said a thing. I waited a few beats.

"Anyone up for a beer?"

They all nodded and mumbled something about Bud Lights and Coronas. Normally, I would have pushed them in another direction beer-wise but figured they'd heard enough preaching for the day, so I just went behind the bar and got what they wanted. I drew myself a pint of the pilsner—we teachers are constantly modeling proper behavior—and we all clinked glasses and said, "To Ricky!"

"Not too many places to sit," I said.

"No problem," Robby said, and then allowed himself his first good look around the place. His eyes got all misty again as he took in all the folks who came to pay tribute to his brother and he smiled. "Wow. This is something else, man. Ricky would've loved this shit."

"These guys loved him, Robby." I put my hand on his shoulder. "You think your mom will stop by? Mrs. Mac—the owner here—wants to pay her respects."

"I don't know, Ray. She barely made it through the burial. She went home with my aunt"—he pointed his thumb at his cousins—"their mom, and I think they were just gonna sit in the backyard under the apple tree and drink tea. I told her I'd give her a call in a few hours, see how she's doing."

"Okay. In the meantime, there's the food." I pointed at the pool table that had been converted to a buffet table. "You know where the bar is. You guys can settle in wherever you find a spot. I'm gonna bounce around and see if anybody needs anything."

Robby grabbed my elbow and said, "You got a minute, Ray? I thought we could talk before things got too . . . you know."

"Yeah, sure, Robby. Absolutely."

"Thanks." He turned back to his cousins. "Why don't you guys hang around for a bit? Maybe you can find some girls to talk to."

All four cousins looked around and one of them said, "Don't seem to be too many girls here, Robby."

"Then talk to each other for a while. I gotta ask Ray a few questions."

The cousins took the not-so-subtle hint and went off to the food table just as the Freddies were bringing in trays of hot dogs and burgers. They seemed happy with the timing.

"Can we talk outside, Ray?" Robby asked. "It's a little loud in here."

"Let's go out front. We'll find our own tree to talk under." I saw him looking at our opened beers. "It's a cop bar. No one'll hassle us."

"Cool. Thanks."

On our way out, the guy who'd been eyeing the juke box got our attention. He walked over, and Robby introduced us.

"Raymond Donne," he said. "Jimmy Key."

We shook hands. "Like the Yankee pitcher?"

He laughed. "Like Jimmy Kisparadis, without all the Greek."

"Jimmy served with Ricky over in the desert," Robby explained.

"Really?"

"Yeah," Jimmy said. "Fucking shame. We pulled a lot of personal security details together. Politicians, four-stars, guys like that."

"Sounds exciting."

"We had our moments. You guys on the way out?"

"Just need to talk to Ray in private for a few," Robby said.

"Grab some food and something from the bar. We'll be right back."

"Roger that," Jimmy Key said. "Eat while you can, is what they taught us." He headed off to the food table.

Outside was anything but cool. What little breeze there had been this morning had been replaced by humidity and haze. The rush-hour traffic was in full swing above us on the Brooklyn Queens Expressway, creating a constant buzz and smelling like a gas station.

"This is one thing I don't miss about the city," Robby said. "I'm a couple of miles away from the thruway, and I'm getting kinda used to all that fresh air."

"How far up are you?"

"About three hours' drive from the city. Not too far from Vermont."

"Nice. How much more time you got in school?"

"Graduated in May with a double major in American lit and creative writing." Before I could comment, he said, "I know. In this job market, employers are just busting down my door with offers."

I laughed. "What *do* you do with that particular combination?"

"Right now, I'm managing some rental properties around the college."

I gave that some thought. "You're a super?"

"Not exactly. I collect the rent, find new tenants when the old ones move out, contract out any maintenance that I can't handle—mostly plumbing and electrical stuff—make sure the grass is cut, and I'll be in charge of snow removal in a few months. Stuff like that."

I took a sip of pilsner. "Not quite what you went to school for, huh?"

"Yeah. My dad's probably rolling in his grave—Jesus, that was a stupid thing to say, huh?"

"Don't worry about it." I gestured with my head back at The LineUp. "There's gonna be a whole lot of stupid shit said today. Alcohol and grief bring out the Hemingway in all of us."

"I guess you're right. Anyway, yeah, the job is what it is, but it does allow me time for my writing. The owner of the buildings pays me a small salary, and I got a decent two-bedroom in one of his nicer houses. I turned the extra room into a study, and that's where I get my shit done."

"Sounds like a good deal. Ricky ever get the chance to come up that way and visit?"

"Yeah, he did." He took a long swallow from his Bud Light. "He helped me move in after I got the gig, and earlier this month he spent a couple of days with me. Folded out the couch in the living room, kept the door open between the rooms, bullshitted until we fell asleep. Was like being kids again."

"He say anything to you about his plan to go back to being a cop?"

"Said he was thinking about it, but with all the shit he'd seen in the Middle East, he wasn't sure what he wanted to do. I know he wanted to get out of Mom's and into his own place. I don't think the taxi driver thing was gonna cover that."

I told him about Ricky doing some work for Jack Knight.

"He mentioned that. I teased him about growing a mustache and sporting some sharp sunglasses. Maybe getting a Ferrari."

"It was a bit more mundane than that. He was pretty much taking pictures of accident scenes and witness statements. There was a little missing person stuff, but nothing that was gonna get him his own apartment."

Robby nodded at that, and we both took a drink in the silence. He closed his eyes and craned his neck upward, getting lost for a minute in the hum of the BQE.

"Un-fucking-believable, Ray." He placed the cool bottle against his cheek. "What a shitty way to go, you know? After the years on the force, the time over there, he gets fucking shot down in his own 'hood." He opened his eyes and looked at me. "I know he's my brother and all, but no one deserves that shit."

I looked into my beer.

"What did he wanna talk to you about that night?" Robby asked.

"I was hoping you knew something." I gave him the whole rundown of how Ricky had called me, picked me up, said something about making a mistake, and then all hell breaking loose inside the cab.

Robby closed his eyes, picturing the scene in Ricky's cab. I put my hand on his shoulder and squeezed. We stood like that for half a minute.

"He didn't tell you what the mistake was?"

"No." I pulled out my cell and brought the Latina girl's picture up. "It might have had something to do with her." I handed my phone to Robby. "You know her?"

Robby looked at the picture and shook his head. "No. Who is she?"

"I'm not sure, but she's got some connection to the missing girl Jack Knight's been hired to track down."

"The PI Ricky was working with?"

"Yeah. This photo was on a phone your brother had with him that night. It was the wallpaper—the photo on the main screen—and according to the phone's history, he mostly used it to call one untraceable number."

"Untraceable? Like prepaids? Whatta they call them? Burners?"

"Yeah. You use them until you want—or need—a new one, and toss it."

"Had a sociology professor in college," Robby said. "He swore the decline of American civilization is the result of us becoming more and more a disposable culture. We throw away more shit in this country than most of the rest of the world even has. This girl," he held up my phone, returning to the matter at hand, "you think she was the one Ricky was calling?"

"That's as good a guess as any."

"So the question is—besides *who* she is—why would she need a burner?"

Now it was my turn to smile. "You ever give any thought to being a cop? You sure as hell think like one."

"Don't like guns," he said. "They do bad things to people. That's the writer asking that question."

"I'm sure the cops interviewed you, right?"

"Oh, yeah. They were over at the house yesterday. Asking me and Mom a lot of questions about Ricky and his 'friends and associates.' Did we notice any behavior out of the ordinary? Shit like that."

"What'd you tell them?"

"I could barely tell them shit. Mom wasn't much help either. Ricky was either working or sleeping. They may have lived in the same house, but they didn't see each other all that often."

I thought about that. "What about your cousin? The one who owns the taxi company? He's not one of the ones inside, is he?"

"Nah from my dad's side. He stayed in the back of the church and then split right after."

"How is the driver who was shot doing, do you know?"

"I heard he got out of ICU today." Robby shook his head. "My cousin, Fred, he's a real good guy. Always there to loan you money, take you to dinner when you're low on cash, shit like that, y'know?"

"Yeah?"

"He's also made it a point of giving ex-convicts jobs. He's got a couple working in the garage. Guys from the neighborhood who need a break."

"This driver who was shot . . . ."

"Michael Dillman. Got busted a few years ago for something. Did a couple of years, and when he got out he hit up Fred for a job driving a cab."

"That's a pretty risky hire."

"That's Fred. The guy said it was a one-time, stupid mistake. Owned up to it and convinced Fred to give him a job. He's been clean ever since."

I took another sip of pilsner. It was getting warm. We'd have to head back inside in a few minutes. I did have work to do.

"So, do the cops think this guy's past might have had something to do with the shootings?"

"I don't know, but I'm sure they're gonna check it out, right? I would."

"Your cousin doesn't have a record, does he?"

"Fred?" Robby laughed. "Hell, no. Fred was an altar boy *and* an Eagle Scout. He was the one the family thought would go into politics or something. Worked his way through City College while driving a cab. Learned enough about the business and saved up enough cash to buy into it. Fred never had the time to get into trouble."

"Any idea why his drivers would be targeted?"

"No. The cops are looking into Fred's work with the city to unionize taxi drivers so the taxi owners would increase pay for the drivers and get their franchise fee raised. He knows that business from both ends. Everybody likes Fred."

It's just his drivers someone's not so crazy about.

We stayed silent for a bit and ended up taking our final sips simultaneously. I patted Robby on the back. "Let's go back inside. There're a lot of guys who'll be pissed if they don't get a chance to offer their condolences. You okay with that?"

He raised his bottle. "As long as I got another one of these coming."

"That," I said, "will not be a problem. But this time, I'm getting you a good one."

Chapter 10

BACK INSIDE, THE DECIBEL LEVEL had increased, and someone had started feeding quarters to the jukebox. At the moment, Bruce was singing about heroes, redemption, and saviors rising from the streets. The AC and the ceiling fans were going full tilt. Even so, Mikey looked like he had run a marathon behind the bar but seemed to have everything under control. I couldn't see Debbie at the moment, but I assumed she was somewhere among the huddled masses that had grown since I had gone outside with Robby.

A few of the guests had started smoking, creating a sort of inside haze that mocked the one we'd just left. This was not the time or place to remind these guys that the No Smoking law in New York City had passed some years back. What was I going to do? Call a cop?

I noticed Mrs. Mac coming from the back and I grabbed Robby by the elbow. She gave me a look as if to say, "Is that the brother?" I nodded and she made her way through the smoke and the crowd, getting thanks and quick embraces along the way.

"There's the owner," I said. "Mrs. McVernon. She's a cop's widow and has nothing but love for 'her boys in blue.' This," I gestured with my hand to take in the whole place, "was her husband's dream. Prepare yourself for a big hug."

"I'm half Italian and half Puerto Rican. I've been getting big hugs since they cut the umbilical cord."

Mrs. Mac came over and opened her arms. Like a good boy, Robby did the same and stepped into hers. They held each other as Mrs. Mac whispered something into Robby's ear. He nodded and said, "Thank you."

When they separated, she held Robby at arm's length and appraised him.

"Aren't you just the spitting image of your brother?" she said. As far as I knew, Mrs. Mac barely knew Ricky T and probably would not have recognized him if he had passed her on the street. But, when you're a seventy-year-old cop's widow who owns a cop bar, you could pretty much say what you wanted.

"Yeah," Robby said. "We come from a pretty strong gene pool, I guess."

"Your father must be a handsome man."

"My mother thought so. He passed away some years ago."

"Oh, dear. I'm so sorry. Do you have any more brothers or sisters?"

"No. Ricky and I were it."

Mrs. Mac shook her head. "Oh, listen to me. I must sound horribly nosy. My husband and I never had any children of our own, and sometimes I just . . ."

"No need to apologize. My mom's pretty close with her sister—my cousins are floating around here somewhere—and we've got some relatives still in the neighborhood."

"Good," Mrs. Mac said. "Family is very important in times like these." She looked right at me as she said that last part.

I put my arm around Robby. "I'm gonna get Robby another beer and introduce him around, Mrs. Mac."

"Will your mother be showing up?" Mrs. Mac asked.

"I'm not sure." He told her the same thing he'd told me. "But she does send her regards and her thanks, Mrs. Mac."

"Well, if I don't get a chance to see her, do extend my condolences."

"I will. Thank you."

"Good." She gave Robby one more hug and went back in the direction she'd come from, then disappeared into the sea of mourners. I took the opportunity to duck behind the bar and get another beer for Robby and myself.

"My mother," I said, handing him his Brooklyn Pilsner, "would say you handled yourself with poise."

"Like I said, Ray, it's been a lifetime of weddings, wakes, communions, *quinceñeras*, you name it." He raised his bottle. "Thanks." He took another sip and looked around at the crowd. "Who do I pay for this, by the way? And how much?"

"You know Billy Morris?"

Robby closed his eyes and thought about that. "The barbecue guy?"

"That's him. He's got some sort of connection with a meat guy and he shelled out for the food."

"Wow. That's pretty damned nice."

"That's Billy." I looked around and couldn't see him. "I'll introduce you when he comes around again. As for the bar tab, the guy you wanna thank is—"

"Jack Knight," a voice said behind me. He stuck his hand out to Robby. "I'm the one called the PBA and got them to foot the bill for the drinks. Told those cheap fucks it's the least they could do for an American hero and brother cop."

Robby pumped Jack's hand a couple of times and said, "Wow," again. "This is all pretty amazing. Thank you."

"Your brother was the real deal, Robby. Whoever did this to him better hope they get caught by the Canadian Mounties, 'cause anyone else gets their hands on them, they ain't gonna get much due process."

Robby managed a smile and nodded, not knowing what to make of Jack. Most people who meet him feel the same way.

"Thanks, Jack," he said. "I'm gonna find my cousins and make sure they're staying out of trouble."

"You do that. Don't leave without having one with me, okay?"

"Okay."

As Robby went off in search of his cousins, I turned to Jack. "Why'd you shine him on like that? Mrs. Mac told me you're picking up the bar tab."

Jack held up one index finger to me, turned, and held up the other index finger to Mikey. He stage-whispered the word "Heineken" and turned back to me.

"Look around, Ray," he said. "What do most of these guys think of me?"

I paused and gave him an awkward shrug and an uncomfortable grin.

"I'm an asshole. Maybe not as much as I used to be, but still . . . I worked hard for that rep. These guys don't need to go changing their minds about me. Too much for them to think about." He reached over and grabbed his beer from Mikey. "You remember the last time I was here, Ray?"

"How could I forget?" I sighed, remembering that fight lost me a second date with the beautiful Elsa.

"See?" He grinned. "I was an asshole. Engaging in fisticuffs with another party guest, let alone *you*?" He took a sip of beer and leaned into me. "Started going to AA meetings a few weeks after that."

I looked at his beer.

"Learned I wasn't an alky. Just a drunk. Did get me to start drinking less, though. Kinda got old, waking up in my car, not knowing how I got home. God damned lucky I never killed anyone. That I know of, anyway." He thought about that for a few seconds. "At least, not behind the wheel."

"So, you don't want these guys knowing you're paying for their drinks."

"For what? To get a bunch of phony pats on the back and 'Attaboys'? I'm good. You and Mrs. Mac know. And Ricky T." He raised his glass to the ceiling.

"I didn't know you're religious, Jack."

"I'm not. God can go fuck himself, all I care. Where was he when Ricky was getting all shot up? Sending another tsunami to a third-world country with dark-skinned people that actually believe in Him? The hell kind of all-mighty being is that, Ray?" He made a half circle with his beer. "These guys? They think *I'm* an asshole? Least I don't go dropping the ocean on top of a buncha poor folks or opening up the earth because I'm bored or angry or whatever the hell reason God has for working 'in mysterious ways.' Talk about your assholes. Jesus H, man."

I've known Jack for almost ten years, and for the second time today, not only did he surprise me, this time I found myself agreeing with him.

"Anyway," Jack said, "since we got a minute alone, we need to talk."

"About what?"

"Turns out I *am* gonna need someone tomorrow. I've been trying to get an interview with this witness to an accident for weeks now, and he calls me this morning, says he's back in town, and gonna be in the neighborhood tomorrow."

"What neighborhood?"

"The Burg. He works on and off for a liquor store over there. Bushwick and Grand."

That was the subway stop one past my school's. "Where'd the accident happen?"

"Right there at the corner. My client's truck ran over a pedestrian."

"Jaywalking?"

"I wish. Driver was making a right, didn't see the ped crossing. Fucking guy barely speaks English. He's Russian or something. Gave the cops a one-sentence statement: 'I hit the woman in the crosswalk.' Companies oughta have these guys driving around with lawyers riding shotgun."

"What's so important about this witness?"

"He told me over the phone that the pedestrian—a single working mother—was talking on her cell phone, running for a bus. I need that official."

"Last I checked, Jack, talking on a cell phone and running for a bus were not illegal."

"That don't make a difference, Raymond. Insurance company knows they're gonna pay out the ass. Got a coupla million in liability, and the victim's lawyer is going for it all. My job is to try and reduce the payout. Anything I can find out that makes the victim look less pitiful, the better for my side."

"Really?"

"It's the way the game's played, Ray. Their side makes my guys look like the bad guys, someone's gotta level the playing field a bit." He took a sip of his Heineken. "I'm even checking out what she was wearing that day."

"What? Like she was asking for it?"

Jack laughed. "It was raining when the accident happened, beginning of spring. I wanna know if she was wearing anything that may have reduced her peripheral vision. It's a full investigation. Just like when we were cops."

"Except there are millions of dollars involved."

He looked at his bottle and smiled. "Except for that, yeah."

I gave that some thought until I realized too much thought might lead to a bad taste in my mouth.

"So, what do you need me for?"

"To take the wit's statement. He's gonna be at the liquor store tomorrow at nine. I need his statement in writing and signed. Then I need a whole bunch of shots of the intersection where the accident happened. You got a decent camera?"

"At school, yeah."

"Take as many shots as you can, and have your sister walk you through how to email them to me. I assume you don't know how."

I nodded.

"You'll be done by noon. One the latest. I'll pay you three bills."

"Three hundred dollars? For four hours' work?"

He reached into his pocket and pulled out a wad of cash. He peeled off three hundred-dollar bills and handed them to me. "Trust me, Ray. That's chicken shit compared to what the lawyers bill. They can afford it."

I looked at the money, folded it in half, and slipped it into my front pocket.

"You want this by tomorrow afternoon?"

"Yeah. My contact info's on the card I gave you the other day."

"Let me have another," I said, leaving out the part where I'd given the first one to Uncle Ray. He did so and finished his beer. "Another beer?"

He gave me a look that told me I'd just asked a stupid question. I went behind the bar and got us each another. As I handed his to him, he said, "Got plans for Wednesday?"

I considered that for about ten seconds. "Not that I know of."

"Good." Jack took a long pull from his bottle. "I need to go out to the Island and check in with the Goldens."

"The family of the missing girl?"

"That's the one. Wanna go for a ride and see how the one percent lives?"

"What do you need me for?"

"Charles—Mr. Golden—has asked for a meeting with me and my *associate*. I never told him I was working with Ricky T, and I'm sure as hell not going to mention that he was killed the other night."

"So, you want me to be your associate? Show the Goldens how seriously your agency is taking this case?"

"You've always been a quick study, Ray. It's a lot easier to justify my expenses if I bring a partner along. And, just to comfort that overdeveloped conscience of yours, I'll make the same deal with you I made with Ricky. When you're out there on the streets taking pictures for the insurance cases, ask around about *chica* on Ricky's phone. That way, when Mr. G asks you about your progress, you can give him an honest answer."

I shook my head. "You got this shit down, don't you, Jack?"

"Like I said, Ray. It's the way the game is played. If I don't do it, someone else will, and I'd be a lot less happy than I am now." To his credit, he realized what he'd just said. "Except for Ricky T, y'know?"

"Yeah. Except for him." I took a sip. "What time on Wednesday?"

"Early. Golden's gonna work from home in the morning, then hit his office in the city for a lunch meeting with one of his clients. You know Anthony Blake?"

"The councilman from the Upper West Side, wants to be mayor?"

"That's the one. Calls himself 'The Magician.' He's a client of Golden's."

I shook my head again. "Golden does all right for himself, I guess."

"Wait till you see his house. And his wife. It'll make you feel a lot better about taking his money."

"You're gonna pay me for the ride out to the Island?" I asked, not wanting to bring it up until Jack did.

"Same deal as tomorrow. Three hundred for half a day's work. You'll be sunning yourself on your deck by early afternoon." He gave me the lookover. "Wear what you've got on. What do they call that? Business casual?"

"I call it khakis and a dress shirt."

"Perfect."

"Without even trying." I took another sip. "I'm going to see how things are running around here, Jack. You sticking around for a bit?"

"Yeah. It'll be good to see the guys." He gave the room a quick look. "Some of them, anyway. I'll text you the address and time. So, if I don't see you later, I'll hear from you tomorrow after your interview."

"That's the deal."

"Cool." He looked over at the new tray of burgers and dogs one of the Freddies was just bringing in. "That's got me written all over it," he said, and headed off to the food table. I watched as he ran into Debbie, touched her hand, said something to her, and left her with something resembling a grin on her face.

Fucking Jack.

Chapter 11

A FEW HOURS LATER, THE COPS mourning Ricky T began leaving, and The LineUp's regular crowd started shuffling in. Jack had said his good-byes, but not before giving his credit card info to Mrs. Mac. I was sitting at the bar when Billy Morris came up and put his arm around me. He asked Mikey for a Bud Light and another pilsner for me.

"Heard a funny rumor, Ray," he said. I could smell that one of his last drinks had been a Jack Daniel's. "Wanna hear it?"

"I could use a little funny," I said. "Unless it's about me."

Mikey silently placed our beers in front of us and walked away.

"Damn, son. Your ears musta been burnin'." He picked up his bottle and touched it to my pint glass. "Someone said you were gonna put in some hours with Jack Knight. Play a little PI."

I nodded, sipped, and remembered how impossible it was to keep a secret in a room full of cops. "Just going to interview a witness for him and take some shots of an accident scene, that's all. Then I'll probably head out to the Island with him and act as window dressing for a client. Two days' work and I'll make enough to get out of the city with my girlfriend for a few days."

Billy shook his head. "Not that long ago you two couldn't be in the same room without the shit flyin' all over the place."

"I guess that was before he saved my life."

"That *will* change your opinion of an individual, won't it?"

"It will." I looked up at the silent TV screen, where the Yanks were just starting their game against the Orioles. I thought I might be here for a bit. "How long you planning on hanging around, Billy?"

"Maybe an inning or two. The O's are for-real this year, huh? I mean, here it is August, and they're still hanging around making some noise. Got some good young guys."

"Yeah. It's good to have them back in the hunt."

We both watched as the Yankees pitcher got the Orioles's leadoff batter to swing at a low, outside pitch for strike three. Another hand touched my shoulder, and I spun around to see Edgar. He looked like he'd stopped off at home, showered, and changed before coming out. Probably wanted to look good for all the cops he figured would still be here.

"Edgar," I said. "You remember Billy Morris?"

"Uh, *yeah*," Edgar said as if meeting his favorite ballplayer. He reached across me and shook Billy's hand. "How ya doing, Billy?"

"Good, Emo," Billy said. "Good to see ya."

Edgar gave him an embarrassed shrug and a silent smile. It'd been two and a half years since the two had seen each other. A lot had changed, including Edgar Martinez O'Brien dropping his old nickname.

"Nobody really calls Edgar that anymore, Billy. He's kinda grown out of it, y'know?"

"My apologies, *Edgar*. Musta missed the memo."

"No problem," Edgar said and looked at our drinks. "Guys up for another?"

Before I could answer, Bill drained his bottle. "Always, man. Thanks."

"Excellent." Edgar got Mikey's attention and did the three-finger swirly thing, signaling another round. We both looked up at the TV, where the Yanks had already closed out the top of the first. "Gotta love this starting pitching," he said. "Gotta combined ERA of three-point-five-seven, and an average of five-point-three innings per start, over the past thirty games."

Billy and I exchanged looks, and Billy said, "But who's counting, right?"

It took Edgar a few seconds to get the joke—it usually did—but when it came to him, he gave an exaggerated laugh. Our beers came, along with a tiny can of tomato juice for Edgar to pour into his Bass. He handed Mikey a ten and a five. "Keep it."

"Thanks, Edgar," Mikey said. "You guys eating?"

Billy and I shook our heads, both of us having had our fill of the bar-becue. Mikey pointed with his thumb over his shoulder at the food table. "Help yourself, Edgar. Might be a bit cold, but it's still barbecue."

"Cool beans," Edgar said.

"I think we're out of those," Mikey said.

Again, it took Edgar a bit, but he eventually gave a little laugh and excused himself as he went over to make up a plate. Mikey went back to working the bar, and Billy shook his head and smiled.

"That Edgar," he said, "is one interesting individual."

"You're not gonna get an argument from me," I said. "But I gotta tell you, he's come in real handy the past few years." I told Billy about my involvement in Douglas Lee's murder investigation last year and how Edgar's computer skills helped solve the case. "It was like watching a concert pianist at work."

"Takes all kinds, my mother used to say."

I raised my glass. "Cheers to that."

We drank a little and I noticed Robby heading over to us with his four cousins in the flanking position. I got up off my stool.

"You heading out?" I asked.

"Yeah," Robby said. "Stayed longer than I wanted to. No offense, I just promised my mother we'd be back."

"Give her my condolences. You know, I'm not far from here. You think she'd mind if I swung by some day this week?"

Robby gave that some thought. "Give me your cell number and I'll give ya a call in a day or two. I'm gonna have to head back upstate, and Mom could probably use the company, but I'll leave it up to her, okay?"

"Understood." I wrote down my cell number on a napkin and gave it to him. "Anytime. I'm pretty much open for the next two weeks."

"Cool, Ray. Thanks."

"Where's Ricky's buddy, Jimmy?"

"Had to skip out early, he said. Work tomorrow."

"What's Jimmy do, now that he's back from Iraq?"

"Some sort of security. We didn't really talk that long. I met him for the first time at the church service."

"Right."

We gave each other a quick hug, said we'd be in touch, and he and his four cousins left The LineUp.

"Shit, man," Billy said as the door closed. "That's a tough load to haul."

"Yeah." I thought about how I'd feel if anything ever happened to Rachel. "I can't imagine."

An hour later, I was walking home through McGolrick Park and decided to grab a bench, enjoy the mild evening, and give Allison a call. I was leaving a message on her voicemail when my phone started to vibrate. It was Allison.

"Hey," I said. "I was just leaving you a message."

"I know. I couldn't get to it right away. What's up?"

I told her how the afternoon at Ricky's wake went and my plans for tomorrow's insurance interview for Jack.

I looked at my watch: almost nine. "Can you swing by tonight?"

"I'm still at work. They got me out in the Bronx checking out the other driver, Michael Dillman. The guy who took one in the shoulder?"

"And?"

"And I'm having trouble tracking him down. He's no longer at the address the taxi company gave me, and the lady who answered the buzzer said she didn't even know his name. The phone number he gave on his application's been disconnected."

"Makes your job more interesting."

" 'Interesting' is not the word I'd use for traipsing around the Bronx after dark, trying to get an interview."

"So come home," I said. "Come to *my* home."

There was silence for ten seconds. "You sound a little drunk, Ray."

"I've been at The LineUp all day, Allison. I am a little drunk."

More silence. "I'm gonna pass tonight. I want to see if my office can get me a new address on this guy. Sounds like you gotta get up early anyway and take your pictures. Let's talk tomorrow, okay?"

"Okay," I said, not doing a great job at hiding my disappointment. "I'll call you when I'm done. Early afternoon, probably."

After ending the call, I leaned back on the bench, closed my eyes, and took a deep breath. Okay, I was drunk. Against doctor's orders and common sense. I was dealing with, or *not* dealing with, Ricky's shooting—hell, *my* shooting—by using alcohol. It was my first time watching a friend get killed and my first time being shot at. I'd deal with it any way I chose.

Chapter 12

I WAS HEADING UP THE SCHOOL STEPS bright and early the next morning when I ran into Jim and Josephine Levine, who were on their way out of the building. They were dressed in matching Mets shirts and khaki shorts. Both were sweating as if they'd just stepped out of a shower. I gave Jo a quick kiss and Jim a handshake.

"What are you two doing here?" I asked. "The words 'summer vacation' mean anything to you?"

Josephine gave a quick laugh, pulled her t-shirt away from her chest, and flapped it a few times to air it out.

"Ron's moving my room again," she said. "Called me yesterday."

Good ol' Principal Ron Thomas, I thought. "Why's he doing that?"

"He's moving all the special ed classes up to the third floor."

"Your room's already on the third floor."

"Yeah, but it's one room away from the others," she explained. "He wants all six rooms in what he's calling a 'Special Education Annex.'"

"And your room not being right next to the others . . ."

"Screws up the annex objective."

I gave that some thought. "And he's doing this why?"

"Because," her husband chimed in, "he's the principal and he can."

And Jim didn't even work for the school system. When your wife's put in twenty-five years with the New York City Department of Education, you learn to think the way administrators often do, and little surprises you.

"What about you?" Jo asked. "How come you're not lying around some beach somewhere, drinking really good, really cold beer?"

"I'm doing a little work for a friend." I explained about my assignment for Jack and that I was at school to pick up my camera. I left out the part about Ricky T and was glad that the newspapers had kept my name out of it.

"A little taste of retirement?" Jo said. "Raymond Donne, PI?"

"Just making a few extra bucks so I can hit that beach and have a few of those beers by Labor Day. You guys going away?"

Jim grinned. "That's why we're doing the room now. We're heading down to Miami for ten days. Mets gotta four-game series with the Marlins."

"Don't start, Ray," Jo said before I could. "We can't all be the Yankees and make the playoffs every year."

"Yeah, but Jo," I said, "once a decade might be nice."

They both gave me a polite, shut-the-fuck-up laugh and Jo said, "We gotta hit the car and get some more boxes. Go get your camera, Ray."

"Say hi to Miami Beach for me. See ya in a couple weeks."

As they headed off to their car, I went into the building. As I had expected, it was stiflingly hot, but pleasantly silent. I walked past the office door, which was shut, meaning someone was inside with the air conditioner on. I opened the door and saw Mary clicking away at the computer. She noticed me and gave me a smile.

"New registrations," she explained. "You?"

I pointed upstairs. "My camera."

"Oooh, going away with the cute reporter?"

"Something like that. How are you getting along?"

Mary was one of hundreds of residents of Breezy Point—The Irish Riviera at the tip of Queens—who had lost their homes in Hurricane Sandy two years ago. Now she was living in some part of Brooklyn I'd need a map to get to.

"I'm good, Ray," she said. "Takes some getting used to, but I'm good."

This, coming from a woman who'd lost just about everything she owned to a freak of nature and still went to church every Sunday. I gave her a wave, went up to my office, grabbed the camera, the batteries, and the charger, and headed out to take some pictures and interview a witness.

• • •

It took me about thirty minutes to get the pictures I needed. I went to all four corners, just as Jack had instructed, and took shots in every direction. I had more than a hundred shots. Let the lawyers figure out what they needed and what they didn't; I was just an employee doing a job. It was getting real hot, so I decided to hit the bodega on the corner for an iced tea before I went over to the liquor store and interviewed Willy Hudson, the star witness for Jack's client.

It didn't take long. The Asian woman behind the cash register told me that Willy was in the storeroom, and I listened as she used the intercom to tell him there was someone here who wanted to talk to him. The figure who emerged from the storeroom was not at all what I had expected. Hudson was about six-and-a-half feet tall, rail thin, and his long, gray hair was pulled back in a ponytail. He wore a pair of cut-off jean shorts, a red-and-white flannel shirt with the sleeves rolled up, and a pair of sunglasses. There was a generic pack of cigarettes in his shirt pocket. As he approached me, he gave me a look that said I was not exactly what he had expected, either.

"You Mr. Knight?" he asked, with an accent more New England than East Williamsburg.

"No," I said. "I'm his . . . associate. Raymond Donne." I offered him my hand and he accepted it with a firm grip. "I was hoping you had about twenty minutes to give me a statement about the accident." Hudson looked at the woman behind the counter, who had obviously been listening to our conversation. She nodded. "Fifteen minutes," she warned, "and this is your break, so smoke now if you're going to."

"Thanks, Miriam," Hudson said, not hiding his sarcasm. When we got outside, he slipped the pack of smokes out of his pocket and removed one. "Her English gets a lot better when she's ordering me around." He lit the cigarette, took a long drag, and watched the smoke rise up and disappear.

I took my notepad out of my back pocket and a pen out of my front. "So," I said, not wanting to waste any of Hudson's break time with small talk. "Tuesday, April sixteenth, at about five minutes to nine, you were standing out here?"

"Yep. Waitin' on Miriam to open up. Hadda squeeze under the awning so I didn't get poured on."

"Store opens at nine?"

"Every day, except Sunday, of course."

"And the weather that morning was . . . ?"

He pushed his sunglasses up with his index finger and took another hit from his cigarette. "Like I said: pouring. Nice fog. Couldn't see the tops of the buildings." He pointed over to the thirty-story projects a few blocks away. "Bit of a breeze out of the southwest, that's where the storm was coming in from."

"You a Weather Channel fan?"

"I'm from Maine. Come from a long line of fishermen and lobstermen. You don't pay attention to the weather, you in for some trouble."

"I like Maine," I said, opting for a bit of small talk. "Thinking about heading up that way before the summer's out." I wasn't really, but figured flattery might make the interview go better.

"Yeah. We got all that charm and shit. Like living in a postcard." He took another long drag from his cigarette. "That's why I ain't been around for the past few months. Been helping out with the family business. Making a little of that Red Lobster money, and now I'm back stocking shelves and breaking down boxes."

He picked up on the look I gave him.

"I got a woman down here. She don't wanna move up to Maine, and I don't wanna live my whole life down here. Whatcha call a compromise. I make enough up there a few times a year to afford living down here."

I nodded and said I understood. "So, what did you see that morning as it relates to Susan Thompson?"

"That the lady got run over?"

"Yes."

He reached up and scratched his head. "I was out here, like I said, waiting on Miriam, having a smoke. Seen this lady—Ms. Thompson?—running across the street to catch a bus. Stop's right there." He pointed to the other side of the avenue at the bus stop. "She was yapping away on her cell phone, holding her coffee so it don't spill, in her own special little world, I guess."

"And the truck?"

"Coming from this way." He pointed to the corner. "Guy was waiting for the people to get across and then made the right turn."

"Where was Ms. Thompson when the driver began his turn?"

"Ya mean *exactly?*"

"As close as you can remember."

He rubbed his lower lip. "A few feet outside the crosswalk, running, like I said, trying to catch that bus."

I wrote that down. "She was outside the crosswalk?"

"Yep. I mean, I think she was hit *in* the crosswalk, but when she started 'cross the street, she was outside the lines, y'know?"

I looked out into the street at the crosswalk, its lines fading. I nodded and continued to jot down the notes.

"Hey," Hudson whispered, a secret idea coming to him. "Is there gonna be, like, a reward or something here? Whatta they call it, a witness fee?"

"No, Mr. Hudson. I just need to hear what you saw. Our office"—*listen to me*—"will type up a copy of your statement and have you sign it. We don't pay for testimony."

"'Cause I can say it better'n that, y'know? Throw in some details about how she couldn't see to the left or the right 'cause of her rain gear." Another idea hit him and he tossed the remainder of his cigarette into the street. "Shit, I can be an expert witness on that with all the boat stuff I got up in Maine. I know you guys pay for expert testimony. I seen that on TV."

I was sure he had. Just like every other American who got their law degree from the University of Couch and Cable TV.

"I'm sure the lawyers will be in touch with you if they decide to go that way, Mr. Hudson. I'm just here to take your statement."

"You be sure to let them know that I can make a better statement if they want, and about that expert testimony, okay?"

"I'll do that. Now," I said, "excuse me for asking this next question, but you hadn't been drinking that morning, had you?"

"Why? Someone say I was?"

That wasn't the "no" I was hoping for.

"I'm asking because the other side is going to ask. They may try to connect your job at a liquor store with your own drinking." I chose my next words carefully. "I'm also asking because you were wearing sunglasses inside."

"There a crime about that?"

"No. Are they prescription?"

"Nope. I got perfect twenty-twenty. Whatchoo gettin' at?"

"I'm just thinking like the other lawyers. If I were them, I'd want to know about your vision, your drinking habits, and why you wear sunglasses inside at your job in a liquor store."

He rubbed the stubble on his chin, considering what I'd said. "Well, I wasn't. I do my drinking after lunch and almost never on the job."

"*Almost?*"

"Shit, man. Who's side you on here?"

I wanted to say the side of the truth, but I knew how corny that sounded.

"It's not about sides, Mr. Hudson. It's about asking all the questions and not being surprised at trial." I highly doubted a case like this would ever see the inside of a courtroom, but I felt the need for Mr. Hudson to understand the significance of any statements he was making and anything he chose to leave out. "Lawyers don't like to ask questions they don't already know the answers to."

As he nodded with comprehension, he pulled another cigarette out of his pocket. His second in less than fifteen minutes. How much did he smoke when he *wasn't* working?

"I gotcha," he said. He looked around, took off his shades, and showed me his slightly bloodshot eyes. "I was out a little late last night, with my lady. Don't need Miriam in there giving me shit about coming in hung over, y'know? I ain't been drinking this morning, but I'm still a bit buzzed from last night, that's all."

"Were you 'a bit buzzed' the morning of the accident, Mr. Hudson?"

He moved his head from side to side. "Mighta been, I don't remember. It was a few months ago."

"But you remember where Ms. Thompson was when she was crossing the street, and what she was wearing?"

"There you go again," he said, angry this time. "Acting like I'm the one did something wrong here. I feel like I'm being cross-examined."

"Trust me, Willy" I said, switching to his first name to remind him who was running this interview. "This is nothing like being cross-examined. If Ms. Thompson's lawyers even suspect that you have a drinking problem, they are going to be all over you like holy on the pope. It's best to get it all out in the open now, so—"

"I know," he interrupted. "I know. No surprises. Shit."

I gave him time to think and to take another drag. This guy's lungs must have looked like an old blackboard.

"So," I began again. "Were you under the influence of alcohol on the morning of Tuesday, April sixteenth?"

He slipped his sunglasses back on. "No. I was not."

"And you'll sign a statement that attests to that?"

"I will."

"And you'll swear under oath in a deposition to that?"

"Deposition?" he said. "That's like a pretrial thing, right?"

There was that TV law degree again.

"It's when a lawyer for the plaintiff gets to ask you questions, just like they would in a trial. You'll be sworn in and asked to sign a statement swearing that everything you said was truthful, to the best of your recollection."

"I'm good with that."

"Good." I flipped my notepad shut. "As I said earlier, my office will type this up, and we'll be in touch to have you sign it."

"I have to go to your office for that?"

"No. Mr. Knight or I will come by here or your apartment if you'd like."

"Here's good," he said. "Just call first, okay? Like the day before."

"Absolutely." I stuck out my hand and he took it reluctantly. "Have a good day, Mr. Hudson."

"You, too."

As he turned to head back inside, I remembered the picture on my cell phone. What the hell?

"Ah, Mr. Hudson," I said, pulling my phone out. "One more thing."

He looked over and laughed. "You sound like Columbo. What now?"

I brought up the photo on my phone and held it out for him to get a good look at. "Have you by any chance seen this woman?"

He took one step over and leaned into the phone as if he thought it would bite him. He raised his shades and squinted.

"Yep," he said.

I didn't even try to hide my surprise. "Really?"

"Every night in my dreams. Either her or someone like her. Look around, Columbo. There's beautiful ladies all over."

I took the phone and put it back in my pocket. "We'll be in touch."

"Looking forward to it."

After walking away from the liquor store and Willy Hudson, I wasn't sure what to do next. It was pushing lunchtime, but I didn't want to go home, and it was too early to go to The LineUp. I certainly wasn't going to go door-to-door showing the picture on my phone, hoping to strike gold. Heading into the city and grabbing some lunch with Allison sounded like an idea, but I was sure she was working, so I decided to hold off on that call.

Before I realized it, I had walked about two blocks and found myself in front of a pizza place. This was not my neighborhood, so I'd never been to this restaurant, but it did remind me of one not too far from here where I *had* been. And where I knew just the right person to help me identify the girl on my phone.

If he'd talk to me, that is.

Unlike the last time I'd been here, this time the door was open and nobody gave me any shit as I walked in. And just like the last time I had been here, the place smelled wonderful. The air was filled with the aroma of baking bread, tomato sauce, and roasting garlic. They could bottle that smell, put it in a spray can, and make a fortune. I stepped up to the counter and watched a tall kid wearing a red-and-white baseball cap deftly slip a new pie into the pizza oven. When he closed the oven door, he turned around and said, "What can I get ya?"

I knew I wanted two mushroom slices and a Diet Pepsi, but what came out of my mouth was, "Boo?"

The kid looked at me and showed no recognition at first. He squinted and then a small grin formed. "Teacherman!" he said, sticking his hand over the counter so we could fist bump. "Whatchoo doin' here? Tio didn't say he was 'specting you."

"Damn, Boo. What are they feeding you? You're a foot taller than the last time I was here."

He fingered the little bit of hair he had on his chin. "Tio know you was comin' by?" All business now, and not the pizza kind.

"I was in the neighborhood and wanted some pizza. I also wanted to talk to Tio, so . . ."

"What kind you want?" *Now* it was pizza business.

I looked up at the menu board and saw nothing that changed my mind. "Two mushroom slices and a large Diet Pepsi. Is Tio around?"

Boo separated two mushroom slices from their brothers and put them in the oven. Then he took a large cup, filled it with ice and soda, and handed it to me. "Not my business to know where Tio is, Teacherman. If he ain't 'specting you, he could be anywhere, know what I'm sayin'?"

"Can you call him for me? I kinda need a favor."

Boo took the red-and-white hat off his head and wiped his brow. "I thought you and Tio was all done doin' each other favors."

"We were, but something came up, and I figured Tio could help me out."

Boo shook his head. "Shoulda called first. Can't just drop in 'specting to find Tio around here. He a busy man."

"I'm sure he is, Boo. But maybe you can give him a call while I eat my lunch? Tell him I'm here and want to talk?"

He flashed me that grin again. "Now you wanna favor from *me*?"

"I'll make it up to you. I'm an excellent tipper."

The grin widened. "I remember you thought you was funny."

He took my slices out of the oven. After sliding them onto a couple of plates and putting them on a tray, he handed them to me. "Five bucks," he said.

I looked up at the menu. He should've been charging me seven-fifty. Boo saw me looking at the sign. "Teacher discount."

I handed him a twenty. "You'll make that call?"

He shrugged. "I was gonna give him one anyway, Teacherman. Let him know how the morning went. Maybe I'll mention you here."

"I'd appreciate that."

He gestured with his chin at my food. "Enjoy your lunch."

"Thanks."

I took my lunch over to a booth that had a view of the TV. Last night's Yankees game was on with the sound muted. Just as well; they had lost pretty badly. I sprinkled some hot pepper flakes on my slices and took a bite. Delicious. I remembered the breakfast Boo had made for me last year when I had first come here asking for his boss's help. Boo had a definite future in the food industry.

I was halfway through my second slice when the door to the restaurant opened. I turned to see two young men enter, both wearing New Orleans Saints jerseys, followed by the man I'd come to see. I'd only met him a few times, but was surprised he wasn't wearing his customary Saints jersey. He had on a white polo shirt, tucked into a pair of khakis. He saw me, nodded to his boys, and they exited. Tio walked over to me and I stood up.

"No jersey?" I asked.

"Took it off to take care of some business," he said. "I was upstairs showing some folks an apartment."

"You're into real estate now?"

"I bought the building last year. Owner was letting it go to shit, wanted to spend his final years in F-L-A. We came to an agreement, and now I'm a landlord."

"You never fail to surprise, Tio."

He ignored that. "You here for the lunch special?"

"If it comes with a conversation, yes."

"What if it don't?"

I looked down at the rest of my meal. "It was worth the trip anyway."

"Good answer. Finish up. I'll be right back."

I watched as he walked through the swinging door, past the pizza ovens, and into the back rooms. I sat down and finished eating, and spent another five minutes watching last night's Yankees pitcher getting knocked around. Mercifully, Tio came back and slid into the booth across from me. Now he was wearing his Saints jersey with the not-so-subtle number 1 on it.

"What do you need to conversate about, Teacherman?"

"I need some help finding a girl."

"I know that story."

I laughed, pulled my cell phone out, and handed it to Tio. "This girl."

Tio looked at the picture for a good thirty seconds before speaking.

"She another student of yours?"

"No. I'm . . . helping out a friend. She's the friend of a missing kid, and my friend's looking for the missing kid."

"You quit teaching? Gone all Shaft on me?"

"Just helping out a friend." I told him about Jack Knight and how he'd been hired by the Goldens to find their daughter.

"Yeah," Tio said. "Seen that on TV. You goin' after that fifty G's?"

"Not exactly. I mean, if we find her, yeah, there's that; but right now I'm just trying to get a name to go with that face." I pointed at my phone.

Tio looked at it again. "And this is some face, Teacherman. You know how old this chick is?"

"Based on that picture, around eighteen. I've seen another photo where she looks younger. It's hard to tell."

"I hear that. Know some guys got into trouble 'cause it's hard to tell sometimes. Fourteen'll get you ten, know what I'm saying?"

"So . . ."

"Nope." He handed me my phone. "Don't know who she is, but I'll tell you what. Text that picture to me."

He gave me his number. Tio's phone dinged. Message received. Maybe I wasn't such a techno idiot after all.

"You'll show that around?"

"Do better than that," he said. "I'll send it out to my boys and see who comes up with what. You willin' to share some of that reward?"

"That's not my call, Tio. I'll pose it to my friend and see what he says."

"You do that. Tell him one of my boys comes up with a name to go with that pretty face, it'll cost him."

"Like I said, I'm not the boss."

"That's more'n fair, Teacherman. I'm letting you use my network."

"And I appreciate any help you can throw my way."

"Works both ways. What's that Latin thing? The one that Hannibal Lecter said to Jodie Foster?"

I thought back, and it took five seconds to come up with the quote from *Silence of the Lambs*.

"*Quid pro quo?*"

"That's it. Used to think that sounded like some kinda seafood."

I slid out of the booth, smiling.

"You find me charming or something?" Tio asked, referring to my smile.

I stuck out my hand. "I find you one of the least boring people I've ever met, Tio."

He shook my hand. "I'll take that as a compliment."

"That's how it was meant."

He held his phone out for me to see. "I'll get this out to my peeps. I got your number now, so either way I'll give ya a call in the next two days."

"That'll be great," I said. "Thanks."

"Cool. You be careful now."

"That's always my plan."

He picked up the remains of my lunch and piled it on the tray. "You should come by again, Teacherman. Try Boo's eggplant lasagna. Bring the girlfriend."

"How'd you know I have a girlfriend?"

He just smiled, turned around, and handed my tray to Boo. Without turning around he said, "Later," and disappeared into the back.

Chapter 13

THE TEMPERATURE WAS EASILY IN the mideighties when I left Tio's, and I didn't feel like waiting around for a bus or heading underground to the subway. I decided to walk home. If a bus came along before I got halfway, I'd jump on, but I wasn't counting on it. Midday busses are few and far between. I bought a shaved cherry ice from a guy on the corner and started making my way down the avenue.

Ten minutes later, I had finished my ice and found myself a few blocks from the L train. At the corner of Ainslie and Graham, it dawned on me that this was the street where Ricky T had lived with his mother. I pulled out my cell, googled Mrs. Torres's name, and got the address. I was right. I'm not usually the type to just drop on by without calling, but this time I could honestly play the I-was-in-the-neighborhood bit. The worst that could happen is I'd have gone a few blocks out of my way. If I got the feeling I was unwanted, I'd leave.

Ainslie was a nice tree-lined street with a lot of two-story attached houses. The families who lived on this block had been here for years and were largely Italian. A teacher I used to work with lived on the top floor of one of these houses years ago, and he told me stories about how his land-lady was always knocking on his door with "extra food." He swore she was trying to fatten him up and set him up with her niece. I looked into a few backyards and could see grapevines hanging from trestles, providing not only shade, but also the fruit for homemade wine. Not the image that earned

Williamsburg its reputation for being "the coolest place on Earth." One of the other Williamsburgs.

I stopped in front of the Torres house and noticed that all the curtains were pulled. There was a black wreath on the front door. I thought about heading home and coming back another time. The signs of mourning made me regret my decision to drop by unannounced. Before I could make up my mind, the front door opened and out walked Ricky's brother Robby. He was with Ricky's service buddy I had met the previous day, Jimmy Key. Robby looked surprised to see me and walked over to where I was standing.

"Ray," Robby said, shaking my hand. "Mom expecting you?"

"No," I said. "I was running some errands and thought I'd swing by, but . . ."

"No, it's okay. But Mom just took a sedative and she's out of it. I'm hoping she finally gets some sleep. You remember Jimmy?"

"Sure." We shook hands. "How's it going?"

"It's going," he said. "I meant to ask you yesterday, you the chief's kid?"

"Nephew. You a cop?"

"Private security."

"Back in the city? Big difference from Iraq, huh?"

"Yeah, but some days, I'm not sure which is worse."

"Oh, shit," Robby said and walked back to the house. He reached into the mailbox and pulled out the contents. He came back over to us. "Gotta get the mail before Mom does. Anything addressed to Ricky sets her off again."

He flipped through the envelopes and was about to tuck them inside a catalogue when something stopped him. He got a weird look on his face.

"What's up?" I said.

"I don't know," Robby answered. He let Jimmy and me see the front of the envelope. The return address had a logo that read, "VA Home Loans." It was addressed to Mr. Richard Torres. Strange to see Ricky T's name so formalized.

"Veteran's Administration," Jimmy observed. "Ricky say anything about buying a house?"

Robby shook his head. He opened the envelope and took out the contents. He unfolded and flipped through the pages as Jimmy and I stood there quietly. After a minute, Robby said, "Says he's been approved for a home loan for up to seven-hundred-and-fifty-thousand dollars."

We all let that sink in.

"You knew nothing about this?" I asked Robby.

"He said he wanted to move out of Mom's. But I figured he meant *renting* an apartment, not buying one." He waved the papers in the air. "And for seven hundred and fifty thou? Where the hell was he gonna get the money to make the payments on a seven-hundred-and-fifty-thousand dollar mortgage?"

"Not on a cop's salary," Jimmy said.

"Can I see those papers?" I asked. I took them from Robby and did as he had done: I flipped through them—as if I'd understand something just by touching it. There were two things I did understand: the interest rate was pretty low; and Ricky'd be paying it off for a little under two thousand dollars a month. That would take a while, but put like that, it didn't seem completely out of the realm of possibility. I guessed if he did go back to the cops, he'd be relying on one of the street cops' best friends: Oscar Thomas. *OverTime.* I handed the papers back to Robby. "I guess you don't wanna ask your mom, huh?"

"Ahh, no," Robby said. He folded the papers and slipped them back inside the envelope. "I'll call them up and let them know about Ricky." He looked at his watch. "Maybe I should do that now. I don't want Mom seeing any more mail from these guys. All she needs now is to know Ricky was going to move out and buy his own place."

He stuck his hand out to Jimmy Key and me. "Thanks for coming by, guys. I'll let Mom know you dropped by, Ray."

"Thanks. Tell her I'll call next time."

"Cool." He pointed back at the house. "I'm gonna go make that call."

"Be good, man," Jimmy said. "When you heading back up?"

"Tomorrow. Gotta show an apartment to some college kids, and one of the year-round tenant's toilet keeps backing up. My boss already gave me two more days than I asked for."

"An overflowing toilet waits for no man," I said, but no one laughed.

"Take it easy, guys." Jimmy and I watched as Robby went back inside.

When the front door had shut, Jimmy turned to me. "I don't know about you, but I could really use a beer at this moment."

"Yeah," I said. "A beer right now would not suck."

I watched as Jimmy Key downed half a pint of Brooklyn Pilsner without taking a breath. I was sure I had been that thirsty once, I just couldn't remember when. He saw the smile on my face, returned it with one of his own, and wiped the moisture from his lips.

"Yeah," he said. "I know. I've been back in the States for almost a year now, but this," he raised his pint glass, "was one of those things I didn't appreciate until I couldn't have it, y'know?"

"There's no beer in the Middle East?"

"Not as much as there should be, with all that Muslim stuff, y'know? And what there was? Not so great." He finished the rest of the pint and slid the glass forward on the bar. We were sitting at Teddy's and were lucky enough to get the last two stools before the after-work crowd came in.

I took another sip of my beer. "Welcome back."

"Thanks."

The bartender came over with two more pints and a gorgeous smile of her own. I hadn't noticed how blue her eyes were the first time she'd come over.

"I'm not quite ready yet," I said.

"These are on Felice," she said in a slight Southern drawl. She motioned with her head to the other end of the bar, where the owner was busy on the phone. Felice gave us an exaggerated grin and a thumbs-up, and went back to her call.

"Then . . ." I drained my beer, "I guess I am ready."

The bartender walked away and Jimmy said, "You in with the owner?"

"She likes teachers. And just wait 'til she hears you're a soldier."

"Private security, Ray. Not Uncle Sam's army." He looked over at Felice. "She's cute."

"And married. Happily." I picked up my glass and touched it to Jimmy's. "I'm guessing there's a lot of things you missed while you were over there."

"You don't know the half of it. Every day I wake up since I've been back? I thank the Lord for fresh coffee, cold milk, hot showers, and seeing more of a woman than just her eyes. I think about the shit I used to complain about and feel like a jerk."

"It was that bad?"

"Most of the time and most of the places, yeah." He let that thought hang for a bit as he took a normal-size sip of beer. "Always had the other guys, though, y'know? You couldn't complain 'cause we were all in the same foxhole, right?"

"Doesn't stop some teachers I work with."

He laughed. "Not in the desert, man. When you're in that situation and you're flying your colors, you're part of something much bigger than yourself." He took a quick sip. "I don't care what your politics are, how you feel about being over there, who you pray to when the lights go down, or if you don't pray when the lights go down. Everybody's wearing our flag, and that means a shitload more than the last time you took a shower or did your laundry."

"You better not say that out loud, Jimmy. Sounds like you wanna go back."

"Nah, man. I made my bucks over there. Helped our guys do what they were told to do, we were proud to do it, but it was time to get all of us the fuck outta there. Hope it stays that way."

"How often you work with Ricky T?"

"We'd run into each other once in a while on some of the bigger details. General, or some senator or congressman trying to look all supportive and shit, comes by for a visit, we'd see each other. But that'd be it."

"So," I said, "being law enforcement over there . . . ."

"A lot of the same shit as over here. Except you're not local, y'know? Some of the folks knew why we were there and respected that. Some knew why we were there and didn't. You know what the shittiest part was?"

I shook my head. "No."

"When you're in the desert or patrolling one of the villages? Everybody fits the profile. Adults, kids, fucking grandmothers. I hate to say this, but you never knew who was out to get ya. Back here, at least, you get a description. Suspect's wearing a black hoodie with a red baseball cap. Suspect was last seen wearing bright orange kicks, riding a BMW bike, heading north on Bushwick. Ain't like that over there. I ain't a racist, Ray, but that thing about some people looking all the same, I never got that until I went over. Shit, I'm sure they felt the same way about our guys—a bunch of white guys in green and khaki, carrying heavy-duty firearms, going anywhere we damn-well pleased. On their streets, in their markets. Fuck, we even went into their homes, for God's sake."

"You private guys did that kinda stuff?"

"And more, man."

Jimmy finished his beer and pushed the empty glass away. The bartender came over with two more. This was fast drinking even for me. Jimmy grabbed his pint right away and gave the bartender a flirty grin before she walked away.

"She's cute, too." He let his eyes linger a while. "Visual Viagra, man. That girl could cure erectile dysfunction just by walking into a doctor's office." He took a sip. "You were a cop for how long?"

"About five years."

"So, you're pretty familiar with the Constitution?"

"The parts that I needed to know on the streets, yeah."

"Ain't no Constitution over there. Illegal search and seizure? Twenty times a day. Reasonable cause? 'Be*cause* I said so,' that's my reasonable cause."

"How long were you home before you went back to security work?"

"Two weeks," he said.

"That sounds pretty quick."

"Yeah, I coulda pushed it to a month or two, but I needed to get back. I didn't want the other guys looking at me like I was a broken toy, y'know?"

I nodded. *Broken toy.* Cop talk for someone who couldn't do the job the way he used to. That was one of the main reasons I chose not to go back after my accident. It's one thing to doubt your own ability to do your job, a completely different thing to have other people doubt it. People whose lives literally depended on you. Once that seed is planted, it's hard to dig it back up. For the first time in a long time, I felt pain in my knees.

"That's why I kept pushing Ricky T to get back on the saddle," Jimmy said. "The longer he put it off, the harder it was gonna be for him. And it was getting hard. He had all the symptoms, man. Told me he wasn't sleeping at night, kept looking over his shoulder. Even told me he'd drive by some fares if he thought they looked Middle Eastern."

"Post-traumatic stress," I said. "I went through some after my accident."

He nodded. "You had a fall, right? Chasing a perp?"

I gave him the quick version of my story: from getting cursed at outside the projects all the way up to the fire escape pulling away from the building.

"How'd you get through that? How'd you avoid the full PTSD thing?"

"My uncle said he'd smack the shit out of me if he ever saw me feeling sorry for myself anymore."

Jimmy laughed. "I've heard stories about the Chief and his old-school methods. But what else did you do?"

"Drank a lot. Watched a few months of shitty TV and sat out on my deck staring at the skyline. One day I woke up and was sick of myself. My sister dragged me to my G.P., who prescribed some meds for half a year. But I never saw a therapist or anything." I ran two fingers up and down the side of my frosted pint glass. "Decided to go back and finish college, and after a semester, figured I'd give teaching a shot. I like to think of it as getting to these kids before the cops do."

Jimmy raised his glass. "Good for you, Ray. Like I said, you're a part of something bigger than you. A lot of guys I talk to who've been over there, that's the biggest thing they miss. Feeling like they're part of something important."

"I'm not comparing being a teacher to what you've done, Jimmy."

"I know. But what you're doing has real meaning. I mean, you stand less of a chance of getting shot at—in theory, anyway—but it's important. Ricky had a blind spot when it came to the bigger picture sometimes."

"But he did come around," I reminded him. "Any idea why? Why now?"

"Nope. Just said it was time. His exact words? 'Time to grow the fuck up.' Never had the chance to follow up on that thought."

"Last thing he told me was that he'd made a big mistake."

"First I'm hearing about that." He spun his pint glass around. "What was it like? Being in the car with him when the shooting started?"

"If I say 'otherworldly' do I sound like an asshole?"

"It makes you sound like a civilian, Ray. A regular human being."

"Let's go with that then." My phone rang. I slipped it out of my pocket and recognized Jack Knight's number. I raised the phone to Jimmy and got off my stool. "I gotta take this."

"No problem," he said. "I gotta pee." He disappeared into the back, while I stepped outside to take the call.

"What's up?"

"That's what I'm calling to ask you," Jack said. "How'd the interview with our wit go? He showed, right?"

"Oh, yeah, he showed." I took a breath. "He's not a good witness, Jack—at least, not for the insurance company. He was still buzzed this morning when we spoke. My guess is he was under the influence the morning of the accident."

Jack was silent for a few seconds. "Shit. You took good notes, though?"

"For what it's worth, yeah."

"Okay." More silence. "Forget about emailing the photos and report." *Good, because I had forgotten.* "You can give 'em to me tomorrow. Refresh my memory; you don't got wheels, right?"

"Right."

"All right. I'll pick you up at seven."

I thought about my plan to drink more beer. "That's kinda early, isn't it?"

"Mr. Golden's working from home tomorrow morning. I wanna be there by eight thirty. With traffic and construction and the kinda cash this guy's paying me, I don't wanna keep him waiting."

"Want me to pick up breakfast?"

"Mighty white of you, Ray. Coffee and a buttered cinnamon raisin bagel."

"I'll see you outside my apartment at seven, Jack."

"Later."

I went back inside and found Jimmy Key standing at the end of the bar, whispering something into our bartender's ear. She seemed to be listening quite intensely and then broke out into a laugh that spread through the bar like sunlight. This guy was good. I went over to our stools and waited for him to come back.

When he did, he was folding up a napkin and sticking it in his front pocket.

"Smooth," I said.

"Man," he said, picking up his beer. "Since I've been back, I've been collecting digits like a motherfucker. This back-from-the-Middle-East thing is getting me all kinds of action."

I touched my glass to his. "You deserve it."

"Amen to that. Important call?"

"I'm doing some work for a P.I. The guy that Ricky T was working with."

"Yeah. Ricky told me he was a jerk. You guys called him The Whack?"

"Yeah, but he's changed. A bit. I'm just picking up some hours before school starts."

"I assume you've had the discussion about whether Ricky's work with Jack had anything to do with the shooting."

"Yeah, and right now it doesn't seem like it."

Jimmy considered that. "The shooting happened right around here, right?"

"A few blocks over. On Kent."

Jimmy drained what was left of his beer, pulled a twenty out of his pocket, and placed it on the bar. The bartender came over, flashed her blue eyes, and said, "You're not leaving so early, are you, Soldier?"

Jimmy patted me on the back. "Me and my buddy are gonna take a quick field trip, Sammi. Be back in less than an hour."

She scooped the twenty off the bar, folded it, and placed it in her cleavage. I'd only seen that in movies. "You better be," she said.

"Count on it."

As Jimmy walked me to the door, I said, "Field trip?"

"I wanna see where this all went down."

Chapter 14

A NICE BREEZE OFF THE EAST RIVER almost made me forget what had happened at this spot a few nights ago. No, that's not true. Not even close. I'd never get into another cab for as long as I lived without reliving that night. The smell coming off the river made my stomach clench.

"You were parked here?" Jimmy said.

I patted the faded-blue pickup truck that was parked along the construction fence. "Just about exactly."

"For how long before . . . you know?"

I had to think about that. A lot of that night was blurry. "I'm going to say about five minutes."

Jimmy nodded and leaned against the pickup. He looked up at the brand-new high-rise condos across the way from us and shook his head.

"Jesus," he said. "These gotta be going for close to a mil, huh?"

"I don't read the real estate section, but that's probably a good guess."

His gaze turned east across Kent Avenue, to the side that looked like the Williamsburg that used to be: five-story walk-ups, street-level commercial properties, and an old factory that I was sure would be loft space soon enough.

"Tell me about that night, Ray."

"What do you want to know?"

"Just tell me about that night. Whatever comes to mind."

"You interviewing me, Jimmy?"

He grinned. "You know how us personal-security types are."

This guy could sell shit to a pig. I told him my story.

Three minutes later, he closed his eyes as if contemplating a brainteaser. I waited another minute before he spoke.

"How much time between the driver's-side window breaking and the shit hitting the fan?"

"That's one of the things I'm fuzzy about."

"Ballpark it for me. A minute? Thirty seconds?"

"Less than that. Five seconds? Ten?"

He nodded and looked at the surrounding area again. In fact, he did a very slow full three-sixty. When he had turned around completely, he seemed to have come to some sort of conclusion.

"What?" I said.

He pointed across the avenue at the row of buildings. "Scaffolding," he said, moving his finger a little to the right and holding it there like he was aiming. After a while, I got what he was doing.

Fuck.

"A sniper?" I said, barely believing the word coming out of my mouth.

"There's one way to find out," He started making his way across the avenue. I followed. When we got to the building with the scaffolding, he turned back to where we'd come from. "That's about thirty, thirty-five yards. Not much of a shot if you know what you're doing." He looked up at the metal bars. The next thing I knew, he had jumped up like a gymnast and swung himself up onto the first layer of scaffolding. He did that one more time so that he was now outside the third-floor window. He ran his hand across the metal bar and stopped in the middle. "Smooth spot right here," he said. "Could be where the shooter rested the rifle. Guy had plenty of time. Dead red."

"What?"

"It's a baseball term. It means—"

"I know what it means. A hitter's waiting on a fastball and then he crushes it. What does that have to do with this?"

"Some of the snipers I knew over there, they'd sit around talking about shots they'd taken. That day, last week, whatever. Sometimes I think they made shit up just to top each other, y'know? Some shots were more difficult than others. The easy ones—the ones where their intel told them exactly where and when to be?—they'd call it 'sitting dead red.'"

From the Middle East to Williamsburg.

"You mean the shooter was waiting for Ricky?"

"That's one way of thinking. Or he found him and had time to set up a kill short."

I shook my head, contemplating what he was saying. "What about the other shots?" I answered my own question. "A second shooter." I remembered that possibility coming up at the hospital.

"Taxi was completely shot up you said, right?"

"Yeah."

"Shooter Number Two was in motion."

I watched as Jimmy came down as gracefully as he had climbed up. There was a time I could do that. When he was standing next to me, I said, "They found a body over in the park the other night." I pointed north two blocks. "Older kid on a bike, automatic weapon was found."

"Shock and Awe."

"Huh?"

"First shooter," Jimmy said. "He gets the job done. One shot—there's your shock. Second shooter, his job is to make a lot of noise, confuse the situation."

"Awe." I waited five seconds. "Goddamn it!" I yelled.

"Some people might say God was looking out for you, Ray," Jimmy said. "The shooter coulda chose the sidewalk to do his banging instead of the street. If he had, we wouldn't be having this conversation."

"Some people can go fuck themselves." My head began to spin, and I felt myself starting to hyperventilate. I grabbed the scaffolding for balance and felt Jimmy's hand on my shoulder. Then I threw up. *Fucking beautiful.*

"You gonna be okay?" he asked, taking his hand off me.

I watched the sidewalk swim and nodded. "I'm good."

It took about a minute to put some truth into that statement. I straightened myself up and slowly shook my head.

"Doctor said I shouldn't drink for a few days. Got a mild concussion."

"Doctors say a lot of things. Do you know if they got the ballistics back on Ricky's shooting?"

"I have no idea. They don't keep me in the loop anymore, Jimmy."

"But you know someone who *would* know. Someone you could call and get whatever info you wanted."

"My Uncle Ray," I said, catching on. "But why do you—"

"If we're right about the way the shooting went down, there'll be two different guns involved."

I pulled my cell out, found the contact info for my uncle, and pressed the screen. It took three rings before he picked up.

"Nephew," he said. "How's the head?"

"I'm good. Thanks." He was not going to be happy about the reason for my call. "Gotta quick question I was hoping you could answer."

"Make it a *real* quick one. I'm about to step into a meeting."

I went straight for it. "They get the ballistics back on Ricky Torres?"

Silence. Then, "Why would you want to know that, Raymond?"

"I'm over here at the scene. With a friend of Ricky's, Jimmy Kisparadis. Jimmy Key. He was in the Middle East with Ricky, and he's got a theory about the shooting."

"How nice for you both," Uncle Ray said. "You got thirty seconds to share this theory with me, Raymond."

I did. Uncle Ray remained quiet. I knew the face he was making: part anger, part contemplation. I'd seen it enough times from him in person.

"Shit," he finally said. "I gotta step into the meeting. Afterward, I'll check in with the lead on the case. You remember Detective Royce, right?"

I ignored that dig. "Can you call me and let me know?" Now I was really pushing it.

"Seems like we need to have a little talk anyway. This guy, why's he involved with this?"

"Like I said, he was over in the Middle East with Ricky and stayed friends with him back here. We got to talking and—"

"You both just ended up at the crime scene."

"Something like that, yeah."

More silence. "It's a good theory, Raymond. Tell your new buddy I said so. You can also tell him to keep his nose out of an active investigation. Do I need to say that goes double for you?"

"No. Thank you."

"Go home now and rest your head." He hung up.

I turned to Jimmy. "He'll look into it. Said it was a workable theory, but didn't like that it came from me. I mean you."

Jimmy shrugged. "As long as he's taking it seriously, I don't care."

"Me, either." I was lying. I was in for a good, old-fashioned butt chewing sometime in the near future.

We walked across the street and stopped in front of the new condos. I looked up at the blue tower and could just imagine the views from way on high. When my thoughts came back to Earth, another one hit me.

"Let's check out the inside," I said.

"Why?" Jimmy asked.

"Humor me for a minute. Your present gig come with a badge?"

"Yeah. Why?"

"Good. Come on."

We stepped over to the entrance and were greeted by a uniformed doorman, who came out from behind a desk that looked designed to take heavy fire.

"Help you, gentlemen?" he asked.

I nodded at Jimmy to flash his badge. He did. "Sales office open?"

"Yes, sir. Is there a problem?"

"Can you direct us to the sales office, please."

"I'll do better than that," he said, and went back behind the desk. "I'll call the sales manager down. That okay?"

"That'll be fine."

The guy picked up the phone, said something I couldn't hear, and then hung up. He gave Ricky and me a big smile. "One minute, sirs."

Sixty seconds later, a well-groomed man in what had to be a very expensive suit appeared from behind the marbled wall. He stepped over to us, checked out our clothing—short-sleeved shirts, shorts, and sneakers; apparently not what he expected two cops to wear—and offered us his hand.

"Officers," he said. "Alberto Diaz, Sales Manager. How may I help you?"

Seeing that this was my play, Jimmy stayed quiet. I took a few seconds to make sure what I wanted to say came out sounding like a cop.

"You're aware," I started, "of the shooting that happened the other night?"

"How could I not be?" Diaz said. "But I already spoke with a detective on Saturday. I don't believe I have anything worthwhile to add."

"There's been a new development. We have reason to believe that the victim—Mr. Torres—was interested in purchasing an apartment here."

"No one mentioned that to me," Diaz said defensively.

"Like I said, Mr. Diaz. It's a recent development. Is there any way you can check and see if Mr. Torres had applied?"

He considered that. "He was a police officer, I was told."

"Yes."

He chose his next words carefully. "No offense, but we don't get many police officers filling out applications here."

"Nor schoolteachers or firemen I guess either, huh?"

"No." He gave a small uncomfortable laugh. "I'm afraid not."

"Would you mind checking for us anyway? I know it sounds unlikely, but we'd like to rule it out. Should we go up to your office?"

"No need." He pulled a phone out of his jacket. His was better than mine. "Torres, right?"

"*Richard* Torres."

Diaz worked his keyboard as Jimmy and I gave each other a look. Mine was one of those it's-worth-a-try looks. Jimmy's was more of the what-the-fuck variety. After a half minute, Diaz grunted, "Huh."

"You find something?" I asked.

"I did. A Mr. Richard Torres filled out a preliminary application a few weeks ago for a two-bedroom apartment." He moved his nimble thumbs across the keyboard again and said, "That's a nine-hundred-thousand-dollar apartment." Diaz gave us both a look, then touched the screen again and scrolled down. "Says here he was inquiring about the total monthly cost after putting down twenty percent."

Twenty percent?

"That's a hundred and eighty thousand dollars," I said out loud.

Jimmy let out a low whistle as Alberto Diaz checked his screen again.

Was this what Ricky T wanted to show me? And what did the girl in the photograph have to do with this, if anything? I heard Ricky's voice in my head again.

"I made a mistake, Ray."

What the hell kind of mistake involves a beautiful girl and an apartment that Ricky T should have no way of affording? The only possibilities I could come up with right away were not good ones. Guys like Ricky don't just happen to have twenty percent of nine hundred thousand bucks at their disposal. I remembered the piece of mail his brother had shown us. How Ricky was eligible for a three quarters of a million-dollar loan.

It was starting to come together why he was suddenly in a big hurry to return to the force. He needed to get back to work—real work—if he were even considering a place like this.

"Is that all, officers?" Diaz asked. "I have a client I need to get back to."

"Yeah," I said. "That's all for now. Do you have a card, Mr. Diaz?"

He pulled one out of his jacket pocket and handed it to me. "I'm here Monday through Friday. Weekends by appointment."

"Thanks. We'll be in touch."

He didn't look too thrilled at that possibility. I watched him walk away and Jimmy looked at me. "How did you know?"

"I didn't." I waved to the guy behind the desk. He was on the phone and waved back. We exited the building. "It just didn't make any sense why Ricky would drive all the way over here to tell me whatever it was he wanted to tell me."

"You saying it makes sense now?"

"Not yet. It brings up a lot of questions. But there's one that's really starting to burn me."

"What's that?"

"How did the shooter know when and where to find Ricky T?"

Chapter 15

IT TOOK LESS THAN TEN MINUTES to walk back to Teddy's. I had made a phone call along the way and was not surprised to see Edgar already sitting at the bar. He had his laptop with him, and he was drinking Bass Ale with tomato juice. I made the standard introductions, and Edgar did not disappoint.

"Like the Yankee pitcher?" he asked as Jimmy and I grabbed stools on both sides of Edgar.

"I'll explain later," I said.

Sammi the bartender came over with two pints of Brooklyn Pilsner. The look on her face made it quite clear it was Jimmy she remembered, not me. I wasn't even sure I registered on her radar. While she and Jimmy flirted, I turned to Edgar.

"Thanks for showing up, Edgar. You got here pretty quick."

"I was just getting off when you called." He giggled at the unintended sexual association. He did that a lot. "Anyway, what d'ya need to know?"

"GPS," I said.

"Global Positioning System," he answered. "I thought we'd been through all this, Raymond. You need another lesson on how it works?"

"I know how it works, Edgar. What I want to know is how taxis use them."

"Ahh." He took a sip of his ale. "They pretty much all use them now. All the fleets, anyway. If you own and operate your own cab, you probably don't need it as much. It's how the owners keep an eye—so to speak—on their drivers. Make sure they're not making unrecorded stops, taking fares and not turning on the meter, shit like that."

"Who monitors the system?"

"In real time? Whoever's back at the station or the depot, whatever they call 'em. But its real application is to check the driver's record of his shift against the GPS. If they don't match, your driver might soon be looking for a new job."

"So, the company knows where the driver is at all times?"

"In theory, yeah," Edgar said. "But whoever's back at the office, or the garage, isn't usually checking the system in real time. That's more for the car service guys who need to know who's closest to the airport to pick up a fare or someone who needs a pickup from home. Saves time and money. The taxicabs? They just pick up hails. There's no need to keep an eye on the system except for the occasional check-in."

"Like when a cabby's going on break?"

"Or filling up, or heading out of the city. Yeah."

Ricky was on a break when he picked me up Saturday morning. *Did he call it in? Did someone back at the shop know where he was?*

"Can someone hack into a cab's GPS?"

"*Hack?*" Edgar said. "Good one, Ray."

"Edgar?"

"I've told you this before, Ray. Anything that goes out over the Internet or uploads to a satellite can be hacked. Would take someone with something *approaching* my kind of skills and equipment to do it, but yeah, it's real doable. Why?"

I wasn't sure I wanted to share that with Edgar yet, so I let the question hang in the air. But halfway through his next sip it came to him. He swallowed hard.

"You think someone was tracking your friend the other night," he said.

"I'm not there yet. I'm not anywhere. I'm just considering the possibility."

"The possibility of what?" Jimmy joined the conversation as his new admirer remembered she had customers at the other end of the bar.

"Edgar's my . . . techie friend." I patted Edgar on the knee. "Explain."

He did. Jimmy listened intently and didn't ask questions. I assumed with his security experience, he knew a lot of what Edgar was talking about already. When Edgar finished, Jimmy nodded and gave a small smile.

"What is it you do, man?" he asked, obviously impressed with Edgar.

"Communications for the Transit Authority."

Jimmy smiled and said, "He's the one who should be working for The Whack, Ray, not you."

Edgar gave me a strange look. "What's that mean, Ray?"

I told him how I was picking up some extra cash, basically by running a few interviews for Jack's PI enterprise. He was not happy with me.

"The guy's an . . . asshole, Ray." He looked at Jimmy. "Excuse me."

"That's okay, man. I've heard pretty much the same about the man."

"It's not important," I said. "Let's focus here." I turned to Jimmy. "Do you know if the cops have interviewed Ricky's cousin yet?" To Edgar, I said, "Ricky's cousin co-owns the fleet Ricky drove for."

"I don't know," Jimmy said. "But we can find out."

"I'm not asking my uncle again. I'm gonna be missing a chunk of my ass as it is for that last phone call."

"I'll call a buddy over at the nine-oh," Jimmy said. "I'm sure they've spoken to the guy. He was Ricky's boss."

"But have the cops thought about checking the GPS?" I asked.

"That," Jimmy raised his glass, "is a good question." He touched my glass with his. "Good call, Ray. You're still good at this shit."

"You don't know the half of it," Edgar said.

"And he doesn't need to know now, Edgar." To Jimmy I said, "I'll tell you some stories over a bunch of beers another time." I looked at my watch. "In the meantime, why don't you seal the deal with Sammi there." I pulled a twenty out and placed it on the bar to cover Edgar's and my drinks. I wasn't planning on sticking around to see if Sammi cleavaged it. "Edgar. Swing me home? I got an early day tomorrow."

He finished his drink and stuck out his hand. "Nice to meet you, Jimmy."

"Same here, Edgar. Keep up the good work."

"You bet I will," Edgar said.

"Let's touch base tomorrow," Jimmy said to me. "Put our heads together again."

"I'll do my best to call you."

He looked over at the bartender and back to me. "Not too early, okay?"

"Enjoy responsibly."

"I always do."

Edgar double-parked in front of my building and kept the engine running. I would have asked him up, but I was tired and looking at an early morning.

"Thanks," I said. "For the ride and the lesson."

"Always glad to be of service, Ray," Edgar said. "That Jimmy guy seems pretty cool, huh?"

"About as cool as they come, Edgar." I opened up the car door. "I'll talk to you in a day or two."

"Looking forward to it."

As I watched him pull away, I got my keys out and my cell phone rang. It was my uncle's personal phone.

"That was quick," I said.

"It's what I do, Raymond," Uncle Ray said. He waited for a few seconds before speaking again. "Turns out at least part of your theory is correct."

"Two different bullets?"

"The one they took out of Ricky's head was a thirty-aught-six. It's consistent with the Springfield, a sniper rifle commonly used in law enforcement and the military. That, by the way, was the only wound Ricky suffered."

I could hear the shots again, the windows coming apart.

"And the others in Ricky's cab?"

"Beretta Px4 semiautomatic pistol. Crime scene found fifteen in and around the vehicle. I'll say this again, Nephew: You are one lucky fuck."

I'll keep that in mind when the dreams come back tonight.

"Did you find anything out about the other shootings? The other cabbie in Long Island City—Michael Dillman, was it?—and the kid next to the semiautomatic in East River Park?"

"You're pushing it, kiddo."

"Damn it, Uncle Ray. I was there. This is not just me sticking my nose where it doesn't belong."

"Easy there, Raymond. Three separate shootings means three separate detectives for the moment. We'll coordinate tomorrow and get it all together."

"Just tell me: that kid they found in East River Park the other night?"

"What about him?"

"Was he killed with a thirty-aught-six?"

Uncle Ray was quiet, so I continued. "The gun he had. Was it a Beretta Px4 semiautomatic pistol?"

"Yep. Magazine holds fifteen. If he was the second shooter, he blew a whole mag on you and didn't stop to reload."

"If he was the second shooter," I said, "someone really wanted him dead."

"See now, Nephew. That's something for the *cops* to figure out, not for you to concern your *civilian* self with."

"I hear you, Uncle Ray. I'm just thinking out loud."

"You always hear me, Ray. It's the thinking that worries me."

"Well, don't." I put my key into the lock. "I'm just going upstairs now and calling it an early night."

"You with the lady friend?"

"No, but that might change."

"Good night, Raymond."

"Good night, Uncle Ray. And thanks," I said before hanging up.

I was halfway up the stairs to my place when the phone rang again. Allison.

"If you're calling to come over, the answer's yes."

"I wish I could, Ray," she said. "I'm still working. I'm getting my notes together on the shootings, and I still have an author profile from last week to do."

"Maybe tomorrow then. Dinner?"

"Pencil me in. How're you feeling?"

"Had a . . . bit of a slight dizzy spell this afternoon, but I'll give you all the gory details tomorrow."

"Okay," she said.

"Don't work too late."

"Tell that to my boss."

"Good night, Ally."

"Good night, Ray."

I stepped into my apartment and checked my landline. No messages. *Good*. I went to the fridge, took out a can of Diet Pepsi and two slices of cold pizza from three days ago. I took it all outside and sat at my table. The sky behind Manhattan was orange, the sky above me filling with clouds. I ate my dinner silently and thought about Ricky T, automatic weapons, and all the ways we've come up with to kill our fellow humans.

And how lucky I was supposed to feel.

Chapter 16

BY THE TIME WE GOT OFF the Meadowbrook Parkway, it was pushing eight thirty, and Jack was growing increasingly worried about pissing off Mr. Golden by being a few minutes late. During the ride out, I told him about the ballistics reports on Ricky T and the dead kid in East River Park. He told me he was waiting to hear back from his guy at the nine-oh regarding the other cabbie's shooting.

Jack made a hard left off Sunrise Highway and drove deeper into suburbia. I gathered up all our breakfast junk, placed it in a bag, and tossed it in the backseat.

"It's not a garbage dump, Ray," Jack said.

"You wanna walk into Golden's house with it?"

He answered by stepping on the gas and running a red light. After a few lefts and a couple of rights, he drove onto a dead-end street. *Excuse me, a cul-de-sac.* The houses here were markedly larger than the ones we had passed just a few blocks ago and were varied in style. With a little more effort, one of them could have been the world's largest Taco Bell. Each one looked out onto a canal or off to the Atlantic. The one Jack parked in front of might as well have had a big sign outside that read: WE HAVE MORE MONEY THAN YOU.

Across the street was a red Dumpster filled to the spilling point in front of a house under repair. I got out of the car, walked over to the Dumpster, and tossed the remains of our breakfast into it. I was sure it was against some ordinance or other, but now my trash was mixing with better company.

Jack locked his car electronically and looked at his watch.

"Okay," he said. "Eight twenty-eight. Not bad."

"Good job." I took in a lungful of ocean air. "Smells like money to me."

Unlike the neighbors' houses, the Goldens' did not have a circular driveway. It did, however, have two impressive Japanese maple trees bordering the front steps. The house was painted gray and had a widow's walk on top. We started walking up the stone path that led to the massive front door, when Jack put his hand on my elbow.

"Let me do the talking. If he asks you something directly, obviously you can answer, but you're here as my support personnel, you got that?"

"Can I ask for a ride in his boat?"

"That's funny, Ray. Let's make that the last funny thing you say for the next hour or so, okay?"

"I'm cool, Jack. I'll be good and quiet."

He spread his arms out, palms up. "All I'm asking."

After pressing the doorbell, we waited. I took the time to run my hand across the wood. This thing would take a bullet. The small windows in the door were a combination of stained and smoked glass. I couldn't see through them, but I picked up some motion on the other side and stepped back.

A sturdy woman of about fifty opened the door. She wore a blue polo shirt neatly tucked into a pair of freshly ironed khakis. She had on a nice pair of boat shoes and was wiping her hands on a towel. She looked like one of the Polish women I see around Greenpoint, and when she spoke, I was pretty sure I had my geography correct.

"Mr. Knight?" she asked.

"Yes," Jack said. "Mr. Golden is expecting us."

"Come," she said, and ushered us quickly inside. Either she was afraid of letting the air-conditioning out or didn't want the neighbors to see us. When she closed the door, she said, "Follow."

We followed her up two steps that led into what I think people who live in these kinds of houses call the main room. It was almost all windows and provided a stunning view of the waterway out to the ocean. In the distance, I thought I could make out the Jones Beach Theater. I'd seen my share of concerts there, having grown up about twenty minutes away. This, however, was my first visit to a mansion.

"Sit," the woman said, and motioned to the couch and chairs in the room. I realized with a small smile that her last three sentences had been one-word commands. Maybe she trained dogs back in the old country. She went away just as briskly, I assumed to get the master of the house.

I picked a seat on the couch that allowed me to look out the windows. There was a slight mist hanging just above the water, a blanket that the sun would burn off in an hour or two. Jack went up to the window and shook his head.

"This is the shit, Ray," he said. "This is the shit."

"I'm glad you approve, Mr. Knight."

Jack and I both turned to see a man in his midforties enter the room. He had on a light blue suit and white shirt. No tie. Maybe he was the kind of guy who put the tie on in his office. He was holding a large mug of what I guessed was coffee. I stood as he approached me and stuck out his free hand.

"Charles Golden," he said.

"Ray Donne."

He held on to my hand as if trying to check my pulse through my palm. "You are Mr. Knight's associate?"

"Yes."

I guess I passed his test because he turned to Jack. "Thank you for being prompt. I'm working from home this morning, but have to leave by noon."

I wasn't sure how anybody who didn't know the whereabouts of his sixteen-year-old daughter could even think about work, but this was not my world.

"Eight thirty means eight thirty."

"Excellent." Golden motioned for us to take our seats. We did, and he did the same. "Can I get you anything?" He raised his mug. "Coffee? Juice?"

"We had breakfast on the way," Jack said. "But thank you."

"So . . ." Golden placed his coffee on the table next to him and then slapped his thighs. "You mentioned a new development. Another avenue of investigation?" He sounded almost as if he enjoyed saying that.

"Yes, sir. We've discovered a more recent picture of your daughter's friend, who we believe to be from Williamsburg. We are currently making that picture available to our connections, both at the local precinct and on the street."

"Excellent," Mr. Golden said.

"Did you remember to ask you wife about Angela ever mentioning going to this girl's house or apartment?"

Golden shook his head. "She just mentioned the parties. I don't believe she ever said whose parties they were."

Jack nodded. "And you've spoken with all her friends out here to see if anyone knew this girl?"

"We have, the school has—at least the kids who are around for the summer—and the police have. No one seems to have seen Angela with this girl."

And if they had, I thought, the local youth might not be so forthcoming. This was not a neighborhood of parents who wanted their offspring associating with kids from the unhip side of Williamsburg.

Golden pulled out his cell phone, checked it, and then placed it on the table next to his coffee. He gave me a long look; I felt like an antique being appraised.

"What's your background with Jack?"

Before I could answer, Jack jumped in. "Ray and I were NYPD together, Mr. Golden. He knows the streets of Williamsburg as well as any of my associates, and he also has quite a lot of experience with kids in crisis."

All of that was basically true but somehow *sounded to me like a lie.*

Golden nodded approvingly. "Do you have a card, Ray?"

"You can reach Ray through me, Mr. Golden."

Golden gave Jack a look, reminding us both who was footing the bill here.

"I like to be able to contact all the players, Jack." To me he said, "May I have your cell phone number, Ray?"

I gave it to him. As I was doing so, a woman stepped up into the room. She was at least ten years younger than Mr. Golden. She was wearing a pink sweatsuit and had her blonde hair pulled back. Her blue eyes could have given the Atlantic outside her house a run for its money. Golden stood as she entered.

"Sweetie," he said, kissing her on the cheek. "Should you be up so early?"

"I'm fine, Charles." She looked at Jack and me. We both stood at the same time. "Good morning, gentlemen," she said. "Hello, Jack."

"Good morning, Mrs. Golden." He noticed her looking at me and introduced us.

She nodded and took a seat next to her husband. He put his hand on her left leg and motioned for us to sit back down.

"I know you can't tell by looking, gentlemen, but my wife is pregnant."

"Congratulations," Jack and I said in unison. Jack added, "You look great, Mrs. Golden. How far along are you?"

She took a beat before saying, "Three months."

Jack and I both shook our heads like guys do when hearing details like that. The woman who let us in earlier came into the room and stood silently.

"Agnes," Mrs. Golden said. "Coffee, please."

"Ma'am," Agnes said and left.

"Jack and Ray were just updating me on Angela, Jewels," Mr. Golden said. "I'll fill you in later."

"Yes," she said. "Thank you both."

"You can thank us when we bring her home. And we will. Is there anything that you've thought of since I last spoke with your husband?"

The Goldens looked at each other. Mrs. Golden said, "No. I'm sorry."

"No need to apologize. It's just that in cases like this, sometimes people remember a small detail that seems unimportant at the time. You've been through a lot, and now with the pregnancy, your mind is probably all over the place."

She nodded. "It is."

"If you think of anything, no matter how insignificant it may seem, tell your husband. He'll tell us," Jack looked at Mr. Golden, "and we'll consider it."

"Thank you," she said.

"It's what we do," Jack said.

I found myself surprised by how good Jack was at this.

"Well," Mr. Golden said as he stood up. "I've got a phone conference in my den in a few minutes. If there's nothing else . . ."

Jack got up and I followed his lead. "We'll be in touch, Mr. Golden."

I almost asked if we could check out Angela's bedroom, but kept my mouth shut as Jack had instructed me. Besides, I figured, Jack had probably already done so. It's the first thing you do when a kid goes missing.

"Gentlemen." Mr. Golden gestured toward the door like a game show host. On our way, we passed Agnes bringing Mrs. Golden her coffee. Agnes did not say good-bye, keeping her total syllables addressed to us at under ten.

After shaking hands and agreeing to talk the next day, Jack and I were outside, standing on the front steps, taking in the neighborhood.

"You grew up out here, right?"

"On Long Island. But not this part. We had to bike or drive to the water."

Jack took in a deep breath and closed his eyes. Now that our meeting was over, he seemed more relaxed, enjoying the surroundings.

"Check that out," he said, pointing to a dock across the way from where he'd parked the car. "That's funny shit."

I looked over and couldn't see what was so funny.

"The owl," he said. "The plastic owl perched on the post."

I squinted and noticed the owl for the first time. It was grayish brown and seemed to be an extension of the post on which it sat. Jack must have had pretty good eyesight to pick that up. Another investigative skill he possessed.

"What's so funny about it? I see them in the city. They're supposed to scare the pigeons away."

He spit out some air. "You spend all this fucking money—two million on that house, at least—to live by the water, to commune with nature. And then you spend another lousy ten bucks to do what? Scare away the seagulls so they don't shit on your precious dock?"

"You saying they don't work?"

"Not if they're just sitting there, Ray." He laughed. "Let's say you're a seagull and you wanna land on Mr. Moneybag's dock over there."

"Okay."

"I'll admit, maybe the first time the seagull sees the fake owl, he thinks better of it and decides to do his business somewhere else. But after a while, don't you think a seagull of even average intelligence is gonna figure out the owl's never moved?" He laughed again and pointed. "I think I see some bird shit on the owl's head."

I nodded. "You get what you pay for, I guess."

"Buy a fucking gun, shoot one of those flying rats, and leave the body. The rest of them will get the idea." Jack opened the driver's side door. "You wanna go see the big guy's boat?"

"Do we have the time?"

"Lots."

"Shit," Jack said, pulling up to another STOP sign and slapping his steering wheel. "It's all these damned lefts and rights and these cutesy nautical names."

We'd been driving around for almost ten minutes trying to find the marina that was supposed to be five minutes from the Goldens' house. Jack had been there before, but this was not his home turf.

"Make a right," I said.

"Why, Ray? Why a right?"

"Why not?"

He made a right, took that street a few blocks, and we hit another STOP sign. "Now what, Magellan?"

I rolled down my window and stuck my head out. I looked up at the clouds and noticed the direction they were floating. I took a deep breath of the sea air. "Make a left and go about a quarter of a mile."

"What? You know something I don't know?"

I pointed in front of us. "I'm just good at reading."

Jack looked to where I was pointing: a faded sign with the word MA-RINA written in faded blue paint and an arrow pointing to the left. ¼ MILE was written below the arrow.

"Smartass," Jack said and left some tire behind as he made the left turn.

There was no sign telling us whether we could park in the marina, so Jack played it safe by parking just outside the entrance, in front of a closed restaurant with a FOR SALE sign in the window. We walked through the entrance of the marina and were met by the cool ocean breeze again. Must be nice to experience this on a daily basis.

We moved toward the line of boats docked in their individual slots. Jack checked them out and found the one he was looking for.

"That's Golden's." He pointed to the biggest boat in the line.

"Nice."

We got closer and I saw the word SILENCE written in blue script on the back.

"Weird name for a boat," Jack said. "Wonder what it means."

"Silence is golden," I said.

Jack looked at me and smiled. "Pretty sharp there, Ray. You should be a teacher when you grow up. Maybe even a cop."

I gave him a weak smile. "He runs a public relations firm, right?"

"Yep. Pretty snazzy one, too, from what I've seen."

"The name makes sense two ways then."

"Really?"

"The obvious one." I paused for effect. "And the not-so-obvious."

I waited as he thought about it. When he didn't come up with it, I spoke.

"Public relations. It's not just what you want people to know about you, it's also what you *don't* want them to know about you."

"You do something good," Jack said, "you want that news getting out there."

"And the opposite is true for when you don't do so good."

"Silence *is* golden." He laughed. "Hell, for me, *Golden* is golden."

"Help you, gentlemen?"

We turned to see a guy walking toward us. He was carrying a cooler and placed it down at the back of one of the other boats. He was dressed all in blue: denim work shirt, oil-stained jeans, and an old pair of blue sneakers. It looked like he had forgotten to shave . . . three days ago. He took the cigarette out of his mouth and let out a long stream of smoke. Then he licked his fingers, extinguished the hot coal on the end, and placed the remaining cigarette in his shirt pocket. Didn't take much to figure this guy for the caretaker.

"We're all full up, if that's why you're out here," he said. "You can fill out an application in the office, if you want. Gotta waiting list, though, so . . ."

"Actually," Jack said, "my partner and I were just interested in checking out Mr. Golden's boat."

"Partner?" the guy said. "You two cops?"

"Private. We're working for the Golden family. I'm Jack Knight." He handed the guy a card and pointed over his shoulder. "This is Raymond Donne."

I gave a little wave, but he was too busy looking at Jack's card to notice.

"Cool," he said, slipping the card into the same pocket that held his recently dead cigarette. "I'm Lowtide. Kinda take care of things around here."

"Lowtide?" I said.

"Well," he said. "It's not the name on my birth certificate, if that's what you're asking. My real name's Louis Tedeschi, but nobody calls me that except my family, and they're all dead except my sister in California, so, I guess, really nobody but my sister calls me that. I'm just Lowtide."

"Okay," Jack said. "You know the Golden family, Lowtide?"

"Oh, yeah. I know all the boat owners out here. Got to. That's how I knew you two weren't residents."

"So you know about their daughter?"

He shook his head. "Angela, yeah. That's a damn shame. She's an angel, that one. Think that's why they named her Angela."

"You ever see her out here by herself. On the boat?"

"You mean without her folks?"

"That's what I mean."

He paused for a beat. "Yeah, a few times. She'd bring a couple of friends out here and they'd eat lunch on the boat or something. Do the fireworks on the Fourth, stuff like that."

"Any boys?" I asked.

"A few. But never alone." He stressed that part. "She wasn't that type of girl. Some of her friends mighta been, but not Angela."

"Any friends stand out?" Jack asked.

Lowtide shook his head. "That's just what the cops asked me and I said no. They were just your average rich kids hanging around Daddy's boat, you know?"

Jack said he did. "Any . . . minority kids?"

"Minority?" Lowtide said and then whispered, "You mean like Jews?"

"No," Jack said, barely stifling a laugh. "She have any black or Hispanic friends that you mighta seen with her on the boat?"

"Nope," he said. "Just the regular white kids from the neighborhood." He seemed to catch himself as those words came out, and he said, "Not 'regular.' I mean just the kids from around here is what I mean. Kids she went to school with."

Jack reached out and put his hand on Lowtide's shoulder. "I know what you mean, man. It's okay." Jack took out his phone and showed it to Lowtide. "You ever see this girl out here?"

Lowtide studied the picture for a few seconds. "Nope."

Jack looked back at the Golden's boat. "How often do the Goldens take the boat out, would you say?"

"Almost every weekend," Lowtide said. "Sunday mornings. Mr. G likes to get out on the water early. He'll call the day before, and I'll have his cooler and his fishing gear ready to go. I even put fresh bait in the cooler. He's a good tipper."

"That's good to know," Jack said, obviously thinking of the fifty-thousand-dollar tip he was hoping would be coming his way soon. "Thanks a lot, Lowtide. You've been a big help."

"You're welcome, Mr. Knight." I could see another thought forming on his face. It took a while before it came out. "Hey, as a private eye," Lowtide began, "you gotta keep confidential, right?"

"Any information I gather relating to my clients—unless I find out they're about to do somebody some harm—is between me and my client."

Lowtide looked around as if making sure there was no one in the area who could hear him. Besides Jack and me—there wasn't.

"Mr. Golden," he said. "He's been coming out here to sleep some nights."

"Alone?"

It took Lowtide a few seconds to get Jack's implication. "Oh, yeah. Absolutely. I wasn't trying to say . . . no, absolutely. Alone."

Jack lowered his voice. "Any idea why he'd sleep out here by himself?"

Lowtide nodded. "Sometimes, some of the folks come out here when it's real hot. Sleep on the boat. But Mr. Golden? Got the feeling he doesn't like being around the house too much these days. Especially now that the wife is pregnant, y'know? I don't care how big your house is. It gets crowded real quick when the wife's pregnant. And . . . the times they're out here together? They don't always talk so nice to each other."

"Have they been out here together since Angela went missing?" I asked.

"No. Matter of fact, they ain't. Guess they want someone at the house at all times case Angela shows up or calls, huh? Isn't that what the cops always say?"

Jack said, "You seem to know a lot about what goes on around here, Lowtide."

"You don't know the half of it. It's like a soap opera sometimes: *As the Prop Turns.* Everybody knows a little bit about everybody's business."

"And you know most of it, right?"

"I guess I do." He seemed pleased with that. "The missus comes out here by herself, too. During the day, when Mr. G's at work. She'll sit on the boat, just staring into space." He shook his head. "Can't imagine not knowing where your kid's at. Coupla times, I seen her sneaking a smoke. Can't blame her, the stress she's under."

"Can't imagine," Jack said and then looked at his watch. "We gotta be heading back to the big city, Lowtide." Jack offered his hand. "Thanks again."

"Anytime," Lowtide said. "You guys be careful."

"Count on it."

Jack and I watched as Lowtide made his way to the other end of the dock. We started walking back to the car, this time around the parking lot instead of across it. We stopped in front of an area of sand with four deck chairs. The folks here had made their own little beach, roughly the size of a classroom at my school. I turned back to face the water. The breeze was bringing in a low level of clouds, and there was the smell of distant rain. It was almost like being on top of a mountain.

"You figure out why they call him Lowtide, Ray?"

"Because he works by the water? And his name's Lou Tedeschi?"

Jack stopped looking at the water and turned to me. "That's half of it."

"What's the other half, Jack? Why Lowtide?"

"Because low tide is when the things that are usually hidden under the water wash up on shore, where you can see them," Jack said. "And sometimes, Ray . . . ?"

"Yeah?"

"It smells like shit."

Chapter 17

BACK ON THE PARKWAY, JACK WAS weaving his car in and around the slower-moving vehicles—the ones doing only ten miles above the speed limit—when his phone rang. It was between us, mounted onto the dashboard. He pressed a button, which not only answered the call but also put it on speakerphone.

"Jack Knight," he said.

"Jack," the caller said. "Willy."

"Willy D! My favorite bagpiper." He turned to me and mouthed, "A guy from the nine-oh." Back to Willy: "Whatcha got for me, bro?"

"I spoke with the lead on the case," Willy said. "They got the ballistics back on all three shootings."

"Lemme guess. They pulled two different slugs from Ricky's case. One of them matches the gun that killed the dead kid in the park, and the other is was from the kid's semiautomatic.

"How'd the fuck you know that?"

"I know many things. Did someone reinterview Ricky's cousin, Fred, yet? The owner of the cab fleet?"

"Nope. He's a pillar of the community and lawyering up."

Jack said, "What's the word on the other cabbie who was shot Dilman?"

"They finally tracked down the guy God musta been looking out for. Cab shot to hell, and this guy took a through-and-through in the shoulder. He's cool, didn't see shit, has no reason why anyone would be using him for target practice."

Jack looked at me as if to ask me if I had any questions for Willy D. I gave it some thought, then shook my head no.

"Okay, Willy. Thanks, man." A wicked smile crossed Jack's face. "Hey, Willy. When's your next blow job?"

Silence from the other end while Jack giggled like a sixth grader.

"That joke gets funnier every time you use it, Jack," said the piper. "In fact, a couple of us played the pipes at a funeral just last night. A lieutenant from the Bronx buried his twelve-year-old daughter. Fucking cancer. Believe that shit?"

That sobered Jack up. "Childhood cancer," Jack said. "God's way of saying, 'I don't really exist.'"

"It ain't all God's fault, Jack. See ya soon."

"Not if I see you first."

He turned the phone off. "This don't look good for Ricky, Ray."

"Ricky's dead, Jack. How good *can* it look?"

"It's *not* supposed to look like he was targeted. But, shit. I know you've been hanging with the kiddies for a few years, but to us cops, Ricky getting one to the head by the same gun that takes out the kid kinda makes it look like this *was* about Ricky, and the kid was supposed to shoot up cabs as a diversion."

I knew damned well what it looked like. I just didn't want to think about it. I told Jack about Ricky and the condos next to where he was killed.

"How'd he think he could afford that?" Jack asked. "He wasn't getting *that* much work from me." Jack merged onto the Long Island Expressway and immediately slowed down with the traffic. "Fucking LIE. World's longest parking lot."

"Ricky never said anything to you about coming into some money?"

"Nada. Just that he was gonna put his papers in to get back on the force. But that don't pay enough for a two-bedroom condo in that building."

We rode in silence for the next mile or so. Jack turned up the AC, cracked the window, and lit a cigarette. Our own mini-version of global climate change.

"Shit, Ray," Jack finally said.

"What?"

"I hate to think this way, but you think there's a chance that Ricky was playing me? That he located the *chiquita*, found Angela Golden, and was going behind my back to collect the reward money?"

"Ricky? No way, Jack. You knew him better than I did. You hired him because you trusted him so much."

"Yeah, but he was different, man. After he came back. That shit can play with your head, you're not careful."

I thought about what Jimmy Key had said yesterday. How Ricky'd been having some trouble adjusting to life back in the states and how it was a good sign that he was going back to the cops.

"I don't know, Jack. I don't see it."

"But it's a possibility, right?"

"Shit, everything's *possible*. But . . ."

Whatever it was I was going to say next just trailed off and vanished out the window with Jack's cigarette smoke. I looked at the hundreds of cars in front of us and almost became mesmerized by their windows. All intact. All normal. Just like my life was a few nights ago. I got this buzzing feeling in my arms, so I closed my eyes and tried to focus on my breathing. I must have dozed off because, before I knew it, Jack was pulling up in front of my apartment.

"All right," he said. "Good day's work." He looked at his watch. "Shit, it's not even noon. Good *half* day's work." He reached into his shirt pocket and pulled out some money. "Here ya go, Ray. Three hundred."

I took it. "That's a lot of money, Jack."

"You up for more work this week?"

"Yeah, I might be. Let me check my schedule and I'll get back to you."

"Your schedule?" Jack laughed. "You don't gotta be at work until the day after Labor Day. What schedule?"

"I do have a life outside of school, Jack. Let me call Allison, see what her week looks like."

"Oh, forgot about the girlfriend." Again he sounded like a seventh grader.

"I'll see what's up with her and I'll get back to you, okay?"

"Okay, Ray." He shook my hand. "I got the work, so just give me the word. You did good today."

"I was window dressing."

"It was more than that, but I'm not gonna waste time complimenting you."

"I wouldn't expect you to."

"Then we're good."

He pulled away. I went to the corner and got an iced coffee and the paper. I brought both upstairs and fell asleep on the futon before finishing either one.

I was dreaming about swimming underwater and getting attacked by some sort of electric eel or stingray. It stung me in the side and wouldn't let go. I'm not sure how long that was going on before I woke up enough to realize it was my cell phone buzzing in my pocket.

"Hello?"

"Don't tell me I woke you, tough guy," Allison said. "I know you had to work a few hours this morning, but jeez, it's only three o'clock."

"I dozed off," I said as I sat up. "How are you?"

"Good. I got a little news for you about the shooting the other night, if you're interested."

I sat up straighter. "Ricky's shooting?"

"No," she said. "The other driver in Queens. Michael Dillman."

"What about him?"

"Turns out he had a record."

I knew that. "For what?"

"Illegal trafficking of tobacco products across state lines. Did five years upstate and just got released back in February."

"How long had he been driving for the company?"

"Since March," Allison said. "Been clean since then, it seems. Meets with his parole officer on schedule, even pisses in a cup once a month."

"He was a user?"

"When they caught him, they found a little marijuana and some coke in his possession. It was barely enough to bust him on intent to distribute. He pleaded out on those and got the five years for the smokes. I think the urine samples were just to break his balls a bit. Remind him he got off easy."

I loved it when Allison talked like a cop.

"Found out something else that may interest you."

"What's that?"

"It seems Mr. Dillman—Little Mike they called him—was superstitious."

"Okay . . ."

"He liked to drive the same cab each shift. Insisted on it."

"What does that have to do with—?"

"The night of the shootings," Allison said, "his regular cab was having engine trouble. He had to drive another car or not take a shift."

"I'm still not seeing why this is important."

"He takes another car and about an hour later, the mechanic's got the other one fixed. Your buddy Ricky comes in—he was running late—and takes *that* one out. He, apparently, was *not* superstitious. Maybe he should have been."

"Because . . ." I said, dragging the word out. "Fuck! The GPS."

"What about the GPS?"

I told her what Edgar had explained to me about how the cab companies used the system to keep track of their drivers and how the system could be hacked into. It came to me as I heard myself speaking.

"If someone hacked into the GPS," I said, "they may have thought they were tracking Little Mike instead of Ricky."

Allison and I stayed quiet, pondering what the hell that meant.

"Which," Allison said, "brings up two very interesting questions."

"How did they know which cab Dillman liked to drive?"

"And who wanted him dead?"

"Yeah." I gave that some thought. "How did you find out about Dillman being superstitious with his cab?"

"I spoke to the mechanic at the garage. They have a small fleet. Six medallions."

"Does the mechanic have access to the GPS system?"

"I didn't ask, Ray."

"Do me a favor?"

"It depends."

"Call the lead detective—Royce over at the nine-oh—with this info. Explain to him how you came across it and leave my name out of it."

He does this thing when he's out campaigning.

"Uncle Ray?"

"I've already pushed it with him and Royce." I went on to explain my trip to the scene with Jimmy Key and Ricky's application for a six-figure condo. I left out the suspicions that info brought up.

"You've been a busy boy, Ray."

"Idle hands. By the way, what do you know about Charles Golden?"

She waited a beat. "Golden and Associates, Charles Golden? The PR guy with the missing daughter?"

"That's the one. What do you know about him?"

"Only what he wants me to know, Ray. If public relations were an Olympic sport, this guy would be on the Wheaties box. Why?"

I told her about my trip to Long Island and meeting the man himself.

"Shouldn't you be taking it easy?—I thought Jack just wanted you to interview witnesses in Brooklyn and take some photos of accident scenes."

"He also wanted a two-man presence at Golden's home this morning."

"Well, my friend, you have been to the castle. He's the go-to guy in a crisis and the king of positive press. He's repping Tony Blake, y'know? The guy wants to be mayor so badly he's getting a huge jump ahead of whoever else decides to run. The next election's not for a while and already we're hearing about what a great councilman he is. Good thing he's got the bucks to back him up."

I laughed. "I love when these 'Men of the People' leave out the part about being able to buy and sell the people they wish to represent."

"That's where Golden comes in. He'll get it out there that Tony Blake went to community college and strategically leave out the part about how he couldn't get into any other college because he was so stoned through-out his high school career."

"Why do they call him 'The Magician'?"

"He does this thing when he's out campaigning. Table tricks. You know, with cards, cups, and shit? He's pretty good."

"You've seen the act?"

"Oh, yeah. Then he turns it into, 'As mayor, I'll make special interests disappear and the city debt will vanish.' People—voters—love that shit."

"Style over substance," I said.

"At least at this point." She paused. "You sure you're okay?"

"Yeah, why?"

"You sound a little . . . off, and it's not like you to sleep during the day."

"I'm fine, Ally." That came out a little sharp, almost like I wasn't as fine as I thought. I breathed. "Am I going to see you tonight?"

"I believe you will. How about I come over to your place, we order in some takeout, and you rip my clothes off?"

"Let me check my schedule."

"Keep checking, tough guy. The offer may get pulled at any moment."

"In that case, I'm free. Seven?"

"Seven."

After we hung up, I thought about what she'd said. I wasn't the kind of guy who took midday naps, but I was tired from getting up early and not getting enough sleep last night. I shook that off, looked at my clock, and figured I had enough time to swing by the gym and get back home for a shower before Allison got here.

Chapter 18

IT WAS MY FAVORITE TIME TO work out at Muscles's: midafternoon. There were only two other clients there. One was a serious lifter, judging from the size of his biceps and the amount of weight he kept adding to the machines. He had a big tattoo on his left arm. I couldn't quite make it out, but from across the gym it could have been a can of spinach. The other was a woman of about thirty who seemed to be in pretty good shape, except for a slight belly. She was working with the trainer/manager Muscles had recently hired to pick up some of the day-to-day slack around his gym while he was out doing off-site personal training sessions more and more these days. My guess was the woman was a new mom from one of the nearby million-dollar condos, working off the pregnancy weight.

"Keep your eye on what you're doing, Ray," Muscles instructed. "I don't want you undoing all this good stuff because you can't focus."

"Sorry," I said, lowering the leg weights on my machine. "Daydreaming a bit. How long have you been crouching there?"

"Long enough." He looked down at his clipboard and smiled. "You've increased the weights by ten pounds since last week. Nice, Ray."

I did another few reps. "It hurts a little."

"It's supposed to, but not too much." He ran his index finger slowly down the clipboard and nodded. "You keep this up, I'm gonna have trouble busting your balls much longer."

"And what a shame that would be."

Over on the other side of the room, the big guy finished a set and slammed the weights back into place, hard and loud. I guess I flinched, because Muscles reached out and put his hand on my shoulder. I noticed an increase in my heart and breathing rates.

"You okay?"

"I'm good," I said yet again, not even convincing myself.

"I keep telling Felix to go easy with my equipment. Want me to talk to him?"

"No, I'm g—. It's just . . ."

"Loud noises, I know." Muscles put the clipboard down. "It helps to talk about it, you know."

"Talk about what?"

Muscles waited before responding. "Some of the guys from the nine-oh were in the other day. They told me you were there when Ricky got his ticket punched. Right next to him?"

"Yeah." I swung my legs off the machine. "I'm really fine, but I've been a bit freaked out about it the last few days."

"Ya think? Jesus, Ray. It's supposed to freak you out. How come you didn't want me to know?"

"I come here for *physical* therapy. I didn't want to lay this on you, too."

He thought about that, and I wondered if I had offended him. If I had, he didn't let it show. "That's a good point."

"What is?"

"Physical therapy and mental—*emotional*—therapy. You should talk to someone. I got a few folks I can refer you to."

"I talk to Allison."

"You're not supposed to be screwing your therapist, Ray."

"She's not my—oh. I guess that's your point, huh?"

He tapped his temple with his index finger. "Quick. You've done such a good job getting your body back, close to where it was. But I don't think you've paid enough attention to your head. You ever see anyone after the accident?"

"No."

"That sounds like you." He gave my leg a gentle slap. "It's never too late, Ray. Especially now, after what you've just been through. Let me guess. You've been thinking a lot more about your fall since the shooting."

"Yeah," I said. "But that's only natural, right?"

"Of course it's natural. That doesn't mean you shouldn't get some help. You know how many guys I get in here—ten, twenty years on the job—they got themselves believing everything's gonna be fine, soon as they get their strength back?"

"I know the speech, Muscles. There are two types of strength: physical and emotional. I watch PBS."

"Everybody knows, but not everyone does something about it, Ray. I don't care how great a shape your body's in, if the mind falls too far behind, it ain't worth shit."

"I'm surprised to hear you say that."

"You shouldn't be. I've been preaching the mind/body connection for years. You've just been so focused on the body part—and I'm proud of you for that, don't get me wrong. Maybe it's time to start working on the mind." He got up out of his crouch. "Any fool can look at himself in the mirror and be happy with what he sees. Takes a certain kinda courage to see who's really looking back."

He was right. One thing about Muscles: he doesn't talk much, but when he does, it's mostly the truth that comes out. That might have been the main reason his business kept growing year after year. That and all the condos going up.

"Go do your twenty on the treadmill," he said. "I'm gonna get a card from the office for you."

"Thanks." I moved over to my next assignment. Since I had started coming back here again three years ago, Muscles had me walking backward on the treadmill for at least twenty minutes a session. Something about the medial meniscus behind both knees benefitting more from this type of motion than the standard forward walking. Like most things Muscles told me to do, I didn't understand it all, but knew enough to follow his directions. Maybe it was time to turn around.

Halfway through the twenty-minute backward walk on an incline, Muscles came up and slipped a card into the machine's cup holder.

"She's good," he said. "Dr. Amy Burke. She's on the Upper West Side and takes your insurance. I recommended her to Ricky."

"Ricky was seeing a shrink?"

"I recommended her. If he was seeing her, we didn't talk about it."

"Aren't there any good therapists in Brooklyn?"

"Lots," he said. "It took Ricky a while to agree to see one; and when he did, he didn't want it to be in the neighborhood. You know how cops are."

I knew what he meant. It wasn't easy for cops to admit they needed help. They convince themselves and their partners they're too tough for that. The last thing they needed was to be seen coming out of a therapist's office.

"And," Muscles continued, "she's got a background in PTSD."

I slipped Dr. Burke's card into my shorts pocket. "I'll think about it."

"Don't think too long, Ray. It goes without saying, you shoulda done this right after your accident."

That was another thing about Muscles: he had a habit of saying a lot of things that could have gone without saying. You can do that when you're able to bench-press a small car. I offered my hand.

"I'll call her," I said. "Thanks."

"Cool. I gotta split."

"Another home visit?"

"It's what keeps this place open, Ray."

I gestured with my head at the attractive new manager. "It does have its upside."

"Focus, Ray." He looked at the timer on the treadmill. "You've still got six minutes and forty-seven seconds left. Then you better hit the cold showers."

Not only was Muscles usually right, he was always exact.

I had just kicked my sneakers off when the downstairs buzzer rang.

I pressed the Talk button. "Yeah?"

"It's Ally."

I stifled the urge to say "Yea!" and pressed the Lock button. It took her less than two minutes to climb the four flights to my place.

We gave each other a hug. I slipped my hand under the back of her T-shirt.

"You're pretty sweaty, tough guy," she said.

"I was hoping to get a shower in before you got here."

She smiled and took my T-shirt off and then hers.

"Well, then," she whispered. "What are we going to do about that?"

Thirty minutes after possibly the greatest shower of my life, Allison and I were sitting on the couch drinking cold Brooklyn Pilsners out of the bottle. As an atheist, I figured this was the closest I'd ever get to Heaven.

"That was nice," she said.

"*Nice?*" I repeated. "You work with words for a living, and the best thing you can come up with is 'nice'?"

She put her beer on the coffee table and swung her leg over so that she was now straddling me. "If I'm too complimentary," she said, "you'll stop working so hard to please me." She kissed me and ran her fingers along my face.

"If this is work, sign me up for another year."

"Just one year?"

"If I'm too complimentary . . ." I said, and then she kissed me again to stop me from finishing the thought.

"You were saying?" She leaned back and took her T-shirt off a second time.

"I don't remember." I leaned in to kiss her breasts. "But it couldn't have been very important."

"There's a good boy. How about we take this into the bedroom?"

"I was thinking about ordering in some Chinese food."

"Afterward," she said, "that would be very nice."

"Excellent idea."

If this were a movie, we would have gotten off the couch in one motion, and I would have carried Allison into my bedroom. But this was real life, and I knew my knees would only let me down if I tried. Ally got up first and grabbed the empty beer bottles to bring them into the kitchen. We both heard two thumps coming from my bedroom.

"What the hell was that?" she asked.

I was pretty sure I knew what it was. I have a sliding glass door in my bedroom that leads out to the common deck area. It's the main reason I keep the curtains pulled. Every once in a while, a bird will fly into one of the windows and either fly away dazed or need to be scooped up and thrown away. The thumps sounded like that, but I didn't ever remember hearing two in close succession.

"Wait here," I said, not wanting Allison to see dead birds and risk ruining the present mood she was in.

I opened my bedroom door and flicked on the light. The curtains were pulled as usual. I stepped over, pulled them aside and looked down. No dead birds. Good. But then I noticed two holes in the curtain as I closed it again and a little bit of glass on the floor. *What the fuck?* I turned around to see Ally in the doorway, now naked.

"What was it?" she asked.

"I'm not sure."

"Oh, well." Allison turned off the overhead, and the light spilling from the hallway framed her beautiful shape. She moved over to my bed and was about to lie down when she said, "Ray?"

"Yeah?"

"What the hell happened to your wall?"

I looked to where she was pointing, grabbed her by the hand, and moved us both out of my bedroom as quickly as I could. I shut the bedroom door and got us both over to the hallway and onto the floor.

"Ray?"

I didn't answer her. I just reached out, grabbed my landline, and dialed 911.

Chapter 19

LESS THAN TEN MINUTES AFTER I'd dialed 911—and made it very clear I was *Chief Raymond Donne*'s nephew—my apartment was crawling with cops. From what I could gather from their conversation and radio chatter, there were also quite a few on the rooftops across the street. The two thumps Allison and I had heard were not misguided birds; they were sniper shots that ended up in the wall behind my bed. Had we been in bed when the shots were fired, neither one of us could have called anyone.

From the kitchen I looked over at Ally, who was sitting on the bed giving a statement to one of the five detectives who showed up. For some reason they would not share with me, I was to give my statement to a sixth detective whenever he showed up. When he finally came through the front door of my apartment, I realized why they had made me wait.

"Mr. Donne," Detective Royce said as he entered the kitchen. "I see things have calmed down a bit since we last spoke."

We "last spoke" a little more than two years ago, after Frankie Rivas safely returned home to his grandmother's apartment. Royce was the lead in the investigation of Frankie's father's murder. He had known I was a more-than-interested bystander in that case and had made it quite clear—nephew of Chief Donne or not—he'd much rather I stuck to teaching and let the cops do what cops do best.

"Detective Royce," I said, offering my hand. "Nice to see you again."

Royce looked at the three uniformed officers crowding me in the kitchen and asked them to step out. When they complied, Royce gave me the same look he had given me throughout the Frankie Rivas case.

"What the fuck, Mr. Donne?" he whispered. "Who the hell did you piss off this time?"

"I honestly don't know, Detective. My girlfriend and I were just ready to . . . call it a night, when we heard the shots."

He looked over my shoulder at the other detectives in my bedroom with Allison and shook his head. "So, you have no idea why someone would be shooting at you?" He raised his hand. "And before you answer, understand that I know you were in the cab with Officer Torres the night *he* was shot and killed."

Beneath his obvious anger, I also detected some genuine concern. He had let me slide two years ago by not looking too closely at my story or Frankie's. Which was good, because neither story would have withstood much scrutiny. Royce was a stand-up guy, but that didn't mean he liked to be messed with.

"Listen," I said, "no one's more confused about this shit than I am, Detective. I've been minding my own business since Frankie and—"

"Please. What about last year after that other kid of yours was stabbed under the bridge?"

"I was just helping out Dougie Lee's mom. That was the extent of my involvement."

"Bullshit. You don't remember that cops talk to each other? Murcer called me after you got involved to ask me for advice on how to handle you."

Detective Murcer was now, once again, my sister's boyfriend.

"What'd you tell him?"

"To keep you on a very short leash." He took a breath and looked as if he desperately needed one of those cigarettes he had quit smoking shortly before we met two years ago. "But this here, Mr. Donne? There is no leash short enough. This is some serious shit."

"You don't think I know that?" I pointed over to Allison. "That's my girlfriend, Detective. I wouldn't do anything to put her in danger."

"Someone clearly disagrees with you."

I looked around at all the cops filling my apartment. "I assume the working theory is this has something to do with Ricky T, right?"

"Yeah, Mr. Donne. You could assume that."

"And the kid with the bike and the semi the other night? At the park?"

"How the fuck do you know about Kwan Myers?!" He shook his head. "Okay, you and me are going down to the station, and you're going to tell me everything—and I mean *everything*—you know or think you know about what's going on here."

"He doesn't need to go to the house for that, Detective."

Royce and I both turned as Uncle Ray came into the kitchen and suddenly made the room crowded again. Neither of us acted surprised to see him.

"Chief Donne," Royce said as he shook my uncle's hand. "Good to see you again, sir. It's been a while."

"Yes," Uncle Ray said and put his huge hand on my shoulder. "Raymond, have you told the detective everything you know about this situation?"

I looked from my uncle's eyes to Royce's. "Yes."

"There you have it, Detective."

Royce's lips disappeared slowly and he shook his head.

"Sir," Royce said as steadily as he could manage, "I believe when we get the ballistics back that we'll be able to connect this shooting with the murder of Richard Torres and Kwan Myers in the park the other night. I also believe your nephew," he gave me a look, "may know more than he . . . thinks and would be a great help in this investigation."

That took a lot for Royce to say. My uncle was not used to people standing up to him, and it showed on his face and in the way he spoke his next words.

"I understand, Detective Royce," he said. "And I have no desire to impede your investigation; nor does my nephew. But if he says he's told you everything he knows, I am inclined to believe him. We both know that if he is brought into the station to give a formal statement, the odds of this appearing in the morning papers increases tenfold. I do not wish to see that happen." He lowered his voice to a conspiratorial whisper. "As it is," he gestured with his head toward Allison, "his girlfriend's a reporter, and it's going to be a challenge keeping this quiet. If you know what I mean."

Royce considered that and nodded. Allison looked over at me, no idea she was part of our conversation.

"Okay." He looked at me. "You have a safe place to stay for a few days, Mr. Donne?"

"My girlfriend's, yeah."

Royce reached into his pocket and pulled out a card. "Seems like we've done this before, doesn't it?" He gave me a look that said he knew I wasn't telling the entire truth and wasn't sure how much I'd told my uncle. "Tomorrow, I expect a phone call recounting all the events in your life from your friend's murder up to and including this evening. Out of respect for your uncle, we'll postpone you having to make a formal statement at the station."

"I appreciate that, Detective."

"As do I," my uncle added.

We all shook hands, and Royce excused himself to confer with his colleagues. My uncle grabbed me—hard—by the elbow and guided me over to the kitchen windows.

"You are telling everything you know, right, Raymond?"

"I don't know all that much."

"You're making that clearer every day." He let go of my elbow. "I asked around about your new friend, Jimmy Key."

"What? Why'd you do that?" I asked.

Ignoring me, Uncle Ray went on, "Did a lot of Personal Security Detail over in Iraq. Hung around with the VIPs. He's good. "

"Seemed that way to me."

"Well, after all, you've shown such good judgment lately."

"Give me a break, Uncle Ray." I rubbed my tired eyes. "Yes, I was with Ricky the night he was killed, and I headed over to the scene with Jimmy Key. Which, you're welcome, resulted in some pretty good info. Besides that, I've kept my nose out of it."

"What about your work with Jack Knight?"

I told him about interviewing the accident witness and some vague details about our trip out to the Island—leaving out, for now, the part about Ricky T's and my search for Angela Golden and her Latina friend. As if to compensate for my deception, I also mentioned that I had an extra six hundred bucks in my pocket.

"Let's hope you live to spend it, huh?" He patted me on the back. "Okay, pack some clothes for the next few days. I'm gonna have one of the squad cars take you to Allison's. Where is she again?"

"Manhattan. Lower East Side."

"Good. You got an extra set of keys to this place?"

I reached into the junk drawer, pulled my spare set out, and handed them to my uncle. They were attached to a Brooklyn Brewery bottle opener, which did not escape my uncle's keen sense of detection. He shook his head.

"You should expand your horizons, Nephew. Try some nice wine every once in a while."

"Maybe when I get to be your age, Uncle Ray."

"Let's hope that happens," he said. "Now, go pack."

The two uniforms, Allison, and I pulled up to Allison's apartment building in a squad car less than half an hour later. I was about to open the car door, when the officer in the passenger seat said, "One minute, Mr. Donne."

Allison and I watched while he got out of the car, scouted out the area, and gave a look at the neighboring buildings and their roofs. When he was satisfied, he opened Allison's back door and asked us to step out. He took Allison's key, opened the front door to her building, and asked Allison which floor her apartment was on.

"Fifth. Is this really necessary, Officer . . . ?" Allison asked.

"Carney, ma'am. Chief Donne's orders. So, yes, it is necessary."

Allison was about to argue, when I put my arm around her. "Shh."

We rode the elevator up in silence. When we reached Allison's floor, Officer Carney held up his hand, stepped out, and looked left and right. I guessed the halls were clear because he waved us out. "Apartment number, ma'am?"

"Allison," she corrected. "Five H."

We followed him to her apartment, and the whole thing played out again. Carney opened the door, directed us to stay outside as he went in, and a minute later allowed us to enter. He stepped over to the window that took up most of her living room wall and looked out. He then pulled the curtain shut.

"Bedroom?" he asked. Allison pointed and he went off.

"This is a bit much, Ray," she said after Carney left the room.

"I'd agree with you except for the two bullet holes above my bed."

She had no answer for that. Carney stepped back into the living room.

"Anybody else have keys to your place, ma'am? I mean, Allison."

"Just Ray. And the super."

"Good. Keep the shades drawn at all times, and do your best to keep away from your windows." He pulled out a card. "My partner and I will be outside. You need us, call."

"Is that nec—" Allison stopped herself, realizing the obvious answer. "Can I get you guys anything?"

"No, thank you. I noticed the bodega on the corner. We'll be fine." He tipped his hat. "You two have a good night."

"Thanks." I walked him to the door. After locking it, I turned to Allison. "I don't know about you, but I feel pretty safe now."

"And hungry," she added. "Lemme see what's in the fridge."

It turned out that she had some leftover Thai, baked ziti, and half a six-pack of decent Mexican beer. We ate our international makeshift meal in front of the TV, where nothing on the all-news channels rivaled what had happened during the past few hours of our lives. We turned off the set and cleared away our mess.

"You ready for bed?" she asked.

"I'm a bit too wired to sleep, I think."

She smiled. "I didn't say anything about sleep, Ray."

Now it was my turn to smile. "You still want to . . . ?"

"It's gonna take more than a sniper attack to get me out of the mood I was in before, tough guy."

I wrapped my arms around her. "I'm impressed."

She reached under my T-shirt. "You will be. . . ."

As we took each other's shirts off and held each other's shaking bodies, we both knew what was about to happen next was not entirely about sex.

Chapter 20

ALLISON'S CLOCK RADIO WENT OFF at six thirty. After texting her boss last night that she would be coming in to work late, she had forgotten to turn the alarm off. When quiet returned to her bedroom, she wrapped herself around me and—I swear—she cooed. That moment was broken by my cell phone going off. My first thought was: Who the hell would be calling me at this hour? But after the events of last night, I decided to pick up. I rolled over, found my phone on the bedside table, and checked the screen: BLOCKED.

Then don't fucking call me at six thirty-one in the morning.

"Hello?" I said, not even attempting to sound upbeat.

"Mr. Donne?"

"Yes?"

"Charles Golden. How are you this morning?"

Fucking exhausted, I thought. *You?*

I sat up. "Fine, sir," I said. "Is everything okay?"

"I'm on my way to my office for an early meeting, and I was hoping you'd be good enough to swing by this morning."

Allison turned over and gave me the who-the-hell-is-that? look. I mouthed "Charles Golden," and she sat up as if the guy had just entered the room.

"Sure," I said. "What time is your meeting over?"

"Actually, I'd like to see you *before* the meeting, if I may. How does seven thirty sound to you?"

I looked over at Allison and weighed my options.

He detected the pause. "I assume you are on the same hourly rate that Mr. Torres was on, is that correct?"

So he knew about Ricky. "What's this all about, Mr. Golden?"

"Be in my office at seven thirty, Mr. Donne, and I'll pay triple whatever Jack pays you for an hour of your time."

I was moving up in the world.

"That's very tempting, Mr. Golden. I'll—"

"Excellent. I'll have breakfast waiting for us." He hung up.

After I put the phone back on the table, Allison said, "What did he want?"

I told her and she whistled.

"Keep this up and you can quit that day job."

I laughed. "You don't mind? I know you're going in late."

"Mind? I'm jealous. Would it be gauche if I gave you my resume?"

"You'd go to work for this guy?"

"Only if I were willing to take a pay increase and get an expense account. Are you kidding me? I told you, this guy's the king of public relations. The people who work for him do pretty much what I do, except for a whole lot more money and in better clothes."

I grabbed at her Brooklyn Brewery T-shirt. "I like your clothes."

"This is your shirt." She slapped my hand away. "And you like what's *under* my clothes." She rolled out of bed. "I'll put the coffee on. You shower. If you're meeting with Charles Golden at seven thirty, you better be there at seven twenty-five."

I was about to say something, but like most smart boyfriends, I decided to keep my mouth shut and do what I was told.

Charles Golden's office was everything Allison had prepared me to expect. It took up two floors of an old warehouse in the meatpacking district of Manhattan's West Side. All the walls were made of glass, and the first and second floors were connected by a wrought-iron spiral staircase. The digital display behind the receptionist's desk informed me that the time in New York City was seven twenty-seven. It also gave the time in seven other cities around the world.

Charles Golden was a man with international influence.

As I stepped over to the receptionist, she stood. "Mr. Donne. Mr. Golden is waiting for you in his office." If Golden was trying to make a good first impression on his visitors, he had succeeded. She seemed to have chosen her light green business suit not only to match her eyes, but also to accent the amount of time she spends at the gym. She pointed to her left, where I could see the man himself on the phone. "How do you like your coffee?"

"A little half and half. No sugar. Thank you."

"Go right on in."

I walked toward his office and passed a group of five having an animated discussion behind a glass wall. I couldn't hear a word, but they looked like a bunch of smart people discussing something of great importance. Golden waved me in as I reached his door. He gestured for me to take a seat and made a rolling motion with his hand, telling me he was wrapping up this phone call.

"Tell Mr. Hwang that works for me if it works for him," he said. "I'm here until six, New York time." He listened. "Yes." He hung up and looked at his watch. "Mr. Donne, thank you for getting here on such short notice."

"Did you let Jack know I'm here?" I asked.

"I'll leave that up to you." He reached into his pocket, pulled out some money, and handed it to me. "Let's get this out of the way."

"Thank you." I took the bills and put them in my front pocket without looking at them. It was a power play on his part; he was letting me know he had enough pocket money to pay me for a day's work. I wondered what I'd find if I checked between the cushions of his couch. "I'm afraid I don't understand why you didn't invite Jack to this meeting."

He was about to explain when the receptionist came in with our coffees and half a dozen croissants on a serving tray. She placed the tray down on his desk within reach of both of us. "Will there be anything else, Mr. Golden?"

"Not at the moment, Natalie. Thank you." After Natalie left, he pushed the tray toward me. "The croissants are quite good, Mr. Donne. From downstairs."

I took one and sipped from the coffee cup I assumed was mine.

"How closely did you work with Richard Torres, Mr. Donne?"

That was a tricky question. I took a bite of the croissant and another sip of coffee as I contemplated a decent answer.

"How do you mean?" was all I could come up with.

"When you were on the job," he said. "Isn't that what policemen say?"

"The ones on TV mostly, yeah."

"When you were both cops, how closely did you work with him?"

"We went through the academy together," I said. "We were assigned to the same precinct for a few years."

"How about during your employment with Mr. Knight?"

I watched as he took a sip of his coffee and the tiniest of bites from a croissant. His eyes told me he was a man who didn't ask many questions he did not know the answers to.

"Something tells me you already know that."

He smiled and tried to look embarrassed. It didn't work.

"You caught me. I pulled some research on you after you left the house yesterday."

"I'm not sure I've ever been researched."

"It wasn't hard. Especially for a man in my position." He leaned forward. "You're a schoolteacher, Mr. Donne. And as far as I can tell, you've been in Jack Knight's employ for . . . exactly two days—not including today. You are a former police officer, your uncle is Chief Raymond Donne, and you were in the car when Mr. Torres was shot and killed early Saturday morning." He held up his hand, stopping me from asking the obvious. "Information is my currency. It's what I deal in, day in and day out, twenty-four/ seven/three-sixty-five. There's not much I don't know or can't find out."

"I've heard as much," I said.

"From Allison Rogers, I assume. She's a decent reporter and an even better writer. A few years from now, she might be hearing from my human resources people."

"She'd like that."

"I know." His smile was approaching glib. I liked the embarrassed one better. "Information is power, Mr. Donne, and power is money. I'm very good at what I do—and surround myself with similar people—because of one reason."

I waited the acceptable amount of time to help make his pause dramatic and said, "And that is . . . ?"

"I am one curious motherfucker," he said. "And I could tell within five minutes of meeting you yesterday, we have that in common."

"How so?"

"I could smell it. The same way I imagine you can smell a child in crisis. Judging from what I've read about you in the papers the last few years—and what did not make the papers—you enjoy sticking your nose into places others may not want you to. Most New York City schoolteachers do not make the papers once, Mr. Donne. It seems to be a hobby of yours."

"I wouldn't put it that way. I just happened to be in the right—or wrong—places a few times."

He took another sip of coffee. "You are not the kind of man who just *happens* to be anywhere. Take the other night, for example. Why were you in Mr. Torres's cab at two in the morning?"

"He said he needed to talk to me. He needed my help."

He slapped his desk. "Exactly my point. You didn't just happen to be there. You were helping out a friend." He touched the side of his nose. "You smelled a crisis, didn't you?"

Again, I wasn't sure how to answer that, so I stalled and took another sip of coffee. I didn't like being on this side of Charles Golden's desk, and considered giving his money back and walking out. I chose another tactic.

"With all due respect, Mr. Golden, I'm smelling something now. You were clearly in a rush to speak with me. Maybe it's time you got to the point. Please."

He nodded. "I like that. Don't take any shit from me, and definitely don't let me control the conversation. Not completely, anyway." He pointed his finger at me. "I like you, Mr. Donne. I was right about you."

I stayed silent and looked out his glass wall. The meeting across the way was breaking up, and I wondered what time those folks had started their day. Thirty seconds more of this bullshit runaround, I told myself, and I was out of here.

"Did Mr. Torres mention anything to you regarding me and the search for my daughter, Mr. Donne?"

Finally. "No," I said. "He did not."

"Would it surprise you if I told you I had a deal with Mr. Torres, separate from the one I have with Mr. Knight?"

"Yes, it would. That doesn't sound like Ricky."

"So he did not mention this deal to you?"

I shifted in my seat. "I think I just answered that, Mr. Golden."

"You did." He took another bite of croissant and seemed to be studying the uneaten part. "Would you care to know what the deal was?"

"I *am*," I said without missing a beat, "a curious motherfucker."

Golden laughed, loud enough for a few of his employees to look in from the other side of the glass. I figured he didn't laugh that often, especially these days. Behind the glass wall, I felt like an exotic fish in a tank.

"Excellent," he said. "You do not disappoint, Mr. Donne."

"I'm sure that depends on whom you speak to."

"Yes." He got up out of his chair and went to his window, which looked out—between two other buildings—on the Hudson River. His shoulders went up and down as if he were taking a deep breath, considering how much information to share with me. "Mr. Torres made it clear to me he had an approach to finding my daughter that Jack Knight did not. I assumed it had something to do with his knowledge of the neighborhood in which he grew up." He turned to face me. "He led me to believe that he had a 'line on' this mysterious friend of my daughter's, who claimed to be from Williamsburg."

"Claimed?"

"We only have my daughter's word that this girl was from where she said she was from. Verification, Mr. Donne, is quite important in my business."

"The business of finding your daughter," I said, "or all this?"

"Both," he said, his voice turning cold. "Make no mistake. I have to show a strong front while I'm with my employees and my clients, but my little girl is missing, and I will do anything to ensure her safe return."

"Including cutting a deal behind the back of the guy you hired to find her?"

Golden placed his hands on the back of the chair. "And so much more. This is my daughter."

I watched his hands grip the back of his chair as if he were trying to rip it apart. This was the primal side of him: the side of a father unwillingly separated from his child. I stood up.

"I'm sorry to disappoint you. I do not have the same 'line' Ricky had. I have a picture of her friend and whatever other information Jack has. I do know the streets of Williamsburg rather well and may have a connection or two I can share with Jack." I thought of Tio. "That's all I can offer you."

Golden looked me in the eyes and slowly released his grip on the chair. He stepped around his desk and offered me his hand.

"Fair enough." He looked over my shoulder and smiled. "My next appointment is here." He led me toward his office door. As he opened it, I recognized his next appointment. These days, it would be hard not to. The slicked-back blond hair, striking blue eyes, and that toothpaste-commercial smile. Tony Blake, city councilman and maybe the next mayor of New York City.

"Chuck," Tony Blake said as he stepped over to us. "Nice to see you so early on this beautiful day." He turned to me. "And who is this prospective voter?"

I stuck out my hand. "Raymond Donne, Councilman. A pleasure."

He pumped my hand. "You don't know me yet," he joked. I could tell he was thinking about something and, sure enough, the next thing out of his mouth was, "Chief Donne's boy, right?"

"Nephew."

"Yes, of course. The schoolteacher. Thank you for doing what you do, Mr. Donne. The New York City public schools are what's going to help bring this city back to its former glory, and nobody's more vital to that than our teachers."

"The kids have a part in it," I said. "And the parents."

He laughed. "I'm going to remember that."

"He means," Golden joined in, "he's going to steal it."

"How did you know I was a teacher, Mr. Blake?"

"Tony, please," he said. "I confess. I know much about your uncle. I can't imagine anybody who wants to be mayor of this fine city not knowing much about Chief Donne. In fact," he said, a light bulb going off over his head, "I'll be seeing the chief tonight at a fund-raiser."

"He didn't mention it to me."

Golden said, "It's for a group called One More Mission. It helps returning Iraq and Afghanistan vets who are struggling to adjust to life stateside."

I thought of Ricky T.

"You should come, Mr. Donne," Blake said. "As my guest. It would be an honor."

This guy was good.

"In fact," Golden said, "bring Ms. Rogers with you." Golden stepped over to his receptionist, whispered something, and she handed him an envelope. He came back over to me. "All the info's in here. It's not formal, but wear a suit and tie."

Yes, Dad.

"I'll give Allison a call as soon as I get downstairs."

"Excellent. Until tonight then." He took Blake by the elbow. "Shall we?"

Blake gave me his hand. "Do you enjoy magic, Mr. Donne?"

The Magician. "In small doses."

"Great." He slipped his hand out of mine and reached up to my ear. "Would it surprise you if I pulled a coin out of here?"

"Only slightly."

He grinned. "Then I won't bore you." He took his hand back and was holding two tickets to the night's event. I couldn't help but smile. "I'll see you this evening, Mr. Donne."

"Looking forward to it," I said as I pocketed the tickets.

As I thought in the elevator about Blake's trick, I reflexively made sure I still had the tickets . . . and my wallet.

I got down to the street and realized I had no plans for the rest of the day. Across the street having a cigarette, a limo driver leaned against his car and spoke on his cell. Had to be Blake's. I called Allison to see if she wanted to go to the benefit.

"Are you kidding me? Charles Golden and Tony Blake give you a personal invite, and you're asking if I'm interested in going?"

"So that's a 'yes'?"

"That would be a *big* 'yes,' Raymond. I'm even tempted to call my editor."

"Don't. Let's just enjoy the benefit and not bring work into it."

"Look who's talking, tough guy."

I got to the corner and looked back toward the Hudson. When I turned, the limo driver was watching me. At least, I thought he was. It was probably just an after-effect from the bullet holes in my bedroom wall. I felt a walk coming on.

"Just bring some business cards, then, okay?" I said. "You can hand them out to any movers and shakers we happen to meet."

"Deal. Where is this shindig?"

I pulled the invite out of my pocket and read it to her. She waited a moment and then let out an audible breath.

"What?" I asked.

"How much did Golden give you today?"

"Three hundred. Why?"

"Because you're going to take that and finally get yourself a suit, Ray."

"I was hoping to put that toward a long weekend with you."

"That's sweet. But that was before we got invited to the benefit."

"I don't even know where to buy a suit, Allison."

"Where are you right now?"

I told her, and she gave me a list of five places off the top of her head. "They're not the best," she said, "but three hundred will just about do it."

"For a suit?"

"You're playing in the big leagues now, Ray. Time to dress like it."

An idea came to me. "Any on the Upper West Side?"

"A few. Why?"

"Can you go to my bag and see if you can find a card for a Dr. Burke?"

"Give me a sec." A minute later she said, "Got it." She read me the number and I entered it into my phone. "You going to a therapist?"

"She was seeing Ricky. I was thinking of speaking with her. I can take a slow walk along the river, pick up a suit, and hopefully meet with Dr. Burke."

It occurred to me now I did have plans for the day.

"Okay," Allison said. "Call me when you're done, and we'll meet back at my place and get ready for the benefit."

"Sounds good."

After walking past Chelsea Piers, the *Intrepid,* the cruise ships docked along the Hudson, and the recently renovated Hell's Kitchen piers, I found myself up by the Seventy-ninth Street Boat Basin. I looked at the houseboats, amazed that people actually lived on them in spaces way smaller than my apartment. A few yachts were docked: rich people swinging by for a visit.

I took a seat on a bench under a tree and dialed Dr. Burke's number. She picked up after three rings.

"Amy Burke."

"Dr. Burke," I said. "My name's Raymond Donne. I am—*was*—a friend of Ricky Torres. I understand he was a patient of yours."

"He was. How can I help you, Mr. Donne?"

"I was hoping you had a few minutes to speak with me."

"About what?"

"About Ricky," I said.

"I'm not at liberty to discuss my patients without their consent. And considering the circumstances, I'm sure you understand."

I looked up at the tree I was under. A starling had landed on the branch above me. He looked down, saw that I had nothing to offer, and flew away.

"Can we just meet for a cup of coffee, Doctor? I won't take up much time."

I watched the boats rocking up and down while she thought about that. She didn't make me wait long.

"I can give you fifteen minutes, Mr. Donne. But I need to remind you ahead of time, I'm very limited in what I can discuss with you."

"I appreciate that. Tell me when and where."

"There's a coffee shop on Seventy-ninth, a few stores off Broadway, the south side of the street." She gave me the name. "Let's say one-oh-five."

"I appreciate it, Dr. Burke."

"Please be prompt, Mr. Donne. I have a busy afternoon."

"One-oh-five," I repeated. "I'll be there."

We hung up and I looked at my watch. I had a little over three hours and exactly three hundred dollars to get myself a suit. I set off to do just that.

According to my cell phone, it was one-oh-six when the woman I assumed was Dr. Amy Burke walked down the steps to the seating area in front of the café. I stood.

"Sorry I'm late," she said. "I got a last-minute phone call."

"Not a problem. I appreciate your meeting with me." I looked down at the table. "I went ahead and got two large coffees. I have no idea how you take it."

"How *would* you know?" She sat down. "This is fine. Thank you. I see you've been shopping," she said, noticing the bag draped over the back of an empty seat at our table."

"New suit."

As she took her first sip of coffee, I got a good look at the woman Ricky T had been telling his problems to. She had reddish-blond hair, which was pulled back from her face the way a therapist's hair should be. I put her age at about ten years older than my own. She had soft green eyes that I'm sure made her clients feel quite comfortable and supported during their sessions.

"So," she said, "you're Raymond Donne?"

"You make it sound like you've heard of me."

"Ricky spoke of you, yes. You seemed to be someone he could trust. He didn't have many people like that in his life."

"I got that feeling," I said. "How long had he been seeing you?"

"About six months, weekly. I can tell you he was suffering from symptoms of post-traumatic stress disorder, but I'm sure you knew that."

"Yeah. The last I spoke with him"—I left out the part about that being five seconds before he was killed—"he seemed very anxious and told me something about making a big mistake."

She nodded. "Did he tell you what the mistake was?"

"He didn't get the chance."

She remained silent, but her eyes told me she understood. After both of us sipped our coffees, she said, "How much did he talk about his time in Iraq?"

"Not much." I explained that we hadn't been in touch as much as I would have liked and that our last conversation was the first one we'd had in many months.

"PTSD sufferers will do that. They often find themselves unable to speak to those to whom they feel closest. I find that to be the case often in my patients who return to jobs that require a tough mental attitude."

"Like a cop."

"More than any other. Firefighters are a close second."

I wondered where schoolteachers landed on that list.

"Did Ricky tell *you* what the mistake was?"

She took a deep breath and let it out slowly. "This is the area where I am very limited as to what I can tell you, Mr. Donne."

"Call me Raymond, please. What *can* you tell me, Doctor?"

She looked at her coffee. "He was planning on telling you about his time in Iraq. Specifically, he was going to discuss with you what we both considered to be the major event of his time over there."

"The cause of the PTSD?"

"There's not *one* cause of PTSD. The disorder can be caused by a series of events that can overwhelm one's ability to resume what he or she considers a normal life. The life they had before the trauma."

I nodded, but felt myself getting impatient. I wanted to know why Ricky had called me that night, and this woman might have the answer.

"I want to make something very clear," Dr. Burke said. "I am only telling you this because Ricky told me he had decided to tell you himself. During our sessions it became clear he needed to trust someone, and you were the one he chose. His own family does not know about this, and he was not ready for them to know. I need you to understand that you are not to discuss this with anyone."

"I understand."

"Good." After another sip, she said, "Ricky had a family over in Iraq."

I was glad I had swallowed my coffee. "Excuse me?"

"He met a civilian. A young Iraqi woman. Fata. Against just about every directive the Marines had drilled into him, he had a relationship with her that led to her becoming pregnant. Obviously, no one over there, besides the girl's family, knew about this relationship. He would have faced disciplinary charges that would have followed him back to the states."

"Probably. So this . . . Fata? She stayed behind after his tour was over?"

"She was killed, Raymond. Ricky wasn't sure which side was responsible, but her village came under attack and she was one of the victims. She was five months pregnant. With Ricky's baby."

"Holy shit," I said.

"Yes. As I'm sure you can understand, Ricky was carrying around a lot of grief on top of a lot of anger. We were working on both. The grief was easier for him to deal with. He had lost someone he had strong feelings for. It was the anger we needed to focus on. Not knowing who was responsible for Fata and the baby being killed confused his emotional state. He felt he needed someone to blame."

"Who was he leaning toward?"

She put her elbows on the table and made a therapist tent with her fingers. "Ricky was a very patriotic man, Raymond. He was proud of his country and proud of his mixed heritage. He told me more than once he felt his family represented what America stands for. When he joined the reserves, he did so out of a great responsibility to his country."

"That sounds like Ricky."

"Like many young people in the same position, he never thought he'd be drafted into combat. But when he was, he went willingly. I wouldn't describe him as gung ho, but he felt he had a duty. Once he was over there—after a few months, he said—he started to question the mission and our military's presence in Iraq."

"I'm sure he wasn't alone."

"No. And after Fata's death, he became increasingly disillusioned with America. For someone like Ricky Torres, that was akin to a devout Catholic being angry with God."

I thought of my mother after my dad's death. My whole family went through a time of serious doubt and questions. My mom got over it; I never did go back to believing; and Rachel struggles with her own beliefs to this day.

"I think I understand," I said.

"Although we still had lots of work to do," Dr. Burke went on, "he was clearly directing his anger toward the country he loved."

I picked up my coffee cup and used a napkin to wipe away the ring it had made on the table. Dr. Burke gave me a look that told me she knew I was stalling.

"You think he was angry enough to act on this anger?" I asked.

"I'm not sure what you mean."

"The mistake he wanted to talk about. I've been giving it a lot of thought and haven't come up with anything. The Ricky I knew before he was deployed would never do anything harmful to anyone, but with this level of anger you're talking about and the PTSD . . . I don't know."

She leaned back and stole a glance at her watch. "Constant stress and anger can change a person. It *will* change a person. Whether it can make a normally peaceful person into one prepared to act upon his anger is an in-dividual issue. There's no set rule. I *can* tell you Ricky was struggling with his identity since he returned home. When you're a soldier, you are doing what you're told to do for the good of the whole. Many soldiers, when they return, feel the loss of belonging to something like that. Ricky was no exception."

"You didn't answer my question, Doctor. Was Ricky a threat to others?"

"I *can't* answer your question, Raymond. I'm a clinical psychologist. You sound as if you want me to be a fortune-teller."

I had no answer. She was right. I was grasping at straws, wanting to figure Ricky out. I looked at my cell phone and realized my fifteen min-utes were up.

"You're right, Dr. Burke. I appreciate the information you were able to share with me. It does help."

"That's why I agreed to meet with you." She took a sip of coffee. "Can I ask you a question now?"

"I don't see why not."

"Are you seeing someone? A therapist, I mean?"

"No," I said. "I'm not. Why do you ask?"

She smiled. "Allow *me* to play detective for a moment?"

"Why not? People let me do it all the time."

She looked at my hands. "You pick at your thumbs and forefingers. I have patients who suffer from anxiety who engage in that type of behavior."

"It's a nervous habit."

"Nervous habits shouldn't make you bleed. It's a form of self-mutilation. A small example, but still."

"So I should be in therapy because I pick my fingers?"

"You also chose to sit facing the street, with your back to the restaurant."

"I wanted to make sure I saw you when you came in."

She ignored that. "You've looked over my shoulder at least a dozen times since I sat down and seem to be quite interested in the buildings across the street. Is it the people passing by? The windows?" She paused. "The fire escapes?"

Damn, this woman was good.

"Ricky told you about my accident?"

"Yes. He didn't go into detail, but he did mention it."

"I fell from a fire escape while chasing a kid. The kid was killed, and I seriously injured my knees. It's the main reason I'm not a cop anymore."

She nodded and smiled. "The *main* reason," she repeated. "And you never saw a therapist after the accident?"

"Does a *physical* therapist count?" I asked, going for humor.

"No," she said, not going for the humor. "Are you in a relationship now?"

"Yes."

"The first one since the accident?"

"Can you tell that from my fingers and the fire escapes?"

Now she laughed. "I'm not that good," she said. "You bought a new suit today. Judging from the name on the bag, someone advised you where to shop. That is the same store where I tell my husband to get his suits, and they're not exactly known for their schoolteacher customer base. So, I just assumed a girlfriend felt you needed some fancy clothes. That fits with a fairly new relationship, probably less than a year."

"I'm impressed. Nine months."

"You have this very guarded side to you I'm sure you don't let most people see. Your concern for your friend, even after his death, shows a sense of responsibility and loyalty. But you don't seem to take care of your own needs." She looked at her watch and stood. "I'm sorry. I know you didn't come here for a five-minute analysis, and I do have to go."

I got up and offered my hand. "Thank you very much, Dr. Burke. For the info on Ricky *and* the five-minute analysis."

"You're welcome," she said and then added, "You have my card."

"It's at my girlfriend's apartment."

That made her smile. "Please thank Muscles for the referral. Have a good rest of the day, Raymond, and take care of yourself."

"I'll do my best, Doctor."

Chapter 21

"DAMN, MR. DONNE." ALLISON RAN HER hands over my new suit. "You clean up real good."

"*Well,*" I said, looking at my reflection in her full-length mirror. I turned sideways and flashed back to my mother shopping with me for my confirmation outfit. I was thirteen and that was the last suit I had owned. "You like the color?"

"Light blue. The salesperson chose wisely."

"What? You don't think I have the sense to pick out the right color?"

"You've got a lot of sense, Raymond. But I've never seen you exercise any in the way you dress." She turned me around, kissed me on the cheek, and appraised me again. "Now you look like somebody loves you."

There was a word neither one of us threw around easily. Or often. I changed the subject by pulling her into a real kiss. "I'm very fond of you, too."

She smacked my butt and went over to her bed to pick up her handbag. She looked beautiful in a black cocktail dress.

"Let's go down and jump in a cab," she said. "I don't wanna miss those jumbo shrimps wrapped in bacon."

"Now you're talking."

•　　•　　•

The Top of the Strand was as ritzy as Allison had said it would be. We were outside enjoying the view of the Empire State Building while we balanced our drinks and the jumbo shrimp. As we drank our beverages—Stoli martini for Allison and a Chelsea Blonde for me—I had to stifle the urge to take out my cell phone and snap pictures. After all these years, I still got a kick out of feeling like a tourist in my own city, but this was not the place or the crowd to let that show. The cold ale and frequent rounds of appetizers would have to be my secret, guilty pleasure.

"What do you think?" Allison asked, slipping her arm through mine.

"It's great."

". . . But . . . ?"

"I can't help thinking about how much this soirée is costing." I looked around at my fellow partygoers; I could almost smell the affluence. "Wouldn't it save a lot of time and money just to write a check directly to the charity and pass on the festivities?"

"Spoken like a true liberal. This," she swept her hand in front of her, "is how you get the well-heeled to part with their cash. The more public the event, the more zeroes at the end of their checks. See that photographer?" She pointed at the guy maneuvering through the well-dressed people and taking pictures. "He's Booker from *The Times*. Check out Sunday's paper. Some of these donors keep score by how many times they get their names and faces in print. If that's what it takes . . ."

"I guess you're right. But I could have taken half the money I spent on this suit and given it to One More Mission. Then you and I could've taken the other half and had a great dinner. It's just—"

"It's just the way it is, Raymond. Drink your beer, eat your shrimp, and enjoy. Don't judge." She kissed me on the cheek and put her lips to my ear. "Besides, the atmosphere and your suit are kinda turning me on."

I controlled my breathing and wrapped my arm around her. "That is another worthy cause."

"Yes." She wrapped her arm around my waist.

"There *is* a hotel just across the street, kids."

Allison and I turned to see my Uncle Ray behind us. He was wearing his dress blues and holding what I assumed to be his drink of choice: Jack Daniel's and Diet Coke.

"Damn, Uncle Ray. You look like a recruiting poster for the NYPD."

"Don't think they haven't asked." He turned to Allison and looked her up and down. "Once again, you prove to be out of my nephew's league. Are you covering this event, or are you an invited guest?"

Before I could answer, Allison said, "Actually, Ray got us the invitation. Do you want to tell him how, Ray?"

As if I had a choice now. "I met with Charles Golden this morning."

"Really," Uncle Ray said. "In what capacity?"

"I told you I was doing a little temp work for Jack Knight."

"Yeah?"

"I know I should've told you earlier, and thanks ahead of time for not giving me any shit, but Jack was hired by Golden to look into the disappearance of his daughter."

His mouth tightened. "You're right, you should have told me earlier."

"Golden asked me to his office this morning to discuss Jack's . . . progress."

Uncle Ray considered that. "Without Jack being present?"

"Yes."

"That sounds a bit strange, Ray. Does Golden have a reason to not trust Jack?" He smirked. "Besides the obvious?"

"Nothing like that. It's just that Golden strikes me as the kind of guy who wants to get to know all the people involved personally, and I guess he thought he could do that better one-on-one without Jack being around."

I left out the part about Golden asking me if I could cut a separate deal with him the way Ricky had. My uncle had that look on his face, telling me he knew I wasn't giving him the complete story, but he was willing to let it go. For now.

"How about you, Uncle Ray?" Allison asked. "Are you here officially?"

"Yes and no," he said. "One More Mission does some great work, and I've supported them for years. I've worked with a lot of cops who've done their bit overseas, and I've seen firsthand what they go through when they come back home." He took a sip of his drink. "I guess I've always felt a little guilty, to be honest. I was stationed in Germany during the last years of Vietnam. Not a lot of action in that part of the world. The biggest risk I faced on a daily basis was getting a paper cut. Don't get me wrong. I served my country. But these guys? They *served* their country."

Allison nodded. "But you've been a cop for what? Thirty years? If that's not serving, I don't know what is."

"I didn't have to come home to a country whose citizens were indifferent—at best—to the shit those guys on the frontline went through. I came back and stepped into a good economy and a job I loved. A lot of today's vets don't have the opportunities I had. These guys are heroes and should be treated like heroes."

"If I didn't know better," I said, "I would say that sounded like modesty."

Uncle Ray grinned. "One: good thing you know better. Two: these guys *make* me feel modest." He took another sip and finished off his drink. "Remember what your old man used to tell you, Raymond?"

"He reminded me often that I had a lot to be modest about."

"What parenting book did he get that out of?" asked Allison.

"Fathers back then didn't read books," Uncle Ray said. "Ray's dad may not've been perfect, but the kid turned out okay, didn't he?"

In spite of my father, I thought. *Not because of.*

Allison grabbed my hand. "Yes. He did."

My uncle looked at the lonely ice cubes at the bottom of his glass. "I'm gonna go mingle with the upper-class taxpayers. Give 'em the thrill of talking to a true crime fighter. You two behave yourselves."

"We'll try," I said.

After he left, Allison squeezed my hand. "I like him, but every time he mentions your dad, I feel you tense up."

"I don't think he can help it."

"I'm talking about *you*, Ray. It's fine, but you've got some unresolved issues you might want to look at."

She was starting to sound like Dr. Burke. Looked like this was my day to be analyzed. "I'm half Irish, Ally. It comes with the territory."

"You blow it off, but it's there. Ignoring it won't help."

"I'm not ignoring it," I said, sounding exactly like I was ignoring it. "I've come to terms with my dad's faults *and* his strengths. That happens when you work with kids who don't even have a father. I think he did the best he could with the skills he had. I'm good with that."

"Okay, tough guy. Just don't be afraid to talk about it."

"With you?"

"With anybody."

I finished my ale, placed it on top of a table, and grabbed Allison around the waist. "Okay. Thanks."

"You're welcome." She looked over my shoulder. "Your new best friend is here."

I turned to see Tony Blake enter the outside area and get immediately swallowed up by the other partygoers. The man who came in with him and stood by his side looked familiar. It took me ten seconds: the limo driver I'd seen outside Golden's office this morning. He was wearing a dark blue suit and looked as if he'd just gotten his daily crew cut. His eyes scanned the room and rested on me for a few seconds, trying to place where he'd seen me before. I pegged him for an ex-cop turned driver/personal security.

As for Blake, he was wearing a different suit than the one he'd had on this morning, and it highlighted the intensity of his blue eyes. I doubted he bought his suit at the same store where I'd bought mine.

"Can you introduce me?" Allison asked.

"When he's done being mobbed, absolutely. I'm not sure he's going to remember me, though. We only met for a few minutes, and by the looks of it, he meets new people—new voters—by the hour."

"Well, in the meantime," she handed me her glass, "fill me up, will ya?"

"Yes, ma'am."

I walked up to the bar and glanced over at Blake. He caught my eye and gave me a can-you-believe-this? look. He did remember me. He looked like a man in his element. Here he was, getting all this attention from admirers with money. Nice job if you could get it.

The bartender handed me our drinks, and I dropped a ten on the bar. Rich people at open-bar charity events are notoriously bad tippers, and I always feel the need to help fill the void. The bartender slipped the bill into his shirt pocket and gave me a smile that said he'd remember me next time.

When I got back to Allison, she was chatting up the photographer from *The Times*. She introduced us, then Booker took a few steps back to take our picture. Allison held up her hand.

"Probably not a good idea, Book. I'm with the competition."

"Not for pub," he said. "For you. I'll send you a copy."

So we smiled, posed, and had our photo taken. He came back over and whispered, "So, what d'ya think of our next mayor?"

"You guys calling the race a year before the primary?"

"I've covered a lot of these guys, and he's got the best infrastructure I've ever seen, even this far ahead of the primary."

"Nice to have money," I said.

"And connections in the business world, good looks, and a wife who looks like a supermodel."

He pointed over to a very attractive blonde in the bar area who reminded me of Charles Golden's wife. She was rocking a sky blue dress, a necklace that rivaled the sun, and appeared to be enjoying her cocktails very much, judging by the way she threw her head back and held on to the bar when she laughed.

"What is she?" I asked. "Twenty-five?"

Booker laughed. "Early thirties. It's amazing what a personal trainer and a little nip and tuck can do, huh? And she has the distinction of being the second Mrs. Tony Blake."

"What happened to the first one?"

Allison said, "A very quiet divorce and settlement. *That's* one of the things you buy when you hire Charles Golden and Associates. The ex hired one of the top divorce lawyers in the city—who lives to make the papers and was preparing for a media event—and before you knew it, *poof*—the whole thing disappeared."

"The Magician," I said.

"Bingo," Booker said and looked at his watch. "Okay, I gotta go and record the next few hours for posterity." He stuck out his hand. "Nice meeting ya, Ray."

"Same." After he left, I said to Allison, "Nice guy, for the competition."

"I think we all know we're lucky to still be in the print biz and feel a sense of camaraderie." She let out a humorless laugh. "At least until we're fighting over what's left of the online news jobs."

"You can always go into teaching."

"Yeah, *that's* gonna happen."

I took another sip from my ale. "Do me a favor and watch this for me." I handed the bottle to Allison. "I need to hit the men's room."

She kissed me on the cheek. "Don't be too long."

I was on my way out the same door we'd entered from when someone called out my name. I turned and saw Tony Blake emerging from his circle of admirers and heading in my direction. His security guy circled around and positioned himself closest to the door. He moved like a guy not wanting to be noticed. Blake stuck out his hand. "Glad you could make it, Mr. Donne." He gave my suit and me a careful look. "You seem quite at home at these functions."

"It's Raymond, Mr. Blake. And not really. The suit's new. It was strongly suggested I purchase it for tonight's event." I motioned with my head at Allison, who was already chatting up another guest.

"Ah, yes," Blake said. "The lovely Ms. Rogers."

"You know Allison?"

"In my position, it helps to know as many journalists as possible."

"She gave me the impression you two have never met."

"We haven't. That doesn't mean I don't know *of* her and her work. If I met everyone I knew, I wouldn't have time for anything else, you know what I mean?"

I didn't, but nodded as if I did. Some loud laughter came from the bar, and Blake and I looked over. Apparently, someone had told Mrs. Blake the funniest joke ever. Blake and his driver gave each other a look, but the driver stayed where he was. I took the opportunity to introduce myself. "Raymond Donne."

He shook my hand. "Nice to meet you, sir," he said. I waited for him to give me his name. He chose to look over at Mrs. Blake instead. I took the time to admire his crew cut. Up close, it looked like the kind that was touched up every morning, giving it that fresh commando look.

"Ex-cop?" I asked.

"No, sir."

"Military?"

"No, sir." Eyes still on the bar area. Who was this guy securing? Mr. Blake or the future candidate's wife?

"Huh," I said. "I had you figured for one or the other."

"I get that a lot."

"Joseph's been with me since I won the city council seat," Blake explained.

"I wasn't aware city councilmembers had personal security."

"Only those of us who can afford it." He laughed. "I have other responsibilities—family business, charities—that require me to be extremely flexible and even more mobile. Joseph's been a big help in that regard. I was lucky to find him."

"I see," I said. Joseph was still observing Mrs. Blake, and I got the feeling from her new fit of laughter that he'd be ushering her out within the hour.

"Flexibility and mobility," Blake repeated. "Two things a mayor needs to serve a city of this size and diversity, don't you agree?"

"Are you practicing a campaign speech on me, Mr. Blake?"

He put his hand on my shoulder. "I'm always campaigning, Raymond. When I'm not serving the fine people of my district, that is."

"Of course."

He looked over my shoulder and waved to someone. "Speaking of which," he said. "You'll have to excuse me, Raymond. There's a gentleman at the bar who has expressed interest in getting in on the ground floor of my campaign. My wife has been good enough to prime the pump, so to speak, and now I need to see if his pockets are as deep as his martini glass." He shook my hand again. "Make sure I meet Ms. Rogers before you leave."

"I'll do that," I said, and off Candidate Blake went to work the bar. I turned to Joseph. "Can I get you anything?"

"I'm fine, sir. Thank you."

"Just out of curiosity, do you call everyone 'sir'?"

He looked at me rather coldly, but I could swear I saw a little uptick on the left side of his mouth, where smiles originate. "Until they give me a reason not to," he answered. "Sir."

"Good answer." I headed back over to Allison, who was just finishing up her second martini. "Another?" I asked as she handed me my ale.

"I thought you were going to the men's room."

"I was. I got sidetracked and the urge passed." I reached for her glass.

"Let me get this one, Ray. I see Blake's up there, and this might be a good time to bump into him."

"He wants to meet you."

"He said that?" she asked, her voice a little high and loud.

"Yeah. Right after school by the swings."

She slapped me on the arm. "Dick. You done with that?"

I drank the rest. "I am now." I handed her the empty. "Do me a favor. I'm going to hit the head after all. Ask the bartender if he's got any Brooklyns hidden away."

Off she went, and I did the same. This time I made it all the way to the men's room, and by the time I got back, Allison was deep in conversation with Tony Blake at the bar. I decided to let her work the guy a bit and set off to mingle.

Over at the food table, I spotted Charles Golden speaking to a guy about my age who apparently spent way more time in the gym than I did, judging by the way he wore his suit. Golden saw me and waved me over.

"Raymond," he said, shaking my hand. "This is Gregory Ericsson, the man behind One More Mission."

"Wow," I said, as we exchanged handshakes. "Congratulations on all your success." I looked around the room. "And on getting a group like this together."

"Thank you. But the success of this event is largely due to Charles."

"Still, your organization does great work. I'm always impressed when someone sees a need—a hole in the system—and fills it."

"That's very kind of you to say," Ericsson said, "but I'm hardly doing this by myself. I've surrounded myself with some very dedicated professionals."

"I'm still impressed."

"Charles tells me you were a cop and now you're a teacher."

"When he's not moonlighting as a private investigator," Golden chimed in.

"*That* is impressive, Mr. Donne." He put his hand on his benefactor's shoulder. "Have you made much progress in finding Charles's daughter?"

I glanced at Golden's face. His eyes now had that distant look one gets when reminded about a reality outside the present moment.

"Some," I said, as much for my sake as Golden's. "I came in a little late, but we've got some solid leads."

"Good." Ericsson looked as if he wished he hadn't brought up the subject. I decided to rescue him by changing it.

"So what makes one join the Marines these days?"

"I joined because my dad was a jarhead and, at the risk of sounding corny, he was my hero. I don't remember wanting to be anything else."

"That's not corny," I said. "That's pretty cool."

"What about you? Your dad a cop?"

"No. A lawyer."

"But your uncle . . ."

"*He's* the reason I became a cop." I looked around and spotted Uncle Ray regaling a group of young ladies with some tale. "I never really thought of it in those terms, but I guess he *was* my hero growing up."

"It piss your dad off when you joined the force?"

"He died when I was thirteen. But, yeah, I think it would have bothered him. Probably one of the reasons I did it."

Ericsson smiled. "We all need something to rebel against, huh?"

"I'm a middle-school teacher. You're preaching to the choir. What about your dad? He still around?"

"Oh, yeah. My mom made him move down to Florida. He's down there whipping a bunch of Sarasota retirees into shape in case Cuba decides to invade."

"First line of defense?"

"That's what he tells me."

A well-dressed young lady came up and touched Ericsson on the arm. "There's someone you need to meet, Greg." She looked at me. "Sorry."

"Not a problem." I shook Ericsson's hand. "Go get 'em."

"Thanks for your support."

After Ericsson left, Golden—I'd forgotten he was still there—tapped me on the upper arm and pointed at Ericsson. "That," he said, "is what makes this business worthwhile, Raymond. I could spend my entire time controlling the flow of information, keeping it in my clients' best interests. But a young man like that . . ." He let that thought drift off into the city sunset. I gave him a few moments.

"Are you okay, Mr. Golden?" I asked. "I don't know how you can enjoy yourself with all that's going on."

He looked me in the eyes. "Is that what you think?" He looked around the room, which suddenly seemed much smaller than a minute ago. "That I'm *enjoying* myself?"

"I guess that was a poor choice of words."

"I am doing what *must* be done. What my clients pay me for. If I spent all my time waiting at home for my daughter to return, I'd blow my brains out." He took a step away and then turned back. There was that primal look again. "Find Angela, Raymond."

I held his gaze. "We're doing our best, Mr. Golden."

"Excellent," he said, staring a hole through my forehead. "Nothing less will be tolerated." He walked away, through the door, and disappeared.

Allison came over with my beer, a Brooklyn Pennant. "You okay?"

"I guess." I took a sip and smiled. I looked over at the bar and raised my glass in thanks. The bartender threw me a salute.

"I don't know," Allison said. "All beer tastes the same to me."

"But you insist on a name-brand vodka?"

"Yes, but that doesn't make me—"

"A vodka snob? Forget it. Let's just enjoy and not question." I took her by the arm and led her over to a couple of seats that had just opened up. As we sat, I said, "Maybe we can finish these and head home?"

"You slowing down on me?"

"Just a little tired. I saw you chatting with Blake. You give him a card?"

"Of course. His wife enjoys her martinis, also, by the way."

"I noticed. You want me to introduce you to Golden?"

She took a sip and shook her head. "Not if you want to leave. I do have to be at work in the morning, and the more I look at you in that suit . . ."

"Drink up." I touched my glass to hers. "I might give you a chance to see how I look out of the suit."

"See? That's how you get a guy naked."

"How's that?"

"Just mention the possibility."

Chapter 22

I WOKE TO ALLISON'S ALARM at six thirty the next morning with Allison's head on my shoulder, a big smile on my face, and the recently acquired knowledge that three hundred dollars for a suit is money well spent. Then I remembered the main reason we had to sleep at Allison's apartment—the two bullet holes in my bedroom wall—and my smile faded. I slipped my arm out from under Ally's head and went to the bathroom. After splashing my face with water, I went into the kitchen to put on a pot of coffee. While waiting for it to brew, I found Ally's laptop and fired it up. I figured I'd check out the *Times* Web site before she got up and caught me cheating with the competition.

I clicked on the Style section, and it didn't take long to find the photos from last night's benefit. Among the pictures of the many well-dressed attendees I did not know, I found a shot of Tony Blake with his arm around Greg Ericsson. Under the photo was a quote from Blake: "The government needs to be doing more for our returning veterans. Greg's an example of how heroes are heroes, no matter where they are."

I wondered how much Charles Golden had to do with those two tightly written and extremely quotable sentences.

I got myself a cup of coffee, plopped down on the couch, and searched the rest of the Web site. Not much going on around the world during the last few weeks of August: the usual political unrest in countries I'd never go to, Congress gearing up for the first battles of the fall, some parts of the country getting too much rain while others were not getting enough, and the usual politicians on both sides of the aisle blaming it on—or denying the existence of—global climate change.

I switched over to Allison's paper's website for two reasons: she was going to be up soon, and their sports section. The Yanks had won again the night before, continuing their late-season optimistic surge to make the playoffs. Football season had snuck up on me again and would be starting in less than three weeks. There was no use denying it: summer was coming to a close, and another school year was almost upon us.

"I assumed you checked the *Times* first?" Allison asked as she came out of her bedroom and kissed me on the head.

"Why do you say that?"

She reached over and clicked on the History tab, exposing my poorly hidden tryst with the enemy.

"It's okay. I do it, too. What are your plans for the day?"

"Not sure. I have to call the precinct, see if it's okay for me to go back to my apartment. Royce still needs a more complete statement from me, too. I was supposed to call him yesterday."

"I don't know, Ray. I'd rather you stay here for a few days."

"I still gotta swing by and pick up some clothes, Ally. I can't just walk around in that suit the whole time."

"Mmmm," she purred. "That might be interesting, Ray."

I stood up and put my arms around her. "I have a brain, too, you know."

"Which," she said, "thanks to the suit, I screwed out last night."

I kissed her. "You talk dirty for a journalist."

"Is that a complaint?"

"It is certainly not a—"

My cell phone rang. I found it on Allison's coffee table and didn't recognize the number, but the 845 area code told me it was from upstate New York. I looked at Ally, shrugged, and answered.

"Hello?"

"Ray?" a hurried voice said.

"Yeah?"

"It's Robby Torres."

I looked at Ally's cable box. It wasn't even seven o'clock yet.

"What's up? Everything okay?"

"I just got a call from my aunt. Mom's house was broken into last night. I'm on my way down."

I could hear he was calling from a moving vehicle. "Is your mother okay?"

"Yeah. She was staying in Maspeth last night with my aunt. The cops called her an hour ago to let her know about the break-in. Where are you?"

"I'm at my girlfriend's. In the city."

"I know it's a lot to ask," Robby said, "but could you head over to my mom's until I get there?"

I wasn't sure what good that would do, but he was Ricky's brother.

"Absolutely. When do you think you'll get there?"

I waited a few seconds as he put together an ETA. "Nine thirty maybe?" he said. "I don't know what traffic's gonna be like when I hit the Bronx."

I could hear the increasing panic in his voice. This was all getting to be too much for him.

"Just take it easy, Robby. Your mom's okay, and you're not going to make things better by rushing down here. I'll call Jack, and we'll meet you at your mom's when you get there. Drive carefully."

"Okay, Ray." I heard him take a deep breath. "Thanks."

"See you in a few, Robby."

After I hung up, I explained the situation to Allison, who had gotten herself a cup of coffee while I was on the phone.

"Jesus," she said. "Like the family hasn't been through enough."

"Yeah."

I dialed Jack's number and got his voicemail. I went over the details as I knew them and said I'd be there in less than an hour. When I put the phone down, Allison was giving me a strange look.

"Why do you have to go over there?"

"Because Robby asked me to. The place'll be crawling with cops, and his mom could probably use some support."

"Your uncle would say you're—"

"You're right," I said, stepping over to the closet where I'd recently started keeping some of my clothes. "And I can't tell you enough how much I appreciate your *not* saying that."

She gave me the exasperated look that I was getting used to. "You think there's a connection between the break-in and what happened to Ricky?"

"More than likely. I mean, there are thieves out there who check the obituaries and try to hit houses during times of personal crisis. But between Ricky's death, the shooting at my place, and now this . . . I don't see how they're not connected."

I put on my shirt and jeans. Allison handed me a pair of sneakers.

"I heard you telling Robby to be careful."

"Yeah?"

"I hope you take your own advice."

"I will, Allison. I'm a careful guy."

"And still, your bedroom wall has two bullet holes in it."

"I'll be careful," I repeated. "Besides, the cops are probably all over the place, and whoever broke in is long gone."

She stepped over and put her arm around me. "Call me."

"Absolutely."

The subways were running well, and I got to Ricky's mom's house in a little more than thirty minutes. When I arrived, the front door was open, and a uniformed cop stood on the front steps. I walked over and said, "Good morning."

"Can I help you, sir?" he asked.

"Yeah, I hope so. Is Detective Royce inside?"

"He is, sir. Is he expecting you?"

"No. He's not. Could you tell him that Raymond Donne is here?" I saw the look on the young cop's face. "Tell him it's the *other* Raymond Donne."

That seemed to do little to lighten his confusion, and he went inside as I stepped back to the sidewalk. The last time I got too close to one of Royce's crime scenes, he made sure I knew it *was* the last time. After a few minutes of waiting on the sidewalk, and not answering questions from Mrs. Torres's neighbors, I saw Royce exit the house. He came over to me with a smile that contained little joy, but I did detect a slight sense of amusement.

"I don't see any coffee in your hands, Mr. Donne," he said. "So I'm not sure what brings you here so bright and early. Unless it's that statement you owe me?"

"Robby Torres called me. Asked me to meet him here."

"For what purpose?"

"Maybe so his mother would see a friendly face."

"You implying my face isn't friendly?"

I took in Royce's face. "Wouldn't dream of it, Detective." I looked past him at the front door. "She in there?"

"Doing an inventory. Seeing if she can figure out what was taken."

"How's that going?"

"It's going," he said. "And no, you may not enter the house."

"I wasn't going to ask."

"Right." He reached into his pocket and pulled out some bills. "Since you *are* here, Mr. Donne, would you mind running over to the avenue and getting me some coffee? I didn't have time on the way, and the responding officers failed to plan for my arrival." He held out a ten-dollar bill.

"It's on me. Just one?"

"Yeah. Large and black. Like me."

"That should be easy to remember."

When I got back five minutes later, I saw Jack Knight talking with the cop stationed on the front steps. Jack saw me, handed the guy a card, and patted him on the back. He came down the steps and walked over.

"That was thoughtful," he said, looking at the three cups in my hands.

"It was," I agreed, holding up the cups for the uniform to see. He came over. "For the detective. The other's yours."

"Yes, sir. Thank you."

After he left, I took a sip of my own coffee and gestured with my chin toward the cop. "Friend of yours?" I asked Jack.

"He is now. And thanks for calling, Ray." He looked at the house. "You know when the break-in happened?"

"No. I was going to ask Royce, but he sent me for coffee instead."

"And you went for it?"

"I figured a fully caffeinated Royce would be more forthcoming."

Jack smiled. "That's the kinda shit you're good at. Wish I could do that."

"What? Think of others?"

"Smoothing the way." He made a sliding motion with his hand. "Me? I gotta flash a little green to get what I need from folks. There's something about you that people like." A thought crossed his face. "Fuck me! I almost forgot. What the hell happened at your place the other night? Someone take a shot at you and your girlfriend?"

"Not quite. And thanks for waiting thirty-six hours to check in on me." I told him about hearing the thuds and finding the bullet holes in the wall above the bed. "If Allison and I had been lying there . . ."

He considered that. "And the curtains were pulled?"

"Yeah. Why?"

"Means the shooter knew the layout of the apartment. He cased your place when the curtains were open and was probably up on the roof across the way when you and your girl got home." He let that sink in. "Cops match the slugs to the one that got Ricky?"

"They haven't told me anything yet. And *my girl*'s name is Allison."

Jack nodded. "That'll work."

We both turned back to the house as we heard the sound of a woman crying. Mrs. Torres was being escorted outside by Detective Royce and another older woman, who I took to be her sister. I started to head toward her when Royce held up his hand like a traffic cop. He walked both women to the parked squad car and opened the back door for them. He then said something I couldn't hear to a uniformed cop, who got into the car and drove off. Then Royce walked over to Jack and me.

"Thought I saw the last of you when you retired, Jack," Royce said.

"I figured you missed me, Detective."

"Like I miss my favorite hemorrhoid. Why are you here?" He turned his glare to me. "Why are either of you here?"

"Friends of the family," Jack said. "Ricky's brother called and asked us to swing by." Jack looked at his watch. "Should be here in a little more than an hour."

Royce nodded. "I understand Torres was working for you."

"He was. Part-time. Interviews, accident scene photos. Minor stuff."

The detective took a sip of his coffee. "So you've gone private, huh?"

"Best decision I ever made," Jack said. "Self-employed is the way to go."

Royce smiled. "You gotta be careful with that, though, I would imagine."

"Why's that?"

"Sometimes when you're self-employed, your boss can be a real asshole."

Jack gave Royce a smile. "That's good. I'm gonna remember that next time I wake up at ten in the morning, make myself a big pot of coffee, turn on my computer, and start billing my clients by the hour."

"What did Mrs. Torres say was taken, Detective?" I asked, tired of the back-and-forth between these two.

"Nothing," he said. "At least not that she could tell."

"How'd they get in?"

"Back basement window, sometime after nine when she left for her sister's in Maspeth, Queens. No home-security system, and none of the neighbors heard a thing. One of them noticed the front door open this morning when they were walking their dog. Any other questions, *Mister* Donne?"

I did have more questions, and I figured it was to my advantage to ask them before Royce got truly bothered by my presence. And Jack's.

"You think there's a connection between the break-in and Ricky?"

"I try not to think about such things until I have time to detect," he said. "But with nothing missing—according to the victim—it does make one think there's another reason the house was broken into."

"Someone was looking for something," Jack said.

"That's a possibility we're looking into."

"It's like a real mystery, huh, Royce?" said Jack. "How do you figure out what the thieves were after when they either got what they wanted or it was never here to begin with?"

"That's a good question, Jack. Was kinda thinking along the lines of checking in with Ricky Torres's employer. See if he could tell me anything. It's called detective work."

Jack nodded. "Employ*ers*. Plural," he said. "Ricky worked for me *and* his cousin."

"I'll start with you."

"I have no idea. Like I said, Ricky was doing minor accident investigations for me." Jack gave me a subtle look, telling me to keep my mouth shut about the work he was doing for Charles Golden. "Nothing that would lead to him getting killed or"—he looked over at the house— "this."

Royce stayed quiet for about ten seconds. "Mr. Donne?"

"I wouldn't know, Detective. The other night was the first time I'd seen Ricky in months."

The look on Royce's face told me we'd said pretty much what he had expected. He reached into his shirt pocket, pulled out a pair of business cards, and handed one to both Jack and me. "You guys know the drill. If you think of anything . . . ."

Jack took the card and handed Royce one of his own. And then, just to prove he hadn't lost all his asshole qualities, said, "You do the same, Detective."

I already had at least one of Royce's cards at home, but took this one and slipped it into my back pocket anyway. "Thanks."

Royce looked at Jack's card and smirked. "You two planning on waiting around for the brother to show up?"

"I told him I would."

"Might save some time if you give him a call and tell him to meet his mother at the precinct. There's not much reason for him to meet me here. He hasn't lived here for . . . how long?"

"Pretty much since he started college over four years ago."

"Right." Royce reached into his pocket and took out his car keys. "Always a pleasure to visit with *ex*-cops."

He started off to his car, when I realized I had one more question for him.

"Royce." He turned. "They match the bullets in my bedroom wall to the one that killed Ricky?"

"Ballistics should have the results this afternoon, Mr. Donne. Your uncle left specific instructions he be notified before anyone else." Royce did a nice job of mixing sarcasm with annoyance. "I'm sure you'll hear from him shortly after."

"Thanks."

He didn't respond and half-a-minute later drove off.

"I think we should've told him about the Golden case, Jack," I said.

"There's another difference between you and me. Information is a valuable commodity. I'm not giving more than I have to unless I'm getting something in return."

"You're starting to sound like Charles Golden."

"I'll take that as a compliment."

"Take it any way you want. . . . I'm hungry. There's a diner on the corner." I raised my cup. "You wanna grab something?"

"Yeah. Whatta we got? An hour before Robby gets to the city?"

"About." My phone rang. It was a 718 number, but I didn't recognize it. "Hello?"

"Teacherman," Tio said. "You up bright and early for a man on vacay."

"Good morning to you, too." I stepped away from Jack. It's not that I didn't want him to hear me talk with Tio—well, maybe it was. Tio was *my* connection and, as Jack said before, information was a commodity. I'd figure out the value of what Tio had, then decide how to—or if I should—share it. "What's the word?"

"Ah, right to the point. I like that about you." He paused for a bit, and I could hear him sipping from a drink. "The word is I got a name to go with the picture of that pretty little *chica* you showed me."

"That was quick."

"That's how I do business, Teacherman. Pizza and whatever, you know? No use making people wait if I can help it."

"I appreciate it," I said, not pushing him on the *business* comment. "What's the name?"

"Sheila E," he said. "Like that drummer chick—used to play with that skinny dude, Prince, from the eighties."

"What does a young guy like you know about the eighties?"

"My mom and dad used to play that shit all the time. Before they split up."

I learned last year that Tio's parents separated when he was young and that his mom had died from AIDS years ago. Life's like that sometimes.

"Cool," I said. "Any idea what the E stands for?"

"Not even sure it's her real name." I took a sip of my coffee as he paused again. "You wouldn't be interested in an address, would ya?"

I almost spit my coffee all over the sidewalk. "You got her address?"

"I got *an* address, Teacherman. Not sure whose it is, but one of my boys said he's seen her around."

"Around the address?"

"And hangin' with the people who live there." He gave me the address, which I entered into my phone. "Thing is . . ."

"Yeah?"

"It's kinda known as a . . . party house, y'know?"

"What's a party house?"

He laughed. "How do I put this so I don't offend your public schoolteacher sensibilities?" he said. "It's a place where you can go to . . . party. In private. You pay to get in and you can drink, you can dance, you can . . . for a little extra dough-re-mi . . . hook up with a young lady—or young man—of your pleasing."

"It sounds like you're describing a whorehouse."

"Except we don't say it like that, though, 'cause then it makes the girls who hang there sound like hos."

I looked over at Jack, who was obviously getting impatient with me. I put the phone down at my side. "Just get me a double-egg and cheese on a roll. I'm good with the coffee." Jack rolled his eyes and gave me a subservient bow, but he went. "Tio," I said, "having sex for money is prostitution no matter what you call the people who are engaging in it."

"There you go, sounding like a cop *and* a teacher. I didn't call you up to play word games, Teacherman. I called to give you some info you asked for."

He was right. "What do I owe you for this, Tio?"

"Hate that word 'owe.' Whyn't you take the info, see what it gets you, and then we'll talk 'bout what it's worth after. Sound fair?"

"More than fair. Thanks, Tio."

"Later."

I put my phone away and thought about what to do next. I had to share this info with Jack, and then we had to check out the address Tio had given me. First, I decided to call Robby and tell him to meet his mother at the precinct. I left a message explaining that there was nothing more to be done at his mom's and to call me when he got to the city.

Jack came back from the diner and threw a brown paper bag at me. He was already chewing on his sandwich. "Hope you like mustard and mayo."

"Perfect." I told him about my call from Tio and showed him the address.

Jack took a sip of coffee and looked at my notepad. "Good shit, Ray. Who's this guy who called you?"

"I'd rather not say, Jack. He likes to keep things on the down low."

Jack gave that about three seconds. "Whatever." He took another bite of his breakfast. "So, we are not sticking around here waiting for Robby?"

"I already called him. We'll talk when he gets to the city."

Jack tapped the address on my notepad. "Let's go for a ride, Mr. Donne."

It took us about ten minutes to get to the address Tio had provided. Jack drove past the place slowly. It was a four-story brownstone that had seen better days, but still seemed to be the best-looking house on the not-yet-gentrified block. We parked down the street.

"Okay," Jack said, "time for a plan. I'm thinking I knock on the door and act like I'm looking for a good time. Mention this Sheila E chick by name; say she comes highly recommended by a friend of mine who's been here before."

"What if they ask for a name?"

"I'll tell him it was Ricky T." Before I could say anything, he said, "It's the truth, ain't it? He didn't exactly give us the name, but he had her picture. Chances are good they know him inside."

I didn't like it, but Jack was probably right. There were a few other things I didn't like. The time of day for one.

"It's kinda early to be looking for . . . 'a good time,' don't you think?" I said.

"I'm a businessman. Heading back home and looking for a quickie before I return home to the wife and rugrats."

It didn't take him long to come up with that. Jack Knight, Method Actor. I couldn't help but be impressed.

"What if they make you?"

"For a cop?"

"You *did* work around here, Jack. The nine-oh's only a mile away, and you weren't exactly known for keeping a low profile."

He put his hands on the steering wheel and closed his eyes as he thought. I looked out the window and watched a girl, who couldn't have been more than seventeen, walk down the block pushing a stroller. The kid was wailing away, but luckily Mom had her earbuds in. Teenage Parenting 101.

"Okay," Jack said, tapping the steering wheel. "Same plan, different approach. *You're* looking for a pre-noon quickie." He faced me. "Think you can sell it?"

"Yeah," I said, trying my best to exude confidence. "What if they don't want to let me in?"

"You beg a little, Ray. I'm sure you've done that before, when you were jonesing for a piece of ass." He reached into his pocket, pulled out some money, and handed it to me. "A little pleading, a little flash of the cash, you're in like a slippery dick." He thought about that and laughed. "Literally."

I looked at the money he'd given me: three hundred-dollar bills. About what my suit cost yesterday. I put the cash in my pocket and pulled out my cell to check the battery. Good to go.

"If I'm not out in ten minutes . . ."

"I'll come charging up those steps like Dirty Fucking Harry," Jack said. He raised his pant leg and showed me his gun. "You want my piece?"

"No, Jack," I said, putting my hand on the door. "I don't want your piece. Just keep your cell phone out. I'm probably gonna be right back anyway."

"Think positive, Ray. That's what got me where I am today."

If that was supposed to inspire me, it missed by a whole lot.

"See ya in a few."

I exited the car and started walking casually up the block to the house. There were very few people on the streets at this hour. I guess those with jobs had already gone, and it was still too early for those who didn't. The parked cars I passed on my way were a good indication of what was happening to this neighborhood. Some were old and battered, the kind you wouldn't cry over if something happened to them; and others were what car dealers would probably call "gently pre-owned" upper mid-range cars: older-model BMWs, two Volvos, and a Saab. The kind of cars that said, "I can do better than this, but I'm still going through my hip stage and just love the diversity of living in Brooklyn."

I stopped in front of the brownstone. Before climbing the steps, I noticed all the windows seemed to be pretty new, and the front door was clearly the envy of its neighbors. I walked straight up to the buzzers. According to the slots, there were eight apartments inside, two per floor. One thing the slots didn't tell me was the names of any of the tenants. Some people like their privacy; others need it. I pressed the one that was labeled "Super" and stood back to wait for a response.

About thirty seconds later, a man's voice came through the intercom. "Who is it?" he asked, coming through loud and clear. Obviously a new intercom system.

I leaned into the speaker. "Chad Curtis," I said, picking the first former Yankee who popped into my head.

"What do you want?"

I couldn't exactly announce what I wanted, so I said, "I was hoping to speak with the . . . manager of the building."

"Ain't no manager," the voice said. "You're talking to the super; and if you're looking for an apartment, we don't got any openings."

"I'm not looking for an apartment." I got real close to the speaker and lowered my voice to just above a whisper. "I'm looking for Sheila."

I waited about ten seconds. "There's nobody by that name lives here, mister. You got the wrong address."

"I was here a while go," I blurted out. "With my friend Ricky?"

Again I waited. "So?"

"I was hoping to see Sheila again. Sheila E."

This time it took a full half minute before I got a response. The front door buzzed, and I pushed it open. I stepped into a foyer that contained a coatrack, a full-length mirror, an old radiator, and some decent carpeting. There was a staircase to my left and a door to my right. The door opened and a Caucasian woman stepped out. She was wearing a long-sleeved work shirt and khaki shorts. Her brown hair was pulled back, and her skin color made me think she'd been enjoying the sun.

"Mr. Curtis?" she asked.

"Chad," I said.

"Chad." She stepped toward me. I could smell the perfume she was wearing. It was not the kind you'd put on if you were planning on spending the day inside, alone. "I'm not sure we've met." She gave me her hand—not her name—and I took it. "You say you were here with a friend how long ago?"

"A little over a month, I guess. With Ricky T."

She repeated the name. "And you met Sheila?"

"Yes."

She nodded. "It's a bit early in the day to be coming by, Mr. Curtis."

"I know and I apologize," I said. "It's just that I'm heading home and—"

"You'd like a little refreshment before you get on the road?"

I put an embarrassed look on my face and smiled as if to say she understood me. "Something like that."

She smiled back. "Where did you park?"

"I found a space up the block." I pointed in the direction opposite of Jack. "Not too close, if you know what I mean."

"I do," she said, sharing in the conspiracy of secrecy. "You have money?"

Right to business now. I reached into my front pocket and pulled out the three hundred dollars. I tried to make it look casual, like I'd done this before. She looked at the money and smiled, but let me hang on to it.

"Why don't you follow me upstairs, Mr. Curtis," she said. "And we'll see what we can do for you."

"Call me Chad, please. Is, uh, Sheila available?"

She took me by the hand and started to lead me up the stairs. "We'll have to see, Chad. If not, we'll find you another suitable girl."

I stopped on the fourth step. "I really came to see Sheila, Miss . . . ?"

"Chad," she said, as if talking to a teenager. "You come by without an invitation, outside our regular hours, requesting a particular girl." She squeezed my hand and rubbed my wrist with her index finger. If she were trying to get my juices flowing, she knew her stuff. "We'll see what we can do to make sure you head home happy. If that does not work for you, you're welcome to come back some other time."

I pretended to give that some thought. "House rules, right?"

She smiled and winked. "I like you, Chad." Damn, she was good at this. I allowed her to lead me the rest of the way up the stairs. When we got to the second floor, she released my hand and walked over to the door on the left. She removed a key from her pocket and unlocked the door, holding it open for me. "Why don't you make yourself comfortable inside, and I'll see what we can do about Sheila."

Not wanting to go into a room I knew nothing about, I said, "I'll wait out here if that's okay?"

She shook her head. "It's not okay, Chad. Like you said: house rules." She opened the door another few inches and waited. I took a deep breath and stepped inside. The door closed behind me and, much to my relief, there was no click of a lock sealing me inside.

The room was laid out like a typical teenager's bedroom. There was a dresser with a huge mirror and a set of shelves containing a large-screen TV, DVR/cable box, and a music system with top-of-the-line speakers. The bed itself was neatly made with a blue-and-white comforter and matching pillows. I walked over to the window and looked out to the backyard. I could see the neighbors' houses across the way and was reminded of Hitchcock's *Rear Window*. Even though the AC was on, I wanted some fresh air, so I bent over to open the window. It was locked. Before I could figure out how to unlock it, the door behind me opened.

I turned, hoping to see the young woman I had seen on Ricky's phone.

Instead, there was a short Hispanic man with a cut-off T-shirt and hairy arms covered in tattoos rather than sleeves. He was smoking a joint and holding a leash, at the end of which was a gray-and-white pit bull.

"So, Mister Five-Oh," he said, blowing out marijuana smoke. "Whatchoo want with my girl Sheila?"

Chapter 23

THERE'S SOMETHING ABOUT pit bulls that makes my scrotum try to play hide-and-seek. It was the exact opposite of the feeling I got when the woman who had escorted me upstairs ran her finger across my wrist. Amazing how moody genitals can be. I tried my best to focus on the guy with the dog, not the dog itself.

"I'm not a cop," I said, as steady as I could manage. I thought about Jack's offer to take his gun with me and wished I'd given it more consideration.

"You either a cop," the dog guy said, "or some other undesirable. Whatchoo askin' about Sheila for?"

"I was here a month ago. We had a good time, and I thought we could do it again. If I'm wrong or it's too early, I can just—" I made a move toward the door. The dog growled. I stopped.

"Who's this Ricky you talking about?"

"He's my friend who brought me here and introduced me—"

"Ricky *was* a cop, man," he said.

I tried to act surprised. "I didn't know that."

"Then you as stupid as you look." He gave me the once-over. "Take off your clothes."

"Excuse me?"

He smirked and shook his head. "You deaf now, too? Take off your fuckin' clothes."

"I don't know what your lady friend told you, but I'm not into that shit. I came for Sheila. You tell me she's not here, I'm out of here, but . . . ."

The guy grinned and looked down at his dog. "Mister," he said, "you either take off your clothes right now, or I have Bates here do it for you. With his teeth."

I looked at Bates and, I swear, he gave me a look like he was hoping I'd choose the second option. I started to unbutton my shirt.

"I get it. You wanna make sure I'm not wired or have a gun on me."

"Yeah," Dog Guy said. "That's it."

I took off my shirt and kicked off my sneakers. After I got my jeans off, I raised my arms and spun around in my boxers and socks.

"I say stop?"

"No, but . . ."

"Bates!" he said, and the dog stood at attention.

"Okay." I started to remove my undershorts. With my penis and what was left of my balls hanging out, I held the boxers up for the guy to see.

"Bates," he said in a softer tone, and the dog relaxed, visibly disappointed. "Putcha clothes back on, mister."

I did as I was told—slowly—and, without asking permission, I took a seat on the edge of the bed. My knees felt like they were about to give out, and I thought I'd been humiliated enough for the morning. I sat there in silence as the man with the dog decided what to do with me.

"Now," Dog Guy said as he reached into his pocket and pulled out his cell phone, "this asshole here?"—he turned the phone to me so I could see a picture of Jack sitting in his car—"*He's* a cop. Used to work 'round here. Wanna tell me whatchoo doin' with him and throwin' Ricky's name around if you ain't a cop?"

I tried to figure out some way to spin this. Some story that would ensure that I left this room—this building—with all the body parts I'd come in with. Dog Guy knew too much for me to try another lie or half-truth. I looked at him and Bates, swallowed, and went with the truth.

"He's a private investigator, hired by the family of a missing girl." I touched my front pocket and Bates growled. "Can I pull out my phone?"

"Slowly," he said.

I did so and went to the photos. I got to Angela Golden's and turned the phone around. "This girl."

Dog Guy leaned forward and studied the picture. "That the girl from TV?" he asked. "The one with the big reward?"

"Yeah. She was recently seen"—I went to the picture of Sheila E and held it out for him to see—"with this girl. I was told her name was Sheila, and she frequented this address."

"Who told you that?"

"I can't tell you that."

"Can you tell Bates?" He stroked the dog's head.

"If I tell you who told me, that person will do more damage to me— and you—than Bates could ever dream of." I wasn't really sure what violence Tio was capable of, and I didn't want to find out.

Dog Guy thought about it. He took another long puff from his joint, licked his fingers, and extinguished the flame. He placed what was left in his pocket.

"He's got juice?" he asked, blowing out smoke. "Your source?"

"More than you wanna deal with." I looked at my cell. "If I don't get out of here in about two minutes, my partner's gonna come in looking for me. And he *does* have a gun. Pretty big one, in fact."

"Big enough to stop Bates?"

"You really wanna find out?" I asked. "Be a waste of a fine canine."

Bates looked at me as if he understood and put his head against his master's leg. Dog Guy just looked at me. We stayed like that for maybe a minute.

"Okay," Dog Guy said. "Lisa said you got some green on you."

I'd played that hand too early. "Yeah."

He reached out. "Gimme what you got."

"In exchange for what?" I asked, acting like I was gaining the upper hand.

"I can tell you about the white girl," Dog Guy said. "And a little about Sheila E. You get to walk out of here—instead of hopping with your hand between your legs—with more info than you came in with. That's what you get."

"That's not much."

"It's better than you got now," he said.

Again, I swore I saw hungry look on Bates's face. I reached into my pocket—slowly—and pulled out the money. Dog Guy leaned over, took it, and slipped it into his pocket.

"Call your boy first," he said. "Don't want him interrupting and getting my dog all upset over nothing, y'know?"

I called Jack and, I swear, he picked up before his phone even rang. "What's going on?" he said. "I'm halfway up the stoop and was about to start knocking."

"I'm good. I'm talking to the . . . manager. Give me ten minutes, okay?"

"The manager? This a music studio or a fuck palace, Ray?"

"I'll explain when I see you. Ten minutes."

"Make it five," he said and hung up.

I put the phone on the bed and looked at Dog Guy.

"Blondie," he said. "What's her name? Golden?" I nodded. "She come by a few times with Sheila. She's all nervous-like. But she's also got this look, like it's a thrill for her, y'know? Sheila told me Blondie's interested in partying, but let's get her used to the place first. I'm cool with that, because the girl was smokin' hot and that gets the customers hot. And if they can't have her, they go for something else. Like a tease, y'know?"

"She's sixteen," I said.

"Hey! I don't check no driver's licenses or IDs, man. Old enough to sit at the table, know what I mean? Anyways," he said as he stroked the area between Bates's eyes with his thumb, "Golden girl shows up two or three times, and just when I decide it's time for her to start really earning her keep, she goes bye-bye."

"And you have no idea where?"

Dog Guy laughed. "If I knew that, you and I wouldn't be conversatin'. What're they giving to get her home? Fifty large? Know how long it takes me to make that kinda cash?"

"You mean, how long it takes your girls, right?"

"You really wanna judge me, Mister PI? I gotcha money in my pocket and Bates here. You best watch yourself. This is *my* house. I give the word, and you're a pile of dog shit tomorrow."

There was a big part of me that wanted to lunge off the bed and grab this guy by the throat. The other part—below the belt—reminded me of his dog. I took a deep breath and slipped my hands under my thighs.

"When's the last time you saw her?" I asked. "The Golden girl."

"Less'n a month ago, I guess. She just stopped comin' by."

"Hard to get good help these days, huh?"

He laughed and pointed at me. "That's good. Not too many guys can be funny in a sitch like this."

"What about Sheila? Can I speak with her?"

"That's gonna cost more'n the three hundred you gave me, mister."

"Why's that?"

"'Cause I ain't seen her since two days after Blondie split on me. Packed up her shit one day and she was gone. Don't know where."

"How close was she to Ricky? The cop."

"He was regular. Two, three times a week, man. Boy had it bad for Sheila. That's good for business mosta the time, but . . . ."

"But?"

"But him being a cop and all, it kept most of the others away from her."

"Ex-cop."

"Makes no diff," Dog Guy said. "Anybody else look at Sheila when that guy was around, they got the eye, man. That cop eye they all got."

"Anybody get the eye more than anyone else?"

"Whaddaya mean?"

"Did you have any customers who seemed particularly annoyed at getting cockblocked by Ricky?"

He thought about that. "Why you askin'?"

"You hear about the shooting the other night? Over on Kent?"

"Heard something about it. And . . ."

"That was Ricky T."

A dim light bulb went off over Dog Guy's head. "And you think it was 'cause of Sheila?"

"Do you?"

"Nah, man. Guys who come here are horny, not killers." He got silent and let Bates sniff his hand. "There was this—ah, shit. Never mind."

"What?"

"I'm not talkin' 'bout my customers, Mister PI. That's the quickest way to lose 'em. You guys know that."

"But there was somebody? Someone who stands out?"

"I told you, man, I'm not gonna—"

"What if no one finds out? What if there was a reward involved?"

"How mucha reward?"

So much for customer confidentiality.

"It would be substantial. You could start off with the ten grand the Cop Shot people offer. If the guy you're thinking of did it."

He shook his head. "I don't know, man. I gotta think on that."

I could see he wasn't going to cough up the name of whomever he thought of, and I worried he might end the conversation if I pushed him any harder on this point. Besides, I didn't have any more money. So I kept going.

"Any idea how old Sheila was?"

"Twenty, I guess. Twenty-one."

"What about a last name? An address?"

"I told you, don't check IDs, man. And *this* was her address. You don't listen real good for a PI."

"I meant for her family."

"She didn't talk about family. She was here for about two years. One day she just showed up with a friend, and she been here ever since. Least 'til she left."

"No idea where she was from?"

"She didn't put it on the job application," Dog Guy said. "Shit, man. Girls come here 'cause they wanna forget where they from. Start all over. Sheila took to the life with a quickness. Started bringing by new girls right after she got here."

"Like the Golden girl?"

"Exactly."

"So she was a recruiter for you?"

That made him smile. "More like a talent scout, know what I'm sayin'? Sheila was real good at picking out girls who'd fit in around here. Girls who didn't mind doing what it takes to earn their way in the big bad city. Start out at Port Authority and head out from there."

That's where most of the busses into New York City ended up, filled with young people—especially young girls—thinking the city would take away all their problems.

"That bank robber guy said it pretty good: you rob banks 'cause that's where the money's at. Wanna find new talent? Bus stations and Amtrak."

And Dog Guy was going to have an unending supply of "talent" for the foreseeable future. I was suddenly very glad I was sitting on my hands.

"I'm going to give you my number," I said, slowly pulling one of Jack's cards out of my pocket.

"What for?"

"In case you wanna reach out about whoever you thought might have been involved with Ricky's shooting."

"A'ight. Don't mean I'm gonna call."

"I understand. Just in case." I wrote my number on the back of the card, handed it to him, and looked at the dog. "Okay if I get up now?"

"Yeah, man. Bates not gonna do nothin' 'less I tell him. You cool."

I eased myself off the bed and headed to the bedroom door. I heard a low growl behind me and just kept moving. I was outside less than a minute later. Jack was across the street leaning against a tree.

"What? You decide to get laid while you were in there?" I guess I was giving off a look or something. "You okay, Ray?"

"I'm fine. I just spent fifteen minutes in a room with a pimp and a pit bull." I looked Jack in the eyes. "I fucking hate pimps and pit bulls."

Jack put his hand on my shoulder. "Me, too, Ray. What'd you find out?"

I was about to tell him when my phone rang.

"Yeah?" I said.

"Ray, it's Robby."

"You with your mom?"

"No, I'm at my aunt's. They're still at the precinct. You got some time maybe?"

"Why?"

"I got something I need to show you."

"Can't you just tell me?"

He paused for a few seconds. "I don't wanna talk about it over the phone. Can you come to my aunt's house?"

"What's the address?" After he gave it to me, I said, "I'm bringing Jack Knight with me, okay?"

Jack gave me a look as Robby said, "Yeah, fine. He can be trusted, right?"

"Absolutely."

"Thanks, Ray."

After I put the phone away, I headed off in the direction of Jack's car.

"What was that about?" he said as he caught up with me.

"That was Robby. He wants us to meet him at his aunt's house."

"What the fuck for?"

"He didn't say, but he sounded a bit shaken up."

"So do you, Ray. What the hell happened inside that house?"

I got to the car and opened the passenger-side door. "We'll talk on the way."

Chapter 24

JACK PUNCHED THE ADDRESS ROBBY had given me into his GPS, and we were in front of the aunt's house in very little time. Robby was waiting for us on the steps and came down as soon as we got out of the car.

Robby and I shook hands. "You remember Jack, right?"

"Sure," Robby said and shook Jack's hand. "Thanks for coming."

"How's your mom?" I asked.

"Still pretty shaken up. She decided to stay here for a few more days." He shook his head. "I'm gonna see if I can convince her to sell the house. My aunt's all about Mom moving in."

"What's so important you had us come out here, Robby?"

Robby took the cell phone that was in his hand and pushed a few buttons. He moved his finger across the screen and handed me the phone.

"I found that in the storage shed behind my house. I was just in there this morning because I remembered that Ricky said he wanted to store some of his stuff and . . . ."

It took a few seconds for the picture to register. When it did, I handed the phone to Jack. He got it quicker than I had.

"Fuck," he said. "How many guns is that?"

"Twenty."

I took the phone back and thumbed to the next picture. It was a second photo of the same green duffel bag, except the guns were in close-up now. This was some serious firepower.

"And you think these are connected to Ricky?"

"He asked for the key when he was up there a coupla weeks ago. I had no idea he was talking about guns, Ray."

"Of course not."

"God, Ray, that's why I was so freaked out when I heard about the break-in at Mom's. I'm thinking now maybe Ricky was mixed up in some bad shit, and it was going to come back on Mom."

"Lemme see that again, Ray," Jack said. I handed him the phone, and he took a minute or so to check out all the pictures. "This is military-grade shit. TEC-Nines. Where the hell did Ricky get his hands on shit like this?"

I made a mistake, Ray. A big one.

"Where're the guns now?" I asked Robby.

"I kept them locked up in the shed. I put a bunch of blankets and tools over them, but I didn't want to move them. I figured you guys would know what to do."

"And Ricky gave you no idea about any of this?"

"No, not a clue. Honest."

Jack put his hand on Robby's shoulder. "We believe you, Robby."

I thought back to my meeting with Ricky's therapist, Dr. Burke. She'd told me Ricky was angry at his country. Angry and confused. Enough to get involved with something like this? *What the hell was this?*

I pulled out my cell phone.

"Who you calling?" asked Robby.

"My buddy, Edgar. You sure they're TEC-Nines, Jack?"

"Why?"

I held up a finger while I listened to Edgar's phone ring.

"Ray," Edgar said. "What's the haps, my man?"

"I need you to check something out for me, Edgar. You at work?"

"Yeah, but I'm about to go on break. Whaddaya need?"

"I want you to find out if there have been any thefts of TEC-Nines from any military bases in the last . . . say, six months."

He was silent for a few seconds. "I'll do what I can, Ray. They usually keep that kinda stuff on the hush-hush. I'm not gonna find much in the papers."

"If it were easy, you think I'd need to call you?"

I could practically hear his smile coming through the phone. Yes, I was souping him up, but Edgar was the only guy I could ask to find this information and not have it come back to bite me in the ass.

"All right, Ray. It's gonna take some time, though. Wanna meet at The LineUp, say, for dinner?"

"Yeah, okay."

Thanks, Ray."

Thanking *me* for doing me a favor. "Thank you, Edgar. See ya later."

"You trust that guy too much," Jack said as I put my phone away.

"He's come through before, Jack. Big-time. And he knows how to keep his mouth shut."

"In the meantime," Robby said, "what are we gonna do about the guns?"

"Keep 'em right where they are," Jack said.

"You think that's safe?" I asked.

"As opposed to moving them and running the risk of getting caught with weapons probably stolen from the U.S. government? Yeah, for right now, it's safe enough. Anybody else have access to that shed, Robby?"

"No. Just me. And I gave Ricky a key."

"Then we leave 'em where they be," Jack said.

The three of us stood there on the sidewalk of Ricky's aunt's house for a few minutes without speaking, but I was pretty sure what we were all thinking: who the hell had Ricky become? Running guns and storing them at his brothers' house, falling for a prostitute, getting involved with an underage rich girl's disappearance? Which was the big mistake Ricky had been talking about?

"I don't know about you, Ray, but I wanna have a chat with that other cab driver who was shot the night Ricky was: Dillman."

I said, "Robby, you got your cousin's number? The one who owns the cab company?"

He thought about that. "My aunt's got his business card inside. On the fridge. Give me a sec." He ran inside.

"This aunt," Jack said, "She's not the cousin's mom?"

"No, Robby told me Fred's from his dad's side."

"Well, Cousin Fred's been keeping a pretty low profile since the shooting. I don't think I've read a word about him in the papers since the first day."

"Probably on the advice of his lawyer and the insurance company. I imagine he's gonna get his ass sued and his business turned inside out."

"Yeah, maybe that's it. But . . . ."

"It might be worth having a conversation with him."

"That's exactly what I was thinking, Ray." He gave me a playful slap on the back. "You're learning, young Skywalker."

Robby came out of the house and handed Jack his cousin's card.

"Have you spoken to Fred since the shootings?" I asked.

"No. He never even spoke to us at the wake or funeral. We're not that close, but he shoulda paid his respects by now."

"I would think, yeah. Anyway, we're going to check on the other driver and then we'll try talking to your cousin."

"No offense, Ray, but shouldn't the cops be doing that?"

"They probably already did. But with the new . . . developments, I'd like to hear Fred's and Dillman's answers to some questions."

Robby hesitated, then started, "The guns . . . ."

"Yeah?"

"Can you keep Ricky out of it?"

"For now," I said. "But I don't see a way around sharing this info with the authorities, one way or another. We're talking about a federal crime here, Robby."

"I know. It's just"—Robby paused to fight back tears—"this'll kill my mom, Ray. She's already halfway there. If Ricky was involved in something wrong, it'll push her all the way."

"We'll do our best to protect her," Jack said.

Jack was more optimistic than I was. At least, he was acting that way for Robby's benefit.

"Okay," Robby said, clearing his throat. "Thanks." He shook our hands. "Be careful, guys."

"Always," Jack said. "Do me a favor and text me those pictures, Robby."

Jack gave Robby his number, and within seconds the pictures of the guns Ricky had stored upstate traveled up into space and landed three feet away on Jack's phone.

"I'll call you tomorrow, Robby," I said.

"Cool."

A car pulling up in front of the house got all of our attention. When the driver got out, I recognized him right away.

"You called Jimmy Key?" I asked Robby.

"Right after I called you guys. I needed help."

I raised my phone. "Let's keep the guns between us for right now, okay?"

"You don't think Jimmy can help?"

"I think the fewer people who know about this, the better."

Jimmy came up to us and shook our hands. I introduced him to Jack. "The PI, right?" Jimmy said, clearly sizing up Jack.

Jack nodded. "That's me. I hear you were over there with Ricky T."

"Brothers-in-arms," he said. "He said you were doing him a solid since he's been back."

"It was mutual," Jack said.

Jimmy turned to Robby. "So what's the emergency, little brother?"

Robby didn't know what to say, so I chimed in. "Turned out to be nothing. He's just pretty shaken up about the break-in."

Jimmy pondered that for a five count and then nodded. "Hate to think I wasted a trip out here, though. Anyone up for a beer?"

"Love to," Jack said. "But Ray and I gotta check out this witness in a case I'm working on. Rain check?"

"Yeah. What about you, Robby?"

Robby nodded. "Sounds good. I need to chill out. Let me just touch base with my mom after she gets back from the precinct. You wanna come in and wait for her and my aunt to get back from Brooklyn?"

Jimmy smiled that smile I'd seen him use on the bartender at Teddy's. "Yeah." He offered his hand to Jack and me. "We're gonna do that beer, boys."

"Absolutely," I said. "Soon."

Robby and Jimmy went into the house, and Jack and I walked over to his car. "I got an idea, Ray."

"Yeah?"

Jack looked at the card Robby had given him. "How about we drop in on cousin Fred instead of calling him?"

"Sounds like you want the element of surprise on our side."

Jack grinned. "See that, Ray? You just said 'our side.'"

I did, didn't I?

The Pulaski Bridge connects Greenpoint to Long Island City over the New-town Creek. Cousin Fred's taxi garage was less than a mile into the bor-ough of Queens. The building was on a busy corner and was painted yellow and black—the colors of New York City taxis. Jack was lucky enough to find a parking spot half a block away, and we walked back. A dark-skinned man was wiping down the outside of a cab and stopped when he saw us approaching.

"Don't got no cars available." He pointed to the intersection. "Best bet's to hail one on the corner."

"Actually," Jack said, flipping open his wallet and displaying his PI license as if it were a badge, "we're here to talk to the owner."

The guy straightened up. "What about?"

"You Fred?"

"No."

"Then it doesn't concern you." Jack paused. "Fred inside?"

"Last I checked," the guy said, and then went back to wiping down his cab.

Jack and I headed over to what we assumed was the office. Whatever the temperature was outside, it was ten degrees hotter inside. A man in a blue work shirt and jeans was standing next to a fan, speaking on the phone. He saw us, turned his back, and very quietly ended his phone call. He turned around and took a good look at Jack and me. "More cops? Don't you guys have anything else to work on?"

"That your lawyer on the phone?" Jack asked.

"I told you guys, I'm done talking. I got nothing more to say."

"We're friends of Ricky's." I noticed he had his name stitched over the left pocket of his shirt. "I'm Raymond Donne, and I was with him the night he was shot, Fred."

Fred sat down in a well-worn chair behind his messy desk. He let out a deep breath and closed his eyes. "Let me guess," he said. "You're Jack."

"The one and only."

"Doesn't change anything. I'm still done talking, especially if you guys ain't even cops."

Jack walked over to Fred's desk, cleared a spot by removing a box, and sat down. Then he took out his phone, pressed and swiped the screen, and turned the phone around for Fred to see. Fred picked up a pair of glasses off the desk and slid them on. It took him a few beats to realize what he was looking at. "So?" he said.

"So," Jack said. "Your late cousin—your *employee*—hid these some-where. They're more-than-likely *stolen* weapons. So, if the cops find out about these weapons and make the connection to your driver—your *cousin*—your business is going to be under much scrutiny, Fred."

Fred stood and looked at the pictures again. "If the cops don't know about these guns," he said, "who found 'em?"

"That's not for you to know. What we wanna know is what Ricky was doing with them."

"How the hell would I—?"

"Fred, Fred, Fred," Jack interrupted. "Please. These guns are connected directly to one of your drivers—our friend and an ex-cop—and your other driver shot last weekend has a record. How long do you think it's gonna take the cops—the Feds—to put two and two together and come up with your company as the common denominator?"

Jack was mixing his math metaphors, but I kept my mouth shut as Cousin Fred's face went from confused to concerned. When he finally spoke again, it was barely above a whisper.

"I don't know about those guns or why Ricky had them. If he and Little Mike were involved in something, they were on their own."

Jack looked at me and back to Fred. "We believe you," he said. "What the Feds are going to believe is a different matter. Did you know that both of your cabs shot up that night had their trunks opened?"

"No."

That's because Jack's lying, I thought.

"Seems like someone was looking for something." Jack held up the phone to show Fred the picture of the weapons. "Not a big leap here."

"I had no idea about—"

"Again, it's not us you're going to have to convince." Jack paused to let that sink in. "If *we* can figure out what was going on here, we've got a much better chance of getting ahead of this and minimizing the damage."

Now Jack was really sounding like Charles Golden.

"We can start," Jack continued, "with you showing us your GPS system."

Without missing a beat, Fred put his hand on the computer screen and turned it toward us. What we saw was a map of the roads and highways of New York City. I couldn't quite figure out how it worked, so I waited.

"All six of our units," Fred said, "are equipped with a GPS module. Their locations are transmitted back here in real time."

"It's that simple?" I asked.

Fred smirked. "It involves GPS satellites and individual vehicle antennas, but yeah, it's all I need to know."

"Anyone else have access to this data?" Jack asked.

"Just me, or whoever's manning the shop."

"And it's twenty-four/seven?"

"Shop's not open all that time, but I can access the system from home or the next day to see where the units have been on the late-night shifts." Anticipating the next question, he said, "I got three units out right now." He punched a couple of keys, the map got much smaller and moved to the left; a satellite photo filled up the right half of the screen. Both sides displayed a red dot with a series of numbers next to it, which I assumed to be the medallion number. "Others ain't on the road right now."

"And only this computer and your home computer can access this data?"

"That's how I've set it up. Why would anyone else wanna know this stuff for?"

"I think someone was tracking your cabs, Fred," I said.

"The guns," Jack added.

"Whoa, whoa, whoa!" Fred said, holding up his hands and springing to his feet. "You can't prove any of that. You trying to put me outta business?"

"Jack was just thinking out loud," I said in an attempt to keep the conversation civil and focused. I looked at Jack; he didn't look happy. "But it's exactly the kind of thinking the cops're going to put together." I took a few seconds to figure out what to say next. I came up with, "We need to talk to Mike. You know where we can find him?"

Fred laughed. "Shouldn't be too hard. Since he got outta the hospital, he's been home *recuperating*. Which means sitting on his ass in front of the TV, drinking Bud Lights."

"He *was* shot, Fred."

"I know, I know." He picked up a piece of scrap paper and pulled a pen out of his breast pocket. He scribbled something down and handed it to me. "Here's his new address. You know where that is?"

"Jack'll find it."

"You're not the only one with GPS," Jack added, snatching the paper from my hand and letting me know he was unhappy I had taken control of the interview.

Fred stepped around his desk, calmer now. "Listen, sorry I got upset about all this shit. It's just, with Ricky dead and Little Mike recuperating, half my fleet's off the streets. And now this." He pointed to the weapons on Jack's phone. "It's all too much, y'know?"

"Don't worry about it," I said.

"What're you gonna do after you talk with Little Mike?"

"Depends on what he tells us. But outta respect for Ricky and his family, if we have to go to the Feds with this, we'll give you a heads-up. That's the best I can do."

Fred gave me a resigned look. "Thanks. How's my aunt doing?"

"Why don't you call her?" I said. "She's at her sister's, here in Queens."

"Better yet," Jack added, "whyn't you swing by with a fucking coffee cake or something. Her son was killed—your cousin." Jack spun around and stormed outside.

I looked at Fred. "That's just Jack's way. Go see your aunt. She'll appreciate it."

"Yeah," Fred said. "Thanks, Ray."

A minute later I was sitting in Jack's car, and he turned the ignition key. I was about to say something, when he held up his hand. "Don't. I just wanna drive over to Mike Dillman's house and see what he's got to say. I'd like to drive in silence."

And so we did.

Finding Mike's apartment building was easy enough. And since the front door was ajar, getting inside was just as easy. Sure enough, Mike was sitting in his living room in front of the TV, a beer in the cup holder of his recliner. All as Fred had led us to expect.

Speaking to him was going to be the difficult part. It looked like someone had put a bullet in the middle of Little Mike's forehead.

Chapter 25

"HOLY FUCKING SHIT," JACK SAID AS he pushed me back into the hallway, drew his gun and joined me against the wall outside. With his foot, he nudged the apartment door all the way open. After ten seconds of nothing, Jack yelled, "NYPD!" More nothing. "Police!" Jack yelled again, this time causing Mike's across-the-hall neighbor to stick her head out.

"Get back inside, ma'am," Jack told her.

"I'm calling the police."

"We *are* the police, ma'am. Shut your door."

She did as instructed, and Jack turned to me. He motioned with his head toward Mike's apartment. "Clear?"

I held up my hand and listened for any noise from inside. There was none, except the sounds of traffic coming through an open window and Mike's TV. I shrugged. "I think so." I took out my phone.

"What the fuck are you doing, Ray?"

"Calling the cops."

"The old bitch across the hall probably already did. This neighborhood, that gives us less than five minutes."

"For what?"

He looked at me like I was stupid and stepped inside the apartment.

I followed him. "I don't think this is a good idea, Jack. It's a crime scene."

And another dead body.

"So I won't touch anything. Just look around."

"For what?"

"When I find it, you'll be the first to know, Ray."

Jack put his gun back in its holster, stepped over to the body on the recliner, and with two fingers checked his neck for a pulse. We both knew there wouldn't be one. "Taking the concept of La-Z-Boy to a new level." With the back of his hand he felt the beer can in the holder. "Warm." He looked around the sparsely furnished living room. "This guy didn't own a whole lot, huh?"

"He's only been out of prison a short time."

"Still. One chair, piece-of-shit couch, and a TV that looks like the one I got rid of ten years ago." He gave the set a closer look. "Least he got cable."

"Bedroom?"

Jack walked over to what had to be the bedroom door. "I'll check it out, Ray. You do the kitchen. We got about a minute or two, I'm guessing."

"Let's make it one, to be on the safe side."

"Right."

I went into the kitchen, grabbed the only dishtowel I could find, and stuck it over my hand. I checked all the cabinets and found them empty. All the dishes this guy owned seemed to be in the drainer. I opened the stove door and did the same to the fridge and the freezer. Nothing out of the ordinary, except the lack of food in both. Maybe he ate out a lot. I was about to close the door to the refrigerator, when I noticed both vegetable crisper drawers on the bottom seemed to be full. I opened them, and each had at least a dozen baseball-sized tomatoes in them. I moved them around with the dishtowel—*Can crime scene techs get fingerprints off a tomato?*— and found an envelope under each group. I removed each one with the very tips of my pinkie and thumb. Through the towel I could feel the envelopes had money inside. I put them back where I'd found them and called Jack.

"No need to yell," he said from over my shoulder, scaring the crap out of me. "Whatcha got?"

I pointed to the crispers. "Two envelopes, cash inside."

"How much?"

"I didn't bother to count, Jack, but by the size of them, it's not petty."

Jack leaned over. I stopped him with a hand on his shoulder.

". . . Ray?" he warned.

"We leave that for the cops. However much it is and wherever it came from, it's evidence. Let's get out of here before the real cops show up."

"You're right," Jack said, straightening up. He put his thumb and forefinger on my wrist and removed my hand from his shoulder. He gave the wrist more than a little squeeze. "Next time you want me to do something—use your words."

"Gotcha."

We were across the street from Mike's apartment for about ten minutes, when it became clear his neighbor had never called the cops. My stomach was tightening up again. I had gotten away with vomiting in front of Jimmy; I was not going for a repeat around Jack.

"We had more time than we thought," Jack said after calling 911 from a pay phone on the corner. He made a point of not mentioning the money in the fridge and hung up. "We coulda found more shit with that time."

"More than the money?"

"And this." Jack pulled something out of his pocket about the size of a stick of gum. He held up a flash drive. "Interesting item for Little Mike to have in his possession, considering he had no computer at his place, huh?"

"It is."

As Jack and I considered that, a blue-and-white pulled up in front of Mike's building. Two uniforms got out and rushed through the entrance. I knew the place would be crawling with detectives, crime scene folks, and EMTs within a half hour. It was time to go.

"What time is your boy Edgar gonna be at The LineUp?"

I looked at my cell. It was almost four. "Less than an hour."

"Let's go grab some beers and dinner. Wanna call him and have him bring his laptop?"

"That's like calling the pope and reminding him to bring his beads."

"Good."

"You sure you're okay to eat?" I asked.

"Why wouldn't I be?"

"Because we just saw a dead body."

He laughed, but not the kind of laugh that said he thought I was being funny. More like the kind of laugh that says, "Shut the fuck up." I did.

We started walking to Jack's car when I realized I should call Allison. We may have had plans for dinner—my memory wasn't so good at the moment—and I wanted to let her know where I'd be. Like most times when I called her these days, I ended up leaving a message. When I was done, Jack grinned at me and made a whipping noise.

"That's funny," I said. "I can't remember the last time I heard a guy with an actual girlfriend make that sound."

He opened his door, looked over the car's roof. "Fuck you, Ray."

We were on our second beers when Edgar showed up. I could tell by the look on his face he was happy to see me, but confused by Jack's presence. Edgar didn't do well with the unexpected. It took a few seconds for the smile on his face to go from anxious to something approaching pleasant surprise. He shook our hands and took the empty stool between us. He got Mikey's attention and ordered a pint of Bass and a small can of tomato juice. When Mikey brought them over, I told him to take it out of my pile of cash on the bar.

"Thanks, Ray," Edgar said. To Jack, he said, "How are you doing?"

"I'm fucking great."

After waiting for some follow-up that never came, Edgar turned back to me. "Ray, I'm sorry, man. I need more time to look into those TEC-Nine thefts. The military intel on this stuff is tight as a drum."

Jack took the flash drive we had found at Mike's out of his pocket. "How much to tell me what's on this thing?"

Edgar looked at it. "You mean how much money?"

"No, how much Chinese silk?"

Edgar's face went back to confused.

"Edgar doesn't charge me when I ask him for a favor, Jack." I put my hand on Edgar's shoulder. "Unless you consider a couple of beers and the occasional burger and fries a fee."

Jack had to take some time to mull that over. In his world, nobody did anything for free. You want something, you pay for it. Somebody wanted something from you, same deal. I liked my world better. By the time Jack had come to terms with that concept, Edgar had his laptop out and booted up. He took his hand and turned it palm up, asking for the drive. Jack gave it to him, and Edgar slipped it in the side.

"This'll take a few secs," he said, and poured a little juice into his beer. "Saw a dead fox today."

"Where the hell do you work again? Parks?"

"MTA. I was underground today checking some signals. Usually I work basic communications, but they were short a guy, so . . ." When no one said anything, Edgar continued. "Fox probably jumped into a truck up-state, jumped out down here, made his way to the subway, and got hit by a train." He paused and I knew a joke was coming. "That's what happens when you don't pay your fare."

I let out a little laugh. Jack remained silent. Edgar didn't notice. When the screen came up, he pressed a few buttons. "This is a GPS program." Edgar ran his fingers over a few more keys. "For a taxi company." He turned to me. "The one Ricky T drove for?"

"Yeah. What can you tell me about it?"

"Where'd you get it?"

"Can't tell you that," Jack said. "Confidential."

Edgar seemed okay with that. "Was it from the owner?"

"No. Why?"

"Because there's no reason for this system to leave the shop. It's for the owner and maybe the dispatcher, if they have one."

"So," I said. "This is a pirate?"

"*Exactamente,* Ray." He fooled around with some more buttons.

"How far back does that thing go?"

"Let me see." Edgar touched a few more buttons while Jack and I took sips from our beers. "Looks like it's on a seven-day program. Sounds normal."

"You mean, we can use that to tell us where the cabs have been over the past week?" Jack asked.

"Well." Edgar paused to drink a little beer. When he put his glass down, he said, "*I* can."

"How much is—?" Jack stopped himself. "What do you want for dinner, Edgar? It's on me."

Edgar's smile took up about three-fourths of his face. He was in blissful business. "Fish and chips would be great, Jack. Thanks."

Jack called Mikey over and gave me a look.

"I'll have the same."

"A round of fish and chips." Jack made a circling motion, pointing to our drinks. "And more of these." When he saw me taking money out of my pocket, he waved it back. "It's on the agency. Charles Golden, actually."

Now we were all smiling.

Halfway through our meal, Edgar announced that he had taken last week's GPS records for all of Fred's working cabs and put them in a PDF. I wasn't sure exactly what that meant, but he explained he could now print out the GPS records.

"Mikey," I said, as he brought us another round. "You mind if we print something out to Mrs. Mac's office?"

"Sure."

"Edgar?" I said.

"I am sending the info to the printer—*now*." He accented that last word with the flair of a concert pianist. Jack shook his head and smirked.

"Mikey," I said. "You mind?"

"Mind? Your man Edgar set the system up." He headed off to the office.

The three of us finished our fish and chips. I looked at the TV above the bar; the Yankees were just about to start. With a beer in front of me and no school for the next week, a rush of late-summer joy came over me. Then I remembered the dead body I'd seen a few hours ago, and what had led Jack and me there.

"Here ya go," Mikey said, placing a quarter inch of paper in front of us. "Happy reading. Another round?" he asked rhetorically, and left to get them.

Jack shoved the stack of printouts over to Edgar. "I wouldn't know what to look for, man. You mind?"

"I'm on it," Edgar said. He grabbed the pile and got off his stool.

"No offense," he said. "But I think better over there." He motioned with his head toward a booth in the corner.

"None taken, Edgar," I said. "Thanks."

When he was gone, Jack said, "Weird guy, but I like him. Sure he won't take any cash for this?"

"Not for this. Not for me. But if you have any private business, I'm sure he would."

Jack nodded. "Guy's got skills."

"That he does. When can you reach out and see what the cops know about Mike's murder?"

"I thought you could do that. Your uncle?"

"My uncle's the last one I'd ask about this. He's already none too thrilled about me working with you."

"Because it's me?" he asked. "Or because it's PI shit?"

"Both, but mostly the PI shit. He's still hurting that I never went back to being a cop. Now that he thinks I'm playing at it, he gives me shit." I took a sip. "Talk to one of your guys at the nine-oh. Detective Royce will obviously get called in on Dillman's case as soon as they connect it to Ricky T."

"That info doesn't usually trickle down to the uniforms, Ray."

"A phone call wouldn't hurt, Jack."

He spun his glass. "Guess you're right, but I wouldn't expect much."

"More than we got now."

"True that."

We went back to our beers in silence for a while. The Yanks were already in a hole with the A's getting their first two batters on base and their RBI leader at the plate. I watched as he moved them both up a base with a warning-track fly ball. With their cleanup guy stepping up, I felt a tap on my shoulder. I turned to see a concerned look on Edgar's face.

"What's up?" I asked.

He took a sheet of paper and put it between Jack and me. I looked at it and noticed he had outlined in yellow what looked like an address.

"Shit," I said.

"What's the matter?" Jack asked.

Edgar pointed at the yellow outline. "That address," he said. "It's right around the block from Raymond's apartment."

Jack shrugged. "So? It's probably a coincidence. Cabs go all over."

"Look at the time and date," I said.

He did. "Yeah?"

"That," I said, "is the day and time someone shot up my bedroom wall."

Jack looked at it again. " 'Shit' is right."

Chapter 26

"CHANGE YOUR MIND ABOUT GOING to your uncle now?"

I was still staring at the yellow line on the printout, thinking about the look on Allison's face when she considered, temporarily amused, what the hell had made two sharp holes in the wall above my bed. Royce said Uncle Ray would get the ballistics report on those bullets this afternoon. *Could I call Uncle Ray about this?*

"Yeah," I said, coming to my senses. "I'll just tell him I got this GPS information after I illegally entered an apartment, stepped all over an active crime scene, and stole a flash drive with evidence. He'll be more than happy to help."

"Hey," Jack said, tapping his finger three times real hard on the highlighted area. "This ain't no coincidence, Ray. Whoever drove this taxi— Ricky T's fucking coworker—was somehow involved in shooting up your crib. I think Chief Uncle Raymond Donne will forgive your transgressions when he hears that."

He was right. This was information that could not be withheld; it was crucial to the investigation, and Detective Royce had to know about it. That didn't mean he had to hear it from m

"You gotta do it," I said.

"Excuse me?"

"You have to bring this informa   o Royce."

"So *I* can explain how *I* illegally   ed an apartment?" he said. "Any idea how easy it is for the NYPD to pull my license, Ray? Any idea how many cops would love to be around for that?"

"You don't have to tell him how you got it. Make some shit up. You got it in the mail or something." A light bulb went off. "Better yet, you asked Ricky's cousin for it, and you noticed the address and brought it right to Royce's attention."

Edgar chimed in. "That's good, Ray. That'll work."

"Because it's so believable that I'd cooperate with the cops," Jack said, sarcasm dripping off every word.

"You know a better way, Jack? I'm all ears over here."

Jack considered that. We both took another swallow of beer. Edgar put his hand on my shoulder and glanced up at the TV. I looked up and saw that the Yanks had gotten out of the bottom of the first with no damage done.

"I'll have to work it out with Cousin Fred," Jack finally said.

"Of course."

"If he doesn't go along with it . . ."

"He's scared shitless the cops are going to implicate him in this mess. Look, we believe him, you said it yourself. I'm sure Fred just wants to find out who really is jamming up his business and who killed his cousin. He's scared now, but Robby says he's a good guy."

"Yeah. He did seem real eager to get himself in the clear, didn't he?"

I looked at my watch. Too late to do anything now.

"So you'll swing by Fred's tomorrow?" I asked Jack. "Make sure he's on board?"

"*We'll* swing by there tomorrow. Early. I got some paperwork to do, and Golden wants to see me again for some reason."

"He didn't seem so good at the benefit last night. He's not doing as well as he wants people to think."

"What benefit?"

Shit. I hadn't told him about that or my meeting with Golden yesterday.

"Something Allison dragged me to," I lied. "A fund-raiser for wounded Marines back from the Middle East."

"Thanks for the update, Ray. Anything else you want to share?"

"Golden called me to his office early yesterday."

"I know," Jack said. "Golden called me after you left. Said he approved."

"That's nice to know. Sorry I didn't mention it."

"You should have, but . . . ." He finished his beer. "I'll pick you up at eight tomorrow. Again, I'll pay you for the day, and you bring the coffee."

"You don't have to pay me. I want to talk Fred into this as much as you do."

"Not paying you for that, Rockford." He stood and pulled some bills from his pocket. "You're coming with me to Golden's."

"He ask for me again?"

"No." Jack peeled off five twenties and placed them on the bar. "But since you guys are so buddy-buddy now, it wouldn't hurt to have you there."

"Okay," I said. "Cool."

"Edgar," Jack said. "Let me have those papers."

"I'm not done going through them yet," Edgar said.

"Doesn't matter." Jack put his hand on Edgar's shoulder. Edgar flinched at the gesture. "You done good. I'll take it from here."

Edgar studied Jack's hand as he considered that. "Okay." He went over to the corner booth to gather the printouts. When he returned, he gave them to Jack without saying anything.

Jack took the papers and looked at the money on the bar. "That's enough for dinner, tip, and one more round of drinks. Thanks for a lovely evening, boys."

After Jack exited the bar, Edgar gave me a look.

"I can see why you guys didn't get along too well when you worked together back in the day, Ray."

"Yeah. Believe it or not, he's better."

"If you say so." He looked back up at the game. "Wanna hang for a few innings? I'll drive you home."

"Yeah." I pulled out my stool. "I can stay for a bit."

"Cool."

We drank a bit more and watched the game for a while. At the end of the inning a thought came to me. I looked over at Edgar's laptop.

"Arrests are a matter of public record," I said.

Edgar gave me his "Duh" face, but was too polite to say that, so he said, "Yeah?"

"Can you pull up Michael Dillman's arrest record? A.K.A. 'Little Mike'?"

Edgar slid the laptop in front of him and started clicking away. In the time it took me to take another sip, he had what we were looking for.

"Voila," he said, turning the screen a few inches so I could see it.

"Michael C. Dillman," I read aloud. " 'Illicit interstate transportation of tobacco products.' That's what I'd heard."

"Buttlegging," Edgar said with a smile. "It's a big business."

I read a little more, and the picture got clearer. It seems Little Mike got pulled over four years ago, driving a truck that was supposed to contain furniture manufactured down south to be sold up north in New York City and New England. Along with the couches, chairs, and dining tables, the highway patrol found over five hundred cartons of cigarettes from Virginia.

"Tough way to make extra money."

"You know what the excise tax is on a pack of cigarettes in Virginia?" Edgar asked. Edgar loved asking questions like that.

"No. But I bet you do."

"Thirty cents. Know what it is in New York?" He waited for me to say something, but I stayed shut. "Five dollars and eighty-five cents. *Per pack.* Do the math, Ray."

I nodded. "I get the idea, Edgar. Buy 'em down in Virginia, sell 'em up here, and pocket a whole bunch of money that's not paid in taxes."

"It's the most-smuggled product in the world." Edgar reads about stuff like this all the time. "They arrested a couple last year who was making five or six K a week selling to buttleggers. They owned some smoke shops down South and sold their merchandise to smugglers, and pocketed a buck a carton. Little Mike was caught with five hundred cartons, which was five thousand packs."

This time I did do a little mental math. The potential profit was amazing.

"Ya think he was back in the smuggling biz, Ray? Maybe that's why he got popped?"

I thought about the picture of at least twenty assault pistols presently hiding under a blanket in an upstate shed that somehow involved Ricky T.

Had Little Mike moved on to transporting something a little more dangerous than cigarettes?

"Could be. Mike got any other busts? Priors?"

Edgar touched a few more keys and shook his head. "Nope. Looks like this was it. Pulled himself a deuce upstate, paroled earlier this year."

I shook my head. "It's like my seventh-grade health teacher told us."

"What's that?"

"Cigarettes will kill you."

Edgar smiled. "Good one, Ray."

"What about the company Mike drove for? They still in business?"

A few more keystrokes. "Yep. Paid a fine, made a donation to the American Lung Association, and kept on trucking. Is that important?"

"It's a question," I said, and then my cell phone rang. I answered without checking the caller ID, hoping it was Allison. "Hello?"

I waited about ten seconds, hearing only what sounded like highway traffic; the caller wasn't saying anything.

"Hello?" I repeated.

"Is this Raymond?" A female voice, just above a whisper.

"Yes. Who's this?"

More silence, more noise in the background. I thought I heard laughter, followed by some car horns.

"I'm a friend of . . ."

I lost the last part to the noise of the horns. Whoever was talking was on a cheap cell phone. One that didn't filter ambient noise as much as amplify it.

"I can't hear you," I said, my voice louder than it needed to be. Edgar gave me a quizzical look. "Who *is* this?" I considered checking the caller ID now, but something in her voice made me press the phone harder to my ear.

"A friend," she said, and five seconds later added, "Of Ricky's."

Whoa. "Okay," I said. "What can I—?"

"You're looking for me."

It sounded almost like she had said I was cooking for her, but I figured it out soon enough. Was this the Latina girl from the photo? Or Angela Golden? I stood up and walked over to the window, leaving a frustrated Edgar on his barstool.

"What's your name?" I asked.

More silence from the girl, but during this round there was the high-pitched whine of motorcycles going by. Crotch Rockets. When that noise Dopplered away, I heard a truck applying its squeaky brakes. My mystery caller was at a service station along some busy highway.

"Who *is* this?" I said for the third time. "What's your name?"

"Marissa," she said.

Marissa? "Are you the girl from the picture on Ricky's phone?"

She waited five seconds. "Yeah. Ricky said I could call you if I was in trouble."

"He was right, Marissa." *So Shiela E was her stage name.* "Where are you?"

More traffic. "I don't know. Some gas station . . . I think it's on the highway. I don't know the name of the town. Do these places even have names? Shit."

"Ask somebody, Marissa."

"What?"

"Ask somebody where you are."

"Why?"

"So I can get you some help. You're in trouble, right?"

"I don't know. I guess, yeah. Hold on."

She must have put the phone down to her side and started moving, because I could hear her talking as the phone moved, catching the wind. I couldn't make out what she was saying, but it sounded like she was asking a man.

"New Baltimore," she said to me. "Never heard of it."

I had. It was up in the Catskills, just south of Albany and not far from where the Thruway meets Interstate 90 into Massachusetts. I'd taken that route a few years ago to catch the Yankees in Boston. It was almost a three-hour ride north of the city. If Marissa was in real trouble, I wasn't sure how much help I could be.

"Marissa," I said sternly. "You need to call the Thruway Police."

"Why?"

"You said you're in trouble. I'm down here in—"

"I said I *might* be in trouble," she snapped.

It was like talking to an eighth grader. "Either way," I said. "You need to call the cops. Tell them what's going on. They can help you better than I can."

"Ricky said to call you if we needed help, not the cops."

Shit. "Who are you with, Marissa?"

"I didn't say I was with anybody. Why do you think I'm with some-one?"

"Are you?"

". . . A friend," she said. "I'm with a friend."

The daughter recently hooked up with a new friend. Puerto Rican, Do-minican, they're not sure.

"Okay. Can you put your friend on the phone?"

"No. Why? No! Why do you wanna talk to my friend?"

"So I can get a better idea of the . . . situation you're in. If you're in immediate danger, I need you to call the cops. Your friend might be—"

"Smarter than me?" she said. "You think I can't tell you what kind of trouble I'm in? You gotta hear it from my friend?"

I took a slow, deep breath. "Then tell me, Marissa. What kind of trouble are you in?"

More silence. Maybe she was taking a few breaths of her own. I kept quiet, not wanting to risk her hanging up on me. I pulled the phone away from my ear quickly to check the caller ID: Blocked. Figured. "What kind of trouble are you in, Marissa?" I repeated calmly.

"I don't know," she finally said. "Big?"

"Define 'big,'" I said.

Another long pause, followed by an audible, shallow breathing.

"I think someone shot Ricky's brother, Robby."

Chapter 27

I WALKED BACK TO EDGAR, WHO WAS staring at his laptop screen. "Call the Highway Patrol and tell them to get some troopers to the service station at New Baltimore. Tell them there's been a shooting." He gave me a look. "Now!" I spoke into the cell again. "Marissa, you need to get inside the restaurant area and wait there. Go up to the counter, have someone call nine-one-one, and do not leave. You and your friend stay at the counter. Do you understand?"

"I think sho," she said. "Yeah."

She no longer sounded like an eighth-grader to me. She sounded as if she were going into shock: rapid breathing, her words slurring. "How did you get there?" I asked.

"To the gas station?"

"Yes, how did you get there?"

"My friend drove me."

"Is she still there with you?"

"Yeah. We took Robby's car and drove here."

And now she's telling me Robby might have been shot?

"Why do you say you *think* Robby's been shot? Did you see this happen?"

"We heard a gunshot," she said. "From behind the house." She took another deep breath. "Some guy came to the house, and Robby told us to hide in the garage. When he didn't come back after a while, we were about to go out. That's when we heard the shot. So we just got in the car, got on the highway, and pulled into the first place that looked safe. Do you think that guy from the house followed us?"

Damn it. "What's the address of Robby's house, Marissa?"

Silence. "I don't know. We just got here—there—yeshterday and . . . I don't know . . . ."

I turned to Edgar again, who was explaining something to someone on the other end of the phone.

"Are they on their way?" I asked.

"Yeah," he said. "But they're not—"

"Can you get an address off a cell number?"

"Yeah. It might take a few—"

I held up a finger to shut him up and went back to Marissa. "Marissa, are you inside yet?"

"I'm at the counter."

"Tell the guy behind the counter you're in trouble and to call 911."

"It's a girl."

"Stay there and do not hang up. I'm going to put you on Hold for a few seconds. Do not hang up." I pressed the buttons that brought me to my recent incoming calls. I scrolled down and read Robby's number to Edgar.

"Got it," he said, and started moving his fingers across his keyboard.

"As soon as you get the address, call the state cops again, and tell them there's been a shooting, and someone may be injured." I pressed another button. "Marissa, you still there?"

"Yes, but I can't find my friend now."

"That's okay for now. Stay at the counter until the cops get there."

"I'm getting cold," she said. "Why am I sweating . . . when I'm cold?"

I thought back to less than a week ago, how I had felt in the emergency room, my body temp alternating between hot and cold, and how hard it was to breathe.

"I think you're going into shock. Grab a seat on the floor by the counter and take some deep breaths."

"Got it!" Edgar said.

"Make the call, Edgar!"

"Why are you yelling?" Marissa asked.

"I'm not yell—are you sitting?"

"Yes. People are looking at me shtrange." Then, nice and loud, she said, "Like they can't mind their own business!"

Good, I thought. The *more attention on her right now, the safer she is.* I wanted to reach through the phone and slap her for not calling for help at Robby's, but there was nothing to be done about that now. *Where—and who—was her friend?*

"Ray," she said. "are you still there?"

"Yeah, Marissa. I'm here." I looked over at Edgar, who was giving me the thumbs-up sign. "Help is on the way. Do you see your friend yet?"

About ten seconds went by. "No, she's not around. You want me to check the ladies' room?" I heard her grunt as if she was getting up. "Maybe she's peeing."

"No," I said sharply. "Stay right where you are until the cops show up."

"Okay. I'm getting tired anyway."

"I need you to stay awake, Marissa."

In the background I could hear the sound of sirens.

"They're here, Raymond. The copsh. Ricky shaid no copsh."

"It's okay, Marissa. When they get inside, give your phone to one of them."

"Okay."

After a few seconds of a conversation I could barely make out, a man's voice came on the phone. He cleared his throat before speaking.

"Who is this?" he asked.

"Raymond Donne. The young lady you're with, her name is Marissa. She called me because she's in trouble and may have witnessed a shooting."

"A shooting?" the guy said. "At the service station?"

"No." I gave him Robby's name and address. "I called the state cops and told them what she told me, but if you could call—"

"I know who to call, Mr. Donne."

I waited while he radioed in the information I had just given him. After he got a response, he came back to me.

"Why did she call you, Mr. Donne?"

Excellent question, Officer. "I'm a friend of a friend. Marissa traveled with a friend to the service station. She's a bit confused about where she is."

He paused, and I heard Marissa yelling in the background. "That would be putting it mildly," he said. "Does she have a history of substance abuse?"

"I have no idea. I think she's in shock."

"You a doctor?"

"No. She said she was starting to feel cold and sweaty, and her speech was getting slurry. She look dizzy to you?"

"She looks high . . . but yeah, I see what you mean. My partner already called for a medical transport unit. They should be here any minute."

"And you're sending an ambulance to the address I just gave you, right?"

A pause. "Yes, sir. That's what we do in a possible shooting situation."

"I'm sorry. I know you know that, I just—"

"And where are you, sir?"

"Williamsburg. Brooklyn."

I waited as he processed that. "She's got no one up here she could call?"

"Yeah, but that's the possible shooting victim."

"Right." Another pause. "All right, Mr. Donne. The wagon's pulling up now. I'm gonna escort Miss—Marissa—to the hospital. You'll be at this number?"

"It's my cell, yeah."

"Someone'll be in touch with you."

"Can you call and let me know about the situation at the house?"

"We don't usually do that, Mr. Donne, unless you're immediate family."

"His *immediate family* was a cop who was just murdered down here in the city," I said too loudly. "Maybe you heard about Richard Torres? The vet?"

It took him a few seconds to respond. "We get the news up here. I'll see what I can do to keep you informed. No promises."

"Thanks." An idea came to me. "Can you do me another favor?"

"Make it quick, Mr. Donne."

"I know it's gonna sound a bit weird, but after you hang up, can you text me a photo of the girl?"

A pause. "Why do you—?"

"I need to make sure she is who I think she is. Trust me, it's important."

Another pause. "You ask a lot for a quarter, Mr. Donne. Next time I'm down in the city, you owe me a beer."

"Make it five. Thank you," I said. "I'm sorry for—"

"Gotta go, Mr. Donne." He hung up.

I stared at my phone, trying to figure out what else I could do from here. The answer came quickly enough: Nothing. Right after that, my phone dinged, telling me I had a text message. It was the photo of Marissa—Sheila E—who was, without a doubt, the girl on Ricky's phone. Not as pretty now that she was going into shock, of course, but it was the same young woman. I must have been staring at the screen longer than I thought, because Edgar touched my shoulder.

"Ray," he said. "You okay?"

"Yeah," I said. "I mean, no. Robby may have been shot." I turned the phone to him so he could see the picture. "That's the girl from Ricky's phone, and I have no fucking idea what's going on." I looked at Edgar and, for what felt like the hundredth time this week, tried to keep the anger out of my voice. "I am the *opposite* of okay, Edgar."

Edgar looked at the picture and scratched his ear. "So she called *you*?"

Now it was my turn to make the "Duh" face.

"Means she has no one else to call," Edgar said. "Now that Ricky's dead."

"Right." I gave that some thought. Who was this Marissa, and why didn't she have anyone else to call? Ricky had obviously told her about me, so why would she wait nearly a week after his murder before reaching out? "Edgar?"

"Yeah?"

"Feel like going for a drive?"

After deciding I was the more sober of the two of us, we filled up Edgar's gas tank, bought two extra-large coffees and a half-dozen donuts, and jumped on the Brooklyn Queens Expressway heading toward the New York State Thruway with me behind the wheel. I was driving over the speed limit with the windows rolled down, the radio playing, and the fervent hope that there would be no cops on the road. There was little traffic heading out of the city, and we were on the Major Deegan and past Yankee Stadium in about half an hour. It was still at least another two hours to New Baltimore, and then we'd have to use the GPS to find Robby's house and the most logical hospital for them to have taken Marissa. That was the closest thing I had to a plan, and I had a couple of hours to try to come up with a better one.

"First," I said out loud, "we get to Robby's house. Maybe he's okay. Marissa was confused, and I don't trust her version in the state she's in." I could hear the hope in my own voice. "I also want to find that shed and see if the guns are still there."

"And if they're not?" Edgar asked.

"I don't know. Second, we find the local hospital. There aren't many up there, so I'm sure they took Marissa to the same one they'd take Robby to, if he's injured." I turned to face Edgar. "Can you get all that info?"

He flipped open his laptop and went to work. "Already got Robby's address. Just let me . . ." At least ten seconds went by. "We got it on the map." He played with the keys a little more. "Looks like our best bet for an area hospital would be Albany Medical Center, unless they take 'em to St. Peter's."

I felt a wave of fuzziness coming on, so I shook my head to keep myself alert. "Let's get to the house first. Maybe by the time we get there, that cop will call back and let us know what's up."

"You really think he'll call back?"

"I don't know, Edgar."

Somewhere just before the Kingston exit, my cell phone rang. It was in the cup holder between Edgar and me, and I asked him to pick it up.

"Hello," he said. "Raymond Donne's phone." He listened. "No, this is his friend, Edgar O'Brien." Another pause and then he said to me, "It's the cop from the service station. You want me to put him on speaker?"

Whaddaya know. "Yeah," I said.

Edgar pressed a button and held the phone about two feet from my face.

"Officer. This is Raymond Donne. Thanks for getting back."

"I'm over here at AMC with your girl—calls herself Marissa, no last name yet—and the EMTs just brought your buddy in: Robert Torres."

AMC. Albany Medical Center. Edgar would have smiled if the news hadn't been so bad.

"How is he?" I asked.

"Don't know exactly. He *was* shot in the shoulder. Far as the EMTs could tell, it was a through-and-through." *That's two through-and-throughs in the shoulders this week.* The trooper continued, "The doc I spoke to said they were gonna operate, get him some blood, and hope he wakes up sooner rather than later. Gunshots can be tricky."

"He was unconscious?"

"He was when we found him, so I'm glad you called when you did." I heard the trooper say something to someone else, and then he said to me, "Sir, it sounds like you're on speaker phone in a car. Are you driving here, Mr. Donne?"

I chose my next words very carefully. "I'm concerned about Robby Torres, Officer. He's a friend. I want to tell his mother I saw her son in person and hopefully give her a good report."

"Whereabouts are you, Mr. Donne?"

"Let me see. Hold on." I needed to think about this and work backward. If I told him the truth, he'd expect me to be at the hospital within the hour. But if I swung by Robby's place to check on the guns first, it would take me at least another half hour to get to the hospital. I thought back to where we were thirty minutes ago and lied, "We're just about to pass through the toll booths at Harriman."

"Okay," he said, but not like he was happy about it. "When you get here, come in through the Emergency Room entrance. I'll probably still be here filling out some paperwork. I'm supposed to call Mr. Torres's family myself, but I understand under the circumstances if you'd like to do that yourself. Tough break about his brother."

"Thank you," was all I could say, my faith in people somewhat restored.

"And can you think of anyone we could call for the girl, besides you?"

"No," I said. "I don't really know her. Did you ever find her friend at the service station?"

"No, we didn't. Marissa's being treated for shock; you were right. So it may have been her imaginary friend."

"How can I find you when I get to the hospital, Officer? Who do I ask for?"

"Me," he said. "Trooper Gamble."

"Thanks, Trooper Gamble."

"No problem," he said.

When we got off at the New Baltimore Travel Plaza, it was time to hit a men's room. There was no sign inside of the excitement I had listened to almost three hours ago. Just a bunch of road-weary travelers getting their fill of crap for the road and maybe a cheesy New York State souvenir. We took care of business, bought a couple of waters, and headed back to the car.

Edgar got behind the wheel this time and handed me his laptop.

"I already put Robby's address in. You know how to work the Maps app?"

"I think so." I proceeded to find out how close to the truth that was.

After navigating for a while, I said, "Shit," then pulled my cell from the cup holder.

"What?"

"I never called Jack." I found Jack's name in my contacts and left him a quick rundown on his voicemail of what I knew, where we were, and where we hoped to be in about an hour. I knew I'd catch some shit for putting off contacting Jack about developments on his own case, and I didn't really have an excuse for taking it all on myself—with a lot of help from Edgar.

A half hour later, our blue Maps dot was nearly on top of the red push-pin. Edgar was planning to pull over just ahead, when we noticed a state trooper's car in front of Robby's house.

"Shit." I hadn't figured that into the equation. "Drive by."

We drove past the house. Edgar took the first right and pulled over.

"Whatta we do now, Ray?"

"Give me a second." I closed my eyes. When I opened them, I saw a well-lit, tree-lined block of good-size, unpretentious houses. What I didn't see was a way to get past the trooper and check out the storage shed.

"Let's go for a walk."

Chapter 28

WE TURNED THE CORNER AND WALKED about halfway down the block to where we figured Robby's house would be on the other side. There was lots of room between the houses, and I didn't see a reason I couldn't hop someone's fence and find the storage shed. There were three possibilities here: one, whoever shot Robby found the guns and took them with him; two, whoever shot Robby didn't find the guns and they were still there; or three, the responding officers found the guns, and Robby was not only in the hospital but also in deep shit. I supposed there was a chance that whoever shot Robby didn't even know about the guns, but I seriously doubted it. I was rooting for the long shot: the shooter never found the guns.

"Okay," I said to Edgar. "Here's how we're going to play this."

I spent the next minute explaining how I'd jump the fence and we'd keep in touch by cell phone. If he saw anybody coming, he'd warn me and I'd be out of there. If I saw any cops in Robby's backyard, I'd turn around and we'd split. Sounded simple enough as I was saying it, but I knew that what I *didn't* know could play a big factor in the way things turned out.

"Either way," I said, "I'm back in less than five."

"Cool," Edgar said.

We bumped fists, and I went off into some unsuspecting suburbanite's backyard. There were lights on in all the surrounding houses, but no one seemed to be outside this evening. I was grateful for that, but if I owned a home up here with a backyard and it was seventy degrees outside, I'd be all over that. But that's me.

Before hopping the four-foot-high fence, I crouched down behind some bushes and listened. My knees complained a little, but not enough to stop me. I couldn't hear any worrisome activity on the other side. Rather than hop, I rolled over the fence, went back into a crouch, and listened. Again, nothing.

I made my way over to what I took to be Robby's storage shed, and it didn't take long—even in the low light—to see that the door was closed. I approached and saw it was locked with a padlock. So if the shooter had taken the guns, he locked up after himself. *Why bother—?*

I heard a man's voice; someone coming from around the side of the house farther from me. I hid behind the shed and held my breath. The voice got louder, but I couldn't hear a second person. I turned off my phone for fear of Edgar's voice coming through too loudly. When the voice got closer, I heard him say, "Over."

Now a second voice crackled over a walkie-talkie, "Sergeant says to give it another half hour and head on back." A radio conversation between cops.

"Roger that," the backyard cop said. I couldn't see his face, but he must have been a newbie; few longtime cops still said "Over" and "Roger" on the radio. But why the hell was he back here and not out front? Did a neighbor look out a window and report someone creeping through the back-yard? The guy didn't sound like he was on high alert. But something had brought him back here. *What?*

My answer came with the unmistakable sound of urine hitting metal. The guy needed to take a leak and chose this spot to do it. That'd make for a great headline: Trespassing Teacher Nabbed by Pissing Cop. I stayed put and was relieved to hear the sound of the cop pulling up his zipper. Now I just hoped he was heading back to his car and not deciding to take a stroll around the yard.

A full minute went by, and I heard nothing else. I crept around the other side of the shed and saw no one. I turned my phone back on and called Edgar.

"What's up?" he whispered. "I thought I lost you there."

"I had a visitor," I said. "What's it like out by you?"

"If your visitor was a cop, he just came out front again. Sorry I missed that earlier. I think he's the only cop here."

"I'm on my way back to the car. Meet me there."

Five minutes later, Edgar stopped the car at the Emergency Room entrance of the hospital.

"Park in the visitor's lot," I said. "Stay there until I call you."

"You sure you don't want me to come in with you?"

"I'm hoping to get some answers in there, Edgar. But first, I'm gonna get hit by a shitload of questions. If you come in, they'll question you, too, and who knows how long that'll go on." I opened the car door. "I'll call you."

"Good luck," he said.

I thought about Robby getting shot, not knowing where the guns were, and Marissa's instability. "It is way too late for luck," I answered.

I got out of the car and entered through the automatic doors. The ER desk was right there, and I saw a state trooper with his hat under his arm, flirting with the admitting nurse. I approached the desk with my hand out.

"Trooper Gamble?" I said.

He turned and gave me the once-over. It took him a few seconds, but he caught on quickly and took my hand. "Mr. Donne?"

"Raymond," I said. "How's Robby?"

"He's out of surgery, and they got him in recovery, so I don't expect he'll be giving us any info real soon. He's listed as critical."

"And Marissa?"

"Last I heard, they've got her sedated on an IV drip. Something about her electrolytes being low, too. The doctors want her more stable before we interview her about the shooting."

I gave the impatient nurse a smile, took Gamble by the elbow, and walked a few feet away from the desk. He glanced at my hand on his arm but went with me.

"Anything else I should know?" I asked.

He gave that some thought. "Like what?"

I wanted to know about the guns, but made something up. "You get the shooter?"

"No," he said. "We're sweeping the neighborhood, but the guy's probably long gone. Like I said, we need to interview this Marissa girl."

"Anything taken?"

"From the house?"

I nodded.

"No idea," he said. "Probably have to wait for Mr. Torres to tell us that, and we've got no idea when that's gonna be."

"Right," I said. I saw nothing in the trooper's face that told me he was hiding something from me. Like, "Oh, yeah. We found a stash of automatic pistols in the storage shed." That was something, at least.

"I need you to answer a few questions *for me*, Mr. Donne," Gamble said.

"Yeah." I looked over at the row of chairs along the wall. There were about a dozen seats, half of them occupied. Two guys were sitting next to each other, both holding ice packs to their heads. Didn't look too serious. Minor car accident, I guessed. A few seats over were a mom with two small children, one of whom sounded as if he were about to cough up a lung. This ER was probably her primary care provider. In the last seat by the wall was a brunette with her head down.

"Can we sit?" I asked. "It's been a long night."

"Sure." Trooper Gamble led me over to a chair so near the brunette I worried about our conversation waking her up. "Where's your buddy? Edgar?"

"He's parking the car."

"I'd like to talk to him as well."

"He's just my ride."

"Yeah, well," Gamble said. "I'll make that call, if you don't mind."

I shrugged. "Absolutely."

He pulled out his pad and flipped it open. "I know we spoke about this over the phone, but I need you to tell me what your relationship is with Marissa and why she called you. Don't leave out anything you think may be unimportant."

It took me less than two minutes to tell him everything I was going to tell him. That's the beauty of a simple story. It's easier to remember which parts you left out—especially the ones that may land someone in jail.

"And you never met her?" Gamble said. "But you have her picture on your phone because the deceased sent it to you?"

"No. His phone got mixed up with mine at the hospital, and when I saw the photo I thought it might be important to the cops, so I took a picture of it with my phone."

"Why didn't you just give the phone to the responding officers?"

"I did," I said, and then realized the more I said, the more I sounded like I was hiding something. I could tell this guy I'd given the phone to Uncle Ray, but I didn't want to get into all that. "It was the concussion. I wasn't thinking straight."

I looked over Gamble's shoulder as a doctor came into the waiting area. I stood up, thinking it was about Robby. Instead, he crouched down in front of the mom and her kids. He took the coughing boy by the hand and led the family away. The two guys with the ice packs gave the doctor a look and he held up his hand, saying something I couldn't hear. The woman at the end never moved. Maybe she was asleep.

"All right, Mr. Donne," Gamble said. "I'm not sure what you wanna do now. Mr. Torres will probably be a guest here for a few days, and the doctors won't allow you to see him or the girl tonight." He looked at his watch. "We're going to hold off calling the family until the morning so you can call first. It's your call, but it's a bit late to be driving back to the city. There's a cheap hotel down the street. Why don't you and your buddy get some sleep?"

I rubbed my eyes. "That's a good idea."

"Maybe you can go splash some water on your face. I need you to stick around here until I speak with Edgar."

"I understand."

"Men's room is over there." He pointed in the direction of the brunette at the end of the row of seats. "Make a right down that hallway. I'll meet you back here after I talk with your buddy, Edgar."

We headed off in opposite directions. I got to the men's room, turned the water on cold, and splashed it on my face. I burped and smelled beer and coffee. I would have paid five bucks for a stick of gum at that point. I went back out in search of a vending machine.

As I passed the brunette, I thought I heard her on her cell phone. On closer inspection, she was talking to herself, and that made me hope she had someone coming to pick her up. I got to my seat, leaned back, rested my head against the wall, and closed my eyes. I was so sleepy, plus the bright lights of the waiting room were getting to me. If Edgar didn't go off on some tangent with Trooper Gamble on how New York State laws compared to those in the city, we would be at the hotel soon.

I heard some footsteps coming toward me and opened my eyes. Expecting a doctor, a nurse, or the trooper, I was wrong on all three. It was the brunette from the waiting room. Now that she was standing, I could see her expectant belly. She stopped when she reached me, covered her face with her hands, and stood above me, crying. I wasn't sure I had it in me to endure one more drama today.

"Can you help me get back home?" she asked through her hands.

Her crying was mixed with a girlish whine. When she took her hands away from her face, I could see now that she wasn't a woman. She was a teenager.

"Don't you need to talk to the nurse?" I stood and looked around for someone. "Should I get the doctor?"

"I wanna go home."

She wiped the tears from under her eyes and brushed her hair out of her face, and I got a better look. Something about her struck me as familiar. I'd seen those blue eyes before, but the dark hair threw me. I didn't think I knew her personally; it was more like I'd seen her on TV.

"I wanna go home," she said. "Can you take me home?"

Holy shit.

I had seen her picture, and those blue eyes and brunette hair were just like her mother's. And, like her mother, she was pregnant.

I was looking into a face worth fifty thousand dollars.

Chapter 29

I STOOD UP AND GENTLY PUT MY ARM around her, easing her down into a chair. She let out a grunt and placed her hands over her bulging belly.

"Angela," I said. "How did you get here?"

"How do you know my name?" she asked, her eyes on the floor.

"I know your dad. How did you get here?"

She picked her head up. "My dad?" she whined again, her voice full of self-pity and fear. "Did he send you here? How did he know where I was?"

"Marissa called me. I'm a friend of Ricky's."

"Oh, yeah. I heard you tell the police guy that." She looked at me through bloodshot eyes. "Ricky's dead."

"I know. They've got Marissa in a room. Let me get you a doctor."

With a quickness that stunned me, she grabbed my wrist. "No. I'm okay. I don't need a doctor. I wanna get Marissa and go home."

"Marissa's not going anywhere until the morning. And before that, she's got a lot of explaining to do." I sat down. "How did you get here?"

"I was in the car," she said. "Waiting for Marissa to come out of the food court thingy." She got silent as the events of the past few hours came back to her. "When the cops and the ambulance came, I thought Marissa was being arrested. When they took her away, I followed them, but they brought her here."

"You followed an ambulance on the highway and made it here okay?"

I thought about how fast she must have been going. "You're only sixteen years old."

She shrugged. "I drive all the time on the Island. My boyfriend takes me over to Jones Beach at night and we just drive around."

I shook my head and looked at her stomach. "Your boyfriend the one who got you pregnant? Isn't he worried about you?"

"No, and he's not my boyfriend anymore." She dropped her head again. "I date older men now."

"And one of them got you pregnant?"

She rubbed her belly. "That's about it, mister . . . what's your name again? Mr. Bun?"

"Donne. I really think you need to have a doctor check you out. At least to make sure the baby's okay."

"They'll call my parents, and then I'll be in real trouble."

As opposed to now.

"Didn't you just ask me to get you home, Angela?"

She shook her head. "Not *home,* home." I waited for her to explain. "Back to the city. To the baby's father. He'll know what to do. He always does."

I looked at the pregnant teenager. "Yeah. I can tell." I stood again. "Listen, there's a state cop out there who's going to want to talk to you about what happened at Robby's tonight."

"No cops."

"You don't really have much of a choice here, Angela. You witnessed a shooting. And for all we know, the shooter's out looking for you and Marissa."

"I didn't witness shit," she said. "We heard a shot and then got the hell out of there, mister."

"You didn't see the guy who came to the door?"

"Nope. Robby told us to hide in the garage."

I was about to tell her I knew that when my cell phone rang. I looked at the caller ID: Jack Knight.

"Hey, Jack."

"The fuck, Ray?" Jack using his dick voice. "What the hell are you do-ing, and why are you doing it without me?"

"Easy, Jack," I said. "Marissa called *me*. She's the girl from Ricky's phone. I made a game-time decision to come up here and called you as soon as I thought of it."

"That shoulda been your *first* thought, Ray. I coulda been there already. Right now I'm stuck on the GWB." He stopped thinking about himself long enough to ask, "How's Robby?"

"Not sure." I looked at Angela Golden. "There's been a new development."

"Explain."

"I'm here at the Albany Medical Center. With Angela Golden."

I could practically hear Jack's face turning red. After about ten seconds, he spoke.

"I knew it!" he yelled. "You *were* going around behind my back—you and your fucking Edgar and Robby, too—looking for her so you could squeeze me out of the reward money."

"Jack," I said. "You're right. I should have called, but—"

"Don't fucking 'Jack' me, Ray. I thought I could trust you."

"Jack," I tried again, "think about it. If I were going behind your back, why would I have called you? I came up here to check on Robby and Marissa."

"And Angela Golden just came up to you and said hi?"

I laughed. "That's exactly what happened." I waited for another outburst. When none came, I said, "And there's more."

"What? You found Amelia Earhart and Jimmy Hoffa, too?"

"She's pregnant."

"Angela Golden?" He took a moment to let that sink in. I wondered if he'd find a way to blame me for that, too. "Angela Fucking Golden is pregnant?"

"I'm trying to get her to see a doctor, but she's scared. And there's a state trooper outside who's gonna be *inside* real quick."

Jack got quiet again as he considered this information. He wasn't going to admit it, but I knew he was thinking about losing the fifty-thousand-dollar reward.

"There a back exit where you are?"

"I don't know, Jack. It's my first time at this hospital."

"Look around," he said. "You're in the ER, right? There's gotta be another entrance or exit you and the girl can leave through."

I did as he said and saw a red EXIT sign at the end of the hallway I'd used to get to the men's room.

"I see it."

"Good. Head out that way, and find a place to hang until I get there."

"What about the state trooper?"

"What about him?" Jack said. "You gave him a statement, right? He gets a look at the Golden girl and we're screwed." *There it was.* "You know what I mean. Our client likes to keep things on the down low. He's gonna freak when he hears the latest, but I want him to hear it from us. The girl's okay, right?"

"I don't know, Jack. I'm not a doctor."

"She bleeding? Screaming out in pain?"

"No."

"Then she's okay enough. Get her away from there and wait for me. I'm still a few hours out, depending on traffic." I heard him lay on his horn. "When I get there, if I think she needs medical care, we'll take her back to the hospital."

"So you get credit for finding her?"

"Yeah, Ray. I've been looking for her for almost a month now. I think I deserve a little something for my efforts, don't you?"

"I'm not saying you don't, Jack."

"Okay." He was silent for a bit. "According to my GPS, there's a hotel right down the block from the hospital."

"I heard."

"Take her there and wait."

"You gonna call Charles Golden?"

"Soon as I get there and eyeball his daughter myself. This guy's all about crossing the t's and dotting the i's. You know that, right, now that you guys are such buddies? I'm not calling him until Angela is in my po—my presence, and I got my eyes on her."

"Okay."

"Glad you approve." He had the dick voice going now. "Call me when you get to the hotel."

Before I could say anything else, he hung up. I looked over at Angela Golden, who was about to doze off. This was a bad time for a nap. I sat down, put my hand on her arm, and she reacted as if I'd stuck her with a cattle prod.

"Fuck!" she said, pulling her arm away. "That my dad on the phone?"

"No," I said. "It was the guy your dad hired to find you. The guy I work for. Your family's been going nuts, Angela."

"Yeah," she said, and for the first time I saw something resembling a smile cross her face. "Daddy gets like that when he's not in control."

"I got that feeling." I stood. "I need you to get up and walk out the back door with me. We're going down the block and into a hotel. Then—"

"I ain't going anywhere with you, Mr. Bun—Dun; whatever that cop said. Especially a hotel."

"Hey," I said, my fatigue and frustration coming through loud and clear. "That works fine for me. I can just leave you here and you can explain everything to the state trooper, who's about to come back. Or I could drive you back over to Robby's house; maybe that nice guy with the gun will come back."

She looked up at me, trying to figure out whether I was bluffing. I'm sure I was too tired to show much of anything on my face.

"Angela, you need to go back to your parents. You're pregnant and alone. Marissa is upstairs, and your boyfriend isn't coming for you, is he? You could take Robby's car and drive back to him. But he doesn't really want you, does he? Otherwise, you wouldn't have run off with Marissa. It's over, Angela. You need to come with me. Now."

She waited a few beats, mulling it over. Finally she decided to get up. Slowly. I couldn't decide if her pregnancy or her passive aggression slowed her down more. She let me know she'd do what I said, but she wasn't happy about it. *Just as long as she came with me.*

I reached for her elbow, and she quickstepped away. "Don't touch me. I can walk out a door by myself."

I held my hand out like a game show host and pointed it at the EXIT sign.

We walked past the nurse's station. The nurse whose flirtations I'd interrupted with Trooper Gamble was working on her computer, a phone cradled in her neck, and she never looked up. I'm not too sure what she would have said anyway. As far as I knew, walking out of an emergency room was no crime. Angela pushed her way through some swinging doors and followed the other EXIT sign that had an arrow pointing to the left. I could see the exit door from where we were and hoped it led out to the same area where Edgar had parked.

"Let me go out first," I said.

"Whatever." She stepped aside and stood with her back against the wall.

The doors opened automatically and I stepped out, looking to my left and my right. I couldn't see Trooper Gamble, so I waved Angela outside. She removed herself from the wall like it was the biggest chore anyone had asked her to do in months. Pregnant teens must be a dream to live with.

We walked together toward the parking lot, and I heard a horn beep to my right. I looked over and saw Edgar wave to me through his window. Even in this light, I could see Edgar was confused that I was with someone. I picked up my pace and was glad when Angela did the same.

Edgar was about to say something, so I stopped him with my hand. "I'll explain at the hotel."

Edgar looked at Angela as I held the rear door open for her. When she got in Edgar said, "Hi," but she didn't answer.

When I got in the passenger seat, I had a brief moment of clarity. I could end this all right now: go find Gamble, call Charles Golden myself, and explain to Jack and Robby and Marissa that I didn't want to be any part of this anymore. Uncle Ray was right: this was a job for the cops. I was a schoolteacher now and had pregnant teens in the projects of Williamsburg I could help the other ten months out of the year. This was my last week of vacation, and I really needed the time to decompress, not to invite more danger into my life.

Instead, I kept facing forward and said, "Drive."

We got to the hotel in less than a minute. As we pulled into the parking lot, I had an idea. If this were the hotel Gamble and Jack recommended, it would also be the first one Gamble checked if he decided to look for me. I told Edgar to turn around and head back the way we'd come.

"Make a left after the hospital," I said. "I wanna put a little distance between us and our last location."

"Why?"

I looked into the backseat, and Angela looked to be dozing again. I motioned with my thumb. "That's Angela Golden, Edgar. The girl—one of the girls—Jack and I have been looking for."

Edgar blew some air out of his mouth. "The one worth fifty G's?"

"Among other things."

"I thought she was blonde."

"Daddy makes me dye it," Angela said from the backseat. "Makes me look more like mom."

We were about a mile past the hospital when I spotted a motel. "This'll do."

Edgar pulled in and I gave him explicit instructions to stay in the car while I checked in. He didn't argue. I got us a double room, toward the back of the motel and away from any street traffic. Once we parked in front of the room, Angela flew out of the car and threw up.

I gave Edgar the room key and went over to where Angela stood, bent over. I put my hand on her back—she didn't shrug me off this time—and waited until she was finished vomiting before speaking.

"If you wanna go back to the hospital, just say the word."

"No." She stood and wiped her mouth with her sleeve. "I'm good. Been doing that for a while now. I don't know why they call it '*morning* sickness.' It should be called 'every-fucking-hour-of-the-day sickness.'"

I gave her a smile she didn't see and patted her back. "Let's go inside."

I knocked on the door. From the other side, Edgar said, "Who is it?"

"The Governor. Open the door, Edgar."

I heard a lock slide and the chain being removed before he let us in. Edgar was a careful guy. Angela headed straight for the bathroom, and Edgar was finally able to give me the what-the-fuck look he had been holding in. I gave him all the details, including my call to Jack. Which reminded me . . .

"Good thinking," Jack said when I explained the reason for the change in lodging. "I'm cruising now, less than an hour out if I don't get pulled over. Any problems?"

"Angela's puking all over the place, but other than that, no."

"No phone calls," he said, ignoring me. "Keep the shades pulled, and don't go out or open the door until I get there."

"Looking forward to it."

After I hung up, Edgar asked, "He pissed?"

"He's . . . excited," I said. "I think it's finally sinking in that this wasn't part of some plan to screw him out of the reward money."

"He thought you—"

"Jack doesn't always think before he speaks, Edgar. He was surprised by the new developments and immediately went into defensive mode. By the time he gets here, he'll be fine."

"I hope so. I don't want him thinking I—"

"It doesn't matter what he thinks. And with the way the events played out, you're getting a third of the reward money."

He took his glasses off, rubbed the lenses with the tail of his shirt, and slipped the glasses back on. "Is that a good idea?" he asked. "I mean, with Jack? He's not gonna be—?"

"I wouldn't have gotten up here without your tech smarts, and if you hadn't been in the parking lot with your car, I wouldn't have been able to get Angela away from the hospital so quickly."

As if on cue, we heard Angela retching behind the bathroom door. This was followed by the toilet flushing and the shower being turned on. She was going to be busy for a while.

"As long as Jack doesn't have a problem with it," Edgar said.

"He won't. If he does, I'll remind him I have Golden's number on my cell, and I could always reach out to him tonight. I'm not completely comfortable with this arrangement as it is. There're about ten different ways this can go south, and one phone call to Golden makes them all go away."

Edgar considered that. Without speaking, he went over to the remote control near the bed and turned on the TV. He found the Yankees game, sat down on the edge of the bed, folded his arms, and watched silently.

This is what he did when he was stressed and didn't want to talk for a while. That would work for me.

I went over to the other bed and lay down. My knees were hanging over the side of the bed, providing me with a fairly decent back stretch. With my eyes closed, I could hear sleep calling. But with Jack expected soon, I stood up and fought to wake up. I did some real stretches now, trying to get the blood flowing.

I walked to the window and sneaked a peek through the curtain. The parking lot was empty, except for Edgar's car, and not very well lit. It felt like we were in the first days of the Witness Protection Program. I closed the curtain, sat in a chair, and grabbed a magazine off the table called *Your Guide to the Capital Region*. I flipped through the pages and looked at ads for restaurants, family fun centers, horse camps, and all the other family-fun activities you find upstate. I put the magazine down and wished for Jack to hurry up. The sooner he got here, the sooner I could end my involvement in this case and get back to my life. I realized I hadn't spoken to Allison in a while.

She picked up after two rings. "Let me guess. You're at The LineUp and want me to swing by?"

"Am I really that predictable?"

"Yes, Ray. But you're cute, so I put up with it. I don't think I can make it tonight." She yawned for effect. "I'm bushed and got an early morning tomorrow."

Not as early as mine.

"Listen," I said. "A lot's happened in the past couple of hours."

"Define 'a lot.'"

"I can't right now."

"Can't or won't?"

I heard the shower stop and a low moan coming from the bathroom.

"What was that noise?" Allison asked.

Shit. "I got the TV on. I have to go, Ally. I'll call you in the morning." I hung up, went to the bathroom door, and said, "You okay?"

I waited a few seconds before Angela stepped out of the bathroom wearing nothing but a towel. She pretended it slipped, then pulled it back up, just above her nipples.

"Golden," she giggled. "I'm the goddamned Golden girl."

She'd be fine for now. I thought about the way I had ended my call with Allison. I decided it was better to get in trouble for hanging up on my girlfriend than for giving her too much information.

I went over to Edgar and pulled him away from the spell of the television and toward the front door.

"What?" he said, as if I had awakened him from a dream.

"We need to get some air," I said. Then to Angela, "Put some clothes on. Pull shit like that again, I'll toss you in the trunk and haul you down to the Island."

"Oooh," she said. "I love when older men talk tough."

I opened the door and pushed Edgar out before I said anything else. We took a few steps away from the door and moved into the parking lot.

"Didn't Jack say not to leave the room?" he asked.

"Yes, he did. But that was before a sixteen-year-old girl came out of the bathroom half-naked in front of two grown men."

Edgar had no idea what I was talking about but pretended he did. "Right . . . . So what do we do now, Ray?"

"We wait out here until Jack comes." I pulled out my cell and checked the time. "Shouldn't be too long."

We both glanced up as a half dozen moths danced around the light in front of the room. "What if someone sees us out here?"

"Good point." I looked over at Edgar's car parked in the dark. "You got your keys on you?"

He took them out of his pocket and jingled them. "Yep."

"Let's go wait in the car. Anybody comes who's not Jack, we'll see him first. Angela tries to leave, we've got the front door covered."

"What if she goes out the bathroom window?"

I smirked. "That's in the movies, Edgar. A shih tzu would have trouble getting through a motel's bathroom window."

Edgar nodded and then giggled. "Shih tzu," he repeated.

"Gimme the keys."

•   •   •

We were in the car for less than ten minutes when Jack pulled into the lot. I got out and Edgar followed. Jack startled when he saw us and made a move toward his belt. Edgar and I raised our hands.

"What the fuck, Ray?" Jack said. "I told you to stay with the girl. *Inside*."

"I know what you told me." I did my best to keep my tone even. I took some bills out of my pocket and handed them to Edgar. "Hit the vending machine, okay? Sports drink if they got it and something with carbs. Angela's gotta be thirsty and hungry." Edgar took off, and I turned my attention back to Jack. "I'm not too keen on being inside a motel room with an underage female who thinks life is clothing-optional."

Jack took in the parking lot. "You see anything out of the ordinary? Anybody call the room?"

"Not while we were in there. We've been out here for ten minutes."

"Okay. That was a good idea about the vending machine. The better Angela looks when Golden gets here, the better for us." He took a deep breath. "Lemme see the girl."

Edgar came back with something blue in a bottle and two bags of pretzels. The three of us walked over to the door of the room. When we got there, I realized I didn't have the key.

"Edgar," I said, holding out my hand.

He looked at my hand. "Yeah?"

We stood like that for a five count before Jack spoke.

"Neither one of you thought to take the key? Fuckin' A, boys." He turned back to the door, separated his middle knuckle from its brothers and rapped lightly. "Angela," he stage whispered. "Open up."

"Who is it?" she teased from the other side.

"Angela," Jack said, louder this time. "I need you to open the door."

He barely finished his sentence when the door swung open and there was very-pregnant Angela, wearing nothing but a shit-eating grin and her underwear. I gave Jack a see-what-I-mean? look, and he shut the door most of the way, careful to keep his foot between the door and the jamb.

"You gotta get some clothes on, darling," he said. "Soon as you do that, we can talk about getting you home."

"My daddy send you?"

"Yes. Now, get dressed so we can come in."

I think I heard her say, "That's no fun," but a minute later, she opened the door again and was wearing her T-shirt and jeans again. "Come on in."

We did.

Angela took a seat on the bed closest to the door. Edgar put the drink and pretzels on the side table and plopped himself down in front of the TV, as Jack and I pulled two chairs over to Angela.

Jack leaned forward. "Are you in any physical pain?" he asked the girl.

"Besides blowing chunks every half hour? No, I'm great." She looked over at the snacks and practically inhaled them, but passed on the drink. "And unless you want me puking blue, I ain't touching that shit."

Jack nodded. "Tell me what happened at Robby's."

She gave him basically the same story I was able to piece together from what she, Marissa, and Trooper Gamble had told me. She stopped at the part where she reached the emergency room in Robby's car. Jack took the whole thing in and gave a small impressed nod. He turned to me.

"And you're sure no one followed you here?"

"I think we'd know already if they had, Jack. We've been here for a little less than an hour, and you're our first visitor."

Again, Jack nodded and glanced at Edgar. "How much does he know?"

"Everything you and I do," I said. "And before you say shit, he splits the reward with us. He's the reason we're all in this room." I'd pay Tio out of my share.

It was clear Jack didn't want to hear that, but it looked as if he'd decided to fight that battle later. I was clear there'd be no battle. Jack reached into his jacket and pulled out his phone.

"I'm going to call your dad now, Angela. I'm going to let him know everything's okay"—he looked at her stomach—"mostly. I'm also going to tell him where we are, and he'll let me know what he wants to do."

"What does that mean?" she asked. "What *he* wants to do?"

Jack stood up and went to the window. He pulled aside the curtain and looked outside before speaking again.

"Your father," he began, "has paid me good money to look for you and is going to pay even better money for your safe return. Now that I've— that you've been found, it's up to him what we do next."

"I don't get a say in this?"

Jack laughed. "I think you've had your say, little lady. You disappear for almost a month and show up pregnant? It's time for the grown-ups to take charge."

Angela scooted back so she was sitting up against the headboard of the bed. She looked at the three grown-ups in the room and smiled.

"It was a *grown-up* who got me pregnant, mister." She rubbed her belly. "What's your name anyway?"

"Jack. Jack Knight."

"Oooh. Like a knight in shining armor coming to my rescue?"

"Something like that, yeah." Jack turned around again and worked his phone. Less than a half minute later, he said, "Mr. Golden. Jack Knight." There was a brief pause as Jack listened. "Yes, sir. I would not be calling you at this hour if I didn't have a good reason." Another pause. "I'm with Angela, sir." I could hear Golden's voice from here. "Outside Albany, and she appears to be in good shape." Jack's brow wrinkled at the next thing Golden said. "I can do that, yes." He turned back and held the phone out to Angela. "Your dad wants talk to you."

She folded her arms. "I'll talk to him when I see him," she said.

Jack's face turned red, and he put his hand over the mouthpiece of the phone. Through gritted teeth, he said, "Your father wants to talk to you. Now."

Angela gave Jack a fuck-you look and closed her eyes. Jack's face lost its color as he tried to figure out how to explain this. He took a deep breath and said, "She's refusing to take the phone, sir." *Good for Jack*, I thought. *The truth.*

"Yes," Jack said and pressed the touch screen. "You're on speaker, Mr. Golden."

"Angela," Golden said. "I want you to take the phone from Mr. Knight and talk to me." His voice had that eerie calmness I've heard from many parents right before they explode. "Now, sweetheart."

Angela opened her eyes, stared at Jack, and stuck out her tongue. She followed that up with a one-finger salute. Nice kid, this Angela Golden. Maybe the dad would pay us another fifty thousand *not* to bring her home.

"Sir?" Jack said after another few seconds.

"You have Skype on your phone, Jack?" Mr. Golden wanted to know. "Face Time or any video conference app?"

Jack looked at Edgar, who quickly grabbed Jack's phone, then nodded yes when he found what he was looking for.

"Yes, sir," answered Jack.

"Put it on, and let me see my daughter. Please."

Edgar silently took back Jack's phone, worked the screen for a minute, and then handed it back to Jack. When Jack still looked confused, Edgar slowly pointed to the screen with his index finger, like a mime performing for the balcony seats. Finally Jack understood, aimed the phone's camera at Angela, and pressed the button Edgar had instructed him to.

Angela immediately covered her face with her hands, prompting Jack to counter a few steps around the bed for a good shot of her stomach. Angela drew up her knees under the covers, hiding her belly, and Jack seemed on the verge of blowing steam out of his ears.

"Thank you, Jack," Golden said with a sigh.

Jack stopped the transmission with the touch of a button.

"Who else is there with you?" Golden continued. "Besides my daughter, of course."

"Raymond Donne, sir. And his . . . colleague, Edgar."

"Edgar?" Golden said, clearly agitated with this information. "Who the hell's Edgar?"

I said, "He's how I got up to Albany and was very instrumental in helping me get your daughter away from the hospital, where I personally think she should still be."

"You invite anyone else along, Raymond?" He was growing increasingly annoyed and taking it out on us. He didn't even ask why his daughter was at the hospital. "Your girlfriend perhaps?"

I stepped closer to the phone. Jack pulled it back and gave me a look to remind me who was paying the bills here. "Be nice," he mouthed.

"No, sir," I said calmly. "But I can call her if you want. This story has all the earmarks of a real career-maker, don't you think?"

"There is *no* story, you son of a bitch. Not until I say so."

"Then," I said, "I suggest you make up your mind quickly about what to do, Mr. Golden. And, with all due respect, sir, a little courtesy would be nice."

"I'm not paying you to give me—" He stopped himself. *Smart man.* "Jack," he said. "Take me off speaker."

Jack did as he was told. "Yes, sir?" He spent the next three minutes listening. When Golden was finished, Jack said, "We'll see you then, Mr. Golden. Room 117 in the back." He put the phone on the table. "Get comfortable, Ray. Golden's on his way north. And he's not too happy with you."

"The feeling's mutual," I said. "So we're supposed to wait for him to get here? How long's that gonna be?"

Jack looked at the digital clock between the beds. I did the same. Almost three thirty in the morning.

"By six thirty," Jack said. "And don't feel obligated to stick around, Ray. You and Einstein over there can go home anytime you want."

I looked over at Edgar, who seemed perfectly happy watching the Yankee rerun. Angela Golden had drifted off in a sitting position; her breathing was getting heavy. I sat in my chair and closed my eyes.

"That's okay, Jack," I said. "I'll wait."

"Whoop-de-fuckin-do," Jack said just before he dragged his chair in front of the door and collapsed into it.

Chapter 30

A COUPLE OF HOURS LATER I was shaken out of a half dream by the buzzing of Jack's phone. All Jack said was, "Yes, sir," and he sprang from the chair and moved it away from the door. He looked through the peephole and opened the door. In walked Charles Golden, wearing a gray suit and blue tie as if this were just another workday. He wasn't alone. Behind Golden stood Joseph, the security guy who worked for Tony Blake. He, too, was dressed for business, but he was wearing sunglasses, which he did not remove when he entered the room.

Jack gave Joseph a look as he shook Golden's hand. Edgar turned off the TV while Golden and Jack both looked over at Angela, who was still sleeping.

"She's been out for hours," Jack explained. "Not a peep out of her."

Golden took in the room. "Yes," he said, something resembling a smile crossing his face. "She's always been a good sleeper." He turned to Blake's guy. "This is Joseph. Joseph, these are Mr. Knight and Mr. Donne."

"We've met," I said. "At the benefit the other night."

Joseph just nodded. Then he turned, looked outside to the parking lot, and shut the door. He stayed in front of it.

"That," Golden said, pointing at Edgar, "is your friend?"

"Hello," Edgar said with the body language of someone who was trying to melt into his chair.

"Yes. Edgar was very help—"

Golden shut me up with a raise of his hand. "I don't care about that, Mr. Donne. If you're worried about the reward money"—he looked at Jack—"I'll round it up to sixty thousand, and the three of you can split that. Fair enough?"

"I'm not worried about the reward money," I said. Jack, on the other hand, looked extremely worried about the reward money. "But, yes, that is fair, Mr. Golden."

"Good." He walked over to the bed and looked down at his daughter. This time, I noticed, he had the look of a father relieved his child was safe. He reached over and gently shook her shoulder. "Angela," he said, just above a whisper. "Angel?"

Angela stirred and let out that low moan kids do when awakened against their will. She rubbed her eyes, and it took her a while to bring them into focus.

"Good morning, Daddy," she said. Just another day in the life of the Golden Family. "Is mom here?"

"No, Angel. It's just me." He sat down next to her. "How are you feeling?"

"Tired." She rubbed her belly. "I'm pregnant."

Golden didn't flinch. "Yes, Angel."

He knew, I thought. All this time she was missing he knew she was pregnant. *Why the hell didn't he—*

As if reading my mind, he said to the room, "My daughter's . . . condition does not get discussed outside of this room. This is a family matter, and it will be handled with the utmost discretion." He looked at Jack, Edgar, and me. "Is that absolutely clear, gentlemen?"

We all said, "Yes."

Golden got off the bed. "Okay," he said. "Here's how this is going to work: Joseph and I will drive Angela down to the city."

"You're not taking her home to Long Island?" I asked.

Golden shot me a look. So did Jack. I was to remain quiet.

"I have a place where I put clients up on occasion. Clients who need to be, let's say, out of the limelight for a few days. I can have a doctor meet us. I believe you've been there, Mr. Donne. Rather recently, in fact."

"I don't know what you're talking about," I said. Jack looked at me as if he believed I did know what Golden was talking about, and he was none too pleased.

"The condo on Kent, Mr. Donne. Where your friend Ricky was interested in purchasing an apartment."

Maybe this guy did know everything.

"That's where you're taking Angela?" Jack asked. "Williamsburg?"

"For a few days, until we can settle this situation." Golden looked around the room. "Angela, do you have anything you need to bring with you?"

She scooted herself up into a full sitting position. "No. It's all at the house."

"The house?" Golden looked to me, and then Jack.

"Robby Torres's house," I explained. "Ricky's brother. That's where she and the other girl, Marissa, were last night. When he was shot—"

Again, Golden waved his hand. "I know about that." He turned to Jack. "What was Robby Torres's role in my daughter's disappearance, Jack?"

"I'm not sure if he had a role in it, sir, other than Marissa asking him to let them hide—stay there." Jack was uncomfortable saying those words to the man who'd been paying him good money to know these things. "Ray and I are heading over to the hospital today to see if we could interview Robby," he said.

We were?

Golden nodded approvingly. "Excellent idea. I want you to interview this other girl, too. Marissa? Find out what she knows, and make sure she understands the consequences of talking to the wrong people."

"What 'consequences' are those, Mr. Golden?" I asked. "That sounds like a threat."

"That came out wrong. I'm tired." Golden smiled. "I mean the girl needs to understand the value of silence. In fact," he turned to Joseph, "maybe we can persuade her to ride down to the city with us. She's from Williamsburg, after all."

Joseph nodded. Edgar glanced at me for a reading of the situation. I ignored him, careful to maintain my poker face.

"She's in the hospital, too," I reminded Golden. "I spoke to her last night by phone, and I wouldn't describe her as a very cooperative person."

"When she hears what I have to offer," Golden said, "I'm sure she'll be very cooperative. Okay." He clapped his hands together, more like a kindergarten teacher than a public relations giant. "We need to get Angela's belongings from Mr. Torres's house. I don't—we don't want anything left there that could connect my daughter to last night's accident."

"Shooting," I corrected him. This guy's spin could make you dizzy.

"Of course. Joseph, you and I will take Angela to Mr. Torres's house to retrieve her things. Mr. Knight and Mr. Donne, I'd like you to go over to the hospital and see if Mr. Torres is in any condition to provide us with any worthwhile information. Then we'll meet you at the hospital to get a report before we head back to the condo in Brooklyn, possibly with Marissa."

"Yes, sir," Jack said, as if visiting Robby had been Golden's idea instead of his. "How do you plan to get into the house?"

Golden exchanged a quick glance with his security guy, Joseph. "We'll find a way. Assuming the police have concluded their investigation."

"Yes, sir." Jack said. "Let's go, Ray. Edgar."

Jack opened the door, and Edgar was the first one out. Jack followed and I was behind him. Something was tugging at the back of my brain—my cop brain—telling me something wasn't quite adding up. I tried to push the tickle forward to my consciousness, but it wouldn't come, so I decided to scratch this itch later.

Before going out, I turned to Charles Golden. "You're welcome," I said.

He gave me a confused look before catching on. "Yes," he said. "I'm glad you found my daughter before this got out of hand."

"Me, too."

I noticed he still never said thank you.

We got to the hospital in less than five minutes. Last night's desk nurse had been replaced, and the benches in the waiting area of the emergency room held only two people: a young couple holding hands and whispering to each other.

Jack approached the woman behind the desk and asked about Robby's status. After telling her that he was Robby's cousin, the nurse clicked a few keys on the computer and moved her lips as she read the info to herself.

"He is awake," she informed us. "Let me page the doctor and see if he's allowed to have visitors." She looked back at the screen. "He's supposed to be transferred to the patient care unit as soon as a room becomes available."

"That's good news," Jack said.

"Yes." She picked up her phone and paged the doctor. "You might want to have a seat," she said, pointing toward the chairs. "I have no idea how long it will take Dr. Price to complete her rounds."

I could tell that didn't sit well with Jack, but he smiled, said "Thanks," and the three of us took seats in the waiting area.

"Should I ask about Marissa?" Jack asked me.

"You gonna tell the nurse she's your cousin, too?" Jack grimaced. "Let's just wait on Dr. Price and see what happens. Maybe Golden can spin a little magic and find out what's up with Marissa."

"If anyone can, he can," Jack said. "You notice how he didn't even flinch when he found out baby girl was preggers? The guy's chill, man."

"Information is Golden's currency, Jack. I got a strong feeling he knew Angela was pregnant all along and has been working on some strategy to protect the family image."

Jack snorted. "It's the twenty-first century, Ray. Teenagers get pregnant all the time." He looked over at the couple sitting a few seats away and whispered, "I bet that's why Romeo and Juliet are here."

"*She's* not the daughter of the King of PR, Jack. What're people going to think if Charles Golden can't even keep his own kid's reputation clean?"

Jack's face told me he knew I had a good point, but he wasn't going to admit it out loud.

"Anyway," he said, "we are officially out of it. We got his daughter back. True, the reward money is five grand less than we expected, thanks to your expansion of the firm," he said, shooting a look at Edgar, "but I'm back to building inspections and interviewing wits the day after tomorrow."

"I'm glad it all worked out for you, Jack," I snorted.

"Come off your high horse, Ray. A week ago you were twenty thousand dollars poorer than you are today. Boo freakin' hoo."

"And Ricky was still alive."

That shut him up. I leaned back and closed my eyes. Allison and I could go anywhere with that kind of cash and spend some much-needed time alone. That thought reminded me I needed to call her. I stood and removed my cell from my pocket. Just then a doctor appeared before us.

Dr. Price looked to be about my age, very blonde, very pretty, and very tired. She held a clipboard against her chest and said, "Mr. Knight?"

Jack jumped up. "That's me, Doc. How's my cuz?"

"Stable," she said, taking in Edgar and me. "Are you aware of the circumstances behind his injury?"

"I know he was shot, if that's what you mean."

"Yes." She looked at the clipboard again and gave it a puzzled look. "I've never seen this before, but when your . . . cousin was brought in last night, his shoulder wound had already been treated."

Now it was my turn to speak. "Excuse me?"

"The admitting physician reported that when he removed the victim's shirt, there was already a dressing on the wound. A rather primitive one, but someone did their best to stabilize Mr. Torres before the EMTs arrived at the scene."

Jack and I exchanged looks. Edgar stood. I'd almost forgotten he was there.

"Does it say there," Edgar pointed at the doctor's clipboard, "how the EMTs were notified there was a shooting?"

Dr. Price looked down at her papers again. "Someone called nine-one-one and reported that someone had been shot."

I saw where Edgar was going with this and jumped in. "Not that there was a gunshot, but that *someone* had been shot?"

"That's how I read this, yes."

Now Jack caught on. "The fucking shooter called nine-one-one." He walked around to let that thought breathe. "The guy shoots Robby—he's got to know the neighbors heard it—but he gets ahead of it and calls it in himself. He figures he's got two or three minutes before the cops and EMTs respond, and just enough time to stabilize Robby. Why?"

"He didn't want him dead," Edgar said.

I looked at Edgar, impressed. I patted him on his upper arm. "Nicely done, man." I turned back to the doctor. "Can we see Robby now?"

"One of you can," she said, and looked at Jack. "Maybe his cousin." She didn't believe that for a minute.

"We're his friends," I admitted. "We came up last night as soon as we heard. I believe his family was to be notified this morning."

Dr. Price smiled. Behind those tired eyes was a spark that told me she could be my ER doc anytime.

"That's very admirable of you," she said. "But it's against hospital policy to allow non-family members to visit a patient in the ICU without family consent."

The three of us considered that. Jack spoke first.

"But he can talk?"

"Oh, yes. He's already asked for coffee and some breakfast."

Jack reached into his pocket, pulled out his cell, and handed it to the doctor.

"Is it against hospital policy to allow ICU patients a phone call?" he asked.

Dr. Price smiled again. "None that I'm aware of. He has your number?"

"Go to my contacts and press 'Ray.'"

"I'll get it to him right away," she said, and went off. As she turned the corner, Jack said, "She can make me turn my head and cough anytime."

"I think you need a different kind of doctor, Jack."

"Yeah, Ray, 'cause you're so normal."

I didn't feel normal. I could tell Jack about my visits with Muscles and Ricky T's therapist and how they got me thinking of my own version of PTSD. Then I thought better of it. If I were going to start talking about my own emotional issues, the first person on the list was not going to be Jack Knight.

My phone rang.

"Robby," I said. "How are you?"

"You're in the lobby, Ray?" Robby croaked.

"Yeah. With Jack and another friend. What happened last night?"

Silence. Then, "Best I can remember, the doorbell rang, I told the girls—You know about the girls showing up?"

"Yeah."

"I told them to go to the garage, and I went to see who it was."

"Who was it?"

"Never saw him before. And I didn't get a good look at him. I was too busy staring at the gun he was pointing in my face."

Right. "He say what he wanted?"

More silence, followed by a deep breath. "I assumed the guns. I think he said something like, 'Where are they?'"

"*They?*" I repeated. Jack tried to take the phone from me but I took a step back. "What did he mean by 'they'?"

"I told him they were in the shed, and he made me go back there with him." He was quiet for a few seconds, and I heard him swallow loudly. "You think maybe he meant the girls?"

"I don't know, Robby. But why did he shoot you? I went to the shed last night and it was locked. Did he get the guns?"

"I don't know." He stopped for a few seconds. "I was scared, Ray. When we got to the back, I pulled my gun on him."

"You did what?" I said, loud enough to bring Jack over to me. "What gun did you pull, Robby?"

"Ricky gave me one when I decided to stay upstate. He said he was worried about me living up in redneck land."

I was trying to process this, but I was real tired. "The cops never found a gun, Robby. Was it registered?"

"Yeah. Ricky insisted on that." He paused. "So the cops didn't find it?"

"No," I said. "Whoever shot you must have taken it." Then I told him the shooter apparently treated his wound.

More silence. "So, he didn't want the cops to know I had a gun, and he obviously didn't want me dead. Nice guy."

Robby started coughing. He may have been feeling a lot better, but getting shot is getting shot, and that takes a lot out of a person. I figured he had told me all he was going to, so I turned back to Jack. "He sounds pretty weak," I said.

Jack put his hand out. "Gimme the phone."

I did, and Jack walked away to talk to Robby in private. Edgar came over to me and did a big roll of his hips into a back stretch.

"I'm ready to hit the road, Ray," he said. "Shit! I gotta call in to work."

Now he walked away, and I was left standing in the waiting area alone when the front doors opened and in walked Charles Golden, his daughter, and Blake's guy, Joseph. Golden stepped over to me as Joseph led Angela over to a chair.

"What did you find out from Mr. Torres?" Golden asked.

I gave him a quick recap. He didn't appreciate the lack of information.

"I need to speak with him," he said.

"Where's Marissa?" Angela asked. No one answered.

"That's not going to happen, Mr. Golden. We were lucky enough to have the doctor take a phone into him. He's too weak to talk much more. He told us what he knows."

"Maybe you didn't ask the right questions, Mr. Donne."

"With all due respect, sir: give it a rest. You're not at a press conference. This is a hospital, and they have rules *even you* have to follow. I think you should focus on getting your daughter home and managing whatever flow of information you wish to manage from there."

Golden blinked his eyes and looked at me as if he were considering what my face would taste like. He took a moment to glance over at his daughter and Joseph sitting against the wall. When he turned back to me, he was calmer.

"You're right, Mr. Donne. We've recovered Angela's possessions from Torres's home. I want to get her down to the Williamsburg apartment and sort things out."

"Good idea," I said, because it was mine. "We'll head home now, too."

"I wanna see Marissa," Angela said.

"Not now, Angel," Golden said. "Mr. Knight and Mr. Donne will see how she is and report back to us."

"We're not going to be able to talk with Marissa, Mr. Golden. We blew our load talking to Robby. Maybe on the ride home, Angela can explain whatever's been going on for the past few weeks."

Golden snorted. "As if she'd talk to me."

I had no answer to that, so I just shrugged. Jack and Edgar had ended their phone calls simultaneously and regrouped with us.

An orderly came over to our group and held up Jack's phone. "From

Dr. Price," he said. Jack took it, slipped it into his front pants pocket, and said, "Thanks."

"Robby said Marissa was told by Ricky to head up here if the shit ever hit the fan," Jack said. "That's how they ended up at Robby's last night. Marissa obviously knew to call Ray."

Golden nodded. "We're leaving, Jack."

"Home?" Jack asked.

"Yes. Raymond suggested that you follow us down to Brooklyn, to the apartment. After last night's events, I think that would be wise in this situation."

"You got it, sir," Jack said.

"Excellent." Golden walked over to his daughter and Joseph, and explained the plan. The two got up and started walking toward the door. "We'll be in the parking lot," Golden said.

"Right behind you."

The nagging question that had been bugging me since we left the hotel finally sprang forward with an intensity that made the top of my head tingle.

"Jack," I said. "Did you give Golden Robby's address?"

"I don't know Robby's address."

"Does Angela strike you as the type of girl who'd remember how to get someplace she'd only been to once in an area she knows nothing about?"

Jack looked confused. "No, Ray. She doesn't. Why?"

I lowered my voice. "How the hell did Joseph know where Robby lived?"

Chapter 31

ALL THREE CARS SWUNG BY A Mickey D's drive-through—an obvious step down for Golden, but we all agreed it was best to stay in our cars—got breakfast, and were on the thruway in less than ten minutes. Jack and I were in his car, which left Edgar pouting and driving solo, but I told him that Jack and I had some things to discuss and that we'd all regroup later at The LineUp. That made him smile.

"So," Jack said after taking a bite from his biscuit sandwich. "How do you wanna play this?"

Excellent question.

"When we get back to Williamsburg," I began, "we need to somehow get Joseph alone, away from Golden and the girl."

"Then what?"

"First thing, we get him to tell us how he knew where Robby's house was."

"What's the second thing?"

"That depends on his first answer, I guess."

I took a bite from my sandwich and thought back to a week ago, when Jack and I were reunited and sharing breakfast from Christina's instead of McDonald's. *I didn't feel twenty thousand dollars richer.* I remembered also that I hadn't called Allison back. I took care of that after another sip of coffee.

"So you're on your way home?" she asked. "Jesus, Ray, you didn't come home last night, and you didn't call to say your place was safe. I didn't know what to think."

I thought about going into some of the last twelve hours' events with her. On the phone. In front of Jack. Instead, I ignored the point. "Should be back by eleven," I said cheerily.

"You're not telling me something, Ray. I can hear it in your voice, and I don't like it."

"I'll explain when I get back, Ally. Trust me on this."

She made me wait ten seconds before she spoke again.

"My place, right? Your place still isn't safe, is it?" she asked.

"Yeah. Your place."

"I can get out of here by five, five thirty."

"Great," I said. "See you then."

After I'd hung up, Jack gave me one of those grins.

"You live a full life, Ray," he said. "A full life."

I closed my eyes, reclined my seat, and enjoyed the jealousy in Jack's voice.

Joseph and Jack parked side by side in the lot behind Golden's condo. Edgar had been directed to park on the street and told to wait. The five of us entered the building through the back door and were greeted by a different doorman than the one Jimmy Key and I had met a few days earlier.

"Afternoon, Mr. Golden," the doorman said as he came out from behind the desk. "Any packages with you today?"

Golden held up his hand, stopping the doorman. "No, thank you. We'll be fine." He pressed the elevator button, and we all made a protective circle around Angela. The doorman went back to his desk—apparently unaware that the brunette girl was Golden's missing daughter. The elevator opened and we stepped in. Joseph pressed the button for the fourteenth floor and turned his back to us.

I gave Jack a look and he gave me an almost imperceptible nod. As casually as I could, I stepped in front of Golden; Jack did the same with Angela. I figured we had about ten seconds to the fourteenth floor if the trip was nonstop. It was. When the door opened, Jack put both hands on

Joseph and pushed him out. I turned, grabbed the Goldens, and said, "Go back down to the lobby."

"What the hell?" Golden yelled.

I heard Jack struggling behind me. "Just do it!" I shouted at the Goldens and backed out just as the elevator door shut. Jack was wrestling with Joseph. Joseph was twisting and turning, trying to get Jack into a headlock. I stepped over to them and, with all my might—and all the frustration of the past week—punched Joseph in the face. It hurt my hand like hell, but it did the job. Jack was able to sweep a stunned Joseph's legs out from under him, wrestle him to the floor, roll him over, then pin Joseph's arms to his sides by sitting on top of him. Now Jack had his gun out and held it against Joseph's head. I lifted Joseph's pants leg and removed a Smith & Wesson from his ankle holster.

"How the fuck did you know where Robby Torres lived?" Jack yelled, inches away from Joseph's face.

"I don't know what—"

Jack smacked him in the head with his gun. He looked like he was going to do it again, so I put my hand on Jack's shoulder to remind him we needed Joseph able to talk.

"How did you know?" Jack repeated.

There was blood coming out of Joseph's nose and mouth, making it hard for him to talk. He turned his head and spit some blood onto the carpet.

"You can tell *us*," I said, "or you can tell the cops. And Blake."

Either way, he was telling the cops. I just wanted the info *now*.

"The girl's phone," Joseph managed to say. "As soon as she turned it back on . . . I was able to track her and her friend. Yesterday."

"So you went up there to get Angela," Jack said. "Why the fuck'd you have to shoot Robby?"

Joseph coughed and again spit up some blood. "He pulled on me," he said. "I just wanted to know where the girls were. He told me they were hiding in the shed and . . . we went through the backyard. He goes to open the door . . . and, I'm like, 'What the *hell*? The girls are hiding in a locked shed?!' He opens the shed and says, 'Here they are.' I went to step inside, and that's when he took out his piece."

Jack smacked Joseph's head, with his palm this time. "So you shot him. He's a kid. A fucking English major, for Christ's sake. You're trained for this shit."

"That's why," Joseph said between heavy breaths, "I shot him in the shoulder. I grabbed his gun and ditched it. I wasn't looking to kill no one. I went up there to get Mr. G's kid and bring her back to the city."

Jack and I looked at each other.

"The city?" I said. "Not Long Island, to her parents?"

Joseph thought about that and said, "I knew about this place. I've been here before with Mr. Blake, when he needed some time away from the missus." He looked at me. "You saw the way she can get."

I nodded, remembering Mrs. Blake's raucous laughter at the gala, which I personally found infectious, not threatening. I looked Joseph in the eyes and decided that, even with a gun pointed at him and blood coming out of his face, he was holding something back—telling us everything we asked, but not everything he knew.

"So," I said, "you called nine-one-one and then what?"

"I got a first aid kit in my car," he said. "Not one of those shitty drugstore ones. A real one. I figured I had some time to stabilize the kid and get the hell out of there before the cops came."

"You're a fucking boy scout, you are," Jack said. "So you get all the way back down to the city, and then what? Golden calls you? You work for Blake."

"I work for whoever Mr. Blake tells me to. Mr. G calls me, says he needs me to do some driving? I do some driving. Spent half the goddamned day making round trips to Albany. Thought I'd come back with fifty thousand bucks worth of kid, but it didn't work out that way, did it?" He looked up at Jack's gun. "You mind now? You got me, don't you?"

"I feel better this way," Jack said, keeping the gun on Joseph, but rolling onto the carpet. "You look around in the shed?"

"Why the hell would I do that?" Joseph asked. "I had to get the hell out of there, and I saw the girls weren't in there."

"No," I said. "But something else was."

He blinked. "I don't know anything about that."

"Which girl's phone did you track?" I asked.

"Whatta you mean?" Joseph said. "The daughter's."

That's what he was holding back.

"Golden ever tell you he had a tracker on his daughter's phone, Jack?"

Jack gave that five seconds of thought. "Nope. He did not. You think that would've come up in conversation, what with all the money he was paying me to find her." Jack stood up, looked down at Joseph, and touched the gun to his head again. "You tracked Marissa's phone, you son of a bitch."

"How the hell—" He stopped when Jack pressed the gun harder to his temple. "Okay," he said. "I tracked the Spanish girl's phone."

"How'd you get her number?" I asked.

"Some guy I know. Said he was looking for her."

"What guy?"

"A friend of the cop who was killed."

Fuck.

"What's his name?" Jack asked.

"Jimmy something," Joseph said. "The last name's Italian or some shit."

I sat down on the floor next to Joseph. "Greek," I said. "Kisparidas." I looked at Jack. "Jimmy Key."

"Who the fuck's Jimmy Key?" asked Jack.

"The guy you met with Robby the other day in front of his aunt's house. Ricky's friend from Iraq." I turned back to Joseph. "You weren't looking for Angela Golden," I said. "You were looking for the guns Ricky'd stashed. And you found them in the shed."

Joseph didn't answer right away. When he got his thoughts together, he said, "I *was* looking for the Spanish girl. I figured what's-her-name would lead me to Golden's kid. When the college kid took me back to the shed, I saw the guns and figured if I couldn't get the girl, least I could get the guns."

"You're Tony Blake's bodyguard." Jack said. "You moonlighting as a gunrunner, Joseph?"

Joseph shook his head.

"Where are the guns now?" I asked.

He didn't answer right away, so I asked him again, this time with my foot next to his ear. I surprised myself as I realized I was ready to cause this guy a lot of pain.

"In the trunk of my car."

Jack laughed. "Son of a bitch." Jack tapped Joseph's head a few times with his gun. "Tell me, Joey. How'd you get involved in all this?"

Joseph got quiet again. Whatever he had to say was sticking in his throat. "This Jimmy guy," he finally said. "He was blackmailing me."

"What the hell for?"

He shook his head and whispered. "Not me. Not exactly."

"Tony Blake," I said. "Jimmy was blackmailing your boss."

Joseph nodded. "Yeah."

"With what?"

No answer. Jack pressed the gun hard against Joseph's temple. "The man asked you a question," he said. "With what?"

Joseph swallowed and got himself up on his elbows. He turned his head to spit once more on the carpet.

"The girl," he said.

The elevator door opened and out stepped Charles and Angela Golden. Before they could begin to comprehend the scene in front of them, my cell phone rang. We were all oddly frozen for the next few moments, caught in a bizarre tableau: the Goldens taking in Joseph, bloody and beaten on the floor; Jack standing above him, gun poised at his head; me sitting on the floor next to Joseph as my cell phone rang and rang. At the time, it made perfect sense to check my caller ID. Edgar was calling.

"What's up?" I answered.

"Raymond," the voice on the other end said. "It's Marissa." A long pause as everyone waited, including me, while I made sense of Marissa's voice coming from Edgar's phone. "I think I'm in trouble again."

"What are you talking about? What did the doctors say?"

"I got discharged."

"You need us to come and get you?"

"Somebody's already got me."

"What does that mean? I'm Kinda busy here, Marissa."

"Hey, Raymond." It was a guy's voice now. If the call had come in five minutes ago, I wouldn't have recognized it. Now I knew exactly who it was. "I think I have something that belongs to you."

I tried to keep my voice steady and calm. "The girl doesn't belong to me, Jimmy. What do you want?"

A few seconds passed, then I heard a voice I knew very well.

"Ray," the voice said. "I'm sorry, man."

Fucking shit. Jimmy Key had Edgar.

Chapter 32

IF THIS WERE A MOVIE, I WOULD HAVE said something threatening along the lines of "If you even think of hurting him . . ." after I heard Jimmy take the phone back.

But this was real, and I was scared shitless for Edgar. I wasn't going to say anything that would bring harm to my friend. Especially since he was only in this position because of me. I got off the floor, switched my cell to speaker so everyone could hear, and said, "What do you want, Jimmy?"

"I want my guns, man," he said. "That's *all* I've wanted for the past week."

"Is that why you killed Ricky?"

"He backed out of our deal, Ray. Mr. Marine turned into a real pussy just when I needed him the most." He took a breath. "I hear that happens when you find out you're gonna be a daddy."

I made a mistake, Ray. A big one.

I looked over at Angela Golden's belly. *No way.* I didn't care how much Ricky had gone through, no way would he—"Marissa?"

"That's what she told our boy, man. They'd been together a short time, and Ricky didn't shoot no blanks."

That's why he was looking for an apartment. He was going to protect *this* family like he couldn't protect the young Iraqi woman and their un-born child from the bombing. But where the hell was he going to get the money for—the guns. Then he must have had a change of heart and backed out. He was too good a guy to abandon his pregnant girlfriend, but much too good a Marine to get involved with smuggling weapons. No wonder he was all twisted around that night in his cab.

"I can't give you something I don't have, Jimmy," I lied.

"But I'm betting you know where they are, Ray."

I looked over at Joseph, still on the carpet. *Good bet, Jimmy.*

"What if I do?"

He laughed. "Like the man on TV says, Ray. 'Let's make a deal.'"

"Just like that? The guns for Edgar and Marissa?"

"Then we're square," Jimmy said.

It couldn't be that easy. I looked at Charles Golden and his daughter, who seemed to have recovered from whatever surprised state they were in when they came off the elevator. I motioned for Golden to take his daughter into the apartment. He was about to argue, but his daughter dragged him down the hallway and out of earshot. For once Charles Golden let someone else take over.

"So you're just going to trust us?" I asked Jimmy, because I sure as hell didn't trust him. "What stops us from turning you in once we get Edgar and Marissa?"

He laughed again. "Ask Blake's boy, Ray. I'll wait. Keep me on the speaker, though. I wanna hear him tell it."

Jack reached down and pulled Joseph off the ground.

Jack shoved him hard against the wall. Joseph almost went down again, but Jack held him up. "Speak, asshole."

"Okay," Joseph said, shaking off Jack's hand. "The fuck's it matter now?" He rolled his neck around, making an audible cracking sound. "The girl?" he said. "Little Miss Golden? Blake's the father of her kid."

Now, that shut us up.

"And how do you know this?" Jack asked.

"Ricky told me," Jimmy's voice came through the phone. "*Marissa* told *him*. Hell, it was Ricky's idea to blackmail the kid fucker in the first place. Seems The Magician likes to make his penis disappear into underage girls. That's how Marissa got to know our future mayor before she aged out."

"And Angela?" I said.

"Met the man through dear old dad. They had a party out at the house on Long Island last year. Blake talked Angela into showing him the family boat after everyone had gone to bed, and . . . well, we've all seen the movies, boys. Let's just say they had an ongoing relationship until he knocked her up."

"Does Golden know?"

Joseph spoke up. "He knew the girl was pregnant. But he had no idea it was Blake, and she wasn't telling."

Now it was coming together. Ricky T was blackmailing Golden *and* Blake. Golden, because his underage daughter's future would be ruined if anyone found out she was pregnant; and Blake, because he was the father. Whatever he was demanding, add his share of the reward money for finding Angela Golden, mix in some profit from smuggling guns, and *Bam!* Ricky T's got himself a down payment on a two-bedroom condo where he was going to keep his new family safe this time. The best laid plans . . . .

"Enough schoolgirl gossip, boys," Jimmy said. "I want my guns. And I've waited too damn long. I got some nasty people waiting on my ass for this."

Poor guy.

"Where are you now?" Jack asked.

Jimmy laughed. "Close enough, Magnum. I'll tell you where I'm *going* to be," he said. "How long will it take you to get my stuff?"

Jack and I looked at each other. The real answer was: however long it takes us on the elevator down to the parking garage. But Jimmy Key was not going to get the real answer.

"Less than an hour," I said.

"Get the guns and call me back in thirty minutes—and I'm not even gonna get into all the do's and don'ts of this situation, you hear me?"

"We hear you," I said.

"Good." He hung up.

I held the phone out for a few more seconds, staring at it as if it were going to provide me with some answers, and then slipped it into my front pocket.

"Now what?" I said.

Jack walked around in a circle, his gun at his side. He closed his eyes while thinking over the news; I kept my eyes on Joseph, who no longer seemed to be a threat. I watched him anyway.

"Okay," Jack said. "The guns are in the trunk, right?"

Joseph mumbled a "Yes."

"We know Jimmy's in the area 'cause he's got Edgar." He gave that some thought. "Shit, he musta followed us up to Albany, got the *chica* after we left, and headed back down here less than a half hour behind us."

"Figuring to use Marissa as a bargaining chip, because she's pregnant with Ricky's kid," I said. "Damn."

"All right," Jack said. "Personally, I don't give a shit about the guns. Our goal here is to get the girl and Edgar back. Agreed?"

I *did* care about the guns getting in the wrong hands someday when I could have prevented it, but not nearly as much as I did about Edgar and Marissa. "Work backward from your goal," Uncle Ray would say.

"Agreed," I said, hoping we'd figure out something better soon.

Jack held out his hand to Joseph. "Gimme the keys."

Joseph looked as if he were about to refuse, but remembered the situation he was in. He reached into his pocket and tossed the keys to Jack.

"What the fuck do we do with him?" Jack asked me.

Sometimes, under pressure, I come up with real good ideas. I hoped this was one of them.

"You still want to protect your boss?" I asked. "Tony Blake, I mean. Not Charles Golden."

He nodded. "That's what he's paying me for."

"Stay here with the Goldens." I turned to Jack before he could object. "I know. It's a shitty option, but it's the only one we got right now."

"What if he decides to split on us?" Jack asked.

"Then the word gets out about his boss, and I help Robby identify Joseph as his shooter." I looked at Joseph. "You down with that?"

He gave me another nod.

"We get the guns to Jimmy Key," I said. "We exchange them for Edgar and Marissa, and then try to think of a way to get the guns back once they're safe."

"Golden's not going to want this info out there either, Ray."

"All he knows is his daughter's pregnant. I hate the idea of Blake getting away with this shit, Jack, but I'd hate it even more if Mrs. Torres were to find out her dead son was into blackmailing and gun smuggling. The papers'll drag Ricky's name through the mud. That family has been through enough."

"How confident are you that you'll be able to figure out how to get those guns back?" Jack asked.

I shrugged. "One thing at a time, Jack."

"Okay, Ray." He didn't like it. "But as soon as I smell things going south, I'm taking care of things myself."

"I can live with that." I turned back to Joseph. "Stay with the Goldens. Take out your phone and call me." I gave him my number, then he dialed and hung up as soon as my phone buzzed so we had each other's numbers. "Let's go, Jack."

I went to the elevator and pressed the Down button. Jack grabbed Joseph by the elbow before he followed. "I even *think* you're fucking with us, you'll be seeing Ricky T real soon."

Joseph looked into Jack's eyes and tried to manage a smirk. It came out as a grimace. He pulled his elbow back and walked away. Jack and I stepped into the elevator and headed down.

"We're handing over guns to the guy who killed Ricky, Ray," Jack said.

"I know, Jack. But if Ricky were here, he'd tell us to protect his kid, you know that. What choice do we have?"

There was no answer to that, because we both knew the answer was "none."

We opened the trunk of Joseph's car, and the guns Robby had photographed and sent us yesterday morning—a lifetime ago—were there: bundled up in the green duffel bag. We did a quick count. All twenty of them—the number Robby had counted—were still there. If what I'd learned from Edgar was correct, we were looking at about forty thousand dollars' worth of assault pistols.

We closed up the bag and shut the trunk. Jack held out his hand. "Let me drive," he said. "Make me feel like I'm the boss again."

I didn't argue. We were out on the avenue in less than a minute. There was Edgar's car, parked directly across the street from where all this had started about a week ago when Ricky was killed.

"Call the man," Jack said. "Let's get this over with."

I dialed the number I had for Jimmy, put the phone on speaker, and he picked up after one ring.

"Musta had the guns close, Ray. Smart."

"Where are we meeting, Jimmy?"

"Right down to business." I listened to a few seconds of silence. "Get on the BQE and head toward Staten Island."

"Then what?" Jack said.

"I'll call back in five minutes," Jimmy said and hung up.

"He's fucking playing games, Ray."

"He's got Edgar and Marissa, Jack. He can afford to."

We hit the BQE, and Jack took the exit for Staten Island. Traffic was pretty light at the moment, and we were cruising along at a brisk forty-five. But anyone who's ever driven this stretch of road will tell you that you never know what the Brooklyn Queens Expressway will throw at you. I hoped Jimmy would call back before we hit any slowdowns.

My phone rang. "Yeah?" he said on speaker.

"Get off at the next exit and head back to the Burg."

"What the hell—" He'd hung up again. Jack slammed the steering wheel with both hands, but took the next exit and got back on the road, going in the other direction. "Fucking shithead," he said. "I don't like this, Ray."

Like I was enjoying myself. "Just stay—" The phone rang again. This time I stayed quiet and waited for Jimmy to speak.

"No pouting now, Ray. Just making sure you didn't reach out to your uncle or anyone and get all clever on me."

"We're good, Jimmy."

"You *are* good, Ray. Take the last exit before the bridge, and head over to the creek. Find a place to park, and I'll call you back in three."

The Newtown Creek: famous for the dumping of toxic waste, weapons used in crimes, and victims of serial killers. Someday it was going to be a real Brooklyn tourist attraction. We drove a few blocks and pulled into a dirt parking lot between two warehouses just as Jimmy called back.

"Stay right there," he said. "I'm right behind you."

We got out of the car and walked to the trunk. I wanted to take a deep breath, but our proximity to the creek made me think twice. A minivan pulled into the lot, Jimmy behind the wheel. No sign of Edgar or Marissa. Jimmy swung the van around and pulled its back up to ours. Then he got out, slid open the side door, and pulled Edgar out. Edgar's face was blank. I'd never seen that look on him before. He was scared.

"Good to see you again, Ray," said Jimmy.

"Go fuck yourself, Jimmy."

Edgar and he stayed by the van. Jimmy pressed a button on his keychain, and his back door opened. Seeing this, Jack opened the trunk of our car.

"Quickly," Jimmy said.

"Wait," I shouted. "Where's the girl?"

"You'll see her after you load in my guns." He motioned with his head at Edgar. "I'm just showing him as a gesture of good faith."

"You're a real gem," Jack said as he loaded the duffel bag into Jimmy's van.

"Now step away, Jack," Jimmy said. "I need to do some counting."

Jack stepped back, and I gave Edgar a look that said everything was going to be all right. Jimmy unzipped the bag, reached inside, and took a minute to inventory its contents. When he turned around, he did not look happy.

"You fucking playing a game with me, Ray?"

"I don't know what you mean," I said. "Those are your guns, right?"

"They're *half* of my guns." He slammed his hand against the side of the van and pulled a gun out of his waist holster with the other. "You don't wanna fuck with me right now, guys!"

"We're not fucking with you, Jimmy," Jack said. "These are what were in the shed upstate. Ricky stashed them at his brother's place."

Jimmy took in that information and grinned. "Pretty good thinking," he said. "But I'm still short twenty guns. That wasn't our deal."

"Our *deal*," I said, "was to give you what we *have* in exchange for Edgar and Marissa. We kept up our end."

Jimmy shook his head. "Not good enough, Ray. Looks as if Ricky's screwing you from the great beyond." He walked over to Edgar and put his hand on his back. Jimmy tapped the gun against Edgar's arm. Edgar closed his eyes and wobbled. I thought he was about to fall when Jimmy pushed him toward us. I caught him, and he collapsed in my arms.

"I get half," Jimmy said. "You get half."

Jack took a step forward and stopped when Jimmy raised his gun.

"I can drop you right here, Jack, and your buddies, too. Both of you take your guns out and toss 'em in the water. Real slow."

I could tell by the look on Jack's face that he was measuring the distance between himself and Jimmy's gun. He was also weighing the odds of reaching for his own piece. They were not good, but Jack was not known for always making the good decision. I said, "Jack." He turned. "Don't."

He stared at me for a bit. Then he reached behind his back, took out his gun, turned around, and threw it into the creek.

"That's it, Jimmy. I'm not carrying," I said before lifting my shirt to show my belt line and my pants legs.

Jimmy nodded. "Now get back in your car."

He held the gun on us while Jack got back in the driver's seat and I helped Edgar into the backseat. I opened my door then stopped.

"What about Marissa?" I asked Jimmy.

"Don't know yet, Ray. I'll see what info I can get from her. If she can get me the rest of my merchandise, she'll be good to go."

"And if she can't?"

He just grinned again. "Don't leave for five minutes, Jack. I see you behind me, and the girl's dead." He pulled something out of his pocket and tossed it to me. A phone. "That's hers," he said. "In case you had any thoughts about tracking us."

Jimmy got into his van and drove away. Jack started the car.

I slipped Marissa's phone into my pocket, leaned inside the car window, and said, "He said not to follow."

"They always say not to follow," Jack said. "Get in."

"We're fucked here, Jack. We're fucked!" I slammed the roof of the car and, for the second time that day, hurt my hand. "I think we gotta call the cops."

Jack shook his head, unwilling to admit defeat. Normally, I'd consider that an admirable quality, but this time that attitude could get people killed.

"Get in the car, Ray," Jack said evenly.

"Jack. I don't think Ricky would want us to put Marissa at risk."

"Ricky's the reason Marissa's *at risk*, asshole. First he gets involved with that scumbag. Then he can't even back out without getting himself killed!" Jack gripped the steering wheel, closed his eyes, and breathed deeply. "Where the hell would he put the other half of the guns? His mom's?"

"No," I said. "He wouldn't take that risk, but I'd bet anything Jimmy's the one who broke into her house."

"Then where?"

I figured if I stalled, just one more minute, any idea Jack had of following Jimmy would be moot. I walked around in a circle outside the car, thinking. When I was done, I got back in.

"I think I have an idea," I said.

"Well," Jack said, putting the car in Drive. "Feel free to share it at any fucking time, Ray."

I did, and Jack left a cloud of dust between us and the creek.

Chapter 33

EDGAR WAS STILL SHAKING WHEN we dropped him off at his car and told him to go home. As much as he dug this detective shit in theory, he apparently needed a vacation from it. Jack took the time to call Charles Golden. Everything seemed to be fine inside the condo. Angela was in one bedroom watching TV, and Joseph was watching the front door. When Golden pressed him for details of our last hour, Jack hung up.

We were parked in Joseph's car down the block from the house we'd been to earlier this week. I rolled my window down as Jack reached under his seat and pulled out another gun.

"I was a boy scout for three weeks," he said. "Always be prepared."

"Now what?"

"You're sure they're in there?" He motioned with his head at the house.

"I'm not sure of anything at this point. But there were few places Ricky felt comfortable after getting back. This is one of them."

Jack nodded. "So we go in, and . . ."

"Last time I had to be *let* in. That's when I met the pit bull. Maybe there's a way in from the back."

Jack opened up his door. "One way to find out." He slipped his gun into the waistband of his jeans as I followed him. "Stay here," he said. "I'm gonna take a quick stroll past the house."

"Be careful," I said. "Dog Guy recognized you last time."

He didn't answer, and I watched as he casually walked past the front of the house and stopped two doors down. He must have seen something, because he started jogging back to me with a grin on his face.

"You ain't gonna believe this."

"What?"

"Front door's open. Just about an inch, but it's open. Radio's on pretty loud."

I thought about that. "Someone must have been in a hurry."

"Looks like your hunch mighta been right." He took out his gun and flattened it against his leg. "Wanna make a home visit?"

"I wanna call the cops."

"We'll call the cops after."

After what? I thought, then followed Jack, who was already running back.

We made our way up the front steps and stopped when we got to the door. We listened for ten seconds but heard nothing but the loud music coming from the radio. Jack eased the door open and we slipped inside, careful not to let the door close behind us. Jack took a glance over my shoulder and mouthed, "What the fuck?"

I turned. Bates, the pit bull that had terrified my testicles a few days ago, was lying on the floor in front of the couch. He was bleeding from his head, clearly dead. His owner, Dog Guy, was in a similar predicament on the couch. I stepped over, saw the pool of blood gathering on the cushion, and felt his neck. No pulse, but the flesh was warm.

I looked at Jack, shook my head, and mouthed the word, "Cops."

He shook his head and pointed to the staircase. He did that walking thing with his fingers, telling me he was going to go upstairs. "Stay here," he whispered, not waiting for an answer. Then Jack climbed the stairs.

I walked around the staircase and found the kitchen. I could still hear the music, but less so. There was a door to the right of the fridge. I assumed it was a pantry or some sort of storage area. It was obviously the newest addition to the kitchen. Through the kitchen windows, I could see the backyards of the brownstones on the other block. I could also see into some of the neighbors' windows. Did they know what went on in this house? Had anyone ever called the cops?

I thought I heard footsteps and turned, expecting to see Jack back from checking out the upstairs. I was wrong. The door next to the fridge opened and out stepped Jimmy Key. He had a duffel bag over his shoulder and held a terrified Marissa by the elbow. In his other hand was his gun. He laughed when he saw me.

"I can see why Ricky went to you for help," he said. "You are one resourceful individual, Raymond." He looked around. "Where's Jack?"

"He's checking out Ricky's mom's house," I lied, surprising myself at how quickly I did so. I looked at the bag over his shoulder and then at Marissa. Jimmy had found his guns. "Now that you got what you want, are you going to live up to your end of the deal?"

He smiled. "*I* found the guns, Ray. So *I* get to keep the girl. At least until I get where I'm going. A little insurance never hurt anyone, right?"

"She's pregnant, Jimmy. Keep her out of it."

He took a step forward and laughed again. I was getting tired of it. "One," he said, "she's in it until I say different. Two, she ain't as pregnant as you thought."

I felt my forehead collapse and my eyebrows try to meet in the middle. "What the hell does that mean?"

"Tell him, *chica*." He shook Marissa by the elbow. "Tell your friend Ray here what you told me."

The look on Marissa's face turned from complete fear to one mixed with shame. When Jimmy shook her again, harder this time, she spoke up.

"I lied," she said, barely above a whisper. "To Ricky." She looked down at the faded tile on the kitchen floor. "I'm not pregnant."

"What?" I said. She didn't lift her head, so I took a step forward. "*What?*"

Jimmy raised his gun, stopping me. "You heard right, Ray. Little Marissa here told a big fat lie to our friend Ricky."

"Why the hell would you do that?"

She looked up. "It got *you* here, didn't it?" she said. "I wanted out. I knew Ricky liked me, he told me after we . . . He told me about his girl in Iraq and the baby. He wanted a family." She stared me in the eyes. Hers were cold now, the shame gone. "So I gave him one."

"You bitch!" came out of my mouth. "You made one up!"

"Easy now, Ray," Jimmy said. "We've all done stuff we ain't too proud of, right? Girl wanted to say good-bye to the life, she did what she knew how to do to get what she wanted. Oooh." He gave a fake shudder. "First female to ever do that? Huh?"

"Jesus," I said to Marissa. "You're the reason Ricky's dead. He never would've gotten himself involved in"—I looked at Jimmy with disgust—"*this* if he didn't feel that he needed to provide for—"

"That's enough, Ray," Jimmy said. "The past is the past. What you need to worry about now is your immediate future. And this girl's."

"Fuck the girl," I said, disgusted now by my words and how true they felt.

"Ricky already took care of that, didn't he?" said Jimmy.

He slipped the bag off his shoulder and placed it on the floor. Without looking, he reached behind him and opened the door he'd come out of and then stepped aside. "I need you to go downstairs, Ray."

I looked over at the door and realized that not only was it brand-new, but it had two locks on it. I mentally kicked myself for thinking it was a pantry.

"You tried to kill me once already, Jimmy, when my girlfriend was over," I said. "Having a bad night that night, were you?"

"If I wanted you dead, Ray, you'd be dead. I had Little Mike on the roof behind your place. He called me when you were in the living room. I put two shots in your bedroom wall just to shake things up."

"It worked," I said. I looked at the door behind him and wanted to keep the conversation going. *Where the fuck was Jack?*

"Why'd you shoot Dillman in the shoulder the night you killed Ricky? And what'd Dillman do to piss you off enough you had to put one between his eyes?"

"The first time? A diversion. Then, I thought he knew where Ricky hid my guns. Turned out he didn't know shit. He became . . . a liability." He pointed to the door with his gun. "Now . . ."

"I'm not going downstairs. I got a feeling I might not be coming back up."

He shrugged. "It's either the basement or . . . ." He showed me the gun again.

"What happens to Marissa?"

"See?" Jimmy said with a smile to Marissa. "He *does* care." Then, to me, "I'm not sure. I'll make that decision when I'm about a hundred miles north of here."

"That where your buyers are?"

"Yep. Some good ol' boys from upstate."

"And you don't care what happens after that?"

"Upstate? I assume they're gonna go hunting with them."

"With TEC-Nines?"

"That's the beauty of the Second Amendment, Ray. Doesn't say what you can or can't *do* with them. Just says you have the right to *bear* them." He pushed the basement door open farther with his foot. "Now, before your boy Jack comes back to fetch you . . . ."

"I'm not his boy," came a voice from below.

Jimmy spun around, his gun held high and the other hand grabbing Marissa by the neck. We all watched Jack come up from the basement, his own gun in the ready position. Had the music not been playing, we would have heard him coming.

Without being asked, Jack said, "Someone built themselves a fantastic . . . what do ya call them? A dumbwaiter? Goes all the way from the top to the bottom. A real selling point. I guess when ya got girls fucking on all floors, some things are must-haves."

"Far enough, Jack," Jimmy said. He placed the gun against Marissa's head. "Drop the piece or I drop the girl."

"You heard Ray, Jimmy. Fuck the girl."

They stared at each other, checking each other's eyes for a bluff. I measured the space between Jimmy and me. It didn't look good.

Jimmy squeezed Marissa's neck, and she let out a moan. Jack continued to stare at Jimmy.

"Okay then," Jimmy said. He swung the gun in my direction. "What about Ray? You wanna fuck him—?"

Jack fired, putting one right between Jimmy's eyes, interrupting the rest of his sentence and pretty much everything else. Jimmy collapsed to the floor and Marissa spun away, moaning and crying. She ran out of the kitchen, and I could hear her crying in the other room.

"Holy fuck, Jack."

"I know," he said, trying to sound calm, but I could tell he was shaken up. He looked down at Jimmy, his eyes wide, and kicked his gun across the floor. "Had to take the shot, right?"

"You could've killed Marissa."

"Like we said, Ray: Fuck the girl."

Yeah, I thought. *But I didn't mean it. Did I?*

Jack reached into his pocket, pulled out the car keys, and tossed them to me. "Get on over to Golden's," he said. "I'll take care of this."

"What does that mean?"

"Go, Ray. I'll call you later." He gave me his best movie star smile and added, "Trust me."

I stood there, stupidly, quietly—in the kitchen of a whorehouse with two dead guys in it—and realized I had no other choice.

After the ten-minute drive to Golden's condo, I was a little less shaken up. The guy behind the desk called upstairs and got permission for me to head on up. I knocked on the door, and Tony Blake opened it. If my hand weren't still hurting from Joseph, I would have punched him in the face, too.

"Come in, Mr. Donne," he said as if he owned the place. After I entered he peered out into the hallway, checking to see if anyone had seen me.

Sitting in the living room were Charles Golden and Joseph, who held an ice pack on his face. I almost pitied Mr. Golden, the only one in the room who didn't know Tony Blake had raped his daughter.

Just then a door down the apartment hallway opened a crack. Angela Golden peered out at me behind glassy eyes. "Marissa's safe, Angela," I said. After a moment, she closed the door till it clicked.

"Where's Jack?" Golden asked.

"Cleaning up a mess," I said. I walked over to Joseph and thought I saw him flinch ever so slightly when I held out his car keys. He took them, avoiding my eyes.

"That's not an answer, Mr. Donne. Jack is still in my employ. As are you."

"It's the only answer you're going to get, Mr. Golden."

"Boys, boys, please," Tony Blake said. "Let's play nice, shall we? Angela is back here and safe. That's what matters."

I looked at Golden and Joseph. "You told him about the guns?" I asked. They nodded. I looked back at Blake. "I'm not in the mood for any spin, Mr. Blake. A lot of shit has gone down over the last twenty-four hours, and you show up when it's all over."

Blake gave me the nobody-talks-to-me-like-that look. I didn't care.

"Thank you for returning Joseph's vehicle, Mr. Donne." Blake said, moving to escort me out.

"I'm waiting for Jack. I'm working for *him*"—I emphasized for Golden's sake—"and I'll go home when he tells me the job is done."

Golden got to his feet. "Your job *is* done," he said. "I'll cut the checks tomorrow, and that will conclude our business."

"With all due respect, sir, I'll wait to hear that from Jack."

Now Joseph stood. "Mr. Golden asked you to leave."

I laughed a nervous laugh. But after seeing two dead bodies, having a gun pointed at me, and dealing with these three guys, any laugh would feel good today.

"You really want to have this discussion, Joseph?"

Before he could answer, Golden's phone rang.

"Yes, Jack," he said, looking at me. "I think he needs to hear that from you. Hold on." He handed me the phone.

"Yeah?" I said.

"You can go home now, Ray," Jack said. "We're good."

"You still at the house?"

"Waiting on the cops, just like we said."

"What about the guns?" I asked.

"All taken care of," he said. "Make sure you read the papers tomorrow. Now go home."

"Okay," I said and handed the phone back to Golden. I left without saying another word or looking back.

Chapter 34

JACK WAS RIGHT: THE WHOLE STORY—BOTH stories—were in the papers the next day. At least the stories fit to print.

Now that it was safe to return to my place, Allison and I had all three papers spread out in front of us on my coffee table as we ate breakfast and watched the muted news on a local station. She seemed mostly okay that none of the stories had her byline on it. I think she felt uneasy about needing to independently verify what I had told her, so she stepped away from being a reporter and fell into being my girlfriend.

Story Number One announced that, more than a month after her disappearance, the missing Golden Girl had been found safe through the relentless efforts of Charles Golden's investigator, Jack Knight. Jack did not mention my name, but he did concede that it was a "team effort involving my entire firm." Jack had learned much from Charles Golden.

There was a picture of a now-very-blonde Angela Golden in an oversized NYU sweatshirt as she and her now-very-pregnant-looking mother entered a black town car. It seemed that mother and daughter were going to Europe to escape the publicity, and to rest and recover. Mrs. Golden had family in Sweden, and there was a distinct possibility that her daughter would go to school there for a while. The Golden's second child—"an unexpected blessing"—would be born overseas, away from the New York media, and Charles Golden would join them soon. Holding the car door for the expectant mother was the unidentified Joseph, who sported a bandage on his forehead and sunglasses hiding black eyes. My guess was that he would be accompanying mother and child to Europe.

"Wow," Allison said. "The guy's good."

"What?"

"You don't know?"

"Know what?"

"Mom's not pregnant, Ray. It's a cover story. They'll go to Sweden—or wherever—stay until Angela has the baby, and then return to the States one big happy. Golden keeps his family's name and his daughter's rep clean and, in the bargain, gets looked at like a stud."

"How do you know she's not—?"

"Remember you told me she said she was three months pregnant?"

"Yeah."

"It took a while for me to get it, but I've had plenty of pregnant girlfriends, Ray. They don't say they're *three months* pregnant. They talk in weeks, right up until the birth. It's all weeks, not months."

"I didn't know that."

"Why would you?" She squeezed my leg: the sweet ignorant male.

Story Number Two reported the discovery of two dead bodies and a cache of assault weapons at a brownstone in Brooklyn. One of the dead—unidentified as of publication—was in his early twenties and heavily tattooed. The other one was temporarily identified as Jimmy Kisparadis, a security consultant recently back from the Middle East. Chief Raymond Donne of the NYPD explained to reporters that this was the unfortunate end to an investigation involving the recently assassinated Richard Torres, who was working undercover with the NYPD's Joint Terrorist Task Force. When pressed for more details, Chief Donne said, "Mr. Torres was a true American hero, both at home and abroad, and his family will be accorded all benefits earned by his efforts."

"How much of that is true?" Allison asked me.

"Enough."

A twenty-two-year-old woman, Marissa Rodriguez, was also found at the scene and was presently being treated at Woodhull Hospital. Chief Donne told reporters that investigators were looking forward to interviewing the young woman and "putting more pieces of this complicated puzzle together."

"Your uncle has a way with words, Ray."

"It runs in the family."

"I'm beginning to find that out," said Allison without humor.

On my way to the kitchen for more coffee, I stopped to look out at the skyline and found myself wondering where Allison and I would go for the last week of my vacation.

"Holy shit," Allison called in from the living room. "Get in here, Ray!"

I ran over to the couch as Allison turned up the volume on the TV. A red BREAKING NEWS sign was at the top of the screen, which showed an aerial view of several small boats in a river. The news ticker beneath the picture read CITY COUNCILMAN TONY BLAKE FOUND NEAR HUDSON RIVER.

Holy shit was right.

". . . unconscious Blake and an unidentified female companion were discovered by city workers who were completing minor repair work along Clinton Cove Park in Manhattan. After the workers called nine-one-one, police quickly identified Tony Blake, businessman, city councilmember, and hopeful 2017 mayoral candidate. Here's what Chief Raymond Donne of the NYPD had to say at a press conference earlier today."

"We got the call around six this morning," my uncle explained to at least a half-dozen microphones. "It's obviously too early to make a definitive statement, but we're not ruling out any possibilities."

"What about the report that Tony Blake's company owned the building in Brooklyn where several guns and two bodies were discovered this morning?" a reporter shouted out.

My uncle smiled. "You know I can't comment on rumors, Annette. Right now, all I can say is we've contacted Mr. Blake's family, and we're conducting a complete and thorough investigation."

They cut back to the reporter. "A spokesman for Councilman Blake's office showed up shortly after Blake was identified."

The shot was now a close-up of Charles Golden's face above the title, "Blake Spokesman." Someone's head would roll for that description.

"There's not much I can add at this moment," Golden said. "We are all obviously confused and concerned by this situation. The family would appreciate the respect of the press and the public at this time. Thank you."

"How will this affect Mr. Blake's mayoral ambitions?" the reporter asked.

Golden just smiled at the camera. "Thank you."

The camera switched to a shot of the reporter again. I muted the TV, trying to hide how much my swollen right hand still hurt from punching Joseph.

"He found out," I said.

"Who found out what?" Allison asked.

I told her about Blake impregnating Angela, and she made the leap to the end of the story all on her own. "Charles Golden set up Tony Blake?"

I sat down next to her, leaned back, and closed my eyes.

"You know I can't comment on rumors, Allison."

She stood. "Fuck it, Ray," she said. I opened my eyes to see a look on her face I'd never seen before. "How much of this did you know, and how long have you known it?"

I sat up. "I found out yesterday about Blake and Angela. I had no idea that Blake's company owned the building in Brooklyn. As for Golden's role in Blake's . . . current 'situation,' I don't know."

She tilted her head at me. "Except that you do."

"What do you want me to say, Ally?" I stood, went to the window, and looked out at my neighbors' rooftops. "I know *some* of the truth, *a lot* of the bullshit, and a few probabilities." I turned to face her. "You mad because *I* didn't tell you or because you didn't know?"

She thought about that. "I don't know. I'm just mad."

"Sorry."

"Me, too, Ray. Me, too." She went into my bedroom, and when she came out she was holding her bag. "I think I need to go."

I went over to her. "You're kidding me. Because . . ."

"Because I don't know how I feel about . . . about this. And I don't want to get into a conversation with you when I'm feeling this way."

"So you're just going to go home?"

"I think that's best right now." She kissed me on the cheek. "I love you, Ray, but I need to go home."

"Okay," I said. "I'll call you tomorrow?"

"Yeah."

"You're still taking the week off, right?"

"Yeah." She squeezed my elbow. "You love me, too. Right, Ray?"

"Of course," I said. "Why would you—?"

"Because you didn't say it, Ray." She stared into my eyes and squinted. "You're supposed to say it right after I do."

She was right. "I'm sorry."

"Me, too."

I watched as she turned and walked out of my apartment. If I could have thought of something else to say, something to stop her from leaving, I would have. But right then and there, I was coming up empty. At least I had twenty-four hours to come up with something before I called her tomorrow.

Yeah, I thought. *Tomorrow.*